Masterpieces
OF
Mystery

Amateurs and Professionals

Selected by ELLERY QUEEN

COPYRIGHT NOTICES AND ACKNOWLEDGMENTS

Grateful acknowledgment is hereby made for permission to reprint the following:

Chambrun and the Electronic Ear by Hugh Pentecost; copyright © 1974 by Hugh Pentecost; reprinted by permission of Brandt & Brandt Literary Agents, Inc.

The Poisoned Dow '08 by Dorothy L. Sayers; from HANGMAN'S HOLIDAY by Dorothy L. Sayers; copyright 1933 by Dorothy Leigh Sayers Fleming, renewed 1961 by Lloyds Bank Ltd., Executors; reprinted by permission of Harper & Row, Publishers, Inc.

The Stripper by H. H. Holmes (Anthony Boucher); copyright 1945 by The American Mercury, Inc., © 1972 by Phyllis White; reprinted by permission of Curtis Brown, Ltd.

The Affair at the Bungalow by Agatha Christie; reprinted by permission of Dodd, Mead & Company, Inc. from THE TUESDAY CLUB MURDERS by Agatha Christie; copyright 1933 by Agatha Christie; copyright renewed 1961 by Agatha Christie Mallowan.

Wally the Watchful Eye by Paul W. Fairman; © 1960 by Davis Publications, Inc.; reprinted by permission of the author.

The Happy Days Club by James M. Ullman; © 1962 by Davis Publications, Inc.; reprinted by permission of the author.

They Can Only Hang You Once by Dashiell Hammett; copyright 1932 by P. F. Collier and Son, renewed 1960 by Dashiell Hammett; reprinted by permission of Harold Matson Company, Inc.

Wild Goose Chase by Ross Macdonald; copyright 1954 by Kenneth Millar; reprinted by permission of Harold Ober Associates, Inc.

File #1: The Mayfield Case by Joe Gores; © 1967 by Joe Gores; reprinted by permission of the author.

About the Perfect Crime of Mr. Digberry by Anthony Abbot; © April Oursler Armstrong, Will Oursler, and Fulton Oursler, Jr.; reprinted by permission of the Estate of Fulton Oursler (Anthony Abbot).

The Devil Is a Gentleman by Charles B. Child; copyright 1947 by C. Vernon Frost, renewed; reprinted by permission of David Higham Associates Limited.

A Winter's Tale by Frances and Richard Lockridge; copyright © 1960 by Frances and Richard Lockridge; reprinted by permission of James Brown Associates, Inc.

Clancy and the Shoeshine Boy by Robert L. Pike; © 1962 by Davis Publications, Inc.; reprinted by permission of Robert P. Mills, Ltd.

Smash and Grab by Henry Wade; copyright 1945 by The American Mercury, Inc., renewed; reprinted by permission of Brandt & Brandt Literary Agents, Inc.

The Motive by Ellery Queen; © 1956 by Ellery Queen; reprinted by permission of Scott Meredith Literary Agency, Inc.

Cause for Suspicion by George Harmon Coxe; copyright 1947, Liberty Magazine, Inc.; reprinted by permission of Liberty Library Corporation.

The Stollmeyer Sonnets by James Powell; copyright 1966 by James Powell; reprinted by permission of Scott Meredith Literary Agency, Inc.

The Botany Pattern by Victor Canning; copyright © 1965 by Victor Canning; reprinted by permission of Curtis Brown, Ltd.

H As in Homicide by Lawrence Treat; © 1964 by Davis Publications, Inc.; reprinted by permission of Robert P. Mills, Ltd.

Nightshade by Ed McBain; copyright © 1971 by Evan Hunter; reprinted by permission of Julian Bach Literary Agency, Inc.

CONTENTS

INTRODUCTION

DEAR READER:

If this book were published in England, it might have been titled *Gentlemen and Players*. The English term derives, we have been told, from the language of cricketing. If we understand the origin correctly, amateur cricketers enter their locker room, or changing room, through a door marked GENTLEMEN; and professional cricketers through a door marked PLAYERS. Hence the application of the phrase to amateurs and professionals.

In a way this volume is a continuation of *Detective Directory*. In Part One of *Detective Directory* (Volume Six in MASTERPIECES OF MYSTERY) we gave you a surprising variety of sleuths to whom detection was an avocation rather than a vocation; they included doctor, lawyer, psychiatrist, insurance agent, magician, priest, teacher, thief, banker, author, artist, as well as correspondence-school, North American Indian, boy, girl, and armchair detectives.

In Part Two of *Detective Directory* (Volume Seven in MASTER-PIECES OF MYSTERY) we added other varieties of crime investigators—waiter, soldier of fortune, tycoon, pathologist, valet, scientist, tailor, baseball umpire, press photographer, railroad detective, and military policeman.

Now, in this extension of *Detective Directory*, we offer still more 'tec types, both amateur and professional. The new amateurs are hotel manager, wine salesman, nun, and spinster; the new professionals include private eyes, industrial spies, skiptracers, and law-enforcement officers who range from commissioner of police to homicide squad and precinct, with inspector, captain, lieutenant, constable, deputy sheriff, medical examiner, and the Royal Canadian Mounted in between.

Happy detecting!

ELLERY QUEEN

CHAMBRUN AND THE
ELECTRONIC EAR

BY HUGH PENTECOST

Hugh Pentecost is the pseudonym of Judson Philips, born in 1903 in Massachusetts. His first short story, "Room Number Twenty-three," was published in 1925 while the author was a student at Columbia University. A founding member of the Mystery Writers of America, Pentecost served as its third president and received its Grand Master Award in 1973. Pentecost has created many series detectives, including the artist John Jericho, Pierre Chambrun, and Uncle George Crowder, all of whom have appeared in *Ellery Queen's Mystery Magazine*. Pentecost lives in Canaan, Connecticut, with his wife, actress Norma Burton, and his teenaged son.

MRS. VEACH, the motherly-looking chief operator on the switchboard at the Beaumont Hotel, was the first one to detect something irregular about the telephone in Room 912. The noise she heard was a faint continuous buzzing the moment the line was open. Mrs. Veach promptly called Jerry Dodd, the Beaumont's security officer.

Dodd listened, gave Mrs. Veach an approving pat on her wide shoulders, and headed for the second floor.

The second floor is where the heart of the Beaumont beats—in the private office of Pierre Chambrun, the legendary resident-manager of America's top luxury hotel. Chambrun is a short square man with bright black eyes buried in deep pouches—eyes that can twinkle with humor and compassion or turn frighteningly cold and hard when the efficiency of the Beaumont is threatened.

The Beaumont is the private world over which Chambrun presides—a small city within one building with its own shops, restaurants, night clubs, cooperatively owned apartments, hospital, safety-deposit vaults, beauty parlors, ballrooms, bars, even its own police force. Chambrun is the "boss," the king with the uncanny ability to know exactly what is going on in his domain everywhere and at all times.

Some people think Chambrun has a kind of built-in radar system of his own, but those of us who work for him know his secret: it is simply that nothing even remotely out of the ordinary is ever kept from him by any of his staff. Jerry Dodd, the wiry little security officer, was perfectly competent to handle the suggestion from Mrs. Veach that the telephone in Room 912 might be bugged, but it wouldn't have occurred to Jerry not to go to Chambrun first.

I happened to be with Chambrun when Jerry reported. I am Mark Haskell, the public-relations man for the hotel and as close to Chambrun as anyone on his staff. My office is just down the corridor from his.

Chambrun listened to what Jerry had to say, then pressed a buzzer on his desk. Miss Ruysdale, his fabulous secretary, appeared in the door to the outer office.

"Card on Room 912, please," Chambrun said. He took a sip

of the Turkish coffee from the cup at his elbow and lit one of his flat Egyptian cigarettes. His eyes narrowed against the smoke.

"You know anything about the occupant in 912?" Chambrun asked Jerry.

"Name—Warren Wilson," Jerry said. "Checked in yesterday. I haven't had a chance to look at his card."

Guests of the Beaumont Hotel might have been a little disturbed to know how complete the record was on them. On their cards were symbols which indicated their credit standing, their marital status, whether or not they were cheating on a spouse, how they handled their liquor. On the card there could be a notation that Chambrun had something special about them in his private file that he didn't want to become general knowledge.

Warren Wilson's card showed that he had not been a guest of the hotel before. We had nothing yet on his habits or his private life. But there was one interesting thing about him. His room had been reserved for him and his credit vouched for by a deputy director of the Central Intelligence Agency in Washington.

"Cloak and dagger," Chambrun muttered. His eyes glittered. "The whole damned country is playing spy games these days, a million phones bugged. Half the world takes it as some sort of amusing parlor game. Who's listening to whom? Not, by God, in this hotel!" He took a deep drag on his cigarette, then ground it out in the ashtray on his desk. "Call Mr. Wilson, Mark, and tell him we'd like to come up to see him."

Mr. Wilson didn't answer his phone. Chambrun decided we would make an examination of Wilson's room whether he was there or not.

There was very little of interest in the room. Wilson had one extra suit, half a dozen shirts, some fresh underwear and handkerchiefs, two rather plain neckties, shaving things in the bathroom. There were no letters, papers or brief cases. Only a slightly aged canvas airplane bag. It was rather less than you'd expect to find in a seventy-dollar-per-day room.

I checked all this out while Jerry searched the room for a bugging device. He found what he was looking for in the telephone instrument itself. He had unscrewed the mouthpiece and sat looking at it, scowling.

"This is it," he said to Chambrun. "Sophisticated little doojig-

9

ger. Sends the sound to a listener somewhere or to a tape recorder somewhere. Like a tiny radio."

"Be careful how you handle it," Chambrun said. "It's so small it couldn't have been installed by a man wearing gloves. There might be a fingerprint on it."

At that moment there was the sound of a key in the door and a man came in. Warren Wilson was, I guessed, in his early thirties. He had sandy hair, cut short, and what was normally a pleasant boyish face. He was angry now.

"Who the hell are you and what are you doing here?" he demanded.

"I'm Pierre Chambrun, the hotel manager," Chambrun said. "This is Mr. Dodd, our security officer, and Mr. Haskell, our public-relations man."

"You're not entitled to be in my room!" Wilson said. He was staring at the phone which Jerry still held, taken apart, in his hands.

"We had reason to think your phone was bugged, Mr. Wilson," Chambrun said. "I didn't choose to wait for you to get back. Show him, Jerry."

Jerry held out the instrument. "Tiny radio device," he said. "Anything you said on the phone went out somewhere. I haven't had a chance to check it, but it may have reported anything that went on in here whether the phone was in use or not."

"That's crazy!" Wilson said. "Who had the room before me? It could have been for them—no chance to remove it."

"Your room was reserved for you by the C.I.A., Mr. Wilson. I assume you work for them," Chambrun said.

Wilson drew a deep breath and fumbled for a cigarette. "I guess there's no point in trying to pretend," he said. "Yes, I work for the C.I.A."

"You care to tell us why you're here at the Beaumont?"

"I can give you a surface explanation," Wilson said. "I'm what you might call a courier. I am carrying documents to be delivered to someone else registered here at the hotel."

"Who?"

Wilson studied the end of his cigarette. "I don't think I can tell you that, Mr. Chambrun. I will say that my contact is supposed to register here at the hotel. He hasn't done so yet."

"So you are waiting for him to show up?"

"Yes."

10

Chambrun glanced at the card in his hand. "You checked in yesterday noon."

"Yes."

"Did you ask for the man you're supposed to meet?"

"Yes."

"Whom did you ask?"

"The man at the desk who registered me."

"Atterbury," Jerry Dodd said. He knew exactly who was on duty every hour of the day.

"Whom did you ask for?" Chambrun asked.

"Sorry. I can't tell you that."

Chambrun turned to me. "Find out, Mark," he said. "Call Atterbury on the housekeeper's phone. We can't use this one." He looked at Wilson. "Atterbury will remember," he said.

Wilson shrugged. "I don't suppose the name matters," he said. "It isn't his real name. I asked for Curt Helwig. The man at the desk told me he had a reservation but that he hadn't checked in."

"And he still hasn't checked in?"

"According to the front desk."

"Have you any idea who might have wanted to overhear your conversations, Mr. Wilson?"

Wilson shook his head slowly. "No idea," he said.

"If you'd had any sensitive telephone calls to make would you have made them on this phone that goes through a switchboard?" Chambrun asked.

"Of course not."

Chambrun was, I saw, controlling his anger. "I don't like this kind of mumbo jumbo going on in my hotel," he said. "The whole damned country seems to be in the hands of idiot children playing spy games. Privacy seems to be a dead privilege. Well, by God, it isn't going to happen in the Beaumont! If somebody will bug your phone, Wilson, they may also try to steal the documents you're carrying. I suggest you put them in the hotel vault."

Wilson grinned. "I put them there right after I registered yesterday," he said. "I intend to leave them there till Helwig shows up."

"Good. Meanwhile we'll remove this device from your phone. When they realize they're not hearing what's going on here that may scare them off. Handle it carefully, Jerry. Remember, we may find a helpful print on it."

11

We left Jerry Dodd with Wilson and went down to the lobby where Atterbury was on duty again. Atterbury wasn't some kind of memory genius, but he did have total recall about Warren Wilson.

"He asked me for a Curt Helwig," Atterbury told Chambrun. "Helwig wasn't registered. Wilson seemed distressed and asked me to check on whether Helwig had a reservation."

"And did he?" Chambrun asked.

Atterbury nodded. "He did—and not quite usual, Mr. Chambrun. The reservation was made by a Washington source we honor without question. Same people who reserved Wilson's room. The thing that was unusual about Helwig's reservation was that they weren't quite sure when he would arrive— yesterday, today, tomorrow, even the day after that. We were to make sure, however, that there was a room for him when he did appear."

"Damn!" Chambrun said.

I knew what irritated him. The Beaumont is not far from the United Nations Building and many foreign diplomats and attachés make the hotel their home-away-from-home. Quite often we are asked by the State Department or the C.I.A. or top White House personnel to provide special accommodations. It isn't always convenient because the Beaumont rarely has any long-range vacancies.

So, more often than not, to accommodate the government, we'd have to turn away a regular guest. We had what we called "house seats," three or four rooms which we kept open, day to day, for emergencies; but these were almost always quickly filled. To hold a room for an indefinite arrival tended to upset our smooth routine.

"Let me know when this Helwig checks in," Chambrun said. "Wilson will pass over his documents—which he tells me are in the vault."

"I put them there—a brief case—myself," Atterbury said.

"Then let's get rid of these two cloak-and-dagger Johns as fast as we can," Chambrun said.

Mr. Wilson and his bugged phone went out of my mind during the rest of that day. I knew Jerry Dodd had removed the electronic gadget from the telephone in 912 and that he was trying to check out its source—that is, the manufacturer. It wasn't, Jerry assured us, a homemade device. There was a fashion show that afternoon that I had to cover and in the evening there was to be a coming-out party in the Grand Ballroom for some debutante chick. These are routines in which a PR man has to involve himself.

It was nearly three in the morning before I finally got to bed in my apartment on the second floor of the hotel. I was bushed, and I went to sleep the moment my head hit the pillow. Actually I hadn't been asleep more than twenty minutes when my phone rang.

I dredged myself up out of some dark void and managed to answer it. It was Mike Maggio, the night bell captain.

"Trouble," Mike said. "You're wanted in the lobby office on the double, Mark."

I mumbled something.

"Robbery," Mike said. "Somebody held up Karl Nevers, the night manager, forced him to open the vault, and took off with God-knows-what."

There had been robberies at the Pierre, the Plaza, the Waldorf-Astoria in the past. We had been waiting for our turn, although we thought our security setup was foolproof.

Behind the front desk in the lobby is a private office for use by the day and night managers. And behind that office is the vault. Only the manager on duty can open it. There's no time lock because guests come in at all times of the day or night with possessions they want to keep safe. Those possessions are mostly jewelry. There have been so many gem robberies around town in plush hotels that we urge guests to keep their gewgaws in the vault. We make it easy for them by having someone who can give them access round the clock. Every room and suite in the hotel has a sign in it urging this precaution.

It seemed that at a few minutes after three, the party in the ballroom being over, a Mrs. Horace Paradine, one of the guests, came to the desk and asked Karl Nevers to place her jewels in the vault. They started through the back office to the vault when someone came up behind them and stuck a gun against Mrs. Paradine's head. Nevers and Mrs. Paradine both described him as medium tall, medium thin; he was wearing a raincoat and had a tan-colored stocking mask over his head and face. Nevers would turn off the alarm system and open the vault or Mrs. Paradine would have her brains blown out onto the office rug.

Nevers is a cool character. He wasn't going to risk Mrs. Para-

13

dine's brains, if any, and he wasn't going to risk his own hide. He also knew exactly what would happen when he turned off the alarm system. There were two ways to turn it off which, Nevers felt certain, the gunman couldn't know. One way was the ordinary turnoff used when a guest came to get something or deposit something. The second way turned off the alarm but set off another. The instant that second way was used a silent-alarm system went into operation. The security office was warned, Chambrun's office and his penthouse apartment were warned, every maintenance office showed a blinking red light, and every doorman was alerted.

At the vault there was no sign of anything except the absence of alarm. Within two minutes of that second turnoff there was almost no way a thief could get out of the hotel undetected. The system was Jerry Dodd's pride and joy and Karl Nevers' comfort in a tense moment.

He used the second turnoff and opened the vault. Stocking Mask forced him and Mrs. Paradine into the vault, the woman sobbing hysterically.

It was a strange business. Mrs. Paradine, by her account, was wearing $100,000 worth of diamonds and other precious stones. The robber had only to snatch them off her, but he didn't.

Instead, the thief opened a couple of small lockboxes and took a handful of jewels without really looking at them.

"He didn't seem to have anything special in mind," Nevers told us. "He didn't examine what he took. Then he went to the box for Room 912, took out a small zippered brief case, told us to go to the end of the vault, went out, and shut us in."

Three minutes later Jerry Dodd opened the vault and let them out. He hadn't met anyone on his way in.

Dr. Partridge, the house physician, was called to deal with the weeping Mrs. Paradine, who had lost nothing. Jerry went to cover all his checkpoints. When I arrived, Chambrun, that hanging-judge look on his face, was in the vault room, waiting with Nevers for Jerry's report.

"It seems quite clear," Chambrun said, "that he wanted it to look like a haphazard robbery, which is why he took a few pieces of jewelry. What he really wanted was Warren Wilson's brief case. We'd better tell Wilson what's happened."

I called Wilson on the phone. He sounded sleepy. I told him what had happened and he was suddenly wide-awake.

14

"Be with you as soon as I can throw on some clothes," he said.

Chambrun fidgeted with one of his flat Egyptian cigarettes, walking around the vault room and actually into the vault itself which was still open. His forehead was drawn together in a concentrated scowl.

"Karl, describe to me again just how he behaved here in the vault," he said, turning to Nevers.

"He forced Mrs. Paradine and me in ahead of him," Nevers said. "He was still holding his gun to her head. Once we were inside the vault he shoved her away and ordered us to the rear of the vault. He was still covering us with the gun, though."

"How did he get the lockboxes open?" Chambrun asked.

"Master key," Nevers said. "He told me to throw him the master key. I did. I wasn't resisting, you understand, Mr. Chambrun. I figured there'd be help any minute."

"You did just the right thing," Chambrun said. "Go on."

"He opened two boxes that were closest to him. He reached in them with his free hand and dug out some pieces of jewelry from each box. He didn't even look at what he had, just stuffed the things in his raincoat pocket. Then he walked directly to the box for 912 and opened it."

"He seemed to know exactly what he was doing?"

"Yes, sir. He opened the box, took out the small brief case, tucked it under his arm, then backed out of the vault and shut us in."

Chambrun took a deep drag on his cigarette. "There's a raincoat hanging on the hatrack in the outer office. I noticed it when I came in. Is that yours, Karl?"

"No, sir. It was a beautiful night when I came on duty. I didn't wear any kind of coat. I wouldn't leave a coat in the outer office anyway. There's a coat closet for employees, as you know."

"Get that raincoat, Mark," Chambrun said.

The so-called "outer office" is not a space occupied by anyone in particular. It is a place where a guest can talk to the manager on duty, or to the credit manager, or to anyone else he wants to talk to in private. There is a table in the center of the room, several comfortable Windsor armchairs, a telephone on the table, and a hatrack in the corner near the door.

Chambrun rarely misses anything and he hadn't missed the raincoat hanging on the rack. There shouldn't have been a coat there without someone to go with it. It's the kind of detail that is

15

endlessly registering in his mind as he moves around the hotel—something out of place, no matter how inconsequential.

There was nothing special about the raincoat. I carried it back to the vault room and handed it to Chambrun. He felt in one of the pockets and I saw a bright hard look in his eyes. He brought his hand out and in it was a tan stocking mask. He reached in the other pocket and produced a handful of jewelry which he put on the table.

"The brief case was all he wanted," Chambrun said. "Smart operator. He left you and Mrs. Paradine in the vault, took off his mask and coat, left them on the hatrack, and walked out of here with the brief case under his arm, all casual and innocent-looking."

"Not so casual and innocent-looking," Jerry Dodd said from the doorway. We turned to look at him and his face was pale and tense with anger. "Butch Schooley, whose job it was to cover the northwest fire stairs when that Number Two alarm went off, is dead. Neck broken. Looks like a karate expert did him in."

Schooley was one of the night-security staff. He had evidently responded to the Number Two alarm and taken up his position in the northwest fire stairs. There are four inside fire stairs at the Beaumont, one at each corner of the building. They lead from the penthouse level down to the subbasement where the elevator machinery, the heating and air-conditioning units, and the chief engineer's shops were located. From that lower level there were exits to the street.

Schooley's body had been found at the third-floor level by Jerry. Someone had killed him on the way up or down. There was no escape possible from the hotel from the upper levels, so I guessed the murderer had been on the way down to his only way out. I said so.

"No, he didn't get out through the basement," Jerry said. "All the exits were covered down there as soon as the alarm went into effect. The killer is still somewhere in the hotel."

At that moment Warren Wilson joined us. He seemed to have hurried into his clothes, not bothering with a necktie. He looked frightened, I thought.

"Did they really get my brief case?" he asked.

"I'm afraid so," Chambrun said. "But Dodd thinks he's still somewhere in the hotel."

16

"I—I'd better get in touch with my chief in Washington," Wilson said. "If those documents are lost—even long enough to be photographed—I'm a dead duck, along with quite a few other people."

"There's a phone in the outer office," Chambrun said.

"Thanks," Wilson said and went to it.

There was nothing secret about the phone call. Wilson asked the night supervisor on the switchboard to charge it to his room. He gave her a number and I could see that Chambrun made a mental note of it. Presently there was a connection.

"Mr. Tabor?" Wilson asked. "I'm sorry to call you at this time, sir—there's been a robbery at the hotel and the stuff I was carrying is gone—yes, I know that, sir—no, Helwig hasn't checked in yet—I don't know who knew, except the clerk who put it in the vault for me—yes, the manager is here." Wilson turned to Chambrun. "It's my boss, Mr. Clarence Tabor of the C.I.A.," he said. "Would you please talk to him, Mr. Chambrun?"

Chambrun took the phone. I couldn't hear the other half of the conversation, but Tabor seemed to know Chambrun and Chambrun appeared to know him. "Wilson hasn't told you the whole story," Chambrun said. "Earlier today we discovered that the phone in his room had been bugged. What happened tonight was an armed holdup by a masked man who seemed to know exactly what he was looking for in the vault—no, but we don't think that he can have gotten out of the hotel, and he won't get out carrying that brief case. He can't hide it on himself—no, but we are about to bring in the police because one of my people has been killed—I don't give a damn about your top-level secrecy, Tabor! One of my staff has been murdered and I don't intend to hold back for God himself!" He put the phone down hard.

Wilson was mopping sweat off his face although the room was air-conditioned. "A lot of people in high places are going to be in big trouble if we don't get that stuff back fast," he said.

"I'm sick of people in high places who are so concerned with their own power that they have to operate forever undercover," Chambrun said. "I don't care who gets into big trouble."

"Since we have no idea who it is, what's to stop him from just checking out of the hotel with my documents in his luggage?" Wilson asked. "Will you subject everybody to a search before they leave the hotel?"

17

Chambrun's cold eyes seemed to be buried in their deep pouches. "I don't think that will be necessary," he said. He turned to Nevers. "However, Karl, let me know if anyone tries to check out before the normal time this morning. If anyone tries, stall until I get to them."

"Yes, sir."

Chambrun gave Wilson a thoughtful look. "You're a professional, Mr. Wilson, at this sort of thing."

"I don't follow you," Wilson said.

"Spy and counterspy, all perfectly legal, of course. Suppose you knew an enemy agent had important documents in our vault, how would you go about getting them?"

Wilson shrugged. "This fellow knew his job pretty well," he said. "I don't know that I could improve on it."

"Probably not," Chambrun said. "There's just one thing this man didn't know when he was planning."

"Oh?" Wilson said.

"That when the alarm was turned off in the vault a certain way it set off another alarm, a silent one, that warned us the vault was being robbed. He couldn't have anticipated that. He thought he had plenty of time, with Nevers and Mrs. Paradine locked inside the vault. He'd planned his escape by way of the northwest fire stairs and unexpectedly he ran into Schooley. So he had to kill."

"In my experience," Wilson said "there's always something unexpected happening. You have to be trained to act without hesitation in any emergency."

"But this man must have had an escape plan as well as his plan to get into the vault, wouldn't you say?"

Wilson nodded. "They'd be equally important," he said.

"So this man planned to make his escape by way of the northwest fire stairs," Chambrun said. "He only had to walk a few yards across the lobby to the stairway door, carrying the brief case, of course. He assumed there had been no alarm, so he didn't have to move so fast that he'd attract attention."

"Sounds logical," Wilson said.

"He must have checked out the ground pretty thoroughly, wouldn't you say?" Chambrun sounded almost casual.

"As I've said, he was obviously a professional."

Chambrun put out his cigarette in an ashtray on the telephone table. He actually smiled at Wilson. "Since he knew the hotel so well," he said, "why do you suppose our man headed *up*

18

the northwest stairway instead of *down?* There's no escape from the upper levels. He must have known that."

"That's pretty obvious, isn't it?" Wilson said. "He started down, found the way blocked by someone alerted by the alarm he didn't know about, and had no choice but to head up in the hope of escaping somewhere into the upper levels of the hotel."

"And ran into Schooley?"

"Must have," Wilson said.

Chambrun seemed to consider this for a moment. "There could be another explanation," he said. "He always *meant* to go up—to his room."

"Could be," Wilson said, "if he had a room."

"I'm inclined to think he does have a room," Chambrun said. He smiled again. "You know, I've had some experience with crime, Mr. Wilson. I always try to put myself in the criminal's mind and think as he might have thought. I assume these documents he stole would be worth a great deal of money to the thief—perhaps blackmail money?"

"You can say that again," Wilson said.

"Being a professional, this man must have recognized the danger of being caught with the documents in his possession. He'd want to get them off his person just as fast as he could, in case anything went wrong."

"You mean, hide them?" Wilson asked.

"Something like that," Chambrun said. "Of course, if he was caught he'd have some difficulty getting back to the hiding place."

"A confederate?" Wilson suggested.

"Would you share a big financial bonanza with someone else, Mr. Wilson?"

Wilson shrugged. "There might not be any other choice. Not in advance, I wouldn't. If I was caught I might get help from my lawyer, for example. But I wouldn't cut anyone in ahead of time."

"And he would know we'd search the hotel from top to bottom," Chambrun said, "so he'd have prepared a safe hiding place."

"Yes, he would."

I could see Jerry Dodd champing at the bit. Chambrun's theorizing wasn't getting us anywhere and Schooley's killer was still at large somewhere in the hotel.

"And that hiding place would have to be somewhere not far

19

from this vault room if he was to dispose of the brief case quickly." Chambrun turned to Jerry Dodd. "Let's walk over what must have been his escape route, Jerry. He'd walk from here through the outer office. He stopped there to take off his mask and then his raincoat—"

We walked into the outer office, Chambrun pausing by the old-fashioned hatrack. He looked around the office.

"No place to hide a brief case here," he said.

We went out into the lobby. It was buzzing with people, mostly staff, who knew what had happened. Ordinarily there would only have been the cleaning crew there at four thirty in the morning. Chambrun headed toward the northwest fire-door exit, Wilson, Jerry, and I following him. He stopped at the door. Just to the left of it was a large mailbox, with slots for letters and larger packages. Chambrun looked at Jerry.

"Can you open that mailbox, Jerry?" he asked.

"At the risk of spending the rest of my natural life in jail," Jerry said. "That's a Federal offense."

"Let's risk it," Chambrun said.

"What's the idea?" Jerry asked. He didn't like it.

"I'm trying to think like our man," Chambrun said. "I'd have come prepared to get rid of that brief case quickly. It would not be easy to hide. But if I had a large envelope prepared that would hold it, all I'd have to do would be to drop it in a mailbox, addressed to some prearranged post-office box, and let Uncle Sam protect it for me.

"He'd been over the ground. He knew this mailbox was here, only a few yards from the vault room. He probably put the brief case in his prepared, stamped envelope when he discarded his coat and mask in the outer office. He walks, innocent as you please, across the lobby to this box and mails his package, quite openly. Open it up, Jerry."

Jerry produced some kind of kit from his pocket and went to work on the mailbox lock. It evidently wasn't very complicated because he got it open almost at once. The big box was half full and Chambrun fumbled around with the contents. Like a magician pulling a rabbit out of his hat he produced a large manila envelope. He read us the address.

P.O. Box 1724
Grand Central Post Office
New York, N.Y. 10017

Chambrun handed the package to Wilson. "I don't think we should compound our Federal offenses by opening it, Mr. Wilson, but would you guess from the feel of it that we might have your brief case here?"

Wilson took the envelope and felt it carefully. "By God, I think you've found it, Mr. Chambrun," he said.

Chambrun almost snatched the package away from Wilson and he wasn't smiling any more. "Check this for the fingerprints Mr. Wilson just made, Jerry," he said. "I think you'll find that the prints on this package match the one you took off the electronic device on Mr. Wilson's phone."

Jerry opened his mouth to speak, then closed it. Chambrun turned to Wilson.

"You were headed upstairs for your room when you ran into Schooley, weren't you, Wilson? Your fingerprints on that package have blown the ball game. You bugged your own phone to make us think someone else was involved. You had to stage the robbery so that the people in Washington would never think of you as the thief. The subsequent blackmailing of higher-ups would appear to be the work of the man who robbed you."

Wilson was sweating again. He looked around like someone trapped, then made a quick move away from us.

"Hold it right there, Wilson!" Jerry Dodd shouted. He'd produced a gun. "Your body will look like a hunk of Swiss cheese if you take one more step."

A couple of Jerry's security boys took charge of Wilson. We stood, watching him being taken away. He would be charged with homicide and robbery.

"Those C.I.A. boys are taught all kinds of things, including karate," Chambrun said, then sighed. "It was mighty bad luck for Schooley."

"I damn near blew it," Jerry said. "You know there was no fingerprint on that telephone gadget. It was too small to take a clear print."

Chambrun's smile was grim. "But Wilson didn't know that," he said. "I wanted him to make a move, just to be certain."

THE POISONED DOW '08

BY DOROTHY L. SAYERS

Dorothy L. Sayers was born in Oxford, England, in 1893, and received her degree from Somerville College, Oxford, in 1915. She was editor of the periodical *Oxford Poetry* from 1917 to 1919, and herself published two volumes of verse. Her first mystery novel, *Whose Body?* (1923), introduced Lord Peter Wimsey, the aristocratic amateur detective. Wimsey also appeared in *Clouds of Witness* (1926), *Strong Poison* (1930), and several other novels and many short stories. Sayers also produced three mystery anthologies, and wrote religious plays and essays in popular theology. She began working on a new translation of Dante and completed the *Inferno* and the *Purgatorio* before her death in 1957.

"GOOD MORNING, MISS," said Mr. Montague Egg, removing his smart trilby with something of a flourish as the front door opened. "Here I am again, you see. Not forgotten me, have you? That's right, because I couldn't forget a young lady like you, not in a hundred years. How's his lordship today? Think he'd be willing to see me for a minute or two?"

He smiled pleasantly, bearing in mind Maxim Number Ten of the *Salesman's Handbook,* "The goodwill of the maid is nine-tenths of the trade."

The parlormaid, however, seemed nervous.

"I don't—oh, yes—come in, please. His lordship—that is to say—I'm afraid—"

Mr. Egg stepped in promptly, sample case in hand, and to his great surprise found himself confronted by a policeman, who, in somewhat gruff tones, demanded his name and business.

"Traveling representative of Plummet and Rose, Wines and Spirits, Piccadilly," said Mr. Egg, with the air of one who has nothing to conceal. "Here's my card. What's up, sergeant?"

"Plummet and Rose?" said the policeman. "Ah, well, just sit down a moment, will you? The inspector'll want to have a word with you, I shouldn't wonder."

More and more astonished, Mr. Egg obediently took a seat, and in a few minutes' time found himself ushered into a small sitting-room which was occupied by a uniformed police inspector and another policeman with a notebook.

"Ah!" said the inspector. "Take a seat, will you, Mr.—ha, hum—Egg. Perhaps you can give us a little light on this affair. Do you know anything about a case of port wine that was sold to Lord Borrodale last spring?"

"Certainly I do," replied Mr. Egg, "if you mean the Dow '08. I made the sale myself. Six dozen at 192s. a dozen. Ordered from me, personally, March third. Dispatched from our head office March eighth. Receipt acknowledged March tenth, with check in settlement. All in order our end. Nothing wrong with it, I hope? We've had no complaint. In fact, I've just called to ask his lordship how he liked it and to ask if he'd care to place a further order."

"I see," said the inspector. "You just happened to call today in

23

the course of your usual round? No special reason?"

Mr. Egg, now convinced that something was very wrong indeed, replied by placing his order-book and road schedule at the inspector's disposal.

"Yes," said the inspector, when he had glanced through them. "That seems to be all right. Well, now, Mr. Egg, I'm sorry to say that Lord Borrodale was found dead in his study this morning under circumstances strongly suggestive of his having taken poison. And what's more, it looks very much as if the poison had been administered to him in a glass of this port wine of yours."

"You don't say!" said Mr. Egg incredulously. "I'm very sorry to hear that. It won't do us any good, either. Not but what the wine was wholesome enough when we sent it out. Naturally, it wouldn't pay us to go putting anything funny into our wines; I needn't tell you that. But it's not the sort of publicity we care for. What makes you think it was the port, anyway?"

For answer, the inspector pushed over to him a glass decanter which stood upon the table.

"See what you think yourself. It's all right—we've tested it for fingerprints already. Here's a glass if you want one, but I shouldn't advise you to swallow anything—not unless you're fed up with life."

Mr. Egg took a cautious sniff at the decanter and frowned. He poured out a thimbleful of the wine, sniffed, and frowned again. Then he took an experimental drop upon his tongue, and immediately expectorated, with the utmost possible delicacy, into a convenient flower-pot.

"Oh, dear, oh, dear," said Mr. Montague Egg. His rosy face was puckered with distress. "Tastes to me as though the old gentleman had been dropping his cigar-ends into it."

The inspector exchanged a glance with the policeman.

"You're not far out," he said. "The doctor hasn't quite finished his post-mortem, but he says it looks to him like nicotine poisoning. Now, here's the problem. Lord Borrodale was accustomed to drink a couple of glasses of port in his study every night after dinner. Last night the wine was taken in to him as usual at nine o'clock. It was a new bottle, and Craven—that's the butler—brought it straight up from the cellar in a basket arrangement—"

"A cradle," interjected Mr. Egg.

"—a cradle, if that's what you call it. James the footman followed him, carrying the decanter and a wineglass on a tray. Lord Borrodale inspected the bottle, which still bore the original seal, and then Craven drew the cork and decanted the wine in full view of Lord Borrodale and the footman. Then both servants left the room and retired to the kitchen quarters, and as they went, they heard Lord Borrodale lock the study door."

"What did he do that for?"

"It seems he usually did. He was writing his memoirs—he was a famous judge, you know—and as some of the papers he was using were highly confidential, he preferred to make himself safe against sudden intruders. At eleven o'clock, when the household went to bed, James noticed that the light was still on in the study. In the morning it was discovered that Lord Borrodale had not been to bed. The study door was still locked and when it was broken open, they found him lying dead on the floor. It looked as though he had been taken ill, had tried to reach the bell, and had collapsed on the way. The doctor says he must have died at about ten o'clock."

"Suicide?" suggested Mr. Egg.

"Well, there are difficulties about that. The position of the body, for one thing. Also, we've carefully searched the room and found no traces of any bottle or anything that he could have kept the poison in. Besides, he seems to have enjoyed his life. He had no financial or domestic worries, and in spite of his advanced age his health was excellent. Why should he commit suicide?"

"But if he didn't," objected Mr. Egg, "how was it he didn't notice the bad taste and smell of the wine?"

"Well, he seems to have been smoking a pretty powerful cigar at the time," said the inspector (Mr. Egg shook a reproachful head), "and I'm told he was suffering from a slight cold, so that his taste and smell may not have been in full working order. There are no fingerprints on the decanter or the glass except his own and those of the butler and the footman—though, of course, that wouldn't prevent anybody dropping poison into either of them, if only the door hadn't been locked. The windows were both fastened on the inside, too, with burglar-proof catches."

"How about the decanter?" asked Mr. Egg, jealous for the reputation of his firm. "Was it clean when it came in?"

"Yes, it was. James washed it out immediately before it went into the study; the cook swears she saw him do it. He used water

25

from the tap and then swilled it round with a drop of brandy."

"Quite right," said Mr. Egg approvingly.

"And there's nothing wrong with the brandy, either, for Craven took a glass of it himself afterwards—to settle his palpitations, so he says." The inspector sniffed meaningly. "The glass was wiped out by James when he put it on the tray, and then the whole thing was carried along to the study. Nothing was put down or left for a moment between leaving the pantry and entering the study, but Craven recollects that as he was crossing the hall Miss Waynfleet stopped him and spoke to him for a moment about some arrangements for the following day."

"Miss Waynfleet? That's the niece, isn't it? I saw her on my last visit. A very charming young lady."

"Lord Borrodale's heiress," remarked the inspector meaningly.

"A very *nice* young lady," said Mr. Egg, with emphasis. "And I understand you to say that Craven was carrying only the cradle, not the decanter or the glass."

"That's so."

"Well, then, I don't see that she could have put anything into what James was carrying." Mr. Egg paused. "The seal on the cork, now—you say Lord Borrodale saw it?"

"Yes, and so did Craven and James. You can see it for yourself, if you like—what's left of it."

The inspector produced an ashtray, which held a few fragments of dark blue sealing-wax, together with a small quantity of cigar-ash. Mr. Egg inspected them carefully.

"That's our wax and our seal, all right," he pronounced. "The top of the cork has been sliced off cleanly with a sharp knife and the mark's intact. 'Plummet and Rose. Dow 1908.' Nothing wrong with that. How about the strainer?"

"Washed out that same afternoon in boiling water by the kitchenmaid. Wiped immediately before using by James, who brought it in on the tray with the decanter and the glass. Taken out with the bottle and washed again at once, unfortunately—otherwise, of course, it might have told us something about when the nicotine got into the port wine."

"Well," said Mr. Egg obstinately, "it didn't get in at our place, that's a certainty. What's more, I don't believe it ever was in the bottle at all. How could it be? Where *is* the bottle, by the way?"

"It's just been packed up to go to the analyst, I think," said the inspector, "but as you're here, you'd better have a look at it.

Podgers, let's have that bottle again. There are no fingerprints on it except Craven's, by the way, so it doesn't look as if it had been tampered with."

The policeman produced a brown paper parcel, from which he extracted a port-bottle, its mouth plugged with a clean cork. Some of the original dust of the cellar still clung to it, mingled with fingerprint powder. Mr. Egg removed the cork and took a long, strong sniff at the contents. Then his face changed.

"Where did you get this bottle from?" he demanded sharply.

"From Craven. Naturally, it was one of the first things we asked to see. He took us along to the cellar and pointed it out."

"Was it standing by itself or with a lot of other bottles?"

"It was standing on the cellar floor at the end of a row of empties, all belonging to the same bin; he explained that he put them on the floor in the order in which they were used, till the time came for them to be collected and taken away."

Mr. Egg thoughtfully tilted the bottle; a few drops of thick red liquid, turbid with disturbed crust, escaped into his wine-glass. He smelt them again and tasted them. His snub nose looked pugnacious.

"Well?" asked the inspector.

"No nicotine there, at all events," said Mr. Egg, "unless my nose deceives me, which, you will understand, inspector, isn't likely, my nose being my livelihood, so to speak. No. You'll have to send it to be analyzed, of course; I quite understand that, but I'd be ready to bet quite a little bit of money you'll find that bottle innocent. And that, I needn't tell you, will be a great relief to our minds. And I'm sure I very much appreciate the kind way you've put the matter before me."

"That's all right; your expert knowledge is of value. We can probably now exclude the bottle straight away and concentrate on the decanter."

"Just so," replied Mr. Egg. "Ye-es. Do you happen to know how many of the six dozen bottles had been used?"

"No, but Craven can tell us, if you really want to know."

"Just for my own satisfaction," said Mr. Egg. "Just to be sure that this *is* the right bottle, you know. I shouldn't like to feel I might have misled you in any way."

The inspector rang the bell and the butler promptly appeared—an elderly man of intensely respectable appearance.

"Craven," said the inspector, "this is Mr. Egg of Plummet and Rose's."

27

"I am already acquainted with Mr. Egg."

"Quite. He is naturally interested in the history of the port wine. He would like to know—what is it, exactly, Mr. Egg?"

"This bottle," said Monty, rapping it lightly with his finger-nail, "it's the one you opened last night?"

"Yes, sir."

"Sure of that?"

"Yes, sir."

"How many dozen have you got left?"

"I couldn't say off-hand, sir, without the cellar-book."

"And that's in the cellar, eh? I'd like to have a look at your cellars—I'm told they're very fine. All in apple-pie order, I'm sure. Right temperature and all that?"

"Undoubtedly, sir."

"We'll all go and look at the cellar," suggested the inspector, who in spite of his expressed confidence seemed to have doubts about leaving Mr. Egg alone with the butler.

Craven bowed and led the way, pausing only to fetch the keys from his pantry.

"This nicotine, now," prattled Mr. Egg, as they proceeded down a long corridor, "is it very deadly? I mean, would you require a great quantity of it to poison a person?"

"I understand from the doctor," replied the inspector, "that a few drops of the pure extract, or whatever they call it, would produce death in anything from twenty minutes to seven or eight hours."

"Dear, dear!" said Mr. Egg. "And how much of the port had the poor old gentleman taken? The full two glasses?"

"Yes, sir; to judge by the decanter, he had. Lord Borrodale had the habit of drinking his port straight off. He did not sip it."

Mr. Egg was distressed.

"Not the right thing at all," he said mournfully. "No, no. Smell, sip, and savor to bring out the flavor—that's the rule for wine, you know. Is there such a thing as a pond or stream in the garden, Mr. Craven?"

"No sir," said the butler, a little surprised.

"Ah! I was just wondering. Somebody must have brought the nicotine along in something or other, you know. What would they do afterwards with the little bottle or whatever it was?"

"Easy enough to throw it in among the bushes or bury it, surely," said Craven. "There's six acres of garden, not counting the meadow or the courtyard. Or there are the water-butts, of course, and the well." the butler added.

"How stupid of me," confessed Mr. Egg. "I never thought of that. Ah! this is the cellar, is it? Splendid—a real slap-up outfit, I call this. Nice, even temperature, too. Same summer and winter, eh? Well away from the house-furnace?"

"Oh, yes indeed, sir. That's the other side of the house. Be careful of the last step, gentlemen; it's a little broken away. Here is where the Dow '08 stood, sir. Number Seventeen bin— one, two, three and a half dozen remaining, sir."

Mr. Egg nodded and holding his electric torch close to the protruding necks of the bottles, made a careful examination of the seals.

"Yes," he said, "here they are. Three and a half dozen, as you say. Sad to think that the throat they should have gone down lies, as you might say, closed up by Death. I often think, as I make my rounds, what a pity it is we don't all grow mellower and softer in our old age, same as this wine. A fine old gentleman, Lord Borrodale, or so I'm told, but something of a tough nut, if that's not disrespectful."

"He was hard, sir," agreed the butler, "but just. A very just master."

"Quite," said Mr. Egg. "And these, I take it, are the empties. Twelve, twenty-four, twenty-nine—and one is thirty—and three and a half dozen is forty-two—seventy-two—six dozen— that's O.K. by me." He lifted the empty bottles one by one. "They say dead men tell no tales, but they talk to little Monty Egg all right. This one, for instance. If this ever held Plummet and Rose's Dow '08 you can take Monty Egg and scramble him. Wrong smell, wrong crust, and that splash of whitewash was never put on by our cellar-man. Very easy to mix up one empty bottle with another. Twelve, twenty-four, twenty-eight and one is twenty-nine. I wonder what's become of the thirtieth bottle."

"I'm sure I never took one away," said the butler.

"The pantry keys—on a nail inside the door—very accessible," said Monty.

"Just a moment," interrupted the inspector. "Do you say that that bottle doesn't belong to the same bunch of port wine?"

"No, it doesn't—but no doubt Lord Borrodale sometimes went in for a change of vintage." Mr. Egg inverted the bottle and shook it sharply. "Quite dry. Curious. Had a dead spider at the bottom of it. You'd be surprised how long a spider can exist without food. Curious that this empty bottle, which comes in the middle of the row, should be drier than the one at the beginning of the row and should contain a dead spider. We see a deal of curious things in our calling, inspector—we're encouraged to notice things, as you might say. 'The salesman with the open eye sees commissions mount up high.' You might call this bottle a curious thing. And here's another. That other bottle—the one you said was opened last night, Craven—how did you come to make a mistake like that? If my nose is to be trusted, not to mention my palate, that bottle's been open a week at least."

"Has it indeed, sir? I'm sure it's the one I put here at the end of this row. Somebody must have been and changed it."

"But—" said the inspector. He stopped in mid-speech, as though struck by a sudden thought. "I think you'd better let me have those cellar keys of yours, Craven, and we'll get this cellar properly examined. That'll do for the moment. If you'll just step upstairs with me, Mr. Egg, I'd like a word with you."

"Always happy to oblige," said Monty agreeably. They returned to the upper air.

"I don't know if you realize, Mr. Egg," observed the inspector, "the bearing, or, as I might say, the inference of what you said just now. Supposing you're right about this bottle not being the right one, somebody's changed it on purpose, and the right one's missing. And, what's more, the person that changed the bottle left no fingerprints behind him—or her."

"I see what you mean," said Mr. Egg, who had indeed drawn this inference some time ago, "and what's more, it looks as if the poison had been in the bottle after all, doesn't it? And that—you're going to say—is a serious look-out for Plummet and Rose, seeing there's no doubt our seal was on the bottle when it was brought into Lord Borrodale's room. I don't deny it, inspector. It's useless to bluster and say 'No, no,' when it's perfectly clear that the facts are so. That's a very useful motto for a man that wants to get on in our line of business."

"Well, Mr. Egg," said the inspector, laughing. "what will you say to the next inference? Since nobody but you had any interest in changing that bottle over, it looks as though I ought to clap the handcuffs on you."

"Now that's a disagreeable sort of an inference," protested Mr. Egg, "and I hope you won't follow it up. I shouldn't like anything of that sort to happen, and my employers wouldn't fancy it either. Don't you think that before we do anything we might have cause to regret, it would be a good idea to have a look in the furnace-room?"

"Why the furnace-room?"

"Because," said Mr. Egg, "it's the place that Craven particularly didn't mention when we were asking him where anybody might have put a thing he wanted to get rid of."

The inspector appeared to be struck by this line of reasoning. He enlisted the aid of a couple of constables, and very soon the ashes of the furnace that supplied the central heating were being assiduously raked over. The first find was a thick mass of semi-molten glass which looked as though it might once have been part of a wine bottle.

"Looks as though you might be right," said the inspector, "but I don't see how we're to prove anything. We're not likely to get any nicotine out of this."

"I suppose not," agreed Mr. Egg sadly. "But"—his face brightened—"how about this?"

From the sieve in which the constable was sifting the ashes he picked out a thin piece of warped and twisted metal to which a lump of charred bone still clung.

"What on earth's that?"

"It doesn't look like much, but I think it might once have been a corkscrew," suggested Mr. Egg mildly. "There's something homely and familiar about it. And, if you'll look here, I think you'll see that the metal part of it is hollow. And I shouldn't be surprised if the thick bone handle was hollow, too. It's very badly charred, of course, but if you were to split it open, and if you were to find a hollow inside it, and possibly a little melted rubber—well, that might explain a lot."

The inspector smacked his thigh.

"By Jove, Mr. Egg!" he exclaimed, "I believe I see what you're getting at. You mean that if this corkscrew had been made hollow, and contained a rubber reservoir, inside, like a fountain pen, filled with poison, the poison might be made to flow down the hollow shaft by pressure on some sort of plunger arrangement."

"That's it," said Mr. Egg. "It would have to be screwed into the cork very carefully, of course, so as not to damage the tube, and it would have to be made long enough to project beyond the bottom of the cork, but still, it might be done. What's more, it has been done, or why should there be this little hole in the metal, about a quarter of an inch from the tip? Ordinary

31

corkscrews never have holes in them—not in my experience, and I've been, as you might say, brought up on corkscrews."

"But who, in that case—?"

"Well, the man who drew the cork, don't you think? The man whose fingerprints were on the bottle."

"Craven? But where's his motive?"

"I don't know," said Mr. Egg, "but Lord Borrodale was a judge, and a hard judge too. If you were to have Craven's fingerprints sent up to Scotland Yard, they might recognize them. I don't know. It's possible, isn't it? Or maybe Miss Waynfleet might know something about him. Or he might just possibly be mentioned in Lord Borrodale's memoirs that he was writing."

The inspector lost no time in following up his suggestion. Neither Scotland Yard nor Miss Waynfleet had anything to say against the butler, who had been two years in his situation and had always been quite satisfactory, but a reference to the records of Lord Borrodale's judicial career showed that a good many years before he had inflicted a savage sentence of penal servitude on a young man called Craven, who was by trade a skilled metal-worker and had apparently been involved in a fraud upon his employer. A little further investigation showed that this young man had been released from prison six months previously.

"Craven's son, of course," said the inspector. "And he had the manual skill to make the corkscrew in exact imitation of the one ordinarily used in the household. Wonder where they got the nicotine from? Well, we shall soon be able to check that up. I believe it's not difficult to obtain it for use in the garden. I'm very much obliged to you for your expert assistance, Mr. Egg. It would have taken us a long time to get to the rights and wrongs of those bottles. I suppose, when you found that Craven had given you the wrong one, you began to suspect him?"

"Oh, no," said Mr. Egg, with modest pride, "I knew it was Craven the minute he came into the room."

"No, did you? But why?"

"He called me 'sir,' " explained Mr. Egg, coughing delicately. "Last time I called he addressed me as 'young fellow' and told me that tradesmen must go round to the back door. A bad error of policy. 'Whether you're wrong or whether you're right, it's always better to be polite,' as it says in the *Salesman's Handbook.*"

THE STRIPPER

BY H. H. HOLMES

H. H. Holmes was the alternate pseudonym of Anthony
Boucher (William Anthony Parker White, 1911-1968).
He received his bachelor's degree from the University of
Southern California in 1932 and a master's degree in
German from the University of California in 1934. His
first mystery novel, *The Case of the Seven of Calvary,* was
published in 1937. Besides writing mysteries and science
fiction, Boucher was a highly respected critic, editor,
and anthologist in both fields. He reviewed mysteries for
*Ellery Queen's Mystery Magazine, The New York Times Book
Review,* and *The San Francisco Chronicle,* and won three
Edgar awards from the Mystery Writers of America for
his mystery criticism.

HE WAS CALLED Jack the Stripper because the only witness who had seen him and lived (J. F. Flugelbach, 1463 N. Edgemont) had described the glint of moonlight on bare skin. The nickname was inevitable.

Mr. Flugelbach had stumbled upon the fourth of the murders, the one in the grounds of City College. He had not seen enough to be of any help to the police; but at least he had furnished a name for the killer heretofore known by such routine cognomens as "butcher," "werewolf," and "vampire."

The murders in themselves were enough to make a newspaper's fortune. They were frequent, bloody, and pointless, since neither theft nor rape was attempted. The murderer was no specialist, like the original Jack, but rather an eclectic, like Kürten the Düsseldorf Monster, who struck when the mood was on him and disregarded age and sex. This indiscriminate taste made better copy; the menace threatened not merely a certain class of unfortunates but every reader.

It was the nudity, however, and the nickname evolved from it, that made the case truly celebrated. Feature writers dug up all the legends of naked murderers—Courvoisier of London, Durrant of San Francisco, Wallace of Liverpool, Borden of Fall River—and printed them as sober fact, explaining at length the advantages of avoiding the evidence of bloodstains.

When he read this explanation, he always smiled. It was plausible, but irrelevant. The real reason for nakedness was simply that it felt better that way. When the color of things began to change, his first impulse was to get rid of his clothing. He supposed that psychoanalysts could find some atavistic reason for that.

He felt the cold air on his naked body. He had never noticed that before. Noiselessly he pushed the door open and tiptoed into the study. His hand did not waver as he raised the knife.

The Stripper case was Lieutenant Marshall's baby, and he was going nuts. His condition was not helped by the constant allusions of his colleagues to the fact that his wife had once been a stripper of a more pleasurable variety. Six murders in three months, without a single profitable lead, had reduced him to a state where a lesser man might have gibbered, and sometimes he thought it would be simpler to be a lesser man.

He barked into phones nowadays. He hardly apologized when he realized that his caller was Sister Ursula, that surprising nun who had once planned to be a policewoman and who had extricated him from several extraordinary cases. But that was just it; those had been extraordinary, freak locked-room problems, while this was the horrible epitome of ordinary, clueless, plotless murder. There was no room in the Stripper case for the talents of Sister Ursula.

He was in a hurry and her sentences hardly penetrated his mind until he caught the word "Stripper." Then he said sharply, "So? Backtrack please, Sister. I'm afraid I wasn't listening."

"He says," her quiet voice repeated, "that he thinks he knows who the Stripper is, but he hasn't enough proof. He'd like to talk to the police about it; and since he knows I know you, he asked me to arrange it so that you wouldn't think him just a crank."

"Which," said Marshall, "he probably is. But to please you, Sister . . . What did you say his name is?"

"Flecker. Harvey Flecker. Professor of Latin at the University."

Marshall caught his breath. "Coincidence," he said flatly. "I'm on my way to see him now."

"Oh. Then he did get in touch with you himself?"

"Not with me," said Marshall. "With the Stripper."

"God rest his soul . . ." Sister Ursula murmured.

"So. I'm on my way now. If you could meet me there and bring his letter—"

"Lieutenant, I know our order is a singularly liberal one, but still I doubt if Reverend Mother—"

"You're a material witness," Marshall said authoritatively. "I'll send a car for you. And don't forget the letter."

Sister Ursula hung up and sighed. She had liked Professor Flecker, both for his scholarly wit and for his quiet kindliness. He was the only man who could hold his agnostic own with Father Pearson in disputatious sophistry, and he was also the man who had helped keep the Order's soup-kitchen open at the depth of the depression.

She took up her breviary and began to read the office for the dead while she waited for the car.

35

"It is obvious," Professor Lowe enunciated, "that the Stripper is one of the three of us."

Hugo Ellis said, "Speak for yourself." His voice cracked a little, and he seemed even younger than he looked.

Professor de' Cassis said nothing. His huge hunchbacked body crouched in the corner and he mourned his friend.

"So?" said Lieutenant Marshall. "Go on, Professor."

"It was by pure chance," Professor Lowe continued, his lean face alight with logical satisfaction, "that the back door was latched last night. We have been leaving it unfastened for Mrs. Carey since she lost her key; but Flecker must have forgotten that fact and inadvertently reverted to habit. Ingress by the front door was impossible, since it was not only secured by a spring lock but also bolted from within. None of the windows shows any sign of external tampering. The murderer presumably counted upon the back door to make plausible the entrance of an intruder; but Flecker had accidentally secured it, and that accident," he concluded impressively, "will strap the Tripper."

Hugo Ellis laughed, and then looked ashamed of himself.

Marshall laughed too. "Setting aside the Spoonerism, Professor, your statement of the conditions is flawless. This house was locked tight as a drum. Yes, the Stripper is one of the three of you." It wasn't amusing when Marshall said it.

Professor de' Cassis raised his despondent head. "But why?" His voice was guttural. "Why?"

Hugo Ellis said, "Why? With a madman?"

Professor Lowe lifted one finger as though emphasizing a point in a lecture. "Ah, but is this a madman's crime? There is the point. When the Stripper kills a stranger, yes, he is mad. When he kills a man with whom he lives . . . may he not be applying the technique of his madness to the purpose of his sanity?"

"It's an idea," Marshall admitted. "I can see where there's going to be some advantage in having a psychologist among the witnesses. But there's another witness I'm even more anxious to—" His face lit up as Sergeant Raglan came in. "She's here, Rags?"

"Yeah," said Raglan. "It's the sister. Holy smoke, Loot, does this mean this is gonna be another screwy one?"

Marshall had said *she* and Raglan had said *the sister*. These facts may serve as sufficient characterization of Sister Felicitas, who had accompanied her. They were always a pair, yet always spoken of in the singular. Now Sister Felicitas dozed in the corner where the hunchback had crouched, and Marshall read and reread the letter which seemed like the posthumous utterance of the Stripper's latest victim:

My dear Sister:

I have reason to fear that someone close to me is Jack the Stripper.

You know me, I trust, too well to think me a sensationalist striving to be a star witness. I have grounds for what I say. This individual, whom I shall for the moment call "Quasimodo" for reasons that might particularly appeal to you, first betrayed himself when I noticed a fleck of blood behind his ear—a trifle, but suggestive. Since then I have religiously observed his comings and goings, and found curious coincidences between the absence of Quasimodo and the presence elsewhere of the Stripper.

I have not a conclusive body of evidence, but I believe that I do have sufficient to bring to the attention of the authorities. I have heard you mention a Lieutenant Marshall who is a close friend of yours. If you will recommend me to him as a man whose word is to be taken seriously, I shall be deeply obliged.

I may, of course, be making a fool of myself with my suspicions of Quasimodo, which is why I refrain from giving you his real name. But every man must do what is possible to rid this city *a negotio perambulante in tenebris.*

Yours respectfully,

Harvey Flecker

"He didn't have much to go on, did he?" Marshall observed. "But he was right, God help him. And he may have known more than he cared to trust to a letter. He must have slipped somehow and let Quasimodo see his suspicions. . . . What does that last phrase mean?"

"Lieutenant! And you an Oxford man!" exclaimed Sister Ursula.

"I can translate it. But what's its connotation?"

"It's from St. Jerome's Vulgate of the ninetieth psalm. The Douay version translates it literally: *of the business that walketh*

37

about in the dark; but that doesn't convey the full horror of that nameless prowling *negotium.* It's one of the most terrible phrases I know, and perfect for the Stripper."

"Flecker was a Catholic?"

"No, he was a resolute agnostic, though I have always had hopes that Thomist philosophy would lead him into the Church. I almost think he refrained because his conversion would have left nothing to argue with Father Pearson about. But he was an excellent Church Latinist and knew the liturgy better than most Catholics."

"Do you understand what he means by Quasimodo?"

"I don't know. Allusiveness was typical of Professor Flecker; he delighted in British crossword puzzles, if you see what I mean. But I think I could guess more readily if he had not said that it might particularly appeal to me . . ."

"So? I can see at least two possibilities—"

"But before we try to decode the Professor's message, Lieutenant, tell me what you have learned here. All I know is that the poor man is dead, may he rest in peace."

Marshall told her. Four university teachers lived in this ancient (for Southern California) two-story house near the Campus. Mrs. Carey came in every day to clean for them and prepare dinner. When she arrived this morning at nine, Lowe and de' Cassis were eating breakfast and Hugo Ellis, the youngest of the group, was out mowing the lawn. They were not concerned over Flecker's absence. He often worked in the study till all hours and sometimes fell asleep there.

Mrs. Carey went about her work. Today was Tuesday, the day for changing the beds and getting the laundry ready. When she had finished that task, she dusted the living room and went on to the study.

The police did not yet have her story of the discovery. Her scream had summoned the others, who had at once called the police and, sensibly, canceled their classes and waited. When the police arrived, Mrs. Carey was still hysterical. The doctor had given her a sedative, from which she had not yet revived.

Professor Flecker had had his throat cut and (Marshall skipped over this hastily) suffered certain other butcheries characteristic of the Stripper. The knife, an ordinary kitchen-knife, had been left by the body as usual. He had died instantly, at approximately one in the morning, when each of the other three men claimed to be asleep.

38

More evidence than that of the locked doors proved that the Stripper was an inmate of the house. He had kept his feet clear of the blood which bespattered the study, but he had still left a trail of small drops which revealed themselves to the minute police inspection—blood which had bathed his body and dripped off as he left his crime.

This trail led upstairs and into the bathroom, where it stopped. There were traces of watered blood in the bathtub and on one of the towels—Flecker's own.

"Towel?" said Sister Ursula. "But you said Mrs. Carey had made up the laundry bundle."

"She sends out only sheets and such—does the towels herself."

"Oh." The nun sounded disappointed.

"I know how you feel, Sister. You'd welcome a discrepancy anywhere, even in the laundry list. But that's the sum of our evidence. Three suspects, all with opportunity, none with an alibi. Absolutely even distribution of suspicion, and our only guidepost is the word *Quasimodo*. Do you know any of these three men?"

"I have never met them, Lieutenant, but I feel as though I knew them rather well from Professor Flecker's descriptions."

"Good. Let's see what you can reconstruct. First, Ruggiero de' Cassis, professor of mathematics, formerly of the University of Turin, voluntary exile since the early days of Fascism."

Sister Ursula said slowly, "He admired de' Cassis, not only for his first-rate mind, but because he seemed to have adjusted himself so satisfactorily to life despite his deformity. I remember he said once, 'De' Cassis has never known a woman, yet every day he looks on Beauty bare.' "

"On Beauty . . .? Oh yes. Millay. *Euclid alone* . . . All right. Now Marvin Lowe, professor of psychology, native of Ohio, and from what I've seen of him a prime pedant. According to Flecker. . . ?"

"I think Professor Lowe amused him. He used to tell us the latest Spoonerisms; he swore that flocks of students graduated from the University believing that modern psychology rested on the researches of two men named Frung and Jeud. Once Lowe said that his favorite book was Max Beerbohm's *Happy Hypocrite;* Professor Flecker insisted that was because it was the only one he could be sure of pronouncing correctly."

"But as a man?"

"He never said much about Lowe personally; I don't think they were intimate. But I do recall his saying, 'Lowe, like all psychologists, is the physician of Greek proverb.' "

"Who was told to heal himself? Makes sense. That speech mannerism certainly points to something a psychiatrist could have fun with. All right. How about Hugo Ellis, instructor in mathematics, native of Los Angeles?"

"Mr. Ellis was a child prodigy, you know. Extraordinary mathematical feats. But he outgrew them, I almost think deliberately. He made himself into a normal young man. Now he is, I gather, a reasonably good young instructor—just run-of-the-mill. An adult with the brilliance which he had as a child might be a great man. Professor Flecker turned the French proverb around to fit him: 'If youth could, if age knew . . .' "

"So. There they are. And which," Marshall asked, "is Quasimodo?"

"Quasimodo . . ." Sister Ursula repeated the word, and other words seemed to follow it automatically. "*Quasimodo geniti infantes* . . ." She paused and shuddered.

"What's the matter?"

"I think," she said softly, "I know. But like Professor Flecker, I fear making a fool of myself—and worse, I fear damning an innocent man. . . . Lieutenant, may I look through this house with you?"

He sat there staring at the other two and at the policeman watching them. The body was no longer in the next room, but the blood was. He had never before revisited the scene of the crime; that notion was the nonsense of legend. For that matter he had never known his victim.

He let his mind go back to last night. Only recently had he been willing to do this. At first it was something that must be kept apart, divided from his normal personality. But he was intelligent enough to realize the danger of that. It could produce a seriously schizoid personality. He might go mad. Better to attain complete integration, and that could be accomplished only by frank self-recognition.

It must be terrible to be mad.

"Well, where to first?" asked Marshall.

"I want to see the bedrooms," said Sister Ursula. "I want to see if Mrs. Carey changed the sheets."

"You doubt her story? But she's completely out of the— All right. Come on."

Lieutenant Marshall identified each room for her as they entered it. Harvey Flecker's bedroom by no means consorted with the neatness of his mind. It was a welter of papers and notes and hefty German works on Latin philology and puzzle books by Torquemada and Caliban and early missals and codices from the University library. The bed had been changed and the clean upper sheet was turned back.

Professor de' Cassis's room was in sharp contrast—a chaste monastic cubicle. His books—chiefly professional works, with a sampling of Leopardi and Carducci and other Italian poets and an Italian translation of Thomas à Kempis—were neatly stacked in a case, and his papers were out of sight. The only ornaments in the room were a crucifix and a framed picture of a family group, in clothes of 1920.

Hugo Ellis's room was defiantly, almost parodistically the room of a normal, healthy college man, even to the University banner over the bed. He had carefully avoided both Flecker's chaos and de' Cassis's austerity; there was a precisely calculated normal litter of pipes and letters and pulp magazines. The pin-up girls seemed to be carrying normality too far, and Sister Ursula averted her eyes.

Each room had a clean upper sheet.

Professor Lowe's room would have seemed as normal as Ellis's, if less spectacularly so, if it were not for the inordinate quantity of books. Shelves covered all wall space that was not taken by door, window, or bed. Psychology, psychiatry, and criminology predominated; but there was a selection of poetry, humor, fiction for any mood.

Marshall took down William Roughead's *Twelve Scots Trials* and said, "Lucky devil! I've never so much as seen a copy of this before." He smiled at the argumentative pencilings in the margins. Then as he went to replace it, he saw through the gap that there was a second row of books behind. Paperbacks. He took one out and put it back hastily. "You wouldn't want to see that, Sister. But it might fit into that case we were proposing about repressions and word-distortions."

Sister Ursula seemed not to heed him. She was standing by the bed and said, "Come here."

Marshall came and looked at the freshly made bed.

Sister Ursula passed her hand over the mended but clean lower sheet. "Do you see?"

"See what?"

41

"The answer," she said.

Marshall frowned. "Look, Sister—"

"Lieutenant, your wife is one of the most efficient house-keepers I've ever known. I thought she had, to some extent, indoctrinated you. Think. Try to think with Leona's mind."

Marshall thought. Then his eyes narrowed and he said, "So . . ."

"It is fortunate," Sister Ursula said, "that the Order of Martha of Bethany specializes in housework."

Marshall went out and called downstairs. "Raglan! See if the laundry's been picked up from the back porch."

The Sergeant's voice came back. "It's gone, Loot. I thought there wasn't no harm—"

"Then get on the phone quick and tell them to hold it."

"But what laundry, Loot?"

Marshall muttered. Then he turned to Sister Ursula. "The men won't know of course, but we'll find a bill somewhere. Anyway, we won't need that till the preliminary hearing. We've got enough now to settle Quasimodo."

He heard the Lieutenant's question and repressed a startled gesture. He had not thought of that. But even if they traced the laundry, it would be valueless as evidence without Mrs. Carey's testimony. . . .

He saw at once what had to be done.

They had taken Mrs. Carey to the guest room, that small downstairs bedroom near the kitchen which must have been a maid's room when this was a large family house. There were still police posted outside the house, but only Raglan and the Lieutenant inside.

It was so simple. His mind, he told himself, had never been functioning more clearly. No nonsense about stripping this time; this was not for pleasure. Just be careful to avoid those crimson jets. . . .

The Sergeant wanted to know where he thought he was going. He told him.

Raglan grinned. "You should've raised your hand. A teacher like you ought to know that."

He went to the back porch toilet, opened and closed its door without going in. Then he went to the kitchen and took the second best knife. The best had been used last night.

It would not take a minute. Then he would be safe and later when the body was found what could they prove? The others had been out of the room too.

But as he touched the knife it began to happen. Something came from the blade up his arm and into his head. He was in a hurry, there was no time—but holding the knife, the color of things began to change.

He was half naked when Marshall found him.

Sister Ursula leaned against the jamb of the kitchen door. She felt sick. Marshall and Raglan were both strong men, but they needed help to subdue him. His face was contorted into an unrecognizable mask like a demon from a Japanese tragedy. She clutched the crucifix of the rosary that hung at her waist and murmured a prayer to the Archangel Michael. For it was not the physical strength of the man that frightened her, nor the glint of his knife, but the pure quality of incarnate evil that radiated from him and made the doctrine of possession a real terror.

As she finished her prayer, Marshall's fist connected with his jaw and he crumpled. So did Sister Ursula.

"I don't know what you think of me," Sister Ursula said as Marshall drove her home. (Sister Felicitas was dozing in the back seat.) "I'm afraid I couldn't ever have been a policewoman after all."

"You'll do," Marshall said. "And if you feel better now, I'd like to run over it with you. I've got to get my brilliant deductions straight for the press."

"The fresh air feels good. Go ahead."

"I've got the sheet business down pat, I think. In ordinary middle-class households you don't change both sheets every week; Leona never does, I remembered. You put on a clean upper sheet, and the old upper becomes the lower. The other three bedrooms each had one clean sheet—the upper. His had two—upper and lower; therefore his upper sheet had been stained in some unusual way and had to be changed. The hasty bath, probably in the dark, had been careless, and there was some blood left to stain the sheet. Mrs. Carey wouldn't have thought anything of it at the time because she hadn't found the body yet. Right?"

"Perfect, Lieutenant."

"So. But now about Quasimodo . . . I still don't get it. He's the one it *couldn't* apply to. Either of the others—"

"Yes?"

"Well, who is Quasimodo? He's the Hunchback of Notre Dame. So it could mean the deformed de' Cassis. Who wrote Quasimodo? Victor Hugo. So it could be Hugo Ellis. But it wasn't either; and how in heaven's name could it mean Professor Lowe?"

"Remember, Lieutenant: Professor Flecker said this was an allusion that might particularly appeal to me. Now I am hardly noted for my devotion to the anticlerical prejudices of Hugo's *Notre-Dame de Paris*. What is the common meeting-ground of my interests and Professor Flecker's?"

"Church liturgy?" Marshall ventured.

"And why was your Quasimodo so named? Because he was born—or found or christened, I forget which—on the Sunday after Easter. Many Sundays, as you may know, are often referred to by the first word of their introits, the beginning of the proper of the Mass. As the fourth Sunday in Lent is called *Laetare* Sunday, or the third in Advent *Gaudete* Sunday. So the Sunday after Easter is known as *Quasimodo* Sunday, from its introit *Quasimodo geniti infantes* . . . 'As newborn babes.' "

"But I still don't see—"

"The Sunday after Easter," said Sister Ursula, "is more usually referred to as *Low* Sunday."

"Oh," said Marshall. After a moment he added reflectively, *"The Happy Hypocrite. . . ."*

"You see that too? Beerbohm's story is about a man who assumes a mask of virtue to conceal his depravity. A schizoid allegory. I wonder if Professor Lowe dreamed that he might find the same happy ending."

Marshall drove on a bit in silence. Then he said, "He said a strange thing while you were out."

"I feel as though he were already dead," said Sister Ursula. "I want to say, 'God rest his soul.' We should have a special office for the souls of the mad."

"That cues into my story. The boys were taking him away and I said to Rags, 'Well, this is once the insanity plea justifies itself. He'll never see the gas chamber.' And he turned on me—he'd quieted down by then—and said, 'Nonsense, sir! Do you think I would cast doubt on my sanity merely to save my life?' "

"Mercy," said Sister Ursula. At first Marshall thought it was just an exclamation. Then he looked at her face and saw that she was not talking to him.

44

THE AFFAIR AT THE BUNGALOW

BY AGATHA CHRISTIE

Agatha Christie was born in Devon, England, on September 15, 1890. Her father, Frederick Miller, an American, died when she was a child. She was raised by her mother, who, along with their neighbor, Eden Phillpotts, encouraged her to write. Her first published novel, *The Mysterious Affair at Styles* (1920), introduced Hercule Poirot, her famous Belgian detective. Christie's more than eighty novels have been translated into almost every modern language. When she died on January 12, 1976, the Ambassador Theatre in London dimmed its lights before raising the curtain on the 9,612th performance of her play, *The Mousetrap*.

"I'VE THOUGHT OF SOMETHING," said Jane Helier.

Her beautiful face was lit up with the confident smile of a child expecting approbation. It was a smile such as moved audiences nightly in London, and made the fortunes of photographers.

"It happened," she went on carefully, "to a friend of mine."

Everyone made encouraging but slightly hypocritical noises. Colonel Bantry, Mrs. Bantry, Sir Henry Clithering, Dr. Lloyd, and old Miss Marple were all convinced that Jane's "friend" was Jane herself. She would have been quite incapable of remembering or taking an interest in anything affecting anyone else.

"My friend," went on Jane, "(I won't mention her name) was an actress—a well-known actress."

No one expressed surprise. Sir Henry Clithering thought to himself: "Now I wonder how many sentences it will be before she forgets to keep up the fiction, and says 'I' instead of 'She'?"

"My friend was on tour in the provinces—this was a year or two ago. I suppose I'd better not give the name of the place. It was a riverside town not very far from London. I'll call it—"

She paused, her brows perplexed in thought. The invention of even a simple name appeared to be too much for her. Sir Henry came to the rescue.

"Shall we call it Riverbury?" he suggested gravely.

"Oh, yes, that would do splendidly. Riverbury, I'll remember that. Well, as I say, my friend was at Riverbury with her company, and a very curious thing happened."

She puckered her brows again.

"It's very difficult," she said plaintively, "to say just what you want. One gets things mixed up and tells the wrong thing first."

"You're doing beautifully," said Dr. Lloyd encouragingly.

"Well, this curious thing happened. My friend was sent for to the police station. And she went. It seemed there had been a burglary at a riverside bungalow and they'd arrested a young man, and he told a very odd story. And so they sent for her.

"She'd never been to a police station before, but they were very nice to her—very nice indeed."

"They would be, I'm sure," said Sir Henry.

"The Sergeant—I think it was a Sergeant, or it may have been

46

an Inspector—gave her a chair and explained things, and of course I saw at once that it was some mistake—"

"Aha," thought Sir Henry. "I! Here we are. I thought as much."

"My friend said so," continued Jane, serenely unconscious of her self-betrayal. "She explained she had been rehearsing with her understudy at the hotel and that she'd never even heard of this Mr. Faulkener. And the Sergeant said, 'Miss Hel—'"

She stopped and flushed.

"Miss Helman," suggested Sir Henry with a twinkle.

"Yes—yes, that would do. Thank you. He said, 'Well, Miss Helman, I felt it must be some mistake, knowing that you were stopping at the Bridge Hotel,' and he said would I have any objection to confronting—or was it being confronted? I can't remember."

"It doesn't really matter," said Sir Henry reassuringly.

"Anyway, with the young man. So I said, 'Of course not.' And they brought him and said, 'This is Miss Helier,' and—Oh!" Jane broke off open-mouthed.

"Never mind, my dear," said Miss Marple consolingly. "We were bound to guess, you know. And you haven't given us the name of the place or anything that really matters."

"Well," said Jane, "I did mean to tell it as though it happened to someone else. But it *is* difficult. I mean one forgets so."

Everyone assured her that it was very difficult, and soothed and reassured, she went on with her slightly involved narrative.

"He was a nice-looking man—quite a nice-looking man. Young, with reddish hair. His mouth just opened when he saw me. And the Sergeant said, 'Is this the lady?' And he said, 'No, indeed it isn't. What an ass I have been.' And I smiled at him and said it didn't matter."

"I can picture the scene," said Sir Henry.

Jane Helier frowned.

"Let me see—how had I better go on?"

"Supposing you tell us what it was all about, dear?" said Miss Marple, so mildly that no one could suspect her of irony. "I mean what the young man's mistake was, and about the burglary."

"Oh, yes," said Jane. "Well, you see, this young man—Leslie Faulkener, his name was—had written a play. He'd written several plays, as a matter of fact, though none of them had ever been taken. And he had sent this particular play to me to read. I didn't know about it, because of course I have hundreds of plays sent to me and I read very few of them myself—only the ones I know something about. Anyway, there it was, and it seems that Mr. Faulkener got a letter from me—only it turned out not to be really from me—you understand—"

She paused anxiously, and they assured her that they understood.

"Saying that I'd read the play and liked it very much and would he come down and talk it over with me. And it gave the address—The Bungalow, Riverbury. So Mr. Faulkener was frightfully pleased and he came down and arrived at this place—The Bungalow. A parlormaid opened the door, and he asked for Miss Helier, and she said Miss Helier was in and expecting him and showed him into the drawing-room, and there a woman came to him. And he accepted her as me— which seems queer because after all he had seen me act and my photographs are very well known, aren't they?"

"Over the length and breadth of England," said Mrs. Bantry promptly. "But there's often a lot of difference between a photograph and its original, my dear Jane. And there's a great deal of difference between being behind the footlights and off the stage. It's not every actress who stands the test as well as you do, remember."

"Well," said Jane, slightly mollified, "that may be so. Anyway, he described this woman as tall and fair with big blue eyes and very good-looking, so I suppose it must have been near enough. He certainly had no suspicions. She sat down and began talking about his play and said she was anxious to do it. While they were talking, cocktails were brought in and Mr. Faulkener had one as a matter of course.

"Well, that's all he remembers—having this cocktail. When he woke up, or came to himself, or whatever you call it, he was lying out in the road—by the hedge, of course, so that there would be no danger of his being run over. He felt very queer and shaky—so much so that he just got up and staggered along the road not quite knowing where he was going.

"He said if he'd had his senses about him he'd have gone back to the Bungalow and tried to find out what had happened. But he felt just stupid and amazed and walked along without quite knowing what he was doing. He was just more or less coming to himself when the police arrested him."

"Why did the police arrest him?" said Dr. Lloyd.

"Oh, didn't I tell you?" said Jane opening her eyes very wide. "How very stupid I am. The burglary."

"You mentioned a burglary—but you didn't say where or what or why," said Mrs. Bantry.

"Well, this bungalow—the one he went to, of course—it wasn't mine at all. It belonged to a man whose name was—"

Again Jane furrowed her brows.

"Do you want me to be godfather again?" asked Sir Henry. "Pseudonyms supplied free of charge. Describe the tenant and I'll do the naming."

"It was taken by a rich city man—a knight."

"Sir Sidney Kane," suggested Sir Henry.

"That will do beautifully. He took it for a lady—she was the wife of an actor, and she was also an actress herself."

"We'll call the actor Claude Leason," said Sir Henry, "and the lady would be known by her stage name, I suppose, so we'll call her Miss Mary Kerr."

"I think you're awfully clever," said Jane. "I don't know how you think of these things so easily. Well, you see this was a sort of week-end cottage for Sir Sidney—did you say Sidney?—and the lady. And, of course, his wife knew nothing about it."

"Which is so often the case," said Sir Henry.

"And he'd given this actress woman a good deal of jewelry including some very fine emeralds."

"Ah!" said Dr. Lloyd. "Now we're getting at it."

"This jewelry was at the bungalow, just locked up in a jewel case. The police said it was very careless—anyone might have taken it."

"You see, Dolly," said Colonel Bantry. "What do I always tell you?"

"Well, in my experience," said Mrs. Bantry, "it's always the people who are so dreadfully careful who lose things. I don't lock mine up in a jewel case—I keep it in a drawer loose, under my stockings. I daresay if—what's her name?—Mary Kerr had done the same, the jewelry would never have been stolen."

"It would," said Jane, "because all the drawers were burst open and the contents strewn about."

"Then they weren't really looking for jewels," said Mrs. Bantry. "They were looking for secret papers. That's what always happens in books."

"I don't know about secret papers," said Jane doubtfully. "I never heard of any."

49

"Don't be distracted, Miss Helier," said Colonel Bantry. "Dolly's red herrings are not to be taken seriously."

"About the burglary," said Sir Henry.

"Yes. Well, the police were rung up by someone who said she was Miss Mary Kerr. She said the bungalow had been burgled and described a young man with red hair who had called there that morning. Her maid had thought there was something odd about him and had refused him admittance, but later they had seen him getting out through a window.

"She described the man so accurately that the police arrested him only an hour later and then he gave his story and showed them the letter from me. And as I told you, they fetched me and when he saw me he said what I told you—that it hadn't been me at all!"

"A very curious story," said Dr. Lloyd. "Did Mr. Faulkener know this Miss Kerr?"

"No, he didn't—or he said he didn't. But I haven't told you the most curious part yet. The police went to the bungalow of course, and they found everything as described—drawers pulled out and jewels gone, but the whole place was empty. It wasn't till some hours later that Mary Kerr came back, and when she did she said she'd never rung them up at all and this was the first she'd heard of it. It seemed that she had had a wire that morning from a manager offering her a most important part and making an appointment, so she had naturally rushed up to town to keep it. When she got there, she found that the whole thing was a hoax. No telegram had ever been sent."

"A common enough ruse to get her out of the way," commented Sir Henry. "What about the servants?"

"The same sort of thing happened there. There was only one, and she was rung up on the telephone—apparently by Mary Kerr, who said she had left a most important thing behind. She directed the maid to bring up a certain handbag which was in her bedroom. She was to catch the first train. The maid did so, of course locking up the house; but when she arrived at Miss Kerr's club, where she had been told to meet her mistress, she waited there in vain."

"H'm," said Sir Henry. "I begin to see. The house was left empty, and to make an entry by one of the windows would present few difficulties, I should imagine. But I don't quite see where Mr. Faulkener comes in. Who did ring up the police, if it wasn't Miss Kerr?"

"That's what nobody knew or ever found out."

"Curious," said Sir Henry. "Did the young man turn out to be genuinely the person he said he was?"

"Oh, yes, that part was all right. He'd even got the letter which was supposed to be written by me. It wasn't the least bit like my handwriting—but then, of course, he couldn't be supposed to know that."

"Well, let's state the position clearly," said Sir Henry. "Correct me if I am wrong. The lady and the maid are decoyed from the house. This young man is decoyed down there by means of a bogus letter—color being lent to this last by the fact that you actually are performing at Riverbury that week. The young man is doped, and the police are rung up and have their suspicions directed against him. A burglary actually has taken place. I presume the jewels were taken?"

"Oh, yes."

"Were they ever recovered?"

"No, never. As a matter of fact, Sir Sidney tried to hush things up, but he couldn't manage it, and I rather fancy his wife started divorce proceedings in consequence. Still, I don't really know about that."

"What happened to Mr. Leslie Faulkener?"

"He was released in the end. The police said they hadn't really got enough against him. Don't you think the whole thing was rather odd?"

"Distinctly odd. The first question is whose story to believe? In telling it, Miss Helier, I noticed that you incline towards believing Mr. Faulkener. Have you any reason for doing so beyond your own instinct in the matter?"

"N-no," said Jane unwillingly. "I suppose I haven't. But he was so very nice, and so apologetic for having mistaken anyone else for me, that I feel sure he *must* have been telling the truth."

"I see," said Sir Henry smiling. "But you must admit that he could have invented the story quite easily. He could write the letter purporting to be from you himself. He could also dope himself after successfully committing the burglary. But I confess I don't see where the *point* of all that would be. Easier to enter the house, help himself, and disappear quietly—unless just possibly he was observed by someone in the neighborhood and knew himself to have been observed. Then he might hastily concoct this plan for diverting suspicion from himself and accounting for his presence in the neighborhood."

51

"Was he well off?" asked Miss Marple.

"I don't think so," said Jane. "No, I believe he was rather hard up."

"The whole thing seems curious," said Dr. Lloyd. "I must confess that if we accept the young man's story as true, it seems to make the case much more difficult. Why should the unknown woman who pretended to be Miss Helier drag this unknown man into the affair? Why should she stage such an elaborate comedy?"

"Tell me, Jane," said Mrs. Bantry. "Did young Faulkener ever come face to face with Mary Kerr at any stage of the proceedings?"

"I don't quite know," said Jane slowly, as she puzzled her brows in remembrance.

"Because if he didn't the case is solved!" said Mrs. Bantry. "I'm sure I'm right. What is easier than to pretend you're called up to town? You telephone to your maid from Paddington or whatever station you arrive at, and as she comes up to town, you go down again. The young man calls by appointment, he's doped, you set the stage for the burglary, overdoing it as much as possible. You telephone the police, give a description of your scapegoat, and off you go to town again. Then you arrive home by a later train and do the surprised innocent."

"But why should she steal her own jewels, Dolly?"

"They always do," said Mrs. Bantry. "And anyway, I can think of hundreds of reasons. She may have wanted money at once—old Sir Sidney wouldn't give her cash, perhaps, so she pretends the jewels are stolen and then sells them secretly. Or she may be being blackmailed by someone who threatened to tell her husband or Sir Sidney's wife. Or she may have already sold the jewels and Sir Sidney was getting ratty and asking to see them, so she had to do something about it. That's done a good deal in books.

"Or perhaps he was going to have them reset and she'd got paste replicas. Or—here's a very good idea and not so much done in books—she pretends they are stolen, gets in an awful state and he gives her a fresh lot. So she gets two lots instead of one. That kind of woman, I am sure, is most frightfully artful."

"You *are* clever, Dolly," said Jane admiringly. "I never thought of that."

"You may be clever, but she doesn't say you're right," said Colonel Bantry. "I incline to suspect the City gentleman. He'd know the sort of telegram to get the lady out of the way, and he could manage the rest easily enough with the help of a new lady friend. Nobody seems to have thought of asking *him* for an alibi."

"What do you think, Miss Marple?" asked Jane, turning toward the old lady who had sat silent, a frown on her face.

"My dear, I really don't know what to say. Sir Henry will laugh, but I recall no village parallel to help me this time. Of course there are several questions that suggest themselves. For instance, the servant question. In—ahem—an irregular ménage of the kind you describe, the servant employed would doubtless be perfectly aware of the state of things, and a really nice girl would not take such a place—her mother wouldn't let her for a minute.

"So I think we can assume that the maid was *not* a really trustworthy character. She may have been in league with the thieves. She would leave the house open for them and actually go to London so as to divert suspicion from herself. I must confess that that seems the most probable solution. Only if ordinary thieves were concerned, it seems very odd. It seems to argue more knowledge than a maidservant was likely to have."

Miss Marple paused and then went on dreamily.

"I can't help feeling that there was some—well, what I must describe as personal feeling about the whole thing. Supposing somebody had a spite, for instance? Don't you think that would explain things better? A deliberate attempt to get him into trouble. That's what it looks like. And yet—that's not entirely satisfactory. . . ."

"Why, Doctor, you haven't said anything," said Jane. "I'd forgotten you."

"I'm always getting forgotten," said the grizzled doctor sadly. "I must have a very inconspicuous personality."

"Oh, no!" said Jane. "Do tell us what you think?"

"I'm rather in the position of agreeing with everyone's solutions—and yet with none of them. I myself have a far-fetched and probably totally erroneous theory that the wife may have had something to do with it. Sir Sidney's wife, I mean. I've no grounds for thinking so—only you would be surprised if you knew the extraordinary things that a wronged wife will do."

"Oh, Dr. Lloyd," cried Miss Marple excitedly. "How clever of you. And I never thought of poor Mrs. Pebmarsh."

Jane stared at her.

"Mrs. Pebmarsh? Who is Mrs. Pebmarsh?"

"Well—" Miss Marple hesitated. "I don't know that she really comes in. She's a laundress. And she stole an opal pin that was pinned onto a blouse and put it in another woman's house."

Jane looked more fogged than ever.

"And that makes it all perfectly clear to you, Miss Marple?" said Sir Henry, with his twinkle.

But to his surprise Miss Marple shook her head.

"No, I'm afraid it doesn't. I must confess myself completely at a loss. What I do realize is that women must stick together—one should, in an emergency, stand by one's own sex. I think that's the moral of the story Miss Helier has told us."

"I must confess that particular ethical significance of the mystery had escaped me," said Sir Henry gravely. "Perhaps I shall see the significance of your point more clearly when Miss Helier has revealed the solution."

"Eh?" said Jane, looking bewildered.

"I was observing that, in childish language, we 'give up.' You and you alone, Miss Helier, have had the high honor of presenting such an absolutely baffling mystery that even Miss Marple has to confess herself defeated."

"You all give up?" asked Jane.

"Yes." After a minute's silence during which he waited for the others to speak, Sir Henry constituted himself spokesman once more. "That is to say we stand or fall by the sketchy solutions we have tentatively advanced. One each for the mere men, two for Miss Marple, and a round dozen from Mrs. B."

"It was not a dozen," said Mrs. Bantry. "They were variations on a main theme. And how often am I to tell you that I will not be called Mrs. B?"

"So you all give up," said Jane thoughtfully. "That's very interesting."

She leaned back in her chair and began to polish her nails.

"Well," said Mrs. Bantry. "Come on, Jane. What is the solution?"

"The solution?"

"Yes. What really happened?"

Jane stared at her.

"I haven't the least idea."

"*What?*"

"I've always wondered. I thought you were all so clever that one of you would be able to tell *me*."

Everybody harbored feelings of annoyance. It was all very well for Jane to be so beautiful—but at this moment everyone felt that stupidity could be carried too far. Even the most transcendent loveliness could not excuse it.

"You mean the truth was never discovered?" said Sir Henry.

"No. That's why, as I say, you would be able to tell *me*."

"Well, I'm—I'm—" said Colonel Bantry, words failing him.

"You are the most aggravating girl, Jane," said his wife. "Anyway, I'm sure and always shall be that I was right. If you just tell us the proper names of all the people, I shall be *quite* sure."

"I don't think I could do that," said Jane slowly.

"No, dear," said Miss Marple. "Miss Helier couldn't do that."

"Of course she could," said Mrs. Bantry. "Don't be so high-minded, Jane. We older folks must have a bit of scandal. At any rate, tell us who the city magnate really was."

But Jane shook her head, and Miss Marple, in her old-fashioned way, continued to support the girl.

"It must have been a very distressing business," Miss Marple said.

"No," said Jane truthfully. "I think I rather enjoyed it."

"Well, perhaps you did," said Miss Marple. "I suppose it was a break in the monotony. What play were you acting in?"

"*Smith*."

"Oh, yes. That's one of Mr. Somerset Maugham's, isn't it? His plays are very clever, I think. I've seen nearly all of them."

"You're reviving it to go on tour next autumn, aren't you?" asked Mrs. Bantry.

Jane nodded.

"Well," said Miss Marple rising, "I must go home. Such late hours! But we've had a very entertaining evening. Most unusually so."

"I'm sorry you're angry with me," said Jane. "About not knowing the end, I mean. I suppose I should have said so sooner."

Her tone sounded wistful. Dr. Lloyd rose gallantly to the occasion.

"My dear young lady, why should you? You gave us a very pretty problem to sharpen our wits on. I am only sorry none of us could solve it convincingly."

"Speak for yourself," said Mrs. Bantry. "I *did* solve it. I'm sure I am right."

"Do you know, I really believe you are," said Jane. "What you said sounded so probable."

"Which of her seven solutions do you refer to?" Sir Henry teased.

Dr. Lloyd gallantly assisted Miss Marple to put on her goloshes. "Just in case," as the old lady explained. The doctor was to be her escort to her old-world cottage. Wrapped in several woollen shawls, Miss Marple wished everyone good night once more. She came to Jane Helier last and leaning forward, she murmured something in the actress's ear. A startled "Oh!" burst from Jane—so loud as to cause the others to turn their heads.

Smiling and nodding, Miss Marple made her exit, Jane Helier staring after her.

"Are you coming to bed, Jane?" asked Mrs. Bantry. "What's the matter with you? You're staring as though you'd seen a ghost."

With a deep sigh Jane came to herself and followed her hostess up the staircase. Mrs. Bantry came into the girl's room with her.

"Your fire's nearly out," said Mrs. Bantry, giving it a vicious and ineffectual poke. "They can't have made it up properly. How stupid housemaids are. Still, I suppose we are rather late tonight. Why, it's actually past one o'clock!"

"Do you think there are many people like her?" asked Jane Helier.

She was sitting on the side of the bed apparently wrapped in thought.

"Like the housemaid?"

"No. Like that funny old woman—what's her name—Marple?"

"Oh, I don't know. I suppose she's a fairly common type in a small village."

"Oh, dear," said Jane. "I don't know what to do."

She sighed deeply.

"What's the matter?"

"I'm worried."

"What about?"

Jane Helier was portentously solemn as she said, "Do you know what that queer old lady whispered to me before she went out of the door tonight?"

"No. What?"

"She said: '*I shouldn't do it if I were you, my dear. Never put yourself too much in another woman's power, even if you do think she's your friend at the moment.*' You know, Dolly, that's awfully true."

"The maxim? Yes, perhaps it is. But I don't see the application."

"I suppose you can't ever really trust a woman. And I *should* be in her power. I never thought of that."

"What woman are you talking about?"

"Netta Greene, my understudy."

"What on earth does Miss Marple know about your understudy?"

"I supposed she guessed—but I can't see how."

"Jane, will you kindly tell me at once what you are talking about?"

"The story. The one I told. Oh, Dolly, that woman—the one that took Charles from me?"

Mrs. Bantry nodded, casting her mind back rapidly to the first of Jane's unfortunate marriages—to Charles Averbury, the actor.

"He married her; and I could have told him how it would be. Charles doesn't know, but she's carrying on with Sir Joseph Salmon—week ends with him at the bungalow I told you about. I wanted her shown up—I would like everyone to know the sort of woman she was. And you see, with a burglary, everything would be bound to come out."

"Jane!" gasped Mrs. Batry. "Did *you* engineer this story you've been telling us?"

Jane nodded.

"That's why I chose *Smith*. I wear parlormaid's kit in it, you know. So I should have it handy. And when they sent for me to the police station it's the easiest thing in the world to say I was rehearsing my part with my understudy at the hotel. Really, of course, we would be at the bungalow—I just to open the door and bring in the cocktails, and Netta to pretend to be me. He'd never see *her* again, of course, so there would be no fear of his recognizing her. And I can make myself look quite different as a parlormaid; and besides, one doesn't look at parlormaids as though they were people.

"We planned to drag him out into the road afterwards, bag the jewel case, telephone the police, and get back to the hotel. I shouldn't like the poor young man to suffer, but Sir Henry didn't seem to think he would, did he? And she'd be in the papers and everything—and Charles would see what she was really like."

Mrs. Bantry sat down and groaned.

"Oh, my poor head. And all the time—Jane Helier, you deceitful girl! Telling us that story the way you did!"

"I *am* a good actress," said Jane complacently. "I always have been, whatever people choose to say. I didn't give myself away, did I?"

"Miss Marple was right," murmured Mrs. Bantry. "The personal element. Oh, yes, the personal element. Jane, my good child, do you realize that theft is theft, and you might have been sent to prison?"

"Well, none of you guessed," said Jane. "Except Miss Marple." The worried expression returned to her face. "Dolly, do you *really* think there are many like her?"

"Frankly, I don't," said Mrs. Bantry.

Jane sighed again.

"Still, one had better not risk it. And of course I *should* be in Netta's power—that's true enough. She might turn against me or blackmail me or something. She helped me think out the details and professed to be devoted to me, but one never *does* know with women. No, I think Miss Marple was right. I had better not risk it."

"But, my dear, you did risk it."

"Oh, no," Jane opened her blue eyes very wide. "Don't you understand? *None of this has happened yet!* I was—well, trying it on the dog, so to speak."

"I don't pretend to understand your theatrical slang," said Mrs. Bantry with dignity. "Do you mean this is a future project—not a past deed?"

"I was going to do it this autumn—in September. I don't know what to do now."

"And Jane Marple guessed—actually guessed the truth and never told us," said Mrs. Bantry wrathfully.

"I think that was why she said that—about women sticking together. She wouldn't give me away before the men. That was nice of her. I don't mind *your* knowing, Dolly."

"Well, give the idea up, Jane. I beg you to!"

"I think I shall," murmured Miss Helier. "There might be other Miss Marples. . . ."

WALLY THE WATCHFUL EYE

BY PAUL W. FAIRMAN

Paul W. Fairman began his writing career in Chicago, Illinois, in the 1930s. He later moved to New York City and had short stories published in *Cosmopolitan, The Saturday Evening Post, Redbook,* and *This Week.* The author of more than two hundred novels, under his real name and various pseudonyms, Fairman was editor of *Amazing* and *Fantastic* magazines. From 1960 to 1963 he was managing editor of *Ellery Queen's Mystery Magazine.* Four of his short stories were adapted for television shows and two were the bases of science-fiction movies. Fairman died in October 1977.

The Watchful Eye Detective School
Parker Building
New York, New York

Mr. Walter A. Watts
Lettyville, New York

Dear Mr. Watts:

As President of Watchful Eye, I wish to thank you for your application; also, to congratulate you on your decision to move into the highly lucrative field of private investigation. I was greatly impressed by the enthusiasm your letter revealed and for that reason am rushing you Lesson Number One of the ten lessons that make up the Watchful Eye course.

However, in your haste to become one of us, you neglected to enclose the $25 tuition payment. An oversight, of course, so please send it along by return mail. In the meantime, allow me to assure you that our expert instruction, coupled with your obvious drive and ambition, will assure you swift progress.

    Sincerely,

     John Hayden, President

Dear Johnny:

Your letter and the first lesson, *Shadowing the Suspect,* received. Thanks a million, and you were right about my enthusiasm. You were real top-drawer to send the lesson without the loot and I'll get it to you as soon as possible.

You see, I'm clerking in old Tom Barton's grocery store here in Lettyville and old Tom's not exactly loose with the lettuce. But there won't be much delay with the dough because I've got a bonus coming from old Tom for watching the store three weeks ago while he took a two-day trip to Boston.

Now you might wonder why old Tom hasn't kicked in with this cabbage being as it's due me for almost a month. Well, Johnny there's a reason for that. You see old Tom never gives out any green unless he's prodded plenty and I haven't felt like

60

hounding him because he's having a hard time just now. You see, his wife, old Martha, committed suicide while he was in Boston.

As you can imagine, a suicide in a little place like Lettyville—pop. 3,000—is a real big deal. So old Tom has been long-facing it all over town with everybody squirting out the sympathy like they were spraying him down for fleas. Everybody helping him moan it up with hardly a thought for Martha who did the dutch while old Tom was in Boston.

And she didn't wait long, either. He'd hardly pulled out for the railroad depot before she turned on the gas range in their kitchen and sat down for a farewell snooze right in front of it.

That's how it had to happen because the coroner said she'd been dead the whole two days when old Tom got back and found her there with the place full of gas. Nobody went to see her while he was gone because we all thought she was going with him. That was how it was supposed to be but old Tom said she changed her mind at the last minute. Probably, I guess, so she could do this one last thing without old Tom griping and heckling her.

And now the whole town's on his side because they know him better and besides, a lot of them owe him money, his claws being in real estate and mortgages and everything else along with the grocery store I work for him in. And they didn't know old Martha very well. She kept to herself in their house about a mile out of town and people said she was snooty.

But that wasn't true. I delivered groceries out there and met her several times and she was real nice. I think old Tom just kept her there by never giving her a dime for duds and she was ashamed to socialize in the sloppy sister smocks and socks he said were good enough for anybody.

And so, Johnny old man, that explains why I'm a little tardy with the tuition. But I know everything costs money these days and I'm going to lean a limb against old Tom tomorrow and bust out the bonus which I've got coming.

In the meantime I'm cramming like crazy, shadowing suspects all over the place until I've hardly got time to pitch any pash with Pearl. Pearl's my girl. She works at the local utility company and I'm planning to put the handcuffs on her as soon as I finish your course and get my license and come through on a couple of big cases. But I've got to really roll because I'm already 17 and I want to have an office by the time I'm 21 with a few ops on my payroll so I can sit back and mastermind their moves and have more time for Pearl.

Yours in a hurry,

Wally Watts

The Watchful Eye Detective School
Parker Building
New York, New York

Mr. Walter A. Watts
Lettyville, New York

Dear Walter:

Your letter received and I am sending along Lesson Number Two in the series—*The Art of Obtaining Information Indirectly*—even though the check you enclosed was to the amount of only $7.40. My better judgment tells me to withhold the lessons until the total tuition is forthcoming as per contract. But one seldom encounters a push and ambition such as yours so I am forced to stretch a point, knowing you will remit the entire amount as soon as Mr. Barton gets around to paying you your bonus.

In the meantime, please allow me to suggest a little restraint in your activities relative to the course. "Shadowing suspects all over the place"—as you put it—can lead to unhappy complications, what with your lack of experience and the suspects being under no suspicion whatever. Therefore I suggest that you confine yourself to the academic aspects of detection as set forth in the Watchful Eye course, avoiding practical application for now.

Cordially,

John Hayden, President

Dear Johnny:

I'm afraid you got the wrong idea from my last letter—about the bonus from old Tom covering all the tuition. Old Tom paid up when I prodded him but the bonus was only five bucks—I told you he was tight with the tips—and I hadn't figured on that to finish off the finances with you. As a matter of fact, I'm peddling my pig to pay the balance. I live on a small farm out of town with my parents and this pig was the runt of the litter and got the short shake on everything. So Dad gave him to me and I bottle-babied him up to a shoat. Now I'm selling him to Frank

Gilmore, a farmer near here, to clean up our contract.

As to the other part, don't worry about a thing. I've stopped shadowing all and sundry and am concentrating all my skill on old Tom. Because here's a hunch right out of the hat, Johnny, and I know you'll keep it confidential—I'm dead sure old Martha didn't commit suicide. Old Tom gave her the gas himself. So it's murder and I don't know why I didn't figure it before. If you were here and could take a gander at the ghoul, you'd catalogue him for a killer right away. Low, slanty forehead. Beady little eyes. A scowl he puts on every morning like his pants.

Oh, he's the criminal type all right and I'm giving him my undivided attention. Of course, I do need a little more shadowing experience. Old Tom made me realize this when he turned around the other evening and said, "Wally, I'm getting tired of banging my heels against your shins every time I stop short. Can't you find your way around town any more without a guide?" Right away, I soaped him real soft and he isn't suspicious, but as I say, I guess I need a little more experience.

And cracking this case won't be easy. Old Tom's probably got the ticket stubs to show he was in Boston all the time. But don't worry. I'll amputate his alibi and keep you posted.

Meantime, I'm studying Lesson Number Two—learning how to obtain the info on old Tom.

The best,

Wally

The Watchful Eye Detective School
Parker Building,
New York, New York

Dear Wally:

Even though you sent only $4.20 in lieu of the total balance due, I'm rushing you the next lesson—all of them up to and including Lesson Number Six which I beg you to read carefully. Even its title—*Logic: The Basis of Successful Detection*—should be enlightening. This Lesson brings out basic truths—that there is no such thing as a criminal type from a physical standpoint. Some of the finest people alive have slanty foreheads; beady eyes may indicate an abnormal optical condition but nothing more. And if we arrested all the scowlers in this world there wouldn't be enough of us left to feed them.

63

So read Lesson Number Six carefully and stop annoying poor old Mr. Barton. He no doubt has enough to contend with already.

Sincerely,

Johnny

Dear Johnny:

About the $4.20—I sold my pig all right and delivered him and made off with the moola. But that night he stymied his new sty and then funneled out under Mr. Gilmore's fence and hiked home. That's how pampering a pig pays off. Hand-feed one and he's yours forever. So Mom made me give Mr. Gilmore back his dough. But don't worry. I went right out and pressured Pete Polichek, a real pal, into buying my old bike. He's paying the price tomorrow.

Also, thanks for all those lessons in one big lump. They help because I'll get to be a real clever op just that much sooner. But I haven't got Lesson Number Two, about obtaining information, down quite pat yet. I know I'm a little rough in this department because Mr. Ingalls, the insurance man hereabouts, almost saw through my efforts. He said, "Wally, whether or not Tom Barton had a life insurance policy on Martha is none of your business. A man's insurance program is confidential and an agent wouldn't get much business if he talked about his client's coverage."

But that info wasn't really too important. I'm about ready to close in. Old Tom is scowling harder and his eyes are getting beadier every day.

The best,

Wally

The Watchful Eye Detective School
Parker Building
New York, New York

Dear Wally:

Look, old pal, I'll level with you. This isn't a big operation I'm running. The address is just a mail drop and I do it all from my furnished room on Sixth Avenue. So you can see I'm just a young fellow like yourself, trying to better myself and make an honest buck—so please lay off Mr. Barton!

If you want to get sued for your shirt and maybe thrown in

64

the clink it's okay, but my lawyer says I could get the works too. Old Tom might extend his coverage to include me when he gets around to suing for libel or maybe false arrest and heaven knows what.

Anyhow, my lawyer says I could be held legally liable along with you, the way you're probably sounding off up there. So please—*please!*—do me a favor and go back to your pigs and groceries. And forget the balance you owe me—the last few lessons are on the house.

Desperately,

Johnny

Dear Johnny:

I'm going to give your school a big boost, old pal. You can use my name and picture in your advertising and get a lot of business. An ad in the big magazines that would say something like—"After Two Watchful Eye Lessons I Nailed My Boss For Murder."

Because that's about how it happened. Old Tom confessed to everything. He did old Martha in with a few whiffs of gas *before* he went to Boston to establish his alibi. Then when he got back from Boston he turned the gas on for a few minutes to smell up the place, opened the windows, and ran out yelling for help.

Of course none of it could have been proved unless old Tom confessed, even with the twenty-five grand policy on old Martha, because everybody figured him to be a solid citizen. But he did confess and that's that. My first case is all wrapped up, signed, sealed, and delivered! And you can go ahead and put that ad in the magazines.

The best,

Wally

121 Sixth Avenue
New York City

Wally, Old Pal:

It's not fair to leave me hanging this way. I know darned well old Tom didn't break down and confess just because you asked him to. Things don't work out that way in this business. You had more on him than you told me. So let me in on it and then maybe I'll be able to sleep nights again.

Johnny

65

Dear Johnny:

It was that logic lesson you sent that steered me right. Knowing old Tom as I did, it wasn't logical that he'd waste two days' gas on a ten-minute job. And I knew he wouldn't risk a fire by leaving a gas stove going for two whole days.

So Pearl, she's my girl, being employed at the utility company made it easy to check old Tom's gas bills. They always ran around $3.00 a month, give or take a dime. Forty-eight straight hours last month would have shoved it up around 80¢ or $1.00 more than usual. But old Tom's bill for last month read the usual—this time, $3.05.

So old Tom could shill the sheriff and con the coroner all right, but he couldn't make a monkey out of the gas meter. Or maybe he forgot that everything costs money these days, even murdering old Martha.

I'm enclosing a snapshot for that ad you'll want to run like I said. The one on the left is Pearl, my girl. She says hello.

All the best,

Walter A. Watts
(the A is for Alert)

THE HAPPY DAYS CLUB

BY JAMES M. ULLMAN

James M. Ullman was born in 1925 in Chicago, Illinois. He spent ten years in the newspaper business, including editing a suburban paper and working for United Press International and the Chicago *Sun-Times*. He has had four mystery novels published as well as more than forty short stories. His interest in mystery and suspense dates from his childhood. Since 1961 he has been self-employed as an editorial consultant. He lives in Park Ridge, Illinois, with his wife, who is also an editorial consultant.

"TED, I'VE GOT ONE right up your alley," Michael Dane James announced over the telephone.

Ted Bennett, sprawled in a chair beside a customer's man in a broker's boardroom, replied without taking his eyes from the tape moving overhead. "Mickey, if it's another scheme to drift me into a Detroit tool and die plant in the guise of a laborer, climb a tree. I don't care *what* the 1965 Whozit is going to look like."

"It's a defensive assignment," James said, "and won't compromise your principles one bit. One of the nation's biggest mutual funds, with assets of half a billion dollars, thinks its secrets are being systematically stolen by a little investment club in Iowa."

"You're kidding," Bennett chuckled.

"I'm leveling," James went on. "So meet me in front of Sam's at five o'clock. Our Wall Street friends want to talk to us there before they commute home to suburbia. They don't think it would look good for us industrial spies to be seen in their offices."

A sign in the window proclaimed *SAM'S—HOME OF THE 25-CENT MARTINI*. The price prevailed only during the cocktail hour, but as a result the place was jammed, mostly with executives from the financial district. James, a stocky man with horn-rimmed glasses riding his pug nose, and Bennett, tall, lean, and hatless, pushed through the crowd to a rear booth tagged *RESERVED FOR MR. ALLEN*.

Victor Allen, president of the Gibraltar Fund's management group, rose to shake hands. He was big and burly and in 1934 had played tackle for the Green Bay Packers. He introduced James and Bennett to the other occupant of the booth—Stuart Clark, chairman of the fund's stock selection committee.

"Mickey and I," Allen told Clark as they sat down, "banged heads one year in the old N.F.L. We both got out alive somehow. Mickey's an industrial espionage consultant now, and Bennett works for him. Sam, a couple more here."

"Is this," Bennett inquired, settling in a corner, "where you boys decide which stocks the Gibraltar Fund will buy? Booze up and then shove a pin through the Big Board listings in *The Times*?"

"Hardly," Clark smiled. "Let's just say that here we review in more relaxed surroundings decisions made elsewhere."

"Show him the clip, Stu," Allen said.

Clark drew an envelope from his pocket and removed a newspaper clipping. He pushed it across the table. A waiter brought two drinks and set them down.

"This clipping," Clark explained, "was forwarded to us by the branch manager of a brokerage house in Des Moines, Iowa. It's a story from a small daily newspaper, the Canfield, Iowa, *Gazette*. The story is the usual feature that papers print now and then about a local investment club."

" 'The Happy Days Club,' " James read aloud, " 'is composed of fifteen residents of the Westlake subdivision. Its members are drawn from all walks of life.' "

"They seem," Bennett observed, peering over James's shoulder, "to have done rather well."

"There's something remarkable about The Happy Days Club," Clark went on. "That's why my friend in Des Moines sent me the clipping. He sells a lot of shares in our fund, you see, and knows our portfolio. And he noticed in the past eight months that the Happy Days Club has been buying or selling only those stocks which *we* bought and sold."

"It could be coincidence."

"It could be," Allen broke in, "but even more remarkable is the fact that their buying and selling took place *before* we announced we had bought or sold the stocks, and in some cases, *after* we had reached a decision but *before* we had even completed a transaction. That story gives the dates of their sales and purchases and we checked them against our records. The club didn't buy every stock we bought, of course—they don't have that much money. But there's not a single stock in their list that we didn't buy. And not a single stock we sold that, if they owned it, they didn't sell."

"Secrecy," Clark added, "is essential at a certain stage in our business, Mr. James. We're required to report quarterly on our purchases and sales. But we're allowed enough leeway so that we don't have to report on the transactions we're making *at that time*. Our minimum investment in any stock is about two million dollars. Naturally, we don't go into the market and buy two million dollars' worth of stock in one day—the purchase, or

69

sale, is spread out over a period of weeks or months. The brokers we buy through are carefully screened for their ability to keep their mouths shut about what we're doing. Because if word got out that we were putting two million dollars or more into a company a lot of speculators would buy the stock, too, hoping for a killing."

"Secrecy isn't as much of a consideration," Allen explained, "when we buy widely held blue chips like AT&T or Jersey Standard. But it's a prime consideration when we buy into a lesser-known company which we think may become a blue chip in the future. And it's that class of stock, incidentally, which The Happy Days Club has been buying into with us."

"So you believe," Bennett said, "that The Happy Days Club must have a pipeline into the innermost circles of the Gibraltar Fund."

"Exactly," Clark said. "We're not so concerned that these fifteen Iowans are stealing our judgment, so to speak, as we are with the fact there *is* a leak in our organization. If word of our decisions reaches many people before we announce them, the price of every smaller company we start buying into will be bid up to the moon. What's more, we're one of the big funds in the country. If the story ever got out that a little investment club was able to steal information from us, we'd be held up to public ridicule. Someone might even investigate us. You know how things are these days."

James fingered the clipping. "Any of these names—the fifteen club members—strike a responsive chord?"

"None whatsoever."

"Well," James concluded, "I'd say the way to begin would be for Bennett, here, to go right to the source and find out how The Happy Days Club arrives at their decisions. Meanwhile, I'll have Barney, my sound man, see if your phones are being tapped or anything. And I'll run a check on the backgrounds of everyone involved in your stock transactions."

"We don't want to alarm those people in Iowa," Allen said.

"Don't worry," Bennett said. "Bennett will appear in appropriate disguise."

A day later Bennett flew to Chicago, took another plane to Davenport, and then rented a car. He drove south along the Mississippi, reaching Canfield, a river town of some 20,000 population, as dusk fell. He checked in at a motel, wolfed a paper plate of fried chicken at a drive-in, and returned to his room for a good night's sleep.

In the morning he drove to downtown Canfield. He breakfasted on tomato juice and toast, stopped at a news agency for a *Wall Street Journal,* and then, *Journal* and an attaché case in hand, entered the offices of the Canfield Savings and Loan Association. The newspaper clipping had identifed the president of The Happy Days Club as Robert Gordon, a loan officer at the institution.

Gordon, a genial, portly man in his fifties, greeted Bennett with a puzzled smile.

"You say you're from New York? Are you buying real estate in our town, Mr. Bennett?"

"No," Bennett said, shaking Gordon's hand and taking a chair, "I'm a writer. Free-lance. I'm working up a magazine piece on investment clubs."

"You've come a long way for that."

"I know," Bennett explained, "but that's the point. I want to get away from the usual slick big-city and fancy suburban crowd—advertising men and sales executives and all that. I want a good part of my article to deal with the way an investment club works in small-town America, the folks right across the street." He pulled a photostat of the clipping from his pocket. "I've had a clipping service send me everything they could find on small-town investment clubs. And as soon as I read about The Happy Days Club in the *Gazette*, I knew it was the club I wanted to feature in my article."

"I'm flattered," Gordon said. "I'm sure the whole club will be flattered. In what magazine will your story appear?"

"I have a tentative commission from the editors of *View,*" Bennett said, handing Gordon a faked letter written on *View* stationery. "But if they decide they don't want it, I don't expect to have much trouble selling it elsewhere."

"Will there be pictures?"

"Of course. I have my camera at my motel."

"Well won't that be nice," Gordon said, beaming and returning the faked letter. "Tell you what. Meet me for lunch at the American Café around the corner. Meanwhile, I'll phone the members and try to set up a special meeting as soon as possible."

Bennett walked to the Canfield *Gazette* building. He told the managing editor the same story he had told Gordon and got permission to use the newspaper's library for background material on the club and its members.

He spent two hours going over the *Gazette's* clipping files. When at last he left the building, a police car slowly followed him around the corner and down the block to the American Café. Bennett tried without much success to pretend it wasn't there.

"All our members have been contacted," Gordon announced over coffee. "Most of them can make it at my house tomorrow night. They'll be there at eight. But I wish you'd drop in tonight, and have dinner with my family."

"Delighted," Bennett said. "By the way, who makes the buying and selling decisions for your club?"

"We have a three-man selection committee—Cromie, Hubbard, and Price. When anyone has a suggestion for a stock to buy or a reason to sell a stock we hold, it's forwarded to the committee. When we were first organized, the whole membership used to vote on what purchases or sales to make. But recently we've let the committee make the actual decisions, since they say timing may be important."

"Who's chairman of the committee?"

"We have no chairman. Just the three men. But the selections they've been making lately have been doing so well that we haven't changed members of the committee in nearly a year. Before that we had an awful lot of losers."

Bennett had almost reached his car when the police car pulled up behind him and stopped. A tall, husky man in uniform emerged.

"Sir," the officer said, "would you mind coming with us?"

"What's the trouble?"

"No trouble. The Chief wants a word with you."

Bennett shrugged and climbed into the back of the police car. He flipped through his *Wall Street Journal* as they rode to the station in silence.

The Chief of Police, a huge, crew-cutted man of about Bennett's age, late thirties, smiled and nodded toward a chair.

"Sit down, Mr. Bennett. I understand you're a writer."

"That's correct," Bennett said. He put his attaché case and the *Journal* on a radiator under the window and sat down. Inwardly, he debated whether to volunteer to show the Chief the faked *View* letter. Something about the Chief made him decide not to.

"What magazine do you write for?"

"I may do this story for *View*."

"Would you mind naming some other magazines where your work has appeared?"

Bennett rattled off the names of several nationally circulated publications. He felt much as he had one day in 1944, when a German officer asked why a French farm laborer who stubbed a toe should know so many American obscenities. That had been a bad day too.

The Chief wrote the names on a pad. "I don't suppose you'd mind," the Chief asked, "if we checked these out."

"Not at all," Bennett replied. "And now I'd like to know why you've taken such a sudden interest in me."

"Well, it's funny," the Chief explained, "but a lot of people from the big city think we're kind of slow out here. They try to sell our citizens traps for mortar mice and all sorts of things. And this morning one of our citizens called me and said there was a man in town from *View* who wanted to meet the members of The Happy Days Club. He said he was suspicious because he'd heard of confidence men approaching investment clubs in one disguise or another, for the very good reason that people in investment clubs have money to invest. He didn't say *you* were a confidence man, understand. He just asked us to check and make sure you're a writer."

"Who was this caller?"

"I'd rather not tell you."

"You asked me in here on the basis of that?"

"Not entirely," the Chief said. "We've had writers around here before, Mr. Bennett. A year ago, when a farmer outside of town chopped up two mail-order brides and buried them in an onion patch, a lot of writers came down. I called one of those boys—he works out of New York too—and he said he never heard of you. So far nobody else he's asked ever heard of you either—including, by the way, the editor of *View*. And the librarian here has been going through the *Reader's Guide* and she can't find any record of where you ever had anything published. Maybe if you'd tell me the dates where some of your stuff ran, she could look it up, and we could both forget the whole thing."

"At the moment," Bennett said blandly, "I just don't remember."

The Chief considered this. "Well that's too bad," he said. "Now you haven't done anything illegal I know of yet, so I can't charge you and put you in jail. Your name *is* Theodore Bennett—we know because you showed identification when you rented that car in Davenport. We checked. We're great respecters of the law out here. We don't push people around because they're strangers. But the way it is, though, I'm afraid there'll be a squad car or a police officer at your elbow every second you're inside the city limits until I'm satisfied you *are* a writer. So if you want to operate under those conditions, you go right ahead."

Bennett managed a weak grin. "Well," he said, "I'm not going to argue. It's ridiculous. But on the other hand, I'm not going to waste my time giving Canfield and The Happy Days Club national publicity if this is the treatment I receive here." He rose. "I saw a pay phone near the sergeant's desk on my way in. I'll telephone Gordon and call the whole thing off."

"Use my phone."

"Wouldn't think of it. I don't want to waste a cent of your taxpayers' money."

Bennett left the Chief's office. He fumbled clumsily through a telephone book for Gordon's number, taking plenty of time. Then he called Gordon and abruptly informed him he was leaving town and wouldn't write a story about The Happy Days Club after all. He hung up, leaving Gordon in mid-sentence and returned to the Chief's office for his attaché case and *Wall Street Journal.*

"A couple of my boys," the Chief said genially, "will go with you to your motel and see to it you get packed proper and on the right road back to Davenport. If you drive fast, you might reach there before dark."

Two uniformed officers drove Bennett to where he had parked the rented car, then followed him to the motel. Bennett packed in five minutes and checked out. They stayed with him to the city limits, pulling to the curb and watching as Bennett gunned the motor and roared out of sight over a hill.

Bennett drove at high speed for about five miles. In the future, he vowed, he'd provide himself with a solid cover story and appropriate supporting documents no matter how innocuous the assignment seemed. Apparently he had vastly underestimated the sophistication of Iowa investment clubs—and of the Iowa police.

When Bennett came to a strip of roadside stores and drive-ins he bounced to a stop in a gravel parking area. He hauled his attaché case from the back seat and opened it, exposing a transistorized tape recorder built into the bottom. Bennett had activated the recorder before placing the attaché case on the radiator in the Chief's office. No matter how the conversation went, it had seemed a good idea.

Quickly Bennett reversed the tape, pushed the playback button, and lit a cigarette, listening to the point where the Chief had said, "Use my phone."

"Wouldn't think of it. I don't want to waste a cent of your taxpayers' money."

Then he heard the door close as he left the Chief's office to telephone Gordon. And then the Chief did what Bennett had hoped he would do. He picked up his own telephone and dialed a number.

"Hello, Mrs. Price? Chief Waner. Your husband home? Hello. Frank. You were right. He must be some kind of swindler, although I never heard of this investment club approach before. But he sure isn't a writer. Don't worry. We had a little talk and he's leaving Canfield this afternoon. He seemed sensible enough not to try to come back. Thanks. Glad you put me on to this guy before he did any damage."

The Chief hung up.

Frank Price, Bennett knew without having to check his list, was a member of The Happy Days Club. What's more, he was one of the three men on the stock selection committee.

Bennett turned the recorder off and looked around. What he needed now was a woman.

He found her behind a counter in a diner. She was reasonably articulate and, from the way she talked back to truck drivers, she seemed to have plenty of nerve. Bennett had to drink two cups of coffee before the place cleared out and he was alone with her. The cook in the back was engrossed in a telecast of a baseball game.

"Miss," Bennett asked, "can you dial Canfield direct on that pay phone?"

"Yes, sir."

"Well," Bennett said, "I'll give you twenty bucks if you make a call for me. It will take you less than five minutes."

"You're crazy," she said.

He pulled twenty dollars from his wallet and pushed it across the counter. "There it is. No fooling. In fact, I'll make it thirty." He extracted another ten.

"I don't want to get in trouble," the girl said.

"You won't."

"Why don't you call?"

"Because I want someone to impersonate a telephone operator."

"That sounds illegal." She advanced and fingered the bills.

"It is a little illegal," Bennett admitted, "but there'll be no risk for you. You've heard of private investigators, haven't you? I can't tell you any more than that. But if you make the call and hang up, nobody will be able to trace it. And even if they did trace it, you could always say some woman came into the diner and used the phone."

"What do you want me to say?"

"Say, 'This is the long-distance operator. The charge on your call to San Diego is twenty-eight dollars and nineteen cents.' I have reason to believe this party just made a long-distance call, although probably not to San Diego. The party will probably be so mad at you that he'll volunteer information about any long-distance calls he did make this afternoon. If he doesn't, ask him if he made any long-distance calls, and to where. Get the out-of-town number if you possibly can. If you can't get any information after a minute or two, say 'This is Albany 4-5634, isn't it?' He'll say no, because his number is Albany 4-5624. Then say you're sorry you made the error and hang up."

"Albany 4-5624," she repeated, reaching for the thirty dollars. "Okay, hon. I'll go along. Got a dime?"

Twenty minutes later Bennett climbed into his car and drove to the next river town. There he turned right and crossed a bridge over the Mississippi into Illinois. The road wound down the river's foothills and flattened out into farm country. It was dark when Bennett checked in at an eight-unit motel in a tiny junction called Blackford.

There was a telephone booth in the parking lot and Bennett called James from there.

"Where've you been?" James demanded. In the background,

the roar of guns from a television set mingled with youthful screams. "I got a pack of Cub Scouts in my living room and can hardly hear you."

"I got chased out of Canfield," Bennett reported, "by the Chief of Police. He knows I'm not a writer and he thinks I'm a confidence man."

"Some industrial espionage agent you are," James said sarcastically. "What happened? Your false mustache fall off?"

"Wait a minute," Bennett said. "The Chief didn't think this up on his own. He was tipped by a club member named Frank Price. Frank Price is also a member of a three-man committee that decides what stocks the club will buy and sell."

A moment of silence ensued.

"Are you thinking," James asked slowly, "what I'm thinking?"

"It occurred to me at the time," Bennett said, "but I figured it was just one chance in a million."

"Well, the odds are shortening. I'll have Barney work on that angle first thing tomorrow. Where are you now?"

"Blackford, Illinois. I'm going to sack in here tonight."

"You'll never get back to New York, the route you're taking. Drive to some place with an airport and catch a plane. I'll send another agent to Canfield with a better cover."

"I'm at Blackford because I had a girl call Price to find out if he placed any long-distance calls after I was run out of town. She pretended to be a long-distance operator. And Price did make a long-distance call this afternoon. To Eaton, Illinois, which is twelve miles from Blackford."

"It's probably a waste of time."

"Maybe. The girl couldn't get the Eaton number that Price called. But Price has a brother, William, who lives in Eaton. I learned that from some social notes about him in the Canfield *Gazette* morgue. It will only take a day to check the brother and see if he has any connection with the Gibraltar Fund."

"Since you're there anyhow, go ahead. I'll hold up on that other agent. Come to think of it, Price called that Chief of Police so fast when he heard you were in town it's like someone pushed a button. He must have known you were coming. I got a hunch that by this time tomorrow we'll both have arrived at the same conclusion."

In the morning Bennett drove to Eaton and parked on a side street. He walked a block to the business district, entered a drug store, bought a *Wall Street Journal,* and stepped into a telephone booth. He flipped through the book to PRICE, WILLIAM J. and dialed the number.

A woman answered.

"Good morning," Bennett said. "Is your husband there?"

"He's asleep. He's always sleeping at this hour. He doesn't get in until three."

"When can I reach him?"

"Who is this?"

"I represent a firm doing market research for an advertising agency in Peoria. We're surveying all property owners in Eaton."

"Well," she said irritably, "why don't you get him at work, then? He doesn't like to be bothered at home. Call him at the restaurant this afternoon."

"What restuarant is that?"

"Why, Betty's, of course," she said, hanging up.

Bennett hung up and opened the book to the yellow pages. Under "Restaurants" he found a display ad for *BETTY'S— Steaks, Chops, Chicken, Cocktails, Open 8 a.m. to 2 a.m. Bill Price, Prop.*

He left the booth and walked back to the car. He drove to the address listed in the telephone book for the restaurant, getting directions from a small boy on a bicycle. The restaurant would be as good a place to begin an investigation of William J. Price as any.

The restaurant, a roadhouse, had been converted from an old farm building on the outskirts of town. Bennett pulled into the parking lot but didn't get out of his car. He didn't have to. Because a foot-high sign in the window proclaimed: *BETTY'S—HOME OF THE ORIGINAL 25-CENT MARTINI.*

Michael Dane James handed the report to Allen—he, Allen, and Bennett were sitting in James's office.

James explained: "Sam, the owner of that comfortable two-bit cocktail-hour martini joint across from your building, wired your reserved booth for sound. The mike was hooked to a tape recorder in his office. Barney found the mike in ten minutes when he joined us for a drink yesterday. A restaurant or bar owner bugging tables isn't unheard of, you know. Usually they say they're just checking customer reaction to food and service and whatnot. In this case it's obvious one of Sam's motives was to get tips on stocks. His location in the financial district would be a natural for that. His twenty-five-cent martini between five and six would be a lure to bring people in. And when he got the right people—like top decision-makers for one of the nation's big mutual funds—he reserved a booth for you regularly, to make sure he could hear everything you had to say."

"As I get it," Allen said, "Sam's connection with The Happy Days Club was through his brother-in-law."

"That's right," Bennett said. "Sam came from Eaton originally. He and his sister, Betty, ran a roadhouse there. After Sam left for New York, Betty married William J. Price, and he took over the roadhouse. As time went on, and Sam got established here, he started relaying some of his inside stock information to his sister and her husband, William Price. And William, in turn, passed it on to his own brother, Frank, who lived in Canfield. Frank belonged to The Happy Days Club and got on the selection committee. Once on it, it wasn't much of a trick to control it. If necessary, he could take one of the other two committee members into his confidence, and the two of them could always outvote the third member. I'm sure most members of the club had no idea they were using information stolen from the Gilbraltar Fund."

"Sam taped our conversation the day we were in his place and you gave us the assignment," James said. "He knew, then, that Bennett was going to Canfield in one role or another. And he had a brief look at Bennett when you ordered martinis for us. When Sam heard the tape he must have panicked. No doubt he called his brother-in-law, William, who in turned called Frank and warned him Bennett was on the way. So the minute Frank Price learned Bennett was in Canfield, he asked the police to check Bennett, hoping Bennett would be run out of town."

"The mystery is solved," Allen admitted, "but it does leave me with a dilemma."

"I don't think," James smiled, "that The Happy Days Club will follow the Gilbraltar Fund's lead any more. This probably scared the daylights out of William and Frank Price."

"Nevertheless," Allen said, "the problem remains: What do we do about Sam? If we expose him, we may still get all the publicity we've been trying to avoid. And if we say nothing, he'll go on eavesdropping on his patrons."

"If it were up to me," James suggested, "I'd pass the word discreetly to your employees never to go into that place again because it's bugged. The news will get around the financial district fast enough, and Sam's will die a slow but certain death."

"Why," Bennett offered, "don't you just sit there, drink his martinis, and pass along tips on stocks you think will go down instead of up?"

"I like that," Allen grinned. "Between all of us, we could give Sam enough bad advice to bankrupt him in thirty days. But we don't want to hurt any innocent investors—even in Canfield, Iowa. No, I think we'll adopt Mr. James's suggestion."

THEY CAN ONLY HANG YOU
ONCE

BY DASHIELL HAMMETT

Dashiell Hammett (b. May 27, 1894) worked as a news-
boy, freight clerk, railroad laborer, messenger boy,
stevedore, advertising manager, and Pinkerton detective, and served in the Army in World War I, before
becoming a detective-story writer in the late 1920s. His
short fiction appeared in *Black Mask,* and his first novel,
Red Harvest, was published in 1929. His most famous
fictional detectives are Sam Spade, the Continental Op,
and Nick and Nora Charles. When he died in 1961, he
left unfinished an autobiographical novel, *Tulip,* which
was included in a collection of his short stories, *The Big
Knockover* (1966).

SAMUEL SPADE SAID: "My name is Ronald Ames. I want to see Mr. Binnett—Mr. Timothy Binnett."

"Mr. Binnett is resting now, sir," the butler replied hesitantly.

"Will you find out when I can see him? It's important." Spade cleared his throat. "I'm—uh—just back from Australia, and it's about some of his properties there."

The butler turned on his heel while saying "I'll see, sir," and was going up the front stairs before he had finished speaking.

Spade made and lit a cigarette.

The butler came downstairs again. "I'm sorry; he can't be disturbed now, but Mr. Wallace Binnett—Mr. Timothy's nephew—will see you."

Spade said, "Thanks," and followed the butler upstairs.

Wallace Binnett was a slender, handsome, dark man of about Spade's age—thirty-eight—who rose smiling from a brocaded chair, said, "How do you do, Mr. Ames?" waved his hand at another chair, and sat down again. "You're from Australia?"

"Got in this morning."

"You're a business associate of Uncle Tim's?"

Spade smiled and shook his head. "Hardly that, but I've some information I think he ought to have—quick."

Wallace Binnett looked thoughtfully at the floor, then up at Spade. "I'll do my best to persuade him to see you, Mr. Ames, but, frankly, I don't know."

Spade seemed mildly surprised. "Why?"

Binnett shrugged. "He's peculiar sometimes. Understand, his mind seems perfectly all right, but he has the testiness and eccentricity of an old man in ill health and—well—at times he can be difficult."

Spade asked slowly: "He's already refused to see me?"

"Yes."

Spade rose from his chair. His blond satan's face was expressionless.

Binnett raised a hand quickly. "Wait, wait," he said. "I'll do what I can to make him change his mind. Perhaps if—" His dark eyes suddenly became wary. "You're not simply trying to sell him something, are you?"

"No."

82

The wary gleam went out of Binnett's eyes. "Well, then, I think I can—"

A young woman came in crying angrily, "Wally, that old fool has—" She broke off with a hand to her breast when she saw Spade.

Spade and Binnett had risen together. Binnett said suavely: "Joyce, this is Mr. Ames. My sister-in-law, Joyce Court."

Spade bowed.

Joyce Court uttered a short, embarrassed laugh and said: "Please excuse my whirlwind entrance." She was a tall, blue-eyed, dark woman of twenty-four or -five with good shoulders and a strong, slim body. Her features made up in warmth what they lacked in regularity. She wore wide-legged blue satin pajamas.

Binnett smiled good-naturedly at her and asked: "Now what's all the excitement?"

Anger darkened her eyes again and she started to speak. Then she looked at Spade and said: "But we shouldn't bore Mr. Ames with our stupid domestic affairs. If—" She hesitated.

Spade bowed again. "Sure," he said, "certainly."

"I won't be a minute," Binnett promised, and left the room with her.

Spade went to the open doorway through which they had vanished and, standing just inside, listened. Their footsteps became inaudible. Nothing else could be heard. Spade was standing there—his yellow-gray eyes dreamy—when he heard the scream. It was a woman's scream, high and shrill with terror. Spade was through the doorway when he heard the shot. It was a pistol shot, magnified, reverberated by walls and ceilings.

Twenty feet from the doorway Spade found a staircase, and went up it three steps at a time. He turned to the left. Halfway down the hallway a woman lay on her back on the floor.

Wallace Binnett knelt beside her, fondling one of her hands desperately, crying in a low, beseeching voice: "Darling, Molly, darling!"

Joyce Court stood behind him and wrung her hands while tears streaked her cheeks.

The woman on the floor resembled Joyce Court but was older, and her face had a hardness the younger one's had not.

"She's dead, she's been killed," Wallace Binnett said incredulously, raising his white face towards Spade. When Binnett moved his head Spade could see the round hole in the woman's tan dress over her heart and the dark stain which was rapidly spreading below it.

Spade touched Joyce Court's arm. "Police, emergency hospital—phone," he said. As she ran towards the stairs he addressed Wallace Binnett: "Who did—"

A voice groaned feebly behind Spade.

He turned swiftly. Through an open doorway he could see an old man in white pajamas lying sprawled across a rumpled bed. His head, a shoulder, an arm dangled over the edge of the bed. His other hand held his throat tightly. He groaned again and his eyelids twitched, but did not open.

Spade lifted the old man's head and shoulders and put them up on the pillows. The old man groaned again and took his hand from his throat. His throat was red with half a dozen bruises. He was a gaunt man with a seamed face that probably exaggerated his age.

A glass of water was on a table beside the bed. Spade put water on the old man's face and, when the old man's eyes twitched again, leaned down and growled softly: "Who did it?"

The twitching eyelids went up far enough to show a narrow strip of bloodshot gray eyes. The old man spoke painfully, putting a hand to his throat again: "A man—he—" He coughed.

Spade made an impatient grimace. His lips almost touched the old man's ear. "Where'd he go?" His voice was urgent.

A gaunt hand moved weakly to indicate the rear of the house and fell back on the bed.

The butler and two frightened female servants had joined Wallace Binnett beside the dead woman in the hallway.

"Who did it?" Spade asked them.

They stared at him blankly.

"Somebody look after the old man," he growled, and went down the hallway.

At the end of the hallway was a rear staircase. He descended two flights and went through a pantry into the kitchen. He saw nobody. The kitchen door was shut but, when he tried it, not locked. He crossed a narrow back yard to a gate that was shut, not locked. He opened the gate. There was nobody in the narrow alley behind it.

He sighed, shut the gate, and returned to the house.

Spade sat comfortably slack in a deep leather chair in a room

84

that ran across the front second story of Wallace Binnett's house. There were shelves of books and the lights were on. The window showed outer darkness weakly diluted by a distant street lamp. Facing Spade, Detective Sergeant Polhaus—a big, carelessly shaven, florid man in dark clothes that needed pressing—was sprawled in another leather chair; Lieutenant Dundy—smaller, compactly built, square-faced—stood with legs apart, head thrust a little forward, in the center of the room.

Spade was saying: ". . . and the doctor would only let me talk to the old man a couple of minutes. We can try it again when he's rested a little, but it doesn't look like he knows much. He was catching a nap and he woke up with somebody's hands on his throat dragging him around the bed. The best he got was a one-eyed look at the fellow choking him. A big fellow, he says, with a soft hat pulled down over his eyes, dark, needing a shave. Sounds like Tom." Spade nodded at Polhaus.

The detective sergeant chuckled, but Dundy said, "Go on," curtly.

Spade grinned and went on: "He's pretty far gone when he hears Mrs. Binnett scream at the door. The hands go away from his throat and he hears the shot and just before passing out he gets a flash of the big fellow heading for the rear of the house and Mrs. Binnett tumbling down on the hall floor. He says he never saw the big fellow before."

"What size gun was it?" Dundy asked.

"Thirty-eight. Well, nobody in the house is much more help. Wallace and his sister-in-law, Joyce, were in her room, so they say, and didn't see anything but the dead woman when they ran out, though they think they heard something that could've been somebody running downstairs—the back stairs.

"The butler—his name's Jarboe—was in here when he heard the scream and shot, so he says. Irene Kelly, the maid, was down on the ground floor, so she says. The cook, Margaret Finn, was in her room—third floor back—and didn't even hear anything, so she says. She's deaf as a post, so everybody else says. The back door and gate were unlocked, but are supposed to be kept locked, so everybody says. Nobody says they were in or around the kitchen or yard at the time." Spade spread his hands in a gesture of finality. "That's the crop."

Dundy shook his head. "Not exactly," he said. "How come you were here?"

85

Spade's face brightened. "Maybe my client killed her," he said. "He's Wallace's cousin, Ira Binnett. Know him?"

Dundy shook his head. His blue eyes were hard and suspicious.

"He's a San Francisco lawyer," Spade said, "respectable and all that. A couple of days ago he came to me with a story about his uncle Timothy, a miserly old skinflint, lousy with money and pretty well broken up by hard living. He was the black sheep of the family. None of them had heard of him for years. But six or eight months ago he showed up in pretty bad shape every way except financially—he seems to have taken a lot of money out of Australia—wanting to spend his last days with his only living relatives, his nephews Wallace and Ira.

"That was all right with them. 'Only living relatives' meant 'only heirs' in their language. But by and by the nephews began to think it was better to be an heir than to be one of a couple of heirs—twice as good, in fact—and started fiddling for the inside track with the old man. At least, that's what Ira told me about Wallace, and I wouldn't be surprised if Wallace would say the same thing about Ira, though Wallace seems to be the harder up of the two. Anyhow, the nephews fell out, and then Uncle Tim, who had been staying at Ira's, came over here. That was a couple of months ago, and Ira hasn't seen Uncle Tim since, and hasn't been able to get in touch with him by phone or mail.

"That's what he wanted a private detective about. He didn't think Uncle Tim would come to any harm here—oh, no, he went to a lot of trouble to make that clear—but he thought maybe undue pressure was being brought to bear on the old boy, or he was being hornswoggled somehow, and at least being told lies about his loving nephew Ira. He wanted to know what was what. I waited until today, when a boat from Australia docked, and came up here as a Mr. Ames with some important information for Uncle Tim about his properties down there. All I wanted was fifteen minutes alone with him." Spade frowned thoughtfully. "Well, I didn't get them. Wallace told me the old man refused to see me. I don't know."

Suspicion had deepened in Dundy's cold blue eyes. "And where is this Ira Binnett now?" he said.

Spade's yellow-gray eyes were as guileless as his voice. "I wish I knew. I phoned his house and office and left word for him to come right over, but I'm afraid—"

Knuckles knocked sharply twice on the other side of the

room's one door. The three men in the room turned to face the door.

Dundy called, "Come in."

The door was opened by a sunburned blond policeman whose left hand held the right wrist of a plump man of forty or forty-five in well-fitting gray clothes. The policeman pushed the plump man into the room. "Found him monkeying with the kitchen door," he said.

Spade looked up and said: "Ah!" His tone expressed satisfaction. "Mr. Ira Binnett, Lieutenant Dundy, Sergeant Polhaus."

Ira Binnett said rapidly: "Mr. Spade, will you tell this man that—"

Dundy addressed the policeman: "All right. Good work. You can leave him."

The policeman moved a hand vaguely towards his cap and went away.

Dundy glowered at Ira Binnett and demanded, "Well?"

Binnett looked from Dundy to Spade. "Has something—"

Spade said: "Better tell him why you were at the back door instead of the front."

Ira Binnett suddenly blushed. He cleared his throat in embarrassment. He said: "I—uh—I should explain. It wasn't my fault, of course, but when Jarboe—he's the butler—phoned me that Uncle Tim wanted to see me he told me he'd leave the kitchen door unlocked, so Wallace wouldn't have to know I'd—"

"What'd he want to see you about?" Dundy asked.

"I don't know. He didn't say. He said it was very important."

"Didn't you get my message?" Spade asked.

Ira Binnett's eyes widened. "No. What was it? Has anything happened? What is—"

Spade was moving towards the door. "Go ahead," he said to Dundy. "I'll be right back."

He shut the door carefully behind him and went up to the third floor.

The butler Jarboe was on his knees at Timothy Binnett's door with an eye to the keyhole. On the floor beside him was a tray holding an egg in an egg-cup, toast, a pot of coffee, china, silver, and a napkin.

Spade said: "Your toast's going to get cold."

Jarboe, scrambling to his feet, almost upsetting the coffeepot in his haste, his face red and sheepish, stammered: "I—er—beg your pardon, sir. I wanted to make sure Mr. Timothy was awake before I took this in." He picked up the tray. "I didn't want to disturb his rest if—"

Spade, who had reached the door, said, "Sure, sure," and bent over to put his eye to the keyhole. When he straightened up he said in a mildly complaining tone: "You can't see the bed—only a chair and part of the window."

The butler replied quickly: "Yes, sir, I found that out."

Spade laughed.

The butler coughed, seemed about to say something, but did not. He hesitated, then knocked lightly on the door.

A tired voice said, "Come in."

Spade asked quickly in a low voice: "Where's Miss Court?"

"In her room, I think, sir, the second door on the left," the butler said.

The tired voice inside the room said petulantly: "Well, come on in."

The butler opened the door and went in. Through the door, before the butler shut it, Spade caught a glimpse of Timothy Binnett propped up on pillows in his bed.

Spade went to the second door on the left and knocked. The door was opened almost immediately by Joyce Court. She stood in the doorway, not smiling, not speaking.

He said: "Miss Court, when you came into the room where I was with your brother-in-law you said, 'Wally, that old fool has—' Meaning Timothy?"

She stared at Spade for a moment. Then: "Yes."

"Mind telling me what the rest of the sentence would have been?"

She said slowly: "I don't know who you really are or why you ask, but I don't mind telling you. It would have been 'sent for Ira.' Jarboe had just told me."

"Thanks."

She shut the door before he had turned away.

He returned to Timothy Binnett's door and knocked on it twice.

"Who is it now?" the old man's voice demanded.

Spade opened the door. The old man was sitting up in bed.

Spade said: "This Jarboe was peeping through your keyhole a few minutes ago," and returned to the library.

Ira Binnett, seated in the chair Spade had occupied, was saying to Dundy and Polhaus: "And Wallace got caught in the crash, like most of us, but he seems to have juggled accounts trying to save himself. He was expelled from the Stock Exchange."

Dundy waved a hand to indicate the room and its furnishings. "Pretty classy layout for a man that's busted."

"His wife has some money," Ira Binnett said, "and he always lived beyond his means."

Dundy scowled at Binnett. "And you really think he and his missus weren't on good terms?"

"I don't think it," Binnett replied evenly. "I know it."

Dundy nodded. "And you know he's got a yen for the sister-in-law, this Court?"

"I don't know that. But I've heard plenty of gossip to the same effect."

Dundy made a growling noise in his throat, then asked sharply: "How does the old man's will read?"

"I don't know. I don't know whether he's made one." He addressed Spade now, earnestly: "I've told everything I know, every single thing."

Dundy said, "It's not enough." He jerked a thumb at the door. "Show him where to wait, Tom, and let's have the widower in again."

Big Polhaus said, "Right," went out with Ira Binnett, and returned with Wallace Binnett, whose face was hard and pale.

Dundy asked: "Has your uncle made a will?"

"I don't know," Binnett replied.

Spade put the next question, softly: "Did your wife?"

Binnett's mouth tightened in a mirthless smile. He spoke deliberately: "I'm going to say some things I'd rather not have to say. My wife, properly, had no money. When I got into financial trouble some time ago I made some property over to her, to save it. She turned it into money without my knowing about it till afterwards. She paid our bills—our living expenses—out of it, but she refused to return it to me and she assured me that in no event—whether she lived or died or we stayed together or were divorced—would I ever be able to get hold of a penny of it. I believed her, and still do."

"You wanted a divorce?" Dundy asked.

"Yes."

"Why?"

"It wasn't a happy marriage."

"Joyce Court?"

89

Binnett's face flushed. He said stiffly: "I admire Joyce Court tremendously, but I'd wanted a divorce anyway."

Spade said: "And you're sure—still absolutely sure—you don't know anybody who fits your uncle's description of the man who choked him?"

"Absolutely sure."

The sound of the doorbell ringing came faintly into the room.

Dundy said sourly, "That'll do."

Binnett went out.

Polhaus said: "That guy's as wrong as they make them. And—"

From below came the heavy report of a pistol fired indoors.

The lights went out.

In darkness the three detectives collided with one another going through the doorway into the dark hall. Spade reached the stairs first. There was a clatter of footsteps below him, but nothing could be seen until he reached a bend in the stairs. Then enough light came from the street through the open front door to show the dark figure of a man standing with his back to the open door.

A flashlight clicked in Dundy's hand—he was at Spade's heels—and threw a glaring white beam of light on the man's face. He was Ira Binnett. He blinked in the light and pointed at something on the floor in front of him.

Dundy turned the beam of his light down on the floor. Jarboe lay there on his face, bleeding from a bullet hole in the back of his head.

Spade grunted softly.

Tom Polhaus came blundering down the stairs. Wallace Binnett close behind him. Joyce Court's frightened voice came from farther up: "Oh, what's happened? Wally, what's happened?"

"Where's the light switch?" Dundy barked.

"Inside the cellar door, under these stairs," Wallace Binnett said. "What is it?"

Polhaus pushed past Binnett towards the cellar door.

Spade made an inarticulate sound in his throat and, pushing Wallace Binnett aside, sprang up the stairs. He brushed past Joyce Court and went on, heedless of her startled scream. He was halfway up the stairs to the third floor when the pistol went off up there.

He ran to Timothy Binnett's door. The door was open. He went in.

Something hard and angular struck him above his right ear, knocking him across the room, bringing him down on one knee. Something thumped and clattered on the floor just outside the door.

The lights came on.

On the floor, in the center of the room. Timothy Binnett lay on his back bleeding from a bullet wound in his left forearm. His pajama jacket was torn. His eyes were shut.

Spade stood up and put a hand to his head. He scowled at the old man on the floor, at the room, at the black automatic pistol lying on the hallway floor. He said: "Come on, you old cutthroat. Get up and sit on a chair and I'll see if I can stop that bleeding till the doctor gets here."

The man on the floor did not move.

There were footsteps in the hallway and Dundy came in, followed by the two younger Binnetts. Dundy's face was dark and furious. "Kitchen door wide open," he said in a choked voice. "They run in and out like—"

"Forget it," Spade said. "Uncle Tim is our meat." He paid no attention to Wallace Binnett's gasp, to the incredulous looks on Dundy's and Ira Binnett's faces. "Come on, get up," he said to the old man on the floor, "and tell us what it was the butler saw when he peeped through the keyhole."

The old man did not stir.

"He killed the butler because I told him the butler had peeped," Spade explained to Dundy. "I peeped, too, but didn't see anything except that chair and the window, though we'd made enough racket by then to scare him back to bed. Suppose you take the chair apart while I go over the window." He went to the window and began to examine it carefully. He shook his head, put a hand out behind him, and said: "Give me the flashlight." Dundy put the flashlight in his hand.

Spade raised the window and leaned out, turning the light on the outside of the building. Presently he grunted and put his other hand out, tugging at a brick a little below the sill. Presently the brick came loose. He put it on the window sill and stuck his hand into the hole its removal had made. Out of the opening, one at a time, he brought an empty black pistol holster, a partially filled box of cartridges, and an unsealed manila envelope.

91

Holding these things in his hands, he turned to face the others. Joyce Court came in with a basin of water and a roll of gauze and knelt beside Timothy Binnett. Spade put the holster and cartridges on a table and opened the manila envelope. Inside were two sheets of paper, covered on both sides with boldly penciled writing. Spade read a paragraph to himself, suddenly laughed, and began at the beginning again, reading aloud:

" 'I, Timothy Kieran Binnett, being sound of mind and body, do declare this to be my last will and testament. To my dear nephews, Ira Binnett and Wallace Bourke Binnett, in recognition of the loving kindness with which they have received me into their homes and attended my declining years, I give and bequeath, share and share alike, all my worldly possessions of whatever kind, to wit, my carcass and the clothes I stand in.

" 'I bequeath them, furthermore, the expense of my funeral and these memories: First, the memory of their credulity in believing that the fifteen years I spent in Sing Sing were spent in Australia; second, the memory of their optimism in supposing that those fifteen years had brought me great wealth, and that if I lived on them, borrowed from them, and never spent any of my own money, it was because I was a miser whose hoard they would inherit; and not because I had no money except what I shook them down for; third, for their hopefulness in thinking that I would leave either of them anything if I had it; and, lastly, because their painful lack of any decent sense of humor will keep them from ever seeing how funny this has all been. Signed and sealed this—' "

Spade looked up to say: "There is no date, but it's signed Timothy Kieran Binnett with flourishes."

Ira Binnett was purple with anger, Wallace's face was ghastly in its pallor and his whole body was trembling. Joyce Court had stopped working on Timothy Binnett's arm.

The old man sat up and opened his eyes. He looked at his nephews and began to laugh. There was in his laughter neither hysteria nor madness: it was sane, hearty laughter, and subsided slowly.

Spade said: "All right, now you've had your fun. Let's talk about the killings."

"I know nothing more about the first one than I've told you," the old man said, "and this one's not a killing, since I'm only—"

Wallace Binnett, still trembling violently, said painfully

92

through his teeth: "That's a lie. You killed Molly. Joyce and I came out of her room when we heard Molly scream, and heard the shot and saw her fall out of your room, and nobody came out afterwards."

The old man said calmly: "Well, I'll tell you: it was an accident. They told me there was a fellow from Australia here to see me about some of my properties there. I knew there was something funny about that somewhere"—he grinned—"not ever having been there. I didn't know whether one of my dear nephews was getting suspicious and putting up a game on me or what, but I knew that if Wally wasn't in on it he'd certainly try to pump the gentleman from Australia about me and maybe I'd lose one of my free boarding houses." He chuckled.

"So I figured I'd get in touch with Ira so I could go back to his house if things worked out bad here, and I'd try to get rid of this Australian. Wally's always thought I'm half-cracked"—he leered at his nephew—"and's afraid they'll lug me off to a madhouse before I could make a will in his favor, or they'll break it if I do. You see, he's got a pretty bad reputation, what with that Stock Exchange trouble and all, and he knows no court would appoint him to handle my affairs if I went screwy—not as long as I've got another nephew"—he turned his leer on Ira—"who's a respectable lawyer. So now I know that rather than have me kick up a row that might wind me up in the madhouse, he'll chase this visitor, and I put on a show for Molly, who happened to be the nearest one to hand. She took it too seriously, though.

"I had a gun and I did a lot of raving about being spied on by my enemies in Australia and that I was going down and shoot this fellow. But she got too excited and tried to take the gun away from me, and the first thing I knew it had gone off, and I had to make these marks on my neck and think up that story about the big dark man." He looked contemptuously at Wallace. "I didn't know he was covering me up. Little as I thought of him, I never thought he'd be low enough to cover up his wife's murderer—even if he didn't like her—just for the sake of money."

Spade said: "Never mind that. Now about the butler?"

"I don't know anything about the butler," the old man replied, looking at Spade with steady eyes.

Spade said: "You had to kill him quick, before he had time to do or say anything. So you slip down the back stairs, open the kitchen door to fool people, go to the front door, ring the bell, shut the door, and hide in the shadow of the cellar door under the front steps. When Jarboe answered the doorbell you shot him—the hole was in the back of his head—pulled the light switch, just inside the cellar door, and ducked up the back stairs in the dark and shot yourself carefully in the arm. I got up there too soon for you; so you smacked me with the gun, chucked it through the door, and spread yourself on the floor while I was shaking pinwheels out of my noodle."

The old man sniffed again. "You're just—"

"Stop it," Spade said patiently. "Don't let's argue. The first killing was an accident—all right. The second couldn't be. And it ought to be easy to show that both bullets, and the one in your arm, were fired from the same gun. What difference does it make which killing we can prove first-degree murder on? They can only hang you once." He smiled pleasantly. "And they will."

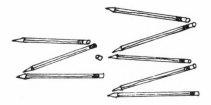

WILD GOOSE CHASE

BY ROSS MACDONALD

Ross Macdonald is the pseudonym of Kenneth Millar, who was born in California on December 13, 1915, and raised in Ontario, Canada. He served in the Navy in World War II and received his doctorate from the University of Michigan in 1951, writing his dissertation on Coleridge. His first mystery novel, *The Dark Tunnel,* was published in 1944. Macdonald's famous private detective Lew Archer appeared in *The Moving Target* (1949) and has been featured in all but two of his subsequent books, as well as several movies and a television series. Macdonald lives in Santa Barbara, California, with his wife, mystery writer Margaret Millar.

THE PLANE TURNED IN towards the shoreline and began to lose altitude. Mountains detached themselves from the blue distance. Then there was a city between the sea and the mountains, a little city made of sugar cubes. The cubes increased in size. Cars crawled like colored beetles between the buildings, and matchstick figures hustled jerkily along the white morning pavements. A few minutes later I was one of them.

The woman who had telephoned me was waiting at the airport, as she had promised. She climbed out of her Cadillac when I appeared at the entrance to the waiting room, and took a few tentative steps towards me. In spite of her height and her blondeness, the dark harlequin glasses she wore gave her an oddly Oriental look.

"You must be Mr. Archer."

I said I was, and waited for her to complete the exchange of names—she hadn't given me her name on the telephone. All she had given me, in fact, was an urgent request to catch the first plane north, and assurances that I would be paid for my time.

She sensed what I was waiting for. "I'm sorry to be so mysterious. I really can't afford to tell you my name. I'm taking quite a risk in coming here at all."

I looked her over carefully, trying to decide whether this was another wild goose chase. Although she was well-groomed in a sharkskin suit, her hair and face were slightly disarranged, as if a storm had struck her a glancing blow. She took off her glasses to wipe them. I could see that the storm was inside of her, roiling the blue-green color of her eyes.

"What's the problem?" I said.

She stood wavering between me and her car, beaten by surges of sound from the airfield where my plane was about to take off again. Behind her, in the Cadillac's front seat, a little girl with the coloring of a Dresden doll was sitting as still as one. The woman glanced at the child and moved farther away from the car:

"I don't want Janie to hear. She's only three-and-a-half but she understands a great deal." She took a deep gasping breath, like a swimmer about to dive. "There's a man on trial for murder here. They . . . they claim he murdered his wife."

"Glenway Cave?"

Her whole body moved with surprise. "You know him?"

"No, I've been following the trial in the papers."

"Then you know he's testifying today. He's probably on the witness stand right now." Her voice was somber, as if she could see the courtroom in her mind's eye.

"Is Mr. Cave a friend of yours?"

She bit her lip. "Let's say that I'm an interested observer."

"And you don't believe he's guilty."

"Did I say that?"

"By implication. You said they *claim* he murdered his wife."

"You have an alert ear, haven't you? Anyway, what I believe doesn't matter. It's what the jury believes. Do you think they'll acquit him?"

"It's hard to form an opinion without attending the trial. But the average jury has a prejudice against the idea of blowing off your wife's head with a twelve-gauge shotgun. I'd say he stands a good chance of going to the gas chamber."

"The gas chamber." Her nostrils dilated, and she paled, as if she had caught a whiff of the fatal stuff. "Do you seriously think there's any danger of that?"

"They've built a powerful case against him. Motive. Opportunity. Weapon."

"What motive?"

"His wife was wealthy, wasn't she? I understand Cave isn't. They were alone in the house; the housekeeping couple were away for the weekend. The shotgun belonged to Cave, and according to the chemical test his driving gloves were used to fire it."

"You *have* been following the trial."

"As well as I could from Los Angeles. Of course you get distortions in the newspapers. It makes a better story if he looks guilty."

"He isn't guilty," she said in a quiet voice.

"Do you know that, or merely hope it?"

She pressed one hand across her mouth. The fingernails were bitten down to the quick. "We won't go into that."

"Do you know who murdered Ruth Cave?"

"No. Of course not."

"Am I supposed to try and find out who did?"

"Wouldn't that be very difficult since it happened so long

97

ago? Anyway, it doesn't really matter to me. I barely knew the woman." Her thoughts veered back to Cave. "Won't a great deal depend on the impression he makes on the witness stand?"

"It usually does in a murder trial."

"You've seen a lot of them, haven't you?"

"Too many. I take it I'm going to see another."

"Yes." She spoke sharply and definitely, leaning forward. "I don't dare go myself. I want you to observe the jurors, see how Glen—how Mr. Cave's testimony affects them. And tell me if you think he's going to get off."

"What if I can't tell?"

"You'll have to give me a yes or no." Her breast nudged my arm. She was too intent on what she was saying to notice. "I've made up my mind to go by your decision."

"Go where?" I said.

"To hell if necessary—if his life is really in danger."

"I'll do my best. Where shall I get in touch with you?"

"I'll get in touch with you. I've made a reservation for you at the Rubio Inn. Right now I'll drop you at the courthouse. Oh, yes—the money." She opened her leather handbag, and I caught the gleam of a blue revolver at the bottom of the bag. "How much?"

"A hundred dollars will do."

A few bills changed hands, and we went to the car. She indicated the right rear door. I went around to the left so that I could read the white slip on the steering column. But the leatherette holder was empty.

The little girl stood up in the front seat and leaned over the back of it to look at me. "Hello. Are you my daddy?" Her eyes were as blue and candid as the sky.

Before I could answer, her mother said: "Now Janie, you know he isn't your daddy. This is Mr. Archer."

"Where is my daddy?"

"In Pasadena, darling. You know that. Sit down, Janie, and be still." The little girl slid down out of my sight. The engine roared in anger. . . .

It was ten minutes past eleven by the clock on the courthouse tower. Superior Court was on the second floor. I slid into one of the vacant seats in the back row of the spectators' section. Several old ladies turned to glare at me, as though I had interrupted a church service.

The trial was more like an ancient tribal ceremony in a grotto. Red drapes were drawn over the lofty windows. The air was dim with human exhalations. Black iron fixtures suspended from the ceiling shed a wan light on the judge's gray head, and on the man on the witness stand.

I recognized Glenway Cave from his newspaper pictures. He was a big handsome man in his early thirties who had once been bigger and handsomer. Four months in jail waiting for trial had pared him down to the bone. His eyes were pressed deep into hollow sockets. His double-breasted gabardine suit hung loosely on his shoulders. He looked like a suitable victim for the ceremony.

A broad-backed man with a straw-colored crewcut was bent over the stenographer, talking in an inaudible voice to the court reporter. Harvey, chief attorney for the defense. I had met Rod Harvey several times in the course of my work, which was one reason why I had followed the trial so closely.

The judge chopped the air with his hatchet face: "Proceed with your examination, Mr. Harvey."

Harvey raised his clipped blond head and addressed the witness: "Mr. Cave, we were attempting to establish the reason behind your—ah—misunderstanding with your wife. Did you and Mrs. Cave have words on the evening of May nineteenth?"

"We did. I've already told you that." Cave's voice was shallow, with high-pitched overtones.

"What was the nature of the conversation?"

"It was more of an argument than a conversation."

"But a purely verbal argument?" Harvey sounded as if his own witness had taken him by surprise.

A sharp-faced man spoke up from the prosecution end of the attorneys' table. "Objection. The question is leading—not to say *mis*leading."

"Sustained. The question will be stricken."

Harvey shrugged his heavy tweed shoulders. "Tell us just what was said then, Mr. Cave. Beginning at the beginning."

Cave moved uncomfortably, passing the palm of one hand over his eyes. "I can't recall it *verbatim*. It was quite an emotional scene—"

Harvey cut him off. "Tell us in your own words what you and Mrs. Cave were talking about."

"The future," Cave said. "Our future. Ruth was planning to leave me for another man."

99

An insect-buzzing rose from the spectators. I looked along the row where I was sitting. A couple of seats to my right, a young woman with artificial violets at her waist was leaning forward, her bright dark eyes intent on Cave's face. She seemed out of place among the frowsy old furies who surrounded her. Her head was striking, small and boyishly chic, its fine bony structure emphasized by a short haircut. She turned, and her brown eyes met mine. They were tragic and opaque.

The D.A.'s voice rose above the buzzing. "I object to this testimony. The witness is deliberately blackening the dead woman's reputation, without corroborative evidence of any kind, in a cowardly attempt to save his own neck."

He glanced sideways at the jury. Their faces were stony. Cave's was as white as marble. Harvey's was mottled red. He said, "This is an essential part of the case for the defense. A great deal has been made of Mr. Cave's sudden departure from home on the day of his wife's death. I am establishing the reason for it."

"We know the reason," the D.A. said in a carrying undertone.

Harvey looked up mutely at the judge, whose frown fitted the lines in his face like an old glove.

"Objection overruled. The prosecution will refrain from making unworthy comments. In any case, the jury will disregard them."

But the D.A. looked pleased with himself. He had made his point, and the jury would remember. Their twenty-four eyes, half female and predominantly old, were fixed on Cave in uniform disapproval.

Harvey spoke in a voice thickened by emotion. "Did your wife say who the man was that she planned to leave you for?"

"No. She didn't."

"Do you know who it was?"

"No. The whole thing was a bolt from the blue to me. I don't believe Ruth intended to tell me what she had on her mind. It just slipped out, after we started fighting." He caught himself up short. "Verbally fighting, I mean."

"What started this verbal argument?"

"Nothing important. Money trouble. I wanted to buy a Ferrari, and Ruth couldn't see any sense in it."

"A Ferrari motor car?"

"A racing car, yes. I asked her for the money. She said that she was tired of giving me money. I said that I was equally tired of taking it from her. Then it came out that she was going to leave me for somebody else." One side of Cave's mouth lifted in a sardonic smile. "Somebody who would love her for herself."

"When did she plan to leave you?"

"As soon as she could get ready to go to Nevada. I told her to go ahead, that she was free to go whenever and wherever she wanted to go, with anybody that suited her."

"And what did you do then?"

"I packed a few clothes and drove away in my car."

"What time did you leave the house?"

"I don't know exactly."

"Was it dark when you went?"

"It was getting dark, but I didn't have to use my headlights right away. It couldn't have been later than eight o'clock."

"And Mrs. Cave was alive and well when you left?"

"Certainly she was."

"Was your parting friendly?"

"Friendly enough. She said goodbye and offered me some money. Which I didn't take, incidentally. I didn't take much of anything, except for bare essentials. I even left most of my clothes behind."

"Why did you do that?"

"Because she bought them for me. They belonged to her. I thought perhaps her new man might have a use for them."

"I see."

Harvey's voice was hoarse and unsteady. He turned away from Cave, and I could see that his face was flushed, either with anger or impatience. He said without looking at the prisoner, "Did the things you left behind include a gun?"

"Yes. A twelve-gauge double-barreled shotgun. I used it for shooting rabbits, mostly, in the hills behind the house."

"Was it loaded?"

"I believe so. I usually kept it loaded."

"Where did you leave your shotgun?"

"In the garage. I kept it there. Ruth didn't like to have a gun in the house. She had a phobia—".

Harvey cut in quickly. "Did you also leave a pair of driving gloves, the gloves on the table here marked by the prosecution as Exhibit J?"

"I did. They were in the garage, too."

"And the garage door—was it open or closed?"

"I left it open, I think. In any case, we never kept it locked."

101

"Mr. Cave," Harvey said in a deep voice, "did you kill your wife with the shotgun before you drove away?"

"I did not." In contrast with Harvey's, Cave's voice was high and thin and unconvincing.

"After you left around eight o'clock, did you return to the house again that night?"

"I did not. I haven't been back since, as a matter of fact. I was arrested in Los Angeles the following day."

"Where did you spend the night—that is, after eight o'clock?"

"With a friend."

The courtroom began to buzz again.

"What friend?" Harvey barked. He suddenly sounded like a prosecutor cross-examining a hostile witness.

Cave moved his mouth to speak, and hesitated. He licked his dry lips. "I prefer not to say."

"Why do you prefer not to say?"

"Because it was a woman. I don't want to involve her in this mess."

Harvey swung away from the witness abruptly and looked up at the judge. The judge admonished the jury not to discuss the case with anyone, and adjourned the trial until two o'clock.

I watched the jurors file out. Not one of them looked at Glenway Cave. They had seen enough of him.

Harvey was the last man to leave the well of the courtroom. I waited for him at the little swinging gate which divided it from the spectators' section. He finished packing his briefcase and came towards me, carrying the case as if it was weighted.

"Mr. Harvey. Can you give me a minute?"

He started to brush me off with a weary gesture, then recognized my face, "Lew Archer? What brings you here?"

"It's what I want to talk to you about."

"This case?"

I nodded. "Are you going to get him off?"

"Naturally I am. He's innocent." But his voice echoed hollowly in the empty room and he regarded me doubtfully. "You wouldn't be snooping around for the prosecution?"

"Not this time. The person who hired me believes that Cave is innocent. Just as you do."

"A woman?"

"You're jumping to conclusions, aren't you?"

"When the sex isn't indicated, it's usually a woman. Who is she, Archer?"

"I wish I knew."

"Come on now." His square pink hand rested on my arm. "You don't accept anonymous clients any more than I do."

"This one is an exception. All I know about her is that she's anxious to see Cave get off."

"So are we all." His bland smile tightened. "Look, we can't talk here. Walk over to the office with me. I'll have a couple of sandwiches sent up."

He shifted his hand to my elbow and propelled me towards the door. The dark-eyed woman with the artificial violets at her waist was waiting in the corridor. Her opaque gaze passed over me and rested possessively on Harvey.

"Surprise." Her voice was low and throaty to match her boyish look. "You're taking me to lunch."

"I'm pretty busy, Rhea. And I thought you were going to stay home today."

"I tried to. Honestly. But my mind kept wandering off to the courthouse, so I finally up and followed it." She moved towards him with a queer awkwardness, as if she was embarrassingly conscious of her body, and his. "Aren't you glad to see me, darling?"

"Of course I'm glad to see you," he said, his tone denying the words.

"Then take me to lunch." Her white-gloved hand stroked his lapel. "I made a reservation at the club. It will do you good to get out in the air."

"I told you I'm busy, Rhea. Mr. Archer and I have something to discuss."

"Bring Mr. Archer along. I won't get in the way. I promise." She turned to me with a flashing white smile. "Since my husband seems to have forgotten his manners, I'm Rhea Harvey."

She offered me her hand, and Harvey told her who I was. Shrugging his shoulders resignedly, he led the way outside to his bronze convertible. We turned towards the sea, which glimmered at the foot of the town like a fallen piece of sky.

"How do you think it's going, Rod?" she said.

"I suppose it could have been worse. He could have got up in front of the judge and jury and confessed."

"Did it strike you as that bad?"

"I'm afraid it was pretty bad." Harvey leaned forward over the wheel in order to look around his wife at me. "Were you in on the debacle, Archer?"

"Part of it. He's either very honest or very stupid."

Harvey snorted. "Glen's not stupid. The trouble is, he simply doesn't care. He pays no attention to my advice. I had to stand there and ask the questions, and I didn't know what crazy answers he was going to come up with. He seems to take a masochistic pleasure in wrecking his own chances."

"It could be his conscience working on him," I said.

His steely blue glance raked my face and returned to the road. "It could be, but it isn't. And I'm not speaking simply as his attorney. I've known Glen Cave for a long time. We were roommates in college. Hell, I introduced him to his wife."

"That doesn't make him incapable of murder."

"Sure, any man is capable of murder. That's not my point. My point is that Glen is a sharp customer. If he had decided to kill Ruth for her money, he wouldn't do it that way. He wouldn't use his own gun. In fact, I doubt very much that he'd use a gun at all. Glen isn't that obvious."

"Unless it was a passional crime. Jealousy can make a man lose his sophistication."

"Not Glen. He wasn't in love with Ruth—never has been. He's got about as much sexual passion as a flea." His voice was edged with contempt. "Anyway, this tale of his about another man is probably malarkey."

"Are you sure, Rod?"

He turned on his wife almost savagely. "No, I'm not sure. I'm not sure about anything. Glen isn't confiding in me, and I don't see how I can defend him if he goes on this way. I wish to God he hadn't forced me into this. He knows as well as I do that trial work isn't my forte. I advised him to get an attorney experienced in this sort of thing, but he wouldn't listen. He said if I wouldn't take on his case that he'd defend himself. And he flunked out of law school in his second year. What the hell could I do?"

He stamped the accelerator, cutting in and out of the noon traffic on the ocean boulevard. Palm trees fled by like thin old wild-haired madmen racing along the edge of the quicksilver sea.

The beach club stood at the end of the boulevard, a white U-shaped building whose glass doors opened "For Members and Guests Only." Its inner court contained a swimming pool and an alfresco dining space dotted with umbrella tables. Breeze-swept and sluiced with sunlight, it was the antithesis of

104

the dim courtroom where Cave's fate would be decided. But the shadow of the courtroom fell across our luncheon and leached the color and flavor from the food.

Harvey pushed away his salmon salad, which he had barely disturbed, and gulped a second Martini. He called the waiter to order a third. His wife inhibited him with a barely perceptible shake of her head. The waiter slid away.

"This woman," I said, "the woman he spent the night with. Who is she?"

"Glen hardly told me anything more than he told the court." Harvey paused, half gagged by a lawyer's instinctive reluctance to give away information, then forced himself to go on. "It seems he went straight from home to her house on the night of the shooting. He spent the night with her, from about eight thirty until the following morning. Or so he claims."

"Haven't you checked his story?"

"How? He refused to say anything that might enable me to find her or identify her. It's just another example of the obstacles he's put in my way, trying to defend him."

"Is this woman so important to his defense?"

"Crucial. Ruth was shot sometime around midnight. The p.m. established that through the stomach contents. And at that time, if he's telling the truth, Glen was with a witness. Yet he won't let me try to locate her, or have her subpoenaed. It took me hours of hammering at him to get him to testify about her at all, and I'm not sure that wasn't a mistake. That miserable jury—" His voice trailed off. He was back in court fighting his uphill battle against the prejudices of a small elderly city.

And I was back on the pavement in front of the airport, listening to a woman's urgent whisper: *You'll have to give me a yes or no. I've made up my mind to go by your decision.*

Harvey was looking away across the captive water, fish-netted with elastic strands of light. Under the clear September sun I could see the spikes of gray in his hair, the deep small scars of strain around his mouth.

"If I could only lay my hands on the woman." He seemed to be speaking to himself, until he looked at me from the corners of his eyes. "Who do *you* suppose she is?"

"How would I know?"

He leaned across the table confidentially. "Why be so cagey, Archer? I've let down my hair."

"This particular hair doesn't belong to me."

I regretted the words before I had finished speaking them. Harvey said, "When will you see her?"

"You're jumping to conclusions again."

"If I'm wrong, I'm sorry. If I'm right, give her a message for me. Tell her that Glen—I hate to have to say this, but he's in jeopardy. If she likes him well enough to—"

"Please, Rod." Rhea Harvey seemed genuinely offended. "There's no need to be coarse."

I said, "I'd like to talk to Cave before I do anything. I don't know that it's the same woman. Even if it is, he may have reasons of his own for keeping her under wraps."

"You can probably have a few minutes with him in the courtroom." He looked at his wristwatch and pushed his chair back violently. "We better get going. It's twenty to two now."

We went along the side of the pool, back toward the entrance. As we entered the vestibule, a woman was just coming in from the boulevard. She held the heavy plate-glass door for the little flaxen-haired girl who was trailing after her.

Then she glanced up and saw me. Her dark harlequin glasses flashed in the light reflected from the pool. Her face became disorganized behind the glasses. She turned on her heel and started out, but not before the child had smiled at me and said: "Hello. Are you coming for a ride?" Then she trotted out after her mother.

Harvey looked quizzically at his wife. "What's the matter with the Kilpatrick woman?"

"She must be drunk. She didn't even recognize us."

"You know her, Mrs. Harvey?"

"As well as I care to." Her eyes took on a set, glazed expression—the look of congealed virtue faced with its opposite. "I haven't seen Janet Kilpatrick for months. She hasn't been showing herself in public much since her divorce."

Harvey edged closer and gripped my arm. "Would Mrs. Kilpatrick be the woman we were talking about?"

"Hardly."

"They seemed to know you."

I improvised. "I met them on the Daylight one day last month, coming down from Frisco. She got plastered, and I guess she didn't want to recall the occasion."

That seemed to satisfy him. But when I excused myself, on the grounds that I thought I'd stay for a swim in the pool, his blue ironic glance informed me that he wasn't taken in.

106

The receptionist had inch-long scarlet fingernails and an air of contemptuous formality. Yes, Mrs. Kilpatrick was a member of the club. No, she wasn't allowed to give out members' addresses. She admitted grudgingly that there was a pay telephone in the bar.

The barroom was deserted except for the bartender, a slim white-coated man with emotional Mediterranean eyes. I found Mrs. Janet Kilpatrick in the telephone directory: her address was 1201 Coast Highway. I called a taxi, and ordered a beer from the bartender.

He was more communicative than the receptionist. Sure, he knew Glenway Cave. Every bartender in town knew Glenway Cave. The guy was sitting at this very bar the afternoon of the same day he murdered his wife.

"You think he murdered her?"

"Everybody else thinks so. They don't spend all that money on a trial unless they got the goods on them. Anyway, look at the motive he had."

"You mean the man she was running around with?"

"I mean two million bucks." He had a delayed reaction. "What man is that?"

"Cave said in court this morning that his wife was going to divorce him and marry somebody else."

"He did, eh? You a newspaperman by any chance?"

"A kind of one." I subscribed to several newspapers.

"Well, you can tell the world that that's a lot of baloney. I've seen quite a bit of Mrs. Cave around the club. She had her own little circle, see, and you can take it from me she never even looked at other guys. *He* was always the one with the roving eye. What can you expect, when a young fellow marries a lady that much older than him?" His faint accent lent flavor to the question. "The very day of the murder he was making a fast play for another dame, right here in front of me."

"Who was she?"

"I wouldn't want to name names. She was pretty far gone that afternoon, hardly knew what she was doing. And the poor lady's got enough trouble as it is. Take it from me."

I didn't press him. A minute later a horn tooted in the street.

A few miles south of the city limits a blacktop lane led down from the highway to Mrs. Kilpatrick's house. It was a big old-fashioned redwood cottage set among tress and flowers above a bone-white beach. The Cadillac was parked beside the vine-grown verandah, like something in a four-color advertisement. I asked my driver to wait, and knocked on the front door.

A small rectangular window was set into the door. It slid open, and a green eye gleamed like a flawed emerald through the aperture.

"You," she said in a low voice. "You shouldn't have come here."

"I have some questions for you, Mrs. Kilpatrick. And maybe a couple of answers. May I come in?"

She sighed audibly. "If you must." She unlocked the door and stood back to let me enter. "You will be quiet, won't you? I've just put Janie to bed for her afternoon nap."

There was a white silk scarf draped over her right hand, and under the silk a shape which contrasted oddly with her motherly concern—the shape of a small hand gun.

"You'd better put that thing away. You don't need it, do you?"

Her hand moved jerkily. The scarf fell from the gun and drifted to the floor. It was a small blue revolver. She looked at it as if it had somehow forced its way into her fist, and put it down on the telephone table.

"I'm sorry. I didn't know who was at the door. I've been so worried and frightened—"

"Who did you think it was?"

"Frank, perhaps, or one of his men. He's been trying to take Janie away from me. He claims I'm not a fit mother. And maybe I'm not," she added in the neutral tones of despair. "But Frank is worse."

"Frank is your husband?"

"My ex-husband. I got a divorce last year and the court gave me custody of Janie. Frank has been fighting the custody ever since. Janie's grandmother left her a trust fund, you see. That's all Frank cares about. But I'm her mother."

"I think I see what it's all about," I said. "Correct me if I'm wrong. Cave spent the night with you—the night he was supposed to have shot his wife. But you don't want to testify at his trial. It would give your ex-husband legal ammunition to use in the custody fight for Janie."

"You're not wrong." She lowered her eyes, not so much in shame as in submission to the facts. "We got talking in the bar at the club that afternoon. I hardly knew him, but I—well, I was attracted to him. He asked if he could come and see me that

108

night. I was feeling lonely, very low and lonely. I'd had a good deal to drink. I let him come."

"What time did he arrive?"

"Shortly after eight."

"And he stayed all night?"

"Yes. He couldn't have killed Ruth Cave. He was with me. You can understand why I've been quietly going crazy since they arrested him—sitting at home and biting on my nails and wondering what under heaven I should do." Her eyes came up like green searchlights under her fair brow. "What *shall* I do, Mr. Archer?"

"Sit tight for a while yet. The trial will last a few more days. And he may be acquitted."

"But you don't think he will be, do you?"

"It's hard to say. He didn't do too well on the stand this morning. On the other hand, the averages are with him, as he seems to realize. Very few innocent men are convicted of murder."

"He didn't mention me on the stand?"

"He said he was with a woman, no names mentioned. Are you two in love with each other, Mrs. Kilpatrick?"

"No, nothing like that. I was simply feeling sorry for myself that night. I needed some attention from a man. He was a piece of flotsam and I was a piece of jetsam and we were washed together in the dark. He did get rather—emotional at one point, and said that he would like to marry me. I reminded him that he had a wife."

"What did he say to that?"

"He said his wife wouldn't live forever. But I didn't take him seriously. I haven't seen him since that night. No, I'm not in love with him. If I let him die, though, for something I know he didn't do—I couldn't go on living myself." She added, with a bitter grimace, "It's hard enough as it is."

"But you do want to go on living."

"Not particularly. I have to because Janie needs me."

"Then stay at home and keep your doors locked. It wasn't smart to go to the club today."

"I know. I needed a drink badly. I'm out of liquor, and it was the nearest place. Then I saw you and I panicked."

"Stay panicked. Remember if Cave didn't commit that murder, somebody else did—and framed him for it. Somebody who is still at large. What do you drink, by the way?"

109

"Anything. Scotch, mostly."

"Can you hold out for a couple of hours?"

"If I have to." She smiled, and her smile was charming. "You're very thoughtful."

When I got back to the courtroom, the trial was temporarily stalled. The jury had been sent out, and Harvey and the D.A. were arguing in front of the judge's bench. Cave was sitting by himself at the far end of the long attorney's table. A sheriff's deputy with a gun on his thigh stood a few feet behind him, between the red-draped windows.

Assuming a self-important legal look, I marched through the swinging gate into the well of the courtroom and took the empty chair beside Cave. He looked up from the typed transcript he was reading. In spite of his prison pallor he was a good-looking man. He had a boyish look about him, and the kind of curly brown hair that women are supposed to love to run their fingers through. But his mouth was tight, his eyes dark and piercing.

Before I could introduce myself, he said, "You the detective Rod told me about?"

"Yes. Name is Archer."

"You're wasting your time, Mr. Archer, there's nothing you can do for me." his voice was a dull monotone, as if the cross-examination had rolled over his emotions and left them flat.

"It can't be that bad, Cave."

"I didn't say it was bad. I'm doing perfectly well, and I know what I'm doing."

I held my tongue. It wouldn't do to tell him that his own lawyer had lost confidence in his case. Harvey's voice rose sharp and strained above the courtroom mutter, maintaining that certain questions were irrelevant and immaterial.

Cave leaned towards me and his voice sank lower. "You've been in touch with her?"

"She brought me into the case."

"That was a rash thing for her to do, under the circumstances. Or don't you know the circumstances?"

"I understand that if she testifies she risks losing her child."

"Exactly. Why do you think I haven't had her called? Go back and tell her that I'm grateful for her concern but I don't need her help. They can't convict an innocent man. I didn't shoot my wife, and I don't need an alibi to prove it."

I looked at him, admiring his composure. The armpits of his

110

gabardine were dark with sweat. A fine tremor was running through him.

"Do you know who did shoot her, Cave?"

"I have an opinion. We won't go into it."

"Her new man?"

"We won't go into it," he repeated, and buried his aquiline nose in the transcript.

The judge ordered the bailiff to bring in the jury. Harvey sat down beside me, looking disgruntled, and Cave returned to the witness stand.

What followed was moral slaughter. The D.A. forced Cave to admit that he hadn't had gainful employment since his release from the army, that his sole occupations were amateur tennis and amateur acting, and that he had no means of his own. He had been completely dependent on his wife's money since their marriage in 1946, and had used some of it to take extended trips in the company of other women.

The prosecutor turned his back on Cave in histrionic disgust. "And you're the man who dares to impugn the morals of your dead wife, the woman who gave you everything."

Harvey objected. The judge instructed the D.A. to rephrase his "question."

The D.A. nodded, and turned on Cave. "Did you say this morning that there was another man in Mrs. Cave's life?"

"I said it. It was true."

"Do you have anything to confirm that story?"

"No."

"Who is this unknown vague figure of a man?"

"I don't know. All I know is what Ruth told me."

"She isn't here to deny it, is she? Tell us frankly now, Mr. Cave, didn't you invent this man? Didn't you make him up?"

Cave's forehead was shining with sweat. He took a handkerchief out of his breast pocket and wiped his forehead, then his mouth. Above the white fabric masking his lower face, he looked past the D.A. and across the well of the courtroom. There was silence for a long moment.

Then Cave said mildly, "No, I didn't invent him."

"Does this man exist outside your fertile brain?"

"He does."

"Where? In what guise? Who is he?"

"I don't know," Cave said on a rising note. "If you want to know, why don't you try and find him? You have plenty of detectives at your disposal. Let them do some work."

"Detectives can't find a man who doesn't exist. Or a woman either, Mr. Cave."

The D.A. caught the angry eye of the judge, who adjourned the trial until the following morning. I bought a fifth of Scotch at a downtown liquor store, caught a taxi at the railroad station, and rode south out of town to Mrs. Kilpatrick's beach house.

When I knocked at the door of the redwood cottage, someone fumbled the inside knob. I pushed the door open. The flaxen-haired child looked up at me, her face streaked with half-dried tears.

"Mummy won't wake up."

I saw the red smudge on her knee, and ran in past her. Janet Kilpatrick was prone on the floor of the hallway, her bright hair dragging in a pool of blood. I lifted her head and saw the hole in her temple. It had stopped bleeding.

Her little blue revolver lay on the floor near her lax hand. One shot had been fired from the cylinder.

The child touched my back. "Is Mummy sick?"

"Yes, Janie. She's sick."

"Get the doctor," she said with pathetic wisdom.

"Wasn't he here?"

"I don't know. I was taking my nap."

"Was anybody here, Janie?"

"Somebody was here. Mummy was talking to somebody. Then there was a big bang and I came downstairs and Mummy wouldn't wake up."

"Was it a man?"

She shook her head.

"A woman, Janie?"

The same mute shake of her head. I took her by the hand and led her outside to the cab. The dazzling postcard scene outside made death seem unreal. I asked the driver to tell the child a story, any story so long as it was cheerful. Then I went back into the grim hallway and used the telephone.

I called the sheriff's office first. My second call was to Frank Kilpatrick in Pasadena. A manservant summoned him to the telephone. I told him who I was and where I was and who was lying dead on the floor behind me.

"How dreadful!" He had an Ivy League accent, somewhat withered by the coastal sun. "Do you suppose that Janet took her own life? She's often threatened to."

112

"No," I said, "I don't suppose she took her own life. Your wife was murdered."

"What a tragic thing!"

"Why take it so hard, Kilpatrick? You've got the two things you wanted—your daughter, and you're rid of your wife."

It was a cruel thing to say, but I was feeling cruel. I made my third call in person, after the sheriff's men had finished with me.

The sun had fallen into the sea by then. The western side of the sky was scrawled with a childish fingerpainting of colored cirrus clouds. Twilight flowed like iron-stained water between the downtown buildings. There were lights on the second floor of the California-Spanish building where Harvey had his offices.

Harvey answered my knock. He was in shirtsleeves and his tie was awry. He had a sheaf of papers in his hand. His breath was sour in my nostrils.

"What is it, Archer?"

"You tell me, lover-boy."

"And what is that supposed to mean?"

"You were the one Ruth Cave wanted to marry. You were going to divorce your respective mates and build a new life together—with her money."

He stepped backward into the office, a big disordered man who looked queerly out of place among the white-leather and black-iron furniture, against the limed-oak paneling. I followed him in. An automatic door closer shushed behind me.

"What in hell is this? Ruth and I were good friends and I handled her business for her—that's all there was to it."

"Don't try to kid me, Harvey. I'm not your wife, and I'm not your judge . . . I went to see Janet Kilpatrick a couple of hours ago."

"Whatever she said, it's a lie."

"She didn't say a word, Harvey. I found her dead."

His eyes grew small and metallic, like nailheads in the putty of his face. "Dead? What happened to her?"

"She was shot with her own gun. By somebody she let into the house, somebody she wasn't afraid of."

"Why? It makes no sense."

"She was Cave's alibi, and she was on the verge of volunteering as a witness. You knew that, Harvey—you were the only one who did know, outside of Cave and me."

"I didn't shoot her. I had no reason to. Why would I want to see my client convicted?"

"No, you didn't shoot her. You were in court at the time she was shot—the world's best alibi."

"Then why are you harassing me?"

"I want the truth about you and Mrs. Cave."

Harvey looked down at the papers in his hand, as if they might suggest a line to take, an evasion, a way out. Suddenly his hands came together and crushed the papers into a misshapen ball.

"All right, I'll tell you. Ruth was in love with me. I was—fond of her. Neither of us was happily married. We were going to go away together and start over. After we got divorces, of course."

"Uh-huh. All very legal."

"You don't have to take that tone. A man has a right to his own life."

"Not when he's already committed his life."

"We won't discuss it. Haven't I suffered enough? How do you think I felt when Ruth was killed?"

"Pretty bad, I guess. There went two million dollars."

He looked at me between narrowed lids, in a fierce extremity of hatred. But all that came out of his mouth was a weak denial. "At any rate, you can see I didn't kill her. I didn't kill either of them."

"Who did?"

"I have no idea. If I did, I'd have had Glen out of jail long ago."

"Does Glen know?"

"Not to my knowledge."

"But he knew that you and his wife had plans?"

"I suppose he did—I've suspected it all along."

"Didn't it strike you as odd that he asked you to defend him, under the circumstances?"

"Odd, yes. It's been terrible for me, the most terrible ordeal."

Maybe that was Cave's intention, I thought, to punish Harvey for stealing his wife. I said, "Did anybody besides you know that Janet Kilpatrick was the woman? Did you discuss it with anybody?"

He looked at the thick pale carpeting between his feet. I could hear an electric clock somewhere in the silent offices, whirring like the thoughts in Harvey's head. Finally he said, "Of course not," in a voice that was like a crow cawing.

114

He walked with an old man's gait into his private office. I followed and saw him open a desk drawer. A heavy automatic appeared in his hand. But he didn't point it at me. He pushed it down inside the front of his trousers and put on his suit jacket.

"Give it to me, Harvey. Two dead women are enough."

"You know then?"

"You just told me. Give me that gun."

He gave it to me. His face was remarkably smooth and blank. He turned his face away from me and covered it with his hands. His entire body hiccuped with dry grief. He was like an overgrown child who had lived on fairy tales for a long time and now couldn't stomach reality.

The telephone on the desk chirred. Harvey pulled himself together and answered it.

"Sorry, I've been busy, preparing for re-direct. Yes, I'm finished now. Of course I'm all right. I'm coming home right away."

He hung up and said, "That was my wife."

She was waiting for him at the front door of his house. The posture of waiting became her narrow, sexless body, and I wondered how many years she had been waiting.

"You're so thoughtless, Rod," she chided him. "Why didn't you tell me you were bringing a guest for dinner?" She turned to me in awkward graciousness. "Not that you're not welcome, Mr. Archer."

Then our silence bore in on her. It pushed her back into the high white Colonial hallway. She took up another pose and lit a cigarette with a little golden lighter shaped like a lipstick. Her hands were steady, but I could see the sharp edges of fear behind the careful expression on her face.

"You both look so solemn. Is something wrong?"

"Everything is wrong, Rhea."

"Why, didn't the trial go well this afternoon?"

"The trial is going fine. Tomorrow I'm going to ask for a direct acquittal. What's more, I'm going to get it. I have new evidence."

"Isn't that grand?" she said in a bright interested tone. "Where on earth did you dig up the new evidence?"

"In my own backyard. All these months I've been so preoccupied trying to cover up my own sordid little secret that it never occurred to me that you might have secrets, too."

"What do you mean?"

115

"You weren't at the trial this afternoon. Where were you? What were you doing?"

"Errands—I had some errands. I'm sorry, I didn't realize you—wanted me to be there."

Harvey moved towards her, a threat of violence in the set of his shoulders. She backed against a closed white door. I stepped between them and said harshly, "We know exactly where you were, Mrs. Harvey. You went to see Janet Kilpatrick. You talked your way into her house, picked up a gun from the table in the hall, and shot her with it. Didn't you?"

The flesh of her face was no more than a stretched membrane.

"I swear, I had no intention—All I intended to do was talk to her. But when I saw that she realized, that she *knew*—"

"Knew what, Mrs. Harvey?"

"That I was the one who killed Ruth. I must have given myself away, by what I said to her. She looked at me, and I saw that she knew. I saw it in her eyes."

"So you shot her?"

"Yes. I'm sorry." She didn't seem to be fearful or ashamed. The face she turned on her husband looked starved, and her mouth moved over her words as if they were giving her bitter nourishment. "But I'm not sorry for the other one, for Ruth. You shouldn't have done it to me, Rod. I warned you, remember? I warned you when I caught you with Anne that if you ever did it to me again—I would kill the woman. You should have taken me seriously."

"Yes," he said drearily. "I guess I should have."

"I warned Ruth, too, when I learned about the two of you."

"How did you find out about it, Mrs. Harvey?"

"The usual way—an anonymous telephone call. Some friend of mine, I suppose."

"Or your worst enemy. Do you know who it was?"

"No, I didn't recognize the voice. I was still in bed, and the telephone call woke me up. He said—it was a man—he said that Rod was going to divorce me, and he told me why. I went to Ruth that very morning—Rod was out of town—and I asked her if it was true. She admitted it was. I told her flatly I'd kill her unless she gave you up, Rod. She laughed at me. She called me a crazy woman."

"She was right."

"Was she? If I'm insane, I know what's driven me to it. I

116

could bear the thought of the other ones. But not her! What made you take up with *her*, Rod—what made you want to marry that gray-haired old woman? She wasn't nearly as attractive as I am."

"She was well-heeled," I said.

Harvey said nothing.

Rhea Harvey dictated and signed a full confession that night. Her husband wasn't in court the following morning. The D.A. himself moved for a direct acquittal, and Cave was free by noon. He took a taxi directly from the courthouse to the home of his late wife. I followed him in a second taxi. I still wasn't satisfied.

The lawns around the big country house had grown knee-high and withered in the summer sun. The gardens were over-grown with rank flowers and ranker weeds. Cave stood in the drive for a while after he dismissed the taxi, looking around the estate he had inherited. Finally he mounted the front steps.

I called him from the gate. "Wait a minute, Cave."

He descended the steps reluctantly and waited for me, a black scowl twisting his eyebrows and disfiguring his mouth. But they were smooth and straight before I reached him.

"What do you want?"

"I was just wondering how it feels."

He smiled with boyish charm. "To be a free man? It feels wonderful. I guess I owe you my gratitude, at that. As a matter of fact, I was planning to send you a check."

"Save yourself the trouble. I'd send it back."

"Whatever you say, old man." He spread his hands disarmingly. "Is there something else I can do for you?"

"Yes. You can satisfy my curiosity. All I want from you is a yes or no." The words set up an echo in my head, an echo of Janet Kilpatrick's voice. "Two women have died and a third is on her way to prison or the state hospital. I want to hear you admit your responsibility."

"Responsibility? I don't understand."

"I'll spell it out for you. The quarrel you had with your wife didn't occur on the nineteenth, the night she was murdered. It came earlier, maybe the night before. And she told you who the man was."

"She didn't have to tell me. I've known Rod Harvey for years, and all about him."

117

"Then you must have known that Rhea Harvey was insanely jealous of her husband. You thought of a way to put her jealousy to work for you. It was you who telephoned her that morning. You disguised your voice, and told her what her husband and your wife were planning to do. She came to this house and threatened your wife. No doubt you overheard the conversation. Seeing that your plan was working, you left your loaded shotgun where Rhea Harvey could easily find it and went down to the beach club to establish an alibi. You had a long wait at the club, and later at Janet Kilpatrick's house, but you finally got what you were waiting for."

His smile widened.

"Does it seem so funny to you, Cave? You're guilty of conspiracy to commit murder."

"I'm not guilty of anything, old man. Even if I were, there's nothing you could possibly do about it. You heard the court acquit me this morning, and there's a little rule of law involving double jeopardy."

"You were taking quite a risk, weren't you?"

"Not so much of a risk. Rhea's a very unstable woman, and she had to break down eventually, one way or the other."

"Is that why you asked Harvey to defend you, to keep the pressure on Rhea?"

"That was part of it." A sudden fury of hatred went through him, transfiguring his face. "Mostly I wanted to see him suffer."

"What are you going to do now, Cave?"

"Nothing. I plan to take it easy. I've earned a rest. Why?"

"A pretty good woman was killed yesterday on account of you. For all I know you planned that killing the same way you planned the other. In any case, you could have prevented it."

He saw the mayhem in my eyes and backed away. "Take it easy, Archer. Janet was no great loss to the world, after all."

My fist smashed his nervous smile and drove the words down his throat. He crawled away from me, scrambled to his feet and ran, jumping over flowerbeds and disappearing around the corner of the house. I let him go.

A short time later I heard that Cave had been killed in a highway accident near Palm Springs. He was driving a new Ferrari at the time.

FILE #1: THE MAYFIELD CASE

BY JOE GORES

Born December 25, 1931, in Minnesota, Joseph Nicholas Gores received a bachelor's degree from the University of Notre Dame and a master's degree from Stanford. He worked for several years as an investigator in San Francisco, and has used this experience as the basis for his series of short stories about the Daniel Kearny Detective Agency. His first novel, *A Time of Predators,* and his short story, "Goodbye, Pops," both won Edgar awards in 1969. Gores's novels include *Dead Skip* (1972) and *Hammett* (1975). He lives in Mill Valley, California.

Tuesday, May 23rd: 8:15 A.M.

LARRY BALLARD WAS HALFWAY to the Daniel Kearny Associates office before he remembered to switch on his radio. After a whine and a blast of static, O'Bannon's voice came on loudly in mid-transmission.

". . . Bay Bridge yet, Oakland Three?"

"Coming up to the toll plaza now. The subject is three cars ahead of me. I'll need a front tail once he's off the bridge, over."

"Stand by, KDM Three-six-six Control calling any San Francisco unit."

Ballard unclipped his mike and pressed the red TRANSMIT button. "This is SF Six. My location is Oak and Buchanan, moving east, over."

"Oakland Three is tailing a red Comet convertible across Bay Bridge, license Charlie, X-Ray, Kenneth Eight-eight-one. The legal owner, California Citizens Bank on Polk Street, wants *car only*—contract outlawed."

Oakland Three cut in: "Wait by the Ninth and Bryant off-ramp, SF Six."

"Control standing by," said O'Bannon. "KDM Three-six-six clear."

O'Bannon set down the hand mike on Giselle Marc's desk, leaving it flipped to MONITOR. He was a wiry red-haired man about forty, with twinkling blue eyes, freckles, and a hard-bitten drinker's face.

"Who's SF Six? The new kid?"

"Right. Larry Ballard. With us a month yesterday." Giselle was a tall lean blonde who had started with DKA as a part-time file girl while in college; after graduation two years before, she had taken over the Cal-Cit Bank desk. "He's a green pea but he's eager and maybe—just maybe—he can think. Kathy's putting him on his own this week."

O'Bannon grunted. "The Great White Father around?"

"Down in his cubbyhole—in a vile mood."

O'Bannon grimaced and laid his expense-account itemization on her desk with great reverence. Giselle regarded it without enthusiasm.

120

"Why don't you ever do your own dirty work, O'B?" she demanded.

Same day: 10:00 A.M.

Ballard was lanky, well-knit, in his early twenties, with blue eyes already hardened by his month with DKA. He was stopped, by Dan Kearny himself, at the top of the narrow stairs leading to the second floor of the old Victorian building that housed the company offices.

"That Comet in the barn?"

"Yes, sir," said Ballard.

"Terrif. Any static?" Kearny was compact and powerful, with a square pugnacious face, massive jaw, and cold gray eyes which invariably regarded the world through a wisp of cigarette smoke.

"I front-tailed him from the freeway. When he parked on Howard Street, Oakland Three and I just wired up the Comet and drove it away."

Kearny clapped Ballard's shoulder and went on. Ballard entered the front office, which overlooked Golden Gate Avenue through unwashed bay windows. Three assignments were in his basket on the desk of Jane Goldson, the phone receptionist with the Liverpool accent: through her were channeled all assignments, memos, and field reports.

Carrying the case sheets, Ballard descended to the garage under the building. Along the right wall were banks of lockers for personal property; along the left, small partitioned offices used by the seven San Francisco field men. He paused to review his new cases before leaving.

The most puzzling one involved a new Continental, financed through Cal-Cit Bank, which had been purchased by a Jocelyn Mayfield, age twenty-three. She and her roommate, Victoria Goodrich, lived at 31 Edith Alley and were case workers for San Francisco Social Services. What startled Ballard was the size of the delinquent payments—$198.67 each—and the contract balance of over $7000. On a welfare worker's salary? Even though her parents lived in the exclusive St. Francis Woods area, they were not cosigners on the contract.

From his small soundproofed office at the rear of the garage Dan Kearny watched Ballard leave. Kearny had been in the game for over half of his forty-three years, and still hadn't

121

figured out the qualities which made a good investigator; only time would tell if Ballard had them. Kearny jabbed an intercom button with a blunt finger.

"Giselle? Send O'Bannon down here, will you?"

He lit a Lucky, leaned back to blow smoke at the ceiling. O'B had come with him six years before, when Kearny had resigned from Walter's Auto Detectives to start DKA with one car and this old Victorian building which had been a bawdy house in the '90s; and reviewing O'B's expense accounts still furnished Kearny with his chief catharsis.

He smeared out the cigarette; through the one-way glass he could see O'Bannon approaching the office, whistling, his hands in pockets, his blue eyes innocent of guile. When he came in, Kearny shook out a cigarette for himself and offered the pack. "How's Bella, O'B?"

"She asks when you're bringing the kids for *cioppino* again."

Kearny indicated the littered desk. "I'm two weeks behind in my billing. Oh . . . this *expense* account, O'B." Without warning his fist smashed down in sudden fury. *"Dammit, if you think . . ."*

O'Bannon remained strangely tranquil during the storm. When Kearny finally ran down, the red-headed man cleared his throat and spoke.

"Giants leading three-two at the bottom of the third. Marichal—"

"What do you mean?" Kearny looked stunned. "What the—"

O'Bannon fished a tiny transistor radio from his pocket, then apologetically removed miniature speakers from both his ears. Kearny gaped.

"You mean—while I—you were *listening to the ball game?*"

O'Bannon nodded dolorously. Speechless with rage, Kearny jerked out the expense-account checkbook; but then his shoulders began shaking with silent laughter.

Same day: 9:30 P.M.

Larry Ballard parked on upper Grant; above him, on Telegraph Hill, loomed the concrete cone of Coit Tower, like a giant artillery piece about to be fired. Edith Alley ran half a block downhill toward Stockton; Jocelyn Mayfield and her roommate, Victoria Goodrich, had the lower apartment in a two-story frame building.

The girl who answered the bell wore jeans and sweatshirt

over a chunky figure; her short hair was tinted almost white. Wide cheekbones gave her a Slavic look.

"Is Jocelyn here?" Ballard asked.

"Are you a friend of hers?" Her voice was harshly attractive.

Ballard took a flier. "I was in one of her Sociology classes."

"At Stanford?" She stepped back. "Sorry if I sounded anti-social. Sometimes male clients get ideas y'know?"

He followed her into the apartment. "You must be Vikki—Josie has mentioned you. You don't act like a social worker."

" 'Say something to me in psychology?' Actually I was a wait-ress down in North Beach before I stared with Social Services."

There were cheap shades at the windows of the rather barren living room, a grass mat on the floor, a wicker chair and a couch, and an ugly black coffee table. The walls were a depress-ing brown. It was not a room in keeping with monthly auto-mobile payments of $200.

"We're going to repaint eventually," Vikki said. "I guess."

Ballard nodded. "Has Josie mentioned selling the Continen-tal?"

"The Continental?" She frowned. "That belongs to Hank—*we* both use my Triumph. I don't think he wants to sell it; he just got it."

"Hank, huh? Say, what's his name and address? I can—"

Just then a key grated in the front door. Damn! Two minutes more would have done it. Now the subject was in the room, talking breathlessly. "Did Hank call? He wasn't at his apart-ment, and—"

"Here's an old friend of yours," Vikki cut in brightly.

Ballard was staring. Jocelyn Mayfield was the loveliest girl he had ever seen, her fawnlike beauty accented by shimmering jet hair. Her mouth was small but full-lipped, her brows slightly heavy for a girl, her brown liquid eyes full-lashed. She had one of those supple patrician figures maintained by tennis on chilly mornings.

"Old friend?" Her voice was low. "But I don't know him!"

That tore it. Ballard blurted, "I'm—uh—representing Cali-fornia Citizens Bank. We've been employed to investigate your six-hundred dollar delinquency on the 1967 Continental. We—"

"You dirty—" The rest of Vikki's remark was not that of a welfare worker. "I bet you practice lying to yourself in front of a mirror. I bet—"

123

"Vikki, hush." Jocelyn was blushing, deeply embarrassed. Vikki stopped and her eyes popped open wide.

"You mean you *did* make the down payment on that car? It's registered in *your* name? You fool! He couldn't make a monthly payment on a free lunch, and you—" She stopped, turned on Ballard. "Okay, buster. Out."

"Vikki, please." Then Jocelyn said to Ballard, "I thought—I had no idea the payments—By Friday I can have all the money."

"I said *out*, buster," Vikki snapped. "You heard her—you'll get your pound of flesh. And that's *all* you'll get—unless I tear Josie's dress and run out into that alley yelling rape."

Ballard retreated; he had no experience in handling a Vikki Goodrich. And there was something about Jocelyn Mayfield— private stock, O'Bannon would have called her. She'd been so obviously let down by this Hank character; and she *had* promised to pay by Friday.

Monday, May 29th: 3:30 P.M.

Jane Goldson winked and pointed toward the Office Manager's half-closed door. "She's in a proper pet, she is, Larry."

He went in. Kathy Onoda waved him to a chair without removing the phone from her ear. She was an angular girl in her late twenties, with classical Japanese features. Speaking into the phone her voice was hesitant, nearly unintelligible with sibilants.

"I jus' rittre Joponee girr in your country very rittre time." She winked at Ballard. "So sorry too, preese. I roose job I . . . ah . . . ah so. Sank you verry much. Buddha shower bressings on you."

She hung up and exclaimed jubilantly, "Why do those stupid s.o.b.'s always fall for that phony Buddha-head accent?" All trace of it had disappeared. "You, hotshot, you sleeping with this Mayfield chick? One report, dated last Tuesday, car in hands of a third party, three payments down—and you take a promise. Which isn't kept."

"Well, you see, Kathy, I thought—"

"You want me to come along and hold your hand?" Her black eyes glittered and her lips thinned with scorn. "Go to Welfare and hint that she's sleeping around; tell her mother that our investigation is going to hit the society pages; get a line on this

124

Hank no-goodnik." She jabbed a finger at him. "Go gettem bears!"

Ballard fled, slightly dazed, as always after a session with Kathy. Driving toward Twin Peaks, he wondered why Jocelyn had broken her promise. Just another deadbeat? He hated to believe that; apart from the Mayfield case he was doing a good job. He still carried a light case load, but he knew that eventually he would be responsible for as many as seventy-five files simultaneously, with reports due every three days on each of them except skips, holds, and contingents.

The Mayfield home was on Darien Way in St. Francis Woods; it was a huge pseudo-colonial with square columns and a closely trimmed lawn like a gigantic golf green. Inside the double garage was a new Mercedes. A maid with iron-gray hair took his card, returned with Jocelyn's mother—an erect pleasant-faced woman in her fifties.

"I'm afraid I'm not familiar with Daniel Kearny Associates."

"We represent California Citizens Bank," said Ballard. "We've been engaged to investigate certain aspects of your daughter's finances."

"Jocelyn's finances?" Her eyes were lighter than her daughter's with none of their melting quality. "Whatever for?"

"She's six hundred dollars delinquent on a 1967 Continental."

"Indeed?" Her voice was frigid. "Perhaps you had better come in."

The living room had a red brick fireplace and was made strangely tranquil by the measured ticking of an old-fashioned grandfather's clock. There was a grand piano and a magnificent Oriental rug.

"Now. Why would my daughter supposedly do such a thing?"

"She bought it for a"—his voice gave the word emphasis— "man."

She stiffened. "You cannot be intimating that my daughter's personal life is anything but exemplary! When Mr. Mayfield hears this—this infamous gossip, he—He is most important in local financial circles."

"So is California Citizens Bank."

"Oh!" She stood up abruptly. "I suggest you leave this house."

Driving back, Ballard knew he had made the right move to bring parental pressure on Jocelyn Mayfield, but the knowl-

125

edge gave him scant pleasure. There had been a framed picture of her on the piano; somehow his own thoughts, coupled with the picture, had made his memory of their brief meeting sharper, almost poignant.

Same day: 5:15 P.M.

Dan Kearny lit a Lucky. "I think you know why I had you come back in, Ballard. The Mayfield case. Are you *proud* of that file?"

"No, sir." He tried to meet Kearny's gaze. "But I think she broke her promise to pay because this deadbeat talked her into it."

"You took a *week* to find that out?" Kearny demanded. "Giselle found out that the subject walked off her job at Welfare last Friday night—took an indefinite leave without bothering to leave any forwarding address."

Kearny paused to form a smoke ring. He could blast this kid right out of the tank, but he didn't want to do that. "I started in this game in high school, Ballard, during the Depression. Night-hawking cars for Old Man Walters down in L.A. at five bucks per repo—cover your own expenses, investigate on your own time. Some of those Okies would have made you weep, but I couldn't *afford* to feel sorry for them. This Mayfield dame's in a mess. Is that *our* fault? Or the *bank's*?"

"No sir. But there are special circumstances—"

"Circumstances be *damned!* We're hired to investigate people who have defaulted, defrauded, or embezzled—money or goods—to find them if they've skipped out, and to return the property to the legal owner. Mayfield's contract is *three months* delinquent and *you* spin your wheels for a whole week. Right now the bank is looking at a seven-thousand dollar loss." He ground out his cigarette and stood up. "Let's take a ride."

Later, ringing the bell at 31 Edith Alley, Ballard warned, "This Victoria Goodrich is tough. I know she won't tell us anything."

Vikki opened the door and glared at him. *"You* again?"

Kearny moved past Ballard so smoothly that the girl had to step back to avoid being walked on, and they were inside. "My name is Turk," he said. "I'm with the legal department of the bank."

She had recovered. "You should be *ashamed,* hiring this

126

person to stir up trouble for Josie with her folks. Okay, so she's two lousy payments behind. I'll make one of them now, and next week she can—

"*Three* payments. And since the vehicle is in the hands of a third party, the contract is void." He shot a single encompassing look around the living room, then brought his cold gray eyes back to her face. "We know Miss Mayfield has moved out. Where is she living now?"

"I don't know." She met his gaze stubbornly.

Kearny nodded. "Fraudulent contract; flight to avoid prosecution. We'll get a grand-theft warrant for her seven-thousand dollar embezzle—"

"Good God!" Vikki's face crumpled with dismay. "Really, I don't know Hank's addr—I mean I don't know where she's gone. I—" Under his unwinking stare, tears suddenly came into her voice. "His wife's on welfare; he's no damn good. Once when he'd been drinking he—he put his hands on me. I guess she's with him, but I don't know where."

"Then what's Hank's last name?"

She sank down on the couch with her face in her hands and merely shook her head. Ignoring her, Kearny turned to Ballard. "Sweet kid, this Mayfield. She *steals* the woman's husband, then a car, then—"

"No!" Vikki was sobbing openly. "It isn't like that! They were separated—"

Kearny's voice lashed out. *"What's his last name?"*

"I won't—"

"Hank *what?*"

"You've no right to—"

"—to throw your trashy roommate in jail? We can and we *will.*"

She raised a tear-ravaged face. "If you find the car will Josie stay out of prison?"

"I can't make promises of immunity on behalf of the bank."

"His name is Stuber. Harold Stuber." She wailed suddenly to Ballard. "Make him stop! I've told everything I know—everything."

Kearny grunted. "You've been most helpful," he said, then strode out. Ballard took a hesitant step toward the hunched, sobbing girl, hesitated, and then ran after Kearny.

"Why did you do that to her?" he raged. "Now she's crying—"

"And we've got the information we came after," Kearny said.

"But you said to her—"

"But, *hell.*" He called Control on the radio. When Giselle answered—he said, "Mayfield unit reportedly in the hands of a Harold Stuber—S-t-u-b-e-r. Check him through the Polk Directory." He lit a cigarette and puffed placidly at it, the mike lying in his lap.

"The only listing under Harold Stuber shows a residence at 1597 Eighteenth Street; employment, bartender; wife, Edith."

"Thanks, Giselle. SF Six clear."

"KDM Three-six-six Control clear."

Driving out to Eighteenth Street, Ballard was glad it had been Vikki, not Jocelyn Mayfield, who had been put through the meat grinder. Vikki wasn't soft, yet Kearny had reduced her to tears in just a few vicious minutes.

The address on Eighteenth Street was a dirty, weathered stucco building above the heavy industrial area fringing Potrero Hill. It was a neighborhood losing its identity in its battle against the wrecker's ball. Inside the apartment house, the first-floor hall wore an ancient threadbare carpet with a design like spilled animal intestines.

"Some of this rubbed off on your true love," said Kearny.

Ballard gritted his teeth. Their knock was answered by a man two inches over six feet, wide as the doorway. His rolled-up sleeves showed hairy, muscle-knotted arms; his eyes were red-rimmed and he carried a glass of whiskey. He looked as predictable as a runaway truck.

Kearny was unimpressed. "Harold Stuber?"

"He don't live here no more." The door began to close.

"How about Edith Stuber?"

The hand on the door hesitated. "Who's askin'?"

"Welfare." When Kearny went forward the huge man wavered, lost his inner battle, and stepped back. The apartment smelled of chili and unwashed diapers; somewhere in one of the rooms a baby was screaming.

"Edie," yelled the big man, "coupla guys from Welfare."

She was a boldly handsome woman in her thirties, with dark hair and flashing black eyes. Under a black sweater and black slacks her body was full-breasted, wide-hipped, heavily sensual.

"Welfare?" Her voice became a whine. "D'ya have my check?"

"Your *check*?" Kearny's eyes flicked to the big man with simulated contempt. He whirled to Ballard. "Johnson, note that the recipient is living common-law with a Caucasian male, height six-two, weight two-twenty, estimated age thirty-nine. Recipient should—"

"Hey!" yelled the woman, turning furiously on the big man, "if I lose my welfare check—"

Kearny cut in brusquely, "We're only interested in your legal spouse, Mrs. Stuber."

Her yells stopped like a knife slash. "You come about Hank? He ain't lived here in five months. When he abandoned me an' the kid—"

"But the Bureau knows he gets in touch with you."

"You could call it that." She gave a coarse laugh. "Last Wednesday he come over in a big Continental, woke us—woke *me* up an' made a row 'bout Mr. Kleist here slee—bein' my acquaintance. Then the p'lice come an' Hank, he slugged one of 'em. So they took him off."

Kearny said sharply, "What about the Continental?"

"It set here to the weekend, then it was gone."

"What's your husband's current residence address?"

She waved a vague arm. "He never said." Her eyes widened. "He give me a phone number, but I never did call it; knew it wouldn't do no good." Behind her the baby began crying; the big man went away. Her eyes were round with the effort of remembering. "Yeah. 860-4645."

Back in the agency car, Kearny lit a cigarette. "If it's any consolation, there's the reason for her broken promise. He gets busted Wednesday night, gets word to Mayfield Thursday, on Friday she quits her job. Saturday she sees him at the county jail, finds out where he left the car, drops it into dead storage somewhere near his apartment, and holes up there to wait until he gets out. Find her, you find the car."

"Can't we trace the phone number this one gave us?"

Kearny gestured impatiently. "That'll just be some gin mill."

The next day the Mayfield folder went into the SKIP tub and a request went to the client for a copy of the subject's credit application. Skiptracing began on the case. The phone number proved to be that of a tough Valencia Street bar. DKA's Peninsula agent found that Stuber had drawn a thirty-to-ninety-day rap in the county jail, the heavy sentence resulting from a prior arrest on the same charge. Stuber said he still lived at Eighteenth Street and denied knowing the subject. A stakeout of the

129

jail's parking lot during visiting hours proved to be negative.

Police contacts reported that the Continental had not been impounded, nor was it picking up parking tags anywhere in San Francisco. Stuber had no current utilities service, no phone listing. The time involved in checking dead-storage garages would have been excessive. By phone Giselle covered Welfare, neighbors around the Edith Alley and Eighteenth Street addresses, the subject's former contacts at Stanford, Bartender's Local Number 41, all the references on the credit application. Ballard supplemented with field contact of postmen, gas station attendants, newsboys, and small store owners.

None of it did any good.

Thursday, June 9th: 7:15 P.M.

Ballard was typing reports at home when his phone rang. He had worked thirteen cases that day, including two skips besides Mayfield; it took him a few moments to realize that it was her voice.

"What have I done to make you hate me so?" she asked.

"I'm all for you personally, Josie, but I've got a job to do. Anyway, if I let up it just would mean that someone else would keep looking."

"I love him." She said it without emotion—a fact by which she lived. "I love him and he said he would leave me if I let them take his car while he's—away. I couldn't stand that. It's the first thing of beauty he's ever possessed, and he can't give it up."

Ballard was swept by a sudden wave of sympathy, almost of desire for her; he could picture her, wearing something soft, probably cashmere, her face serious, her mouth a pink bud. How could Stuber have such a woman bestowed on him, yet keep thinking of a damned automobile? How could he make Jocelyn see Stuber as he really was?

"Josie, the bank objects so strongly to Stuber that they've declared the contract void; as long as he had possession, they'd hold the account in jeopardy. Surrender it. Get him something you can afford."

"I couldn't do that," she said gravely, and hung up.

Ballard got a beer from the refrigerator and sat down at the kitchen table to drink it. After only one meeting and a single phone conversation, was he falling for Jocelyn Mayfield? He felt a deep physical attraction, sure; but it wasn't unsatisfied

130

desire which was oppressing him now. It was the knowledge that he was going to keep looking for the car, that there was no way to close the case without Jocelyn being badly hurt emotionally.

Friday, June 17: 10:15 A.M.

"If I see her mother once more, she'll call the cops," Ballard objected. "Stuber gets out June twenty-ninth. We could tail him—"

"The bank's deadline is next *Tuesday*—the twenty-first," said Kearny. "Then their dealer recourse expires and they have to *eat* their loss—whatever it is. Find the girl, Ballard, and get the car."

The intercom buzzed and Jane Goldson said, "Larry's got a funny sort of call on 1504, Mr. Kearney. She sounds drunk or something."

Kearny gestured and stayed on as Ballard picked up. The voice, which Ballard recognized as Jocelyn's, was overflowing with hysteria.

"I can't stand it any more and I want you to know you're to blame!" she cried. "My parents hate me—can't see Hank on weekends 'cause I know you'll be waiting, like vultures—sho—I did it." She gave a sleepy giggle. "I killed myself."

"You're a lively sounding corpse," said Kearny in a syrupy voice.

"I know who you are!" Surprisingly, she giggled again. "You made Vikki cry. Poor Vikki'll be all sad. I took all the pillsh."

Kearny, who appeared to have been doodling on a sheet of scratch paper, held up a crudely printed note: *Have Kathy trace call.* Ballard switched off, jabbed Kathy's intercom button. Please God, he thought, let her be all right. What had brought her to this extremity?

"I'll trace it," rapped Kathy. "Keep that connection open."

He punched back into 1504. "—Ballard's shoul when I die—lose car, lose Hank, sho—" Her singsong trailed off with a tired sigh; there was a sudden heavy jar. After a moment a light tapping began, as if the receiver were swinging at the end of the cord and striking a table leg. They stared at one another across the empty line.

The intercom buzzed, making Ballard jump. Kathy said, "469 Eddy Street, Apartment 206, listed under Harold Stein—

131

that'll be Stuber. The phone company'll get an ambulance and oxygen over there. Good hunting."

Ballard was already out of his chair. "It's a place on Eddy Street—we've got to get to her!"

As they rocketed up Franklin for the turn into Eddy Street, Ballard said, "We shouldn't have hounded her that way. Do you think she'll be all right?"

"Depends on how many of what she took. That address— between Jones and Leavenworth in the Tenderloin—crummy neighborhood. The nearest dead-storage garage is around the corner on Jones Street. We can—hey! What the hell are you doing?"

Ballard had slammed the car to a stop in front of a rundown apartment building. "I've got to get to her!" he cried. He was halfway out the car door when Kearny's thick fingers closed around Ballard's tie and yanked him bodily back inside.

"You're a repo man, Ballard," he growled. "That might not mean much to you but it does to me, a hell of a lot. *First* we get the car." Ballard, suddenly desperate, drew back a threatening fist. Kearny's slaty eyes didn't flicker; he said, "Don't let my gray hairs make a coward of you, sonny."

Ballard slumped back on the seat. He nodded. "Okay. Drive on, damn you."

As they turned into Jones Street, a boxy white Public Health ambulance wheeled into Eddy and smoked to a stop on the wrong side of the street. At the garage half a block down, Kearny went in while Ballard waited in the car. Why had he almost slugged Kearny? For that matter, why had he backed down?

Kearny stuck his head in the window. "It's easy when you know where to look." He laid a hand on Ballard's arm. "On your way up there call Giselle and have her send me a Hold Harmless letter."

Ballard circled the block and parked behind the ambulance. On the second floor he saw three tenants gaping by the open door of Apartment 206. A uniformed cop put a hand on Ballard's chest.

"I was on the phone with her when she—fainted."

"Okay. The sergeant'll wanna talk with you anyway."

She was on the floor by the phone stand, her head back and her mouth open. Her skin was very pale; the beautifully luminous eyes were shut. A tracheal tube was down her throat so

132

that she could breathe. The skirt had ridden high up one sprawled thigh, and Ballard pulled it down.

"Is she—will she—"

The intern was barely older than Ballard, but his hair already was thinning. "We'll give her oxygen in the ambulance." He opened his hand to display a bottle. "Unless she had something in here besides what's on the label, she should be okay."

Ballard glanced around the tiny two-roomer. There was a rumpled wall bed with a careless pile of paperbacks on the floor beside it; he could picture her cooped up there day after day, while her depression deepened. Above the flaked-silver radiator was a large brown water stain from the apartment upstairs; it was a room where dreams would die without a whimper.

Ballard backed off; instead of talking to the detective in charge he would call her folks so that their own doctor could be at the hospital to prevent it being listed as an attempted suicide.

That afternoon DKA closed the file on the Mayfield case. She was released from the hospital a few days later and returned to 31 Edith Alley. Without really knowing why, Ballard went over there one Tuesday evvening to see her; she refused to come out of the bedroom, and he ended up in the living room, drinking tea with Vikki Goodrich.

"She's grateful for what you did, Larry. But, as far as anything further—" She paused delicately. "Hank Stuber will be out tomorrow." She paused again, her face suddenly troubled. "She's going to surprise him and pick him up in my Triumph; he doesn't know about the Continental. After that I guess she'll be—well, sort of busy."

Leaving the apartment, Ballard told himself that ended it. Yet he sat behind the wheel of his car for a long time without turning the ignition key. Damn it, that *didn't* end it! Too much raw emotion had been bared. . . .

Thursday, June 30th: 8:15 A.M.

Each short journalistic phrase in the *Chronicle,* read over his forgotten restaurant eggs, deepened his sense of loss, his realization that something bright in his life had been permanently darkened.

Police officers, answering a call late last night to 31 Edith Alley, were greeted by Miss Victoria Goodrich, 24, a case worker with San Francisco Social Services. The hysterical Miss Goodrich said that her roommate, Jocelyn Mayfield, 23, and Harold P. Stuber, 38, had entered the apartment at eight P.M. Stuber had been drinking, she said; by ten P.M. he had become so abusive that he struck Miss Mayfield. According to Miss Goodrich he then departed, and Miss Mayfield locked herself in the bathroom.

At eleven P.M. Miss Goodrich called for police assistance. They broke down the locked door to find Miss Mayfield on the tile floor in a pool of blood. Both wrists had been slashed with a razor blade. The girl was D.O.A. at San Francisco General Hospital. Stuber, an unemployed bartender who was released only yesterday afternoon from the county jail, is being sought on an assault charge.

Ballard thought, I've never even seen the son-of-a—I could pass him on the street and not even know it. He felt a sudden revulsion, almost a nausea, at his own role in the destruction of Jocelyn Mayfield. Half an hour later he slammed the *Chronicle* down on Kearny's desk.

"Stuber said he'd leave her if we took the Continental while he was in jail. He left her, all right."

Kearny looked at him blandly. "I've already seen it."

"If we hadn't taken the car—"

"—she would have killed herself next month or next year over some other deadbeat. She was an emotional loser, Ballard, a picker of wrong men." He paused, then continued drily, "It's the end of the month, Ballard. I'd like to review your case file."

Ballard dropped his briefcase on the littered desk. "You know what you can do with your case file, Kearny? You can take it and—"

Kearny listened without heat, then reached for his cigarettes. He lit one and sneered, through the new smoke, "What will you do now, Ballard—go home and cry into your pillow? She's going to be dead for a long long time."

Ballard stared at him, speechless, as if at a new species of animal—the square pugnacious face, the hard eyes which had seen too much, the heavy cleft chin, the nose slightly askew from an old argument which had gone beyond words. A long slow shudder ran through the younger man's frame. Work—that was Kearny's answer to everything. Work, while Jocelyn Mayfield lay with a morgue tag on her toe. Work, while scar tissue began its slow accretion over the wound.

All right, then—work. Very slowly he drew his assignments from the briefcase. "Let's get at it then," he said in a choked voice.

Dan Kearny nodded to himself. A girl had died; a man had had his first bitter taste of reality. And in the process DKA bought themselves an investigator. Maybe, with a few more rough edges knocked off, a damned good investigator.

ABOUT THE PERFECT CRIME OF MR. DIGBERRY

BY ANTHONY ABBOT

Anthony Abbot was the pseudonym of Charles Fulton Oursler, born in 1893 in Baltimore, Maryland. He worked at various occupations, including law clerk and packer in a department store, and performed as a magician in clubs. He worked as a reporter for the *Baltimore American* and in 1918 became editor of *Music Trades* in New York City. His editorial career continued to rise and in 1944 he became senior editor of the *Reader's Digest*. Besides mystery novels written as Abbot, Oursler wrote popular religious works, the most famous being *The Greatest Story Ever Told* (1949). Oursler died in 1952 in New York City.

THE FACTS IN THE CASE of Mr. Digberry have not been disclosed by the New York Police Department. Absurd as the statement may sound, Mr. Thatcher Colt, then Police Commissioner, actually connived with the little man to conceal all evidence of his singular misdeeds. Mr. Digberry was guilty of one felony and deeply involved in a second crime of peculiar fiendishness and horror. Yet he was allowed to go free, with his pockets stuffed with money and his secret utterly safe.

Now, after three years, the Digberry bargain has come to an end. In revealing the circumstances, as I learned them while I was confidential secretary to the commissioner, I am able to give at last a complete account of the murder of one of the most beautiful women in New York.

I first saw Mr. Digberry in the line-up about nine-thirty one scorching August morning. More than a thousand detectives were crowded into the old gymnasium of the Headquarters Building at 240 Centre Street. Across the runway, that Monday morning, passed a defiant parade of lawbreakers. Auto thieves and dope peddlers, gunmen and blackmailers, they came forth, put on their hats and took them off again, stood fullface and profile, and were marched off in custody.

It was in such unholy company that Thatcher Colt and I encountered one of the truly unique conspirators of criminal history.

"Everett P. Digberry!"

Assistant Chief Inspector Flynn barked the name angrily, and a small, bald-headed man, with a fringe of gray hair around his temples and with large, blinking eyes, walked indignantly toward the center of the platform. His gray Palm Beach suit was wrinkled, and against his left side he pressed a stiff straw hat, banded with a gay ribbon of red and blue.

"You were found climbing over the back wall of St. Christopher's Cemetery, the Bronx, at two A.M. on Sunday, and you are charged with carrying a concealed weapon without a license. Are you guilty or not?"

"I would like to explain," began Mr. Digberry. "As a citizen, I demand—"

"Have you ever been arrested before?"

"Never. I can explain everything!"

"You'll have to!" was Flynn's grim assurance. "Where did you get this gun—a thirty-two caliber French Touron? Come on, now, speak up!"

"I haven't the remotest idea where I got it," rasped Mr. Digberry. "All this was due to a letter from the Driller. If you would only listen—"

By by then he was being yanked through the door, and the next suspect faced the lights.

"Tony," whispered Thatcher Colt to me, "get that fellow and bring him to my office. I want to talk to him!"

I glanced at Colt in surprise. But orders were orders, and at ten o'clock I led my man into the commissioner's private office.

"I've just read a report about you, Digberry," Colt stated accusingly. "You've been lying! What were you doing in that graveyard at two o'clock in the morning?"

Mr. Digberry gulped. "I've been trying to answer that all night long, and no one will listen to me! Won't you let me tell my story?"

"Do I understand that you have a letter signed by the Driller?"

"I have, chief!"

"Then go ahead and tell your story in your own way."

"Well you see, to begin with, I'm a wigmaker," explained Mr. Digberry. "I carry on a manufacturing business founded by my grandfather. I produce wigs of mohair, human hair, and of silk and wool, suitable for all characters and impersonations. Also, a complete line of wigs for dolls."

"What has that to do with your recent behavior? You'll have to come to the point!"

"I am now at the point," declared Mr. Digberry. "I am only a victim, chief. You see, I've been spending the summer alone at my home in New Rochelle. My family—I have a wife and six daughters—are at a bungalow in Maine. That's why I've had to face the whole thing alone. This letter—this ghastly letter from the Driller—came at a moment when I needed all my mental resources for my own business. I am about to launch a new idea in the wig field: a soft, flexible cap of silk gauze, with the hair sewn—"

"When did you get this letter?" interrupted Colt.

"One week ago."

"What did it say?"

"It told me I must pay the sum of one thousand dollars or be killed!"

"And how were you to pay this money?"

"I was to wait for directions."

"And you received them?"

"Yes, chief; that's why I was in the graveyard. Three days after the letter arrived, my telephone rang about six in the morning. A harsh voice told me to get the thousand dollars, and on Saturday—really, two o'clock Sunday morning—carry it in a bundle to Waverly Avenue and Gorsuch Street, in the Bronx; to climb over the wall of St. Christopher's Cemetery and go at once to my own family plot. I have three aunts buried in that plot. I was told to lay the money on the middle grave—Aunt Kate's."

"And you did that—without consulting the police?"

"Yes, I did, chief. After all, I have my wife and six daughters to think of. I drew the money out of our savings, laid it on Aunt Kate's grave and ran. But as I ran, I looked back and I saw a tall man pick up the money and disappear among the trees. Then I climbed over the wall and practically dropped into the arms of one of your policemen!"

"But you carried a revolver. Where did that come from?"

"As heaven is my witness, I don't know! I found it in my room about half past ten last Saturday night. I had gone out for a few minutes, and when I returned, I found the gun on the bed. A burglar has been in our apartment house three times recently. Perhaps he left it there. I don't know. But I took it along when I started for the cemetery. I meant to give it to an officer and explain—"

Colt looked incredulous and changed the subject. "From what bank did you get the money?"

"The Drovers and Mechanics in New Rochelle."

Colt glanced at me; a flash of his eyes that was an instruction. Going to another room, I called the manager of the Drovers and Mechanics Bank. Back in Colt's office, I nodded quickly—Colt knew I had confirmed the fact that Mr. Digberry had withdrawn one thousand dollars.

"I'm going to be reasonable with you," Colt told the nervous little man. "Frankly, I don't believe your story about the revolver. I'll give you the benefit of the doubt, but only if you're on the level and help the police."

"I'll do anything—anything."

"Where is your letter from the Driller?" Colt demanded, as he pressed a buzzer.

"In the top left-hand drawer of my wife's bureau at home."

The door opened to admit Captain Israel Henry, the official guardian of Colt's office.

"Send a detective with Mr. Digberry to his home for a letter," ordered Colt. "Bring down all his personal papers—bankbooks, insurance policies. Arrange with the district attorney to delay his appearance before the magistrate. And come back here with the letter."

At the door the captive turned. "Chief, my wife and daughters are coming home tomorrow afternoon. Can't I be released in time to meet them? And can't I get out of this without anybody being the wiser?"

Captain Henry practically tossed him through the door. Meanwhile, Colt had opened a drawer of his desk, lifted out a sheaf of papers and cast them on the blotter.

"The Driller's been causing some excitement, Tony."

"Don't believe I ever heard of him."

"Probably some harmless nitwit, but because of the people involved, I have to take it seriously. Ten of Manhattan's foremost citizens have received letters like the one that fellow just described. The chairman of the Opera Society got the first one. That was two weeks ago. Since then, several friends of mine have received similar threats. Each letter was typewritten and demanded payment of money with death as the penalty for disobedience. Each promised further instructions as to how payment was to be made, and each was signed 'The Driller.' "

"Of course it's a crank!"

"The fantastic entrance of Mr. Digberry into the affair makes me wonder. Remember that all the other letters went to eminent citizens, ranging from John Otts, the bank president, to Margaret Coleman, the coloratura soprano. All persons of position and wealth—except Digberry. And Digberry is a wig-maker!"

Two minutes later, at Colt's summons, Inspector Flynn stalked into the office and Colt explained the situation.

"Get in touch with all these people who received Driller letters, Flynn! Find out if any of them know Digberry or have had any dealings with him."

Within half an hour Flynn phoned me. "Tell the chief I've got a man in my office who knows all about Digberry."

140

"Send him right up!" was Colt's instruction.

The stranger who entered the commissioner's office a minute or two later was young and slender and blond, with keen blue eyes and the grace that expresses athletic strength. He was Captain Edgar Walters, a correspondent for foreign journals, who lived in an East Side riverview apartment.

"I am a friend of Margaret Coleman," the visitor explained. "I was told you wished to question me."

"You know Digberry?"

"Madame Coleman does. I've met him once or twice. Eggy runt, you know—harmless but full of eloquence."

"How does Madame Coleman know Digberry?"

Captain Walters grinned. "Through his art as a wigmaker. He's an enthusiast about his work—a left-handed chap who can draw curious designs. He made Madame Coleman a remarkable wig for her role as Gilda in 'Rigoletto,' and has since made her other wigs. Mr. Digberry has a passion for exactitude. His wigs are most realistic."

Colt nodded thoughtfully and asked, "Where is Madame Coleman now?"

"In Norway."

"But she received one of these letters?"

"It was turned over to me."

"And what is your relation to Madame?"

Captain Walters made an expressive gesture with his hands. "I am what is called a 'ghost.' Madame Coleman's book of memoirs is soon to be published. I'm writing them for her— under her name, of course. We came to know each other when I was publishing a Riviera society and fashion magazine at Menton, and interviewed her there. That was before her divorce—you recall she was married to Lucius Polk Coleman, that jealous old poof-poof? A millionaire, but a hopeless muffle-head. I told her she was a fool to stick to him, and when that blew up—"

"Is the wigmaker trustworthy?"

Captain Walters chuckled. "Honest, yes; harmless, too, but the most garrulous creature alive. I don't know him well, but Madame Coleman finds him stimulating."

When Captain Walters had departed, after seeing the other Driller letters, Colt once more signaled for Flynn.

"I want to keep busy on this case," he told the inspector. "Trace that Digberry revolver. And let's go further with that

141

paper, too—all those Driller notes were on identical sheets. . . . Now, Tony, let's get at this budget report."

But the budget was doomed to be neglected. Just before noon, Colt's phone rang sharply. The commissioner listened a minute, then swore devoutly. He hung up the receiver and reached for his hat. "Woman murdered on Sixty-Fourth Street. One of our men who was at the line-up this morning is on the scene. And what did he find on the mantelpiece but a photograph of our Mr. Digberry!"

I reached for my hat as Colt braced Captain Henry.

"When Digberry is brought back here, hold him incommunicado. See particularly that he learns nothing about this Sixty-Fourth Street murder!"

Drawn up under the porte-cochère on the Broome Street side of Headquarters was the commissioner's car. At the wheel sat the moonfaced Neil McMahon, Colt's chauffeur. With the siren blowing defiance of all the red lights, we raced uptown to the Wedgeworth Arms on Sixty-Fourth Street, a few doors from Central Park.

The crime had been committed in a fourth-floor rear apartment, furnished—two rooms, kitchenette and bath. Here we found a full detail from the Homicide Squad and Doctor J.L. Multooler, an assistant medical examiner.

"We didn't want to move the body until you came, Commissioner," the doctor explained. "You'll find it a peach of a case!"

"What's the woman's name?"

"She was known here as Mrs. Samuel Smith. Probably a fake!"

I am not easily shaken by woeful sights, but the scene that awaited us in that inner room was unnerving.

It was like a living room, but with a bed that collapsed into a wall closet. The door to that closet was now open wide, and the body of the victim was standing bolt upright, facing us—a beautiful blond woman, her face rouged and powdered.

She had been shot through the left temple, and the powder burns showed that the weapon had been held close to her head. It must have been the killer who placed her in this extraordinary position. Her shoeless feet were on the floor; a scarf was tied around her throat and drawn through the bedsprings. Her arms were lifted so that the ripped sleeves of her costly dress were attached to hooks in opposite sides of the closet.

142

Doctor Multooler's voice broke the silence. "I wonder who she really is!"

Colt turned to the surgeon with an amazed expression. "You don't recognize her?" he exclaimed. "This is the body of Margaret Coleman, the coloratura soprano. She was believed to be in Norway."

The commissioner's piercing glances searched the room, rested finally upon an overstuffed armchair drawn up to a window, overlooking a courtyard. The chair faced the singer's body.

Colt studied this chair with patient care.

"Blood on the upholstery," he announced. "She must have been sitting in this chair. The murderer entered the room unheard. He crept up behind her and shot through her left temple."

"But only a left-handed person would do that!" I exclaimed.

To this deduction of mine (of which I felt rather proud), Colt made no answer. Instead, he approached the body once more and lifted its left wrist.

"Bracelet watch with crystal broken," he announced. "That slight bruise over the right eye probably means the body toppled forward, striking the watch on the floor. The hands of the watch stopped at ten minutes past twelve."

"So the time of the murder is fixed," said Doctor Multooler.

Again Colt refrained from comment. Instead, he turned to Captain Allerton of the Homicide Squad.

"Observe that she had recently powdered and rouged her face. Get the trademark name of the powder, rouge and lipstick," directed the commissioner. "There must be samples in this apartment."

As Allerton moved along, Colt turned to a detective from the D.A.'s office.

"Where's that picture of Digberry?"

The detective pointed to the mantel behind us. There, indeed, stood a likeness of the wigmaker of New Rochelle. The picture had been torn across as if by angry hands. The top of it was missing. Colt picked it up with a low whistle of amazement.

Just then Captain Allerton brought in the manager of the Wedgeworth Arms, Percy J. Cooper. Colt questioned him in the outer room.

"When did anyone in this apartment house last see this woman alive?"

"Saturday night, about seven-thirty, when she had a meal served in her room."

"Did she have any visitors that night?"

"Yes, sir. That man there!" The manager pointed to Digberry's photograph.

"Do you know him?"

"I disrecollect his name, but we noticed him around here all the time."

"At what hour was he here on Saturday night?"

"The elevator boy says he got here late. He don't remember just when."

Mr. Cooper had not known his tenant was a famous singer; Margaret Coleman had not been recognized by the employees or tenants. She had come to the Wedgeworth Arms early in June—three days after her reported sailing, as it later developed—and engaged the apartment, paying two months' rent in advance.

"Did Madame have many visitors?"

"A few. One I distinctly remember—a gray-haired man about sixty. They had a terrific row about money. The neighbors heard Madame Coleman crying that she had been robbed and made penniless. I had to object to the noise."

"When was that?"

"About a month ago. I think the gray-haired man—he was short and dapper, I remember, and he carried a stick—came two or three times before, but never after that scene. She stopped at the desk the next morning and apologized. She said the man was her husband and asked me never to let him up in the elevator again."

"And Mr. Digberry—did he come often?" asked Colt, placing the torn photograph in his pocket.

"Nearly every night."

"Who discovered the body?"

"The floor maid. She couldn't get in yesterday, so she decided the tenant did not wish to be disturbed. But this morning, when no one answered her knocking, she went in. Seeing nobody around, she went ahead and cleaned up—until she opened that door!"

Colt dismissed the manager and we returned to the inner room. Inspector Flynn, who had arrived shortly after we did, came forward with something that gleamed dully in his hand. "The bullet that did it," he announced. "It flattened against the wall beside that armchair. My guess would be a thirty-two."

"Send it to the ballistics department," Colt ordered. "Tell them to compare it with the bullets from Digberry's gun."

Hedge, one of the assistant D.A.'s, was conferring with Captain Allerton.

"Our men have searched everywhere," Allerton reported, seeing Colt. "But all Madame Coleman's personal papers are missing. Whoever did it was thorough. No fingerprints, except the lady's."

Colt nodded abstractedly, his eyes once more searching the room for some significant detail. But there seemed to be no visible clues.

"Our men questioned twenty people in flats near this one; nobody heard the shot," continued Allerton. "But on Saturday night there were radios going in a lot of rooms in the house."

Colt's stalking around the room had brought him back to the open closet. The expanse of coiled bedspring filled his gaze. Beginning at the upper left-hand corner, he studied it by inches. Presently he lifted an almost invisible object that had been caught in the bedspring.

It was a gray hair!

On the sleeve of his left arm, Colt placed that threadlike clue. Against the blue serge, he could study it clearly; it was, indeed, a human hair, and yet there was a tiny fragment at one end that was certainly not human; it seemed more like a knotted sliver of white gauze.

I produced a department envelope from my pocket. In this, the hair was sealed and marked for identification.

Meanwhile, Colt was giving Flynn instructions. "Get Madame Coleman's husband. I want to question him downtown. And get the writer—Captain Walters. There are a few things he'll have to clear up. I'd like pictures of both of them. And come down to my office as soon as you can, inspector. I want you there when I talk to Digberry."

But our leaving was still delayed. Captain Allerton had obtained samples of Madame's facial preparations and Colt sat down to study them.

As I waited for him near the door, I felt a clammy hand touch mine. I turned around hastily to find myself staring into the pale eyes of Cooper.

"Take this," he whispered.

He placed in my hands a legal-sized envelope with bulky

contents. A rubber band was around it; the flap was sealed.

"A thousand dollars reward for anyone who finds the guilty man—it might help the hotel's reputation," Cooper gurgled, and darted away.

As soon as we were in the car, I told the commissioner about the money. He merely nodded and shoved the envelope into his pocket. He remained silent until we reached Headquarters at two-thirty.

Digberry was waiting for us. "Where's the letter?" was Colt's first question.

Detective Mulvaney, who stood beside the prisoner, handed over a much-fingered envelope, from which Colt drew out a single sheet of note paper. It was a duplicate of the ten others reposing in the drawer at his right hand.

"This calls for one thousand dollars or death," he commented. "Where is your bank passbook?"

Mulvaney promptly offered a gray-backed booklet, on the front of which appeared the names of Everett P. and Hattie Elizabeth Digberry, and a statement that the account was payable to either, or both, and to the survivor.

Colt flipped the pages; then glanced at the prisoner. "This is a new book. It has just been issued!"

"I lost the old one about three weeks ago. The bank advertised the loss, and then issued this new one."

Colt's eyes were solemn and accusing. "We'll come back to the bankbook matter later. In the meantime, what were your relations with Margaret Coleman?"

Mr. Digberry's cheeks blanched. "She was one of my customers," he replied.

"Wasn't she an intimate friend?"

"Miss Coleman reposed a great deal of confidence in me as an artist in my own line," the wigmaker admitted.

"Is that why she put your picture on her mantel? And is that why you visited her almost every night, when she was supposed to be in Europe?" pursued Colt relentlessly.

The prisoner thrust out his chin. His silence was plainly meant for defiance.

"Are you refusing to answer?"

"I am!" declared Mr. Digberry. "I really am! There's such a thing as professional confidence. Any questions about Madame Coleman she can answer for herself."

"You know better than that, Digberry. You know as well as I

do that Margaret Coleman cannot answer any questions."

"How should I know that? Why can't she?"

"Because she's dead!"

"Dead! Margaret—dead?"

"Murdered!" Colt added. "With a bullet through her head. And you didn't know anything about that, did you?"

"Nothing!" groaned Digberry. "As God is my witness, I knew nothing about it."

"Didn't you visit Margaret Coleman Saturday night?" Colt demanded.

"No! Indeed, no!"

"Where were you?"

"I was in the cemetery."

"Where were you at midnight?"

"I was waiting outside the cemetery until the time to leave the money."

"Anybody see you from eleven-thirty until you were arrested at two?"

"Not a soul."

"And you call that an alibi?"

"I call it hell!" declared Mr. Digberry.

"I'm waiting to know what your relations were with Margaret Coleman."

"She liked me," replied Digberry. "There was nothing immoral in our friendship. She was lonely. So was I. She was tired of her smart friends. She always said she could talk to me. And she admired my work. You know she was divorced?"

"Well?"

"Her husband was Lucius Polk Coleman—a very rich man. When they parted he made a settlement. But even though they were divorced, he still wanted to tell her what to do with her money. Soon the money was all gone. She said she had been cheated out of it. She blamed a man—she would not name him, but I never had any doubt. Literally, Mr. Colt, that poor lady, that truly great musical artist, was broke. Think of that humiliation. Yet she had to keep up appearances. So she pretended to go abroad. Her idea was to save every cent to prepare for next season. But her stocks went down to nothing—literally nothing. And all the time she was working with a man at the bank to punish the man who had robbed her."

"What bank?" interposed Colt.

"The Harrison National."

147

Colt reached for the telephone. In five minutes one of our Wall Street Squad was on his way to the Harrison National Bank. While Colt was talking, Inspector Flynn came in. He saluted and sat down.

"Go on!" prompted Colt, when he had finished phoning.

"I was telling you," resumed Digberry, "how Madame pretended—"

"Never mind. Take a look at this, see if you know what it is."

On his desk Colt laid the envelope containing the gray hair. He extracted the strand with a small pair of pincers.

"I recognize that," Digberry said spitefully. "It's evidently from a very poor wig made by a faker named Wilkins."

"How can you make a positive statement like that?" asked Colt.

"I know by the way that knot is tied. One wigmaker knows another's work."

Colt put away the hair. "Whom did Madame Coleman fear most?"

"Her husband. She was getting evidence to bring action against him."

Flynn chuckled grimly. "Surely you can tell us more than that. For instance, what time did you leave the Wedgeworth Arms on Saturday night?"

"I just told the chief I wasn't there on Saturday night," reiterated Mr. Digberry.

"But the manager saw you!"

"Not me. On Saturday night I had my own worries; I had to put a thousand dollars on Aunt Kate's grave."

"Is that the best you can do?" Colt cried. "All right, Flynn. Take him downstairs and let the boys talk to him!"

"The third degree!" groaned Digberry.

Flynn sent him off, shut the door and walked over to Colt's desk. "Here are the two pictures you wanted. I talked with Walters. He's out of it. At the time this woman was killed, Walters and a friend who spent the night with him were talking with our sergeant on that beat. That's an alibi nobody can smash."

"But what about her husband?"

Flynn sighed. "He sailed at one A.M. Saturday on a liner due in Cherbourg five days from now."

The door closed on Inspector Flynn.

"Get me the address of Wilkins," Colt called to me.

As I hurried to the outer office, I left him, telephone in hand, asking to be connected with the chief of the Paris police. I found the address of Elmer Wilkins, wigmaker, and Colt decided to call upon him.

Mr. Wilkins, a man with ears too big, a nose too long and a mouth too wide, received us with a Chinaman's smile. Before we had spoken, he assured us that his firm was the oldest and most reliable in the United States.

Colt silenced him by stating, "I don't wish to buy any artificial hair today. I'm the police commissioner, and I want information." He drew forth the gray hair. "Now, what can you tell me about that?"

Mr. Wilkins produced a magnifying glass. "Perhaps it's from a wig that was made here," he conceded.

"How long since you made a gray wig?"

"I'll show you my records."

For ten minutes Colt and Wilkins pored over the books. Then I saw Colt produce three photographs from his pocket.

"Recognize any one of these men?"

"Why—why, yes I do. This one—it's the man himself."

"You have a quick eye, Mr. Wilkins. That's all I want to know."

With Wilkins' promise to remain within call, we hurried off. It was now six-thirty P.M.

"Amusing thing!" Colt said. "Just before we left, I had a telephone call from our Wall Street man. He discovered what Coleman was up to in her investigation, and it certainly ties up with that wig."

For the rest of that night and down to the Tuesday-morning breakfast hour Colt labored constantly on the Coleman murder case. Three times that night he talked on the transatlantic telephone with the Paris police. He also held a ten-minute conversation by radiophone with the captain of the liner on which Lucius Coleman had sailed. But not until an hour before midnight did we get a break in the case.

That came with the report of Doctor Multooler. At eleven he called Colt. "The autopsy fixes the time of death within ten minutes of ten o'clock," he announced.

"But Madame's watch stopped shortly after midnight!" gasped Colt.

"Nevertheless, my evidence is positive. I'll send you a full report in writing."

149

Multooler's discovery upset Colt's previous calculations. "I think we'll go up to the abode of Digberry," he announced.

The wigmaker's home was in St. Nicholas Place, not far from the railroad station in New Rochelle. During our swift drive to the suburb, Colt remarked. "That watch must have been stopped by opening the back and depressing the spring. Not a new alibi—but I didn't suspect it."

No more was said until we reached our destination, an old-fashioned, five-story apartment building known as the Gloria Arms. Mr. Digberry leased Suite G, on the second floor, and the janitor willingly let us in. For ten minutes we traversed our prisoner's deserted rooms, but Colt admitted that his search was almost barren.

On our way out, he paused to question the girl in charge of the outmoded lobby switchboard. Yes, she had worked last Saturday night. Yes, she remembered a call for Mr. Digberry around ten-thirty. She finally admitted she had listened in.

"I heard a man say he had a message from Madame Coleman and would like to see Mr. Digberry at once, down at the railroad station. Right after that Mr. Digberry went out. But he came right back. After a little while I saw him go out again, and he didn't come back for quite a while. Even then, he went out later."

As Colt lighted his pipe in the car, his face was grave. "I won't know how to put this thing together," he confessed, "if all Digberry's extraordinary story is proved true. But this much is obvious. If our little bald friend is innocent, then the murderer played him a villainous trick.

"I believe I see through this crime now, Tony—but I don't know yet how to pin it on the murderer. There's one long shot," he added. "Do you remember that Walters had a visitor who spent the night with him? Well, Tony, there's our long shot; if it hits, we might get a perfect case."

When we returned to Headquarters, I sat down at my typewriter. I had three books full of stenographic pothooks on the case, and soon I was absorbed in their transcription. It must have been an hour later when I was disturbed by voices in the commissioner's office. I entered to find Colt seated at his desk. Spread before him were a gray Palm Beach suit and a straw hat with a band of red and blue. Colt was issuing orders to a detective.

"Use the vacuum cleaner on these clothes," directed the

commissioner, "and turn the results over to our laboratory. The chemists know what to look for."

The detective saluted, gathered up the costume and departed.

"I've taken a chance on our long shot, Tony," declared Colt wearily.

It was Tuesday noon—twenty-four hours after the discovery of Margaret Coleman's body. Gathered in Colt's office were Inspector Flynn and Digberry, the commissioner and myself.

Flynn had failed to break down Digberry; nevertheless the inspector was satisfied of the little man's guilt.

"Mr. Digberry, where did you go when you left your house at ten-thirty Saturday night?" Colt demanded.

"I went to the station to see a man who didn't show up."

Flynn snorted. "I think we've stalled long enough with this fellow. I want to charge him with murder!"

"You have no case against me at all!" Digberry cried. "I demand to be represented by a lawyer!"

"You'll need a doctor if you take that tone," Flynn came back. "You wrote those Driller letters. We've traced the paper from the manufacturer to the dealer and found a supply of it in that hair works you run in New Rochelle. And the experts swear all the letters were written on a typewriter in your joint. And the one you wrote to yourself was only to cover up."

"Why should I do such a thing?" shouted Digberry.

Flynn gave a harsh chuckle. "You're asking me? You sent them as a blind, so the police would think the Driller killed Margaret Coleman. And he did. For you're the Driller, Digberry."

"I did *not* kill her!" Digberry screamed. "Why should I kill her?"

"Because you had a love affair with her. You've lied about everything. Here's the report from the bank. It's true that you drew out a thousand dollars. But not as ransom money, in one lump sum, as you said. You've been drawing that cash out in dribs and drabs all summer. While your wife was away, you were spending money on an opera singer. It was high life for you, Digberry, my boy. But now the end of the summer is near. You thought there was only one way to get rid of that woman. So the whole hocus-pocus was just a scheme of yours to kill Margaret Coleman and put the blame on some made-up villain!"

151

"Try to prove that I killed her!" Digberry taunted. "Just try!"

"I can do that, too," Flynn grated. "You had a gun on you, didn't you? Well, the shot that killed Margaret Coleman was fired from that gun."

Digberry whirled to Colt. "Mr. Commissioner, I'm not guilty of these things! How am I to face my wife—"

An attendant was ushering Captain Walters into the office.

"Hello!" he cried. "What's the row?"

"Just a few questions, Captain," began Colt. "I believe you told me yesterday you met Madame Coleman at Menton?"

"Quite!"

Colt stood up and pointed at Captain Walters with the bowl of his pipe. "It's a curious fact," he said, "that the revolver which Mr. Digberry says was left in his apartment by a burglar is one of French manufacture, purchased from a dealer in Menton, and containing a mark recognizable to the police!"

Walters began, "Do you infer—?"

"Tony, open that door!"

I opened a door just behind Colt's desk. Wilkins was standing there.

"Mr. Wilkins," called Colt, "do you recognize in this room any of your recent customers?"

Wilkins nodded. "The little blond fellow over there," he rumbled, pointing to Captain Walters. "He's the man I made the bald wig for the other day."

"See any head in this room that your wig resembled?"

The eyes of the two wigmakers met, and Wilkins roared, "Of course! Why didn't I think of it before? That wig was the dead image of old Digberry's head."

"That will do!" said Colt, and I closed the door after Wilkins, as an attendant led him away. Colt again faced Walters.

"I have your complete history," he announced. "This morning you kindly left your fingerprints on sensitized paper that I gave you when I showed you the Driller letters. Your prints were telephotoed to the police in Europe. You served time in France and Holland for blackmail."

Captain Walters laughed convincingly. "My dear Mr. Colt, you can't connect me with this murder. My alibi is complete. I had no motive and no opportunity."

Colt smiled. "You stole Madame Coleman's money, Walters," he said. "A banking friend of hers helped her to investigate you. The Parisian police co-operated and they told me all about that.

152

Somehow you learned that the singer was in a fair way to send you to Devil's Island. So you decided to kill her!"

"That is preposterous! I refuse—"

"And you decided to make it a perfect crime. A perfect crime demands that the police have a victim. You decided on Digberry after calling on Margaret Coleman. She refused to forgive you. That was when you tore Digberry's picture. You wanted only the upper part of his head—the lower part might have been recognized by Wilkins, a fellow craftsman. For you meant to kill a woman and have it appear that Digberry was her murderer. That was why you had a wig designed to make you resemble Digberry. That was why you bought a duplicate of his Palm Beach suit and his straw hat. We've traced the shops where you made those purchases. Too bad you didn't destroy the suit and hat and wig, but before you got around to it, they were in our hands.

"You dressed up like Digberry and went to the Wedgeworth Arms. It was a hot night; the door was open and you crept in. Mr. Digberry was left-handed, so you fired the fatal shot with your left hand."

"You can't prove one word."

"The concierge in Menton can prove that you owned the revolver with which Margaret Coleman was killed," pursued Colt. "That was the gun you planted in Digberry's apartment by calling him out and then going in yourself. And after that, you thought the job was finished. You had faked the time on the wrist watch; by eleven o'clock, you were at home with your friend. You expected to prove you were home an hour before the crime was thought to be committed. Too bad a hair of your wig caught in that bedspring."

"You have no evidence that will put me on the scene of the crime," Walters snarled.

"Sorry to disappoint you, Walters," Colt replied. "But I really can put you on the scene of that murder. You remember that Margaret Coleman's face was powdered and rouged. She preferred a distinctive powder made by a craftsman in Norway. Madame still had some of it left from more prosperous days. When the killer lifted that body it was inevitable that some of the powder should fall on his clothing. And our chemists found some of it on your suit."

"I've nothing to say," replied Walters thickly, "until I talk with my attorney."

Two detectives came and took him away to a fate that all New York remembers.

When the door had closed, Inspector Flynn rose. "Mr. Commissioner," he protested, "that was wonderful work, but there's still the evidence against Digberry. He did write those letters; he did lie about taking the money out of the bank."

Colt chuckled. "You're right," he agreed. "Mr. Digberry, as Captain Walters told us, has a passion for realism, for exactitude. That is shown in his masterpieces of wigs, and also in his visit to the cemetery."

"But he didn't have a thousand dollars with him, chief—"

"Because he wanted to befriend a lady who had been gracious to him, Mr. Digberry drew on the savings which were the joint property of his wife and himself. Tomorrow, Mrs. Digberry returns. The day of reckoning is at hand. The new bankbook will hide the withdrawals. But what about the balance? Mr. Digberry must explain to his wife what he did with the missing thousand. Hence, he invented these letters and included himself among ten illustrious others."

Flynn began to laugh. But Colt, opening a strongbox in his lower drawer, drew out a sheaf of green paper money.

"The Wedgeworth Arms has posted a reward of one thousand dollars," he explained. "Mr. Digberry, you identified the Wilkins wig—I think you earned the cash and the glory."

"I would like the cash," Digberry admitted. "But chief, my wife mustn't know about this affair. Give the credit to Mr. Flynn."

With his pockets full of money, the wigmaker ran off to meet the train. Colt had promised to keep the facts a deep secret. And so he did—but Digberry, since a widower, has married again and the necessity for silence has passed.

THE DEVIL IS A GENTLEMAN

BY CHARLES B. CHILD

(No photograph available of Mr. Child)

Charles B. Child is the pseudonym of C. Vernon Frost, who was born in London in 1903. He began his writing career at eighteen doing newspaper work and later published many short stories in English pulp magazines. During World War II he was in the RAF and spent three years in Iraq, where he worked with the local police. In 1946, while living in the United States, he created Inspector Chafik J. Chafik of the Bagdad police. His short stories were popular in *Collier's* and were later reprinted in *Ellery Queen's Mystery Magazine*. "Death Had a Voice" and "The Devil Is a Gentleman" are considered among the most outstanding.

THE LITTLE MAN WHO entered the Cabaret of the Great
Caliph, behind the fashionable Saa'dun Quarter of the modern
city of Baghdad, stood for a moment in the shadows, as if he
were shy of this walled garden where patrons sat in booths
discreetly screened by flowering shrubs.

He looked at the stage where an orchestra of various wind
instruments, strings and drums was playing varying rhythms,
while a slender girl sang a single note and then surrounded it
with an arabesque of grace notes. It was music without har-
mony, but the man had not a Western ear and found it pleas-
ing. As the girl began to dance, he walked down a path between
the high wall and the shrubs and entered a booth so un-
obtrusively that the solitary occupant did not notice him.

Inspector Chafik of the Criminal Investigation Department
carefully dusted a chair and said as he sat down, "If the
thoughts of men were public, one would be justified in raiding
this place. And even you, my dear Abdullah, would see the
inside of a cell."

The tall, gaunt man hastily looked away from the stage, but
seeing the smile lurking in the dun-colored eyes of his companion, he raised a hand in protest. "Sir, my concentration was
purely of a professional nature—" Sergeant Abdullah began,
and wriggled in his seat when the Inspector interrupted:

"The purity of it is what I doubt, The girl is indeed gifted."
They both looked at the stage where the dancer turned full
circle with swiftly moving feet and made of her body a reed
rippling in a hot wind of passion.

Watching her, Chafik wondered how many men had been
clay in the flowerlike hands of Khurrem. His records at headquarters described her as a Syrian, but many details of her life
were lacking and this was irritating to the tidy mind of the little
man. He said, voicing his worry, "She has danced in Cairo,
Beirut and Teheran. Her lovers are always military men or
government officials and she ignores others although they are
often wealthier. An odd thread in the pattern, for surely a
woman of this profession is solely interested in money?" He
shrugged and then said, "But on the record one could not
refuse her entry into Iraq. A suspicion is not a fact, and you,

Sergeant Abdullah, will not report to me only with facts."

The sergeant answered as if reading from his notes, "On your orders I have watched this woman for a week. Her favor goes to Major Ali Rasim of the Second Mountain Brigade. He is infatuated and sits nightly in the booth at the top right corner of the garden, where she often joins him."

Inspector Chafik turned his sleek head, the black hair oiled and brushed until it had the sheen of silk. The lights in the garden were dim, but he could see a man in the booth. Major Rasim was the younger son of an aristocratic Baghdadi family and the brigade with which he served was organized for frontier defense. Chafik lighted a cigarette and said, "This is a matter for Military Intelligence. We, as the political and criminal police, are solely interested in civilians."

"Among the civilians, sir, Mohammed Shaalan is captivated by the girl—"

"Shaalan, Mohammed. Eldest son of Ibn Shaalan, a sheik of the Muntafiq." The Inspector was quoting from his records and as he partly closed his eyes he could see the card on which the particulars were entered. "Rich," he went on. "Spends more time in Baghdad than on his father's estate. Weakness, women. Arrogant. Hot-tempered. Is the man here?"

"In the booth opposite." Sergeant Abdullah looked across the cool garden and then said, "He has gone now, but he was there when you arrived. The girl only ignores him."

"Other men?"

"They are as bees around the queen," Sergeant Abdullah said.

"A queen bee," Chafik said, "has an unattractive appearance and is often swollen with eggs. One cannot say Khurrem is unattractive. Or swollen," he added, watching the girl who had finished her dance and was now bowing to the applause. He drew back into the shadows as the dancer left the stage and walked lightly to the booth where Major Rasim was sitting.

"The names of the other men—" began Sergeant Abdullah.

A woman's scream ripped the perfumed peace of the night and was followed by a moment of silence, broken only by the croaking of frogs in the irrigation ditches squaring the lawn. A second scream ran in mocking echoes within the high walls, and as panic gripped the crowd Inspector Chafik said calmly, "Tell the police at the doors to let nobody out. It appears there is entertainment for us at the Great Caliph tonight." He vaulted

157

the shrubs and ran for the booth Khurrem had entered; after one brief glance he turned to the men who crowded at his heels. "Return to your seats," he said. "The police are already here." His voice, not overloud, had the quality of a whip.

Entering the booth, he looked at the girl who crouched against the shrubs with gloved hands to her face; her eyes were black pits. She was about to scream again when the little man caught her wrist and slapped her cheek. "It would be wise to forget hysterics," he said. "I shall have many questions to ask."

Khurrem whispered, "See, see! Oh, God the Merciful! The major—"

Chafik interrupted, "Bodies have no rank or title. They are all equal before God," and going to the table he looked at the man in military uniform who was huddled low in a chair, his chin on his breast, his mouth open.

From the base of the neck at the right shoulder projected the wooden handle of a knife. A small patch of blood stained Major Rasim's light summer tunic. The Inspector ignored the knife and put his hand on the man's heart. Casually, voicing thoughts, he said, "It was to be expected he would be dead, with the knife in such a spot." Lifting his strange, ageless eyes to the girl, who was now quiet, he continued, "Such a thrust could be made with the arm of the killer lovingly around his neck. It could also be made by one standing behind on the path between the bushes and the wall. Was your arm around his neck?"

"I? You suggest—" Khurrem straightened her slender body and said in the husky voice of anger, "My arm was not around his neck. I entered the booth and thought he was sleeping. He drinks too much and you can see the whisky on the table. I spoke to him and then I put my hand on him." She covered her face with her hands.

"And then you saw the knife," Chafik prompted gently.

"Yes, I saw *that*. And only half an hour before we sat and talked."

"So he was killed when you were on the stage and all eyes were on you. Even I was watching you. But what did you see from the stage? Surely you sang for your lover?"

"The booth is in shadow. One cannot see into it from the stage. And who says he was my lover?" There was a challenge in the question, and throwing back her cloud of hair Khurrem looked at the Inspector with hatred tempered by fear.

He answered softly, "I know many things about you and will

158

know more. Come to me tomorrow and bring your passport. The name is Chafik J. Chafik." He turned to Sergeant Abdullah who had just arrived with a squad of police summoned from a near-by station. The sergeant was ordering back a man who had roughly pushed his way through the crowd, but the Inspector said, "Permit Mr. Hassoon to pass. He has a right here." He had recognized the owner of the cabaret.

"What is this? What is this?" demanded Hassoon, hugging his hands to his breast and contorting his thin body into a gigantic question mark. "I have always had a respectable cabaret," he said. "You, Inspector Chafik, know I give good entertainment without vice. Now a woman screams and the police gather like flies on a festering wound—"

"There has not been time for the wound to fester," Chafik said mildly, and moving aside from the body he asked, "You know him, Mr. Hassoon?"

"Major Rasim!" The shrill voice sank to a whisper as the proprietor peered at the body and projecting knife. "Murder? Oh, Compassionate God, what wickedness has this woman caused?" He turned so quickly on Khurrem that Chafik thought he was going to strike her and caught his arm.

"Why do you think the woman is the motive for the crime?" he asked sharply.

Hassoon was calmer now but his voice was edged with anger as he said, "A woman who sings and dances is as honey to men. When she gives her favors to one the evil begins. Perhaps I am in the wrong business," he said looking with distaste from the dancer to the body. He took a handful of salted melon seeds from his pocket and politely offered them to Chafik, who bowed his thanks but preferred his cigarette. "As I have told you, I make every effort to keep the atmosphere of my cabaret clean," Hassoon went on, "but I have often looked on the faces of my guests and found them lustful." He took the husk of a melon seed from his mouth and placed it tidily in an ash tray.

Chafik said dryly, "We appear to share the same opinion. As you are so observant, my dear Mr. Hassoon, can you tell me who was particularly jealous of Major Rasim?"

"There were many, but I have noted one man who looked at him with hatred—but I must be loyal to my guests even if I dislike their ways."

"Major Rasim was also your guest. You must not withhold information."

159

"True. The name I was about to mention was Mohammed Shaalan."

Chafik gave Abdullah a warning look because the sergeant had said, "By God and by God!"

Then the Inspector said quietly, "Let us go to your office, Mr. Hassoon. Abdullah, look for the son of Ibn Shaalan and if he is still in the cabaret bring him to me." He gave the corpse a brief glance. "Obviously the killer took the precaution to wear gloves, but of course test the knife for fingerprints. Detectives are more fortunate in fiction," Inspector Chafik added sadly. . . .

In the office behind the stage, where there were also dressing rooms for the entertainers, the little man sat and waited. He lighted the inevitable cigarette while Hassoon munched melon seeds. Presently the sergeant ushered into the room a sharp-nosed, swarthy man who was dressed in the fine cotton and silk robes of a tribal Arab. The gray headcloth which shaded his face was bound with a cord of braided goat's hair making a double ring about his head, and as his robes swirled Chafik noticed the holster of a gun. Mohammed Shaalan was a young man of handsome appearance, but he was burning with an inner anger and burst out, "Why have I been brought here? My father—"

The Inspector said soothingly, "I have a great respect for the sheik, your father. Please seat yourself. A cigarette?"

"I do not smoke."

"That is wise. I myself smoke too much." He stubbed out the butt smoldering between yellow fingers, spilling husks from the tray on the desk and sweeping them tidily into a wastepaper basket. "You will excuse me asking questions," he said, "but I am obliged to check on everybody who knew Major Rasim—"

"I did not know him! I never wished to know him!" Shaalan clenched his slender hands, and the stone of his signet ring was a red eye gleaming balefully in the electric light.

"Mr. Shaalan, do you know Khurrem the Dancer?"

The young man answered, "The question is indecently personal. I have tried to know her, but she turns her face from me and even sends back my gifts. A cabaret woman should divide her favors," he added vindictively.

"Where were you when Rasim was killed?"

"At my table." Mohammed Shaalan saw the dun-colored eyes of Inspector Chafik become suddenly brilliant, and moistening his lips said, "I cannot be sure. I do not know when he was

160

killed. I left the booth when the girl danced and went to her dressing room."

"Why?"

"Because no woman has ever refused me! Because—" He sprang to his feet with the silk of his undergown rustling and shouted, "I refuse to be questioned by you! My father is powerful, and we of the Muntafiq are true Arabs who do not bow our heads to Baghdadis!"

Chafik did not stop him as he went out the door, but said as it slammed, "We are all Iraqis." The little man shrugged and voicing a thought, murmured, "A very difficult young man. He must be watched." Hearing his own voice he smiled, saying, "I have an unfortunate habit of speaking my thoughts, and you will forget what you heard, Mr. Hassoon. But you wish to speak?"

The proprietor of the Great Caliph was nervously walking the room hugging his clasped hands. "It is so awkward," he said. "So very awkward. But I realize I cannot withhold information."

"You are an excellent citizen, Mr. Hassoon. What is this information?"

"Mohammed Shaalan was not in Khurrem's room. I myself was there, Inspector. I was waiting to warn her that unless she withdrew her favors from Major Rasim, and conducted herself virtuously, I would break the contract and send her back to Damascus. As you so kindly said, I try to be a good citizen. I do not run a house of ill fame," he said between tight lips. "Vice shocks me."

When Inspector Chafik was leaving the cabaret after checking the identities of the patrons, he stopped at the door of Khurrem's dressing room. The girl had been escorted to her hotel, and Chafik entered the room with Abdullah and made a methodical search. The heavy perfume of jasmine made him press his handkerchief to his nose. "Perfume is dangerous," he said to the watchful sergeant. "The fact is well known to manufacturers in America, judging by the advertisements in their magazines."

"So long as there are women there will be perfume, sir."

"As a flower attracts the bees," said Chafik. He picked up the ash tray from the dressing table. "What do you see here, Abdullah?"

"Sir, I see a glass tray three inches square containing the stubs

161

of five cigarettes. They are stained with lipstick and were therefore smoked by the girl." He gave a smile of triumph as he added, "I did not expect to see anything else. Mohammed Shaalan does not smoke."

The Inspector said, "That is true. I offered him a cigarette. Besides, we were told he was not here. What else do you see, Abdullah?"

"I see nothing, sir—"

"I also see nothing. You will note that carefully." And he left the room, followed by Sergeant Abdullah, who was fumbling for his notebook with a puzzled expression on his dark face.

In the morning Inspector Chafik sat on the edge of a chair in the office of the Chief Inspector. His superior, a burly Englishman who was a former Chief Inspector of Scotland Yard, held his present appointment from the Iraqi government. He was a man whose liver gave him an unpredictable temper. He was also justly proud of his department, so when he roared, "A man murdered under your nose and nobody arrested!" Chafik nervously twisted his black *sidarah* and meekly bowed his head.

"There were three hundred guests," he said. "The killer was aided by the confusion. You yourself, Mr. Ellsworth, will be the first to understand my difficulties." He smiled ingratiatingly and went on, "If you will direct me as to my next actions on the basis of my report—"

Ellsworth said, "It's a very thorough report and a black one for Shaalan. My God, Chafik, there'll be the devil to pay if we pick him up for murder! A thing like that might well rouse the Muntafiq."

"I have handled him cautiously for that reason, sir. If only Mr. Hassoon had not been so observant—"

"He did his duty. Now we've got to do ours. And what's this damn fool paragraph in your report about Hassoon?" The Chief Inspector picked up the file and read, "Observes the full ritual of daily prayer, including *coubh, zhor, acr* and *magreb*. Unmarried—" He flung the file down. "His religious habits are his own affair. Tell me about the girl."

"Chief Inspector, she is undoubtedly the agent of a foreign power and used her charms on Major Rasim for obvious reasons. With your permission, I intend to retain her passport until the investigation is completed. And I will use her," Chafik added in a hard voice.

162

"Could she have killed Rasim?"

"She could—and she is an excellent actress."

"He may have threatened to denounce her." Ellsworth drummed the desk and then asked abruptly, "The knife's untraceable?"

"It could have been purchased anywhere. These knives are mass-produced in your country, sir."

"But they don't make 'em to kill people!" The Chief Inspector picked up Chafik's report again and reread the paragraph referring to the weapon. "A thin blade," he said. "External bleeding insufficient to stain the killer's hand. No fingerprints." He shrugged. "It's a tough case, Chafik, and I don't propose to muddle you with suggestions. You have your own methods and perhaps the less I know about 'em the better, I leave it to you."

The Inspector stood and bowed. He said, "Sir, I am honored by your trust and will do my best. But all is with God." He salaamed with the curved fingers of his right hand to his forehead, but when he was in the corridor and had closed Ellsworth's door he murmured, "I leave it to you. I leave it to you. How very nice to be the Chief Inspector!"

In his own office Chafik found the woman Khurrem waiting with Sergeant Abdullah in attendance. She was quietly dressed in the Western style, but a black shawl, like a Spanish mantilla, was draped over her head and from under the folds her great eyes looked out with suspicion and alarm. The sergeant, who was hovering behind her chair, made a gesture as if pleading for clemency but the voice of the Inspector was cold as he said, "You have your passport?"

He took the passport, embossed with the arms of the Syrian Republic, and wrote out a receipt. Khurrem said, "This is outrageous!"

"It is a precaution," answered Chafik. "It does not suit my purpose that you should leave Iraq. You are accustomed to taking orders, Madame, and now I give them."

"You talk riddles. I am only a woman who sings and dances—"

"You do both delightfully!" He turned to a ponderous steel cabinet and took out a file. "The pattern of your life," said Inspector Chafik casually, "has the intricate weave of a Kirman carpet and the more one studies it the more one sees. Your father, who was a Syrian, gave you a Turkish name. You were born in Istanbul and taken to Damascus at the age of ten. You were orphaned four years later and there is a gap in your life until you reappear in Tabriz, Iran, as a cabaret entertainer in the last year of the war."

"Is that a crime?" She put a cigarette into a jeweled holder and Sergeant Abdullah hastened with a match.

Chafik said, "It is not a crime. And as I am a broad-minded man I think no evil of you because you lived with Mr. Ali Muzaffer, a very prominent member of the Left, or Tudeh party." There was a musical rattle of bracelets as Khurrem's hand shook. The little man tapped the open file and continued in the same casual voice, "Here is where the pattern becomes very interesting. You crossed and recrossed the Middle East from Teheran to Cairo, and the men you charmed were military men and government officials, never any others. Those were your orders, Madame?"

"I refuse to answer such a question."

"And rightly so. Of course the connection of the Tudeh party with our very powerful northern neighbor—" Inspector Chafik paused. "Sergeant Abdullah, where are your manners? The lady's cigarette has gone out." He waited a moment and then said gently, "Madame, I am not interested in political matters this time. Only murder. I require a well-trained agent—one so charming as yourself, for instance."

"I? Work for you?" The woman was pale, trembling.

"I am a gentleman," Chafik said, "and it would distress me to retain your passport permanently. Mr. Hassoon might dismiss you from the Great Caliph and then perhaps you would find it difficult to find other work in Baghdad," he added sadly.

Khurrem picked up her long gloves and drew them carefully over her slender hands, the palms of which were touched with henna. "What are your orders?"

"You will continue to entertain at the cabaret, but you will be very kind to Mohammed Shaalan who has long admired you. Other orders will be given later. And you will, of course, be discreetly silent about our talk."

"I think you are the Devil!"

Inspector Chafik rose to his feet and bowed. "That is with God," he said. . . .

Five days after the interview between Inspector Chafik and Khurrem the Dancer, a sandstorm spread a dirty canopy over

164

the Baghdad sky. It was a day of oppressive heat and the air was filled with dust and stinging insects.

In the Nassah Quarter two men stabbed each other over a debt amounting to thirty *fils*. A husband at Kadhimain, wearied of his wife, strangled her and dropped the body in the Tigris, and was caught by the police. In his headquarters on Al-Rashid Street, Inspector Chafik read the reports and said, "One regrets these things, but conditions are excellent for my little plan and tonight, Abdullah, we put it into action."

Shortly before ten o'clock, Khurrem, performing to a half-empty cabaret, received a note slipped into her hand as she left the stage for the booth occupied by Mohammed Shaalan. The Arabic characters which marched from right to left across the paper had a certain tidiness, and left her in no doubt of the writer, although the note was unsigned.

> In the name of God the Compassionate. You will invite Mr. Shaalan to your hotel and proceed there by arabana. You will leave the carriage and enter the hotel ahead of him. Be assured that your virtue will be protected.

Khurrem tore the letter into shreds. Her fingernails were red daggers and her look was dangerous as she tossed her stormy hair and went slowly to the booth where Shaalan was waiting. She passed Hassoon who said, "There are such few guests I am closing early. Please inform your new lover." Khurrem brushed him with her shoulder, a gesture of contempt.

When she passed through the gap in the flowering shrubs she found a smile for Shaalan, but it faded when the Arab said, "I saw a man speak to you! I saw you lean against him!"

The woman said in a husky voice, "Thou fool!" and her small teeth clenched on the stem of the jeweled cigarette holder. Then she opened her bag and took out her gloves. "We close early. I am weary. Will you see me to my hotel?" Partly closing her great eyes she looked at Shaalan through lashes thickened by kohl.

When they left the cabaret an arabana swung out of the waiting line and drew to the curb, and a man in a café across the street went quickly to the telephone. He dialed a number and shortly afterward Inspector Chafik, who was relaxing at his favorite cinema, rose as he felt Abdullah's touch on his shoulder.

The little man said, "Now I shall never know who put the body of the collector of Chinese jade in the parrot cage at the Central Park zoo." He looked over his shoulder at the screen and shook his head regretfully.

The street was almost empty. Dust, weighted with moisture sucked from the river by the day's heat, fell softly and a blue haze obscured the lights. Sergeant Abdullah said, "One eats dust," and Chafik answered, "It is our lot." They walked under the pillared arcade to the top of Al-Rashid Street and turning at a sign which read, MA'MUN HOTEL, entered a dark passage. A door leading to a neglected garden opened and three officers of the Metropolitan Police, their tunics smudges of white in the darkness, saluted smartly.

The Inspector stationed himself behind the partly closed door and polished his nails with a handkerchief. Presently he raised his head as the clop-clop of horses' hoofs sounded up the street, but he did not speak until there was the double crack of a driver's whip. Then he put away the handkerchief, saying, "It is the signal."

As the carriage drew up, Mohammed Shaalan, muffled in his robes against the storm, jumped down and extended his hand to Khurrem. The woman said softly, "Follow me in a few minutes," and went up the passage to the hotel fumbling in her bag. When Shaalan had given money to the driver he waited until the carriage had disappeared into the haze of dust and then glided after Khurrem with the smooth step of the desert dweller.

At that moment a car came up the road and pulled to the curb, and a man crossed the sidewalk with a single leap. The blade of an uplifted dagger darted like a serpent's tongue toward Shaalan's back.

Inspector Chafik threw back the garden door with a twist of his left shoulder and thrust out his arm in the same movement. He felt the burn of steel on his wrist as he wrapped his arm about the throat of the man and flung him violently against the wall of the passage. At the same time Sergeant Abdullah, crouching on the parapet above, descended with his full weight crying, "Thou dog of dogs!"

The three constables rushed from the garden, and the carriage driver, wheeling his horses, joined the confused huddle of struggling bodies.

In a quiet voice Chafik was heard to say, "The ferocity of a

166

pack of wolves is not equal to that of a pack of men. Do not tear him to bits."

The steel jaws of handcuffs closed. Sergeant Abdullah rose from the huddle and said with wonder, "Sir, it is Hassoon!"

"He fitted the pattern," answered the Inspector, and went to look at the thin hollow-eyed man who was now helpless in the grip of the police.

Hassoon was crying, "In the name of God let me kill him as I killed the other lustful dog! The evil in the hearts of men! The honey of women!" And he began to quote from the Koran in a high voice, "By their tokens shall the sinners be known, and they shall be seized by their forelocks and their feet . . . Amid pestilential winds and in scalding water . . ."

The voice changed to gibberish, and Sergeant Abduallah said, "God has touched him. He will not hang, for the madness has always been there. I cover my shamed face because I did not see the truth, that this man who never married and hated lust was himself filled with lust for the woman Khurrem, and so killed those she favored. Yet, sir, a fact and not a theory must have guided you to the truth."

"I told you to note the fact. An ash tray in which we saw nothing but the stubs of cigarettes. You disappoint me, Abdullah!" Inspector Chafik dipped into the prisoner's pockets and showed a handful of salted melon seeds. "As I smoke, so this one nibbles," he said. "So strong the habit that he nibbled in the presence of Major Rasim's corpse and placed the husks of the seeds in the tray on the table. And in his own office was a tray piled with husks. Yet in Khurrem's dressing room, where he said he waited for her, were no husks. Therefore he was not in the room and therefore he lied when he said Shaalan was not there."

"Such deduction has the clarity of a flawless crystal," said Abdullah.

"It was clear because God made it so. And the rest of the story is a pattern of woven threads. Who else but Hassoon could have stolen behind Rasim and made the fatal thrust? He tried to claim another victim by putting suspicion on Shaalan, but that failed and he was again driven to murder. Fortunately prevented," Inspector Chafik added, turning to Mohammed Shaalan.

"By God's mercy—" the young Arab said.

"And by my arm and the men who guarded you from the

moment you left the Great Caliph! You will find the Muntafiq a safer place than the cabarets of Baghdad. Please give my compliments to the sheik, your father." Chafik's nod was a dismissal and Shaalan, wiping the perspiration from his face with the folds of his headcloth, murmured, "I bless your House," and left meekly.

They took away the man Hassoon, who was now chanting from the Koran, "The beauteous ones with large dark eyeballs ... whom man hath never touched, nor any jinn. ..." Inspector Chafik turned to Khurrem who stood in the shadows with her shawl modestly veiling her face. The perfume of jasmine made the little man sigh as he took an envelope from his pocket and gave it to the woman.

"Your passport, Madame." He paused and then said with a note of regret in his voice, "I took the liberty of enclosing a ticket for Damascus by the Nairn Trans-Desert Autobus."

Khurrem said softly, a little laugh catching her throat, "Yes, you are surely the Devil!"

And with his most courteous bow, curved fingers hovering near his *sidarah* in a salaam, Inspector Chafik answered, "But you will agree the Devil is a gentleman—"

A WINTER'S TALE

BY FRANCES & RICHARD LOCKRIDGE

(No photograph available of Frances or Richard Lockridge)

Richard Lockridge was born in St. Joseph, Missouri, in 1898 and married Frances Louise Davis, a native of Kansas City, Missouri, in 1922. The first novel they wrote together, which established Mr. and Mrs. North as a detective team, was *The Norths Meet Murder* (1940). Many critics credit the Lockridges with having popularized the use of humor in mysteries. After his wife's death on February 17, 1963, Richard Lockridge continued other series characters they created together, such as Nathan Shapiro and Merton Heimrich of the New York State Police. He now lives in Tryon, North Carolina, with his second wife, writer Hildegarde Dolson.

AT A QUARTER AFTER ONE ON A Wednesday afternoon in mid-January, Florrie Watson parked her battered sedan and for a moment sat in it shivering, hugging a worn cloth coat around her. But there wasn't any use sitting there dreading it.

So she opened the car door, stepped out into the raging north-west wind, and ran—was half blown, for she was a little woman and not a young woman—to the kitchen door of the big drafty house on the hilltop. She had her key ready, turned it in the old-fashioned lock, tugged the door open, and let the wind slam it to behind her. It made noise enough, she thought, to wake the dead.

It was warm in the house and she took her coat off and hung it up before she did anything else. She found that she was listening for the old man to growl at her, to tell her angrily that she was late again. But there was no sound in the house, except the sound of the wind.

Florrie went into the living room, where she always started, and there was Aaron Stark, lying on the floor, wearing a night-shirt and a bathrobe over it. The low winter sun glared in through a window and he was lying on a rug in a patch of sunlight.

She called his name and then, again, more loudly, "Mr. Stark!" Then she made herself touch him. She had wasted breath calling him.

She had to go back into the bitter wind—it had been eight above when she left home and didn't seem to be getting any warmer—and drive half a mile to the nearest house because there was no telephone in the old Stark house. There had been one until about a year before, but Aaron Stark had quarreled with the telephone company, with everybody—and jerked the instrument out of the wall, carried it out to the road, and thrown it down hard on the pavement. Which, he told Florrie, would teach them.

At the nearest neighbor's house Florrie Watson called the State Police.

The news that old Stark had died alone in his big barn of a house, four miles or so from Van Brunt Center, spread quickly. It was, people said, an awful thing to happen to anybody—to

170

any old man, alone in a big drafty house. When they said "anybody" there was a just perceptible emphasis on "any"—as if the term were being stretched to include Aaron Stark.

That was the way people who lived in the town of Van Brunt felt about Aaron Stark, the old skinflint. People who knew Mary Phipps and her daughter Joan had even harder words for him. A man who won't help out his relatives when they are in bad trouble and he's got plenty is "no kind of a man." This was freely said by friends of Mary Phipps while Stark was alive, and when he was dead there were some who said, and many who thought, that now his money—of which it was generally agreed he had plenty—would go where it was needed, where it would do some good.

Captain M.L. Heimrich, of the Bureau of Criminal Investigation, New York State Police, heard of Stark's death at around eight o'clock Wednesday evening. He went out of the biting cold—the forecast was for zero to ten below in Northern Westchester and Putnam counties, and Heimrich didn't doubt it for a minute—into the warm taproom of the Old Stone Inn at Van Brunt Center. He went, as any sensible man would on such a night, to the bar and Harold, the barman, pouring, said, "Hear about old Stark?"

Heimrich shook his head.

"Dead," Harold said. "Bad thing to happen to *any*body, dying alone that way." And he told Heimrich that the doc—"this new man, Smith; Doc Bender's in town at a meeting or something"—said that Stark had been dead twenty-four hours when he, as acting coroner, examined the body. At least twenty-four hours.

"Except," Harold said, detective to detective, "I'd figure it was longer, because that would make it yesterday afternoon, and what was he doing in a nightshirt in the afternoon?"

Heimrich said "Hmmm" in appreciation of this reasoning. He took his drink over to the fireplace and stood with his back to the fire. "Probably woke up in the morning not feeling so good," Heimrich said, "and had a stroke. He must have been near eighty."

Actually, Heimrich was not too interested; he had known of Aaron Stark, but not known him. Surely Stark had died of natural causes or Heimrich would have heard by now, and death from natural causes, however sudden, is not a concern of Heimrich's. His concern is with homicide.

171

So Heimrich warmed his back, and then the bar telephone rang and Harold said into it, "Yep. Just come in."

Heimrich sighed. He went to the telephone and listened to an official voice. He said, "Okay. May as well start at the house," and finished his drink and put the glass down on the bar. Harold was looking at him. Harold might as well know—everybody would know soon enough. Things get around.

"Stark died of a fractured skull," Heimrich said, and went out of the taproom into the cold night and drove four miles to a hilltop and a lighted house. Little shivers of cold air roamed through it, but it was warm enough. Hot air poured up from an old-fashioned floor register. Heimrich could hear the furnace throbbing in the basement, straining against the cold.

The body had been removed hours before. Two State Troopers were waiting for Heimrich. "Florrie Watson found him," one of them said. "She worked for him. Part time," and was asked if he knew where Florrie Watson lived. He did. She lived a mile and a half down the road.

"Go get her," Heimrich said and the trooper went, and Heimrich looked the house over.

It was a big house, an old house. Little money had been spent on it in many years, Heimrich thought. The wind whined in around loose-fitting windows, and scurried in under the kitchen door. It was surprising that it was as warm as it was, and Heimrich glanced at the thermostat and saw it was set for 80.

He went up a flight of stairs, opened a door, and a rush of cold air met him. The upper floor, evidently, was not used; certainly was not heated. He went down the stairs, opened another door, and looked into darkness. The throbbing of the furnace was louder. He found Stark's bedroom, saw that the bed had been slept in but not made up.

Then the trooper brought in Florrie Watson—Mrs. Florence Watson, a little woman with red hands and straggling gray hair.

"I just thought he'd had a stroke or something," Florrie said. "I didn't dream."

Heimrich was gentle. He was sorry he had to ask her to come out on a night like this.

"This *weather*", she said. "Monday you wouldn't have thought it was January. Like April almost. And then like this."

People will talk about the weather under almost any circumstances, Heimrich thought; they will escape to the trivial, the safe.

172

"Yes," he said. "Where did you find him, Mrs. Watson?"

It had been about there, and she pointed. Near the center of the living room; near the center of an oval hooked rug. "In the sun." She had known at once that he was dead. She had called him, but known it was no good. Yes, the house had been locked when she came. The locks were not snap locks; you had to use the key. She came at one every afternoon, except Sunday, and worked until five, cleaning up and preparing dinner for Stark to warm up later when he wanted it. Breakfast and lunch he got for himself.

Heimrich said, "*Every* weekday? Then—"

"Not yesterday," she said. "I had one of my sick headaches. I started out and almost got here but I felt so sick—well, I just turned around and drove back home." She stopped suddenly. "If," she said, "if I'd come on I—I could have done something. That's what you mean?"

"Now, Mrs. Watson," Heimrich said. "It isn't very likely you could have done anything for him. Just found him already dead, probably. He would have had to let in anyone who came? I mean, he always kept the doors locked?"

Always, so far as she knew. And she had the only extra key she knew about. Not that anybody ever came.

Somebody had come, Heimrich told her. That was clear enough.

"The trooper said he fractured his skull," Mrs. Watson said. "Couldn't he have fallen down and—?"

Heimrich shook his head. Stark had fallen, apparently, on the rug. If he had had a stroke, or merely fainted, he would almost certainly have slumped down, not fallen hard. And fallen on the padding of the rug. A fairly thick rug.

She didn't know. People never came. People didn't like him.

"You didn't like him?" Heimrich asked.

"Not to say liked," Florrie Watson said. "Put up with. It wasn't too far to come and I've got to work some place. Nag, nag, nag all the time, but I got so I didn't listen."

"About the way you worked?"

"About everything. Wasting things, mostly. I don't waste. Not what you'd call waste. But what he called it—Well, he's dead now. The poor old thing."

Speak no evil, however tempted.

"Somebody came," Heimrich said. "Somebody killed him. Who would want to more than anyone else?"

She didn't know. But she hesitated, so Heimrich waited.

"Well," she finally said, "I don't like to say it. The girl said some mean things to him. Monday afternoon, that was. I don't know as I blame her, but—"

The girl was Joan Phipps, Aaron Stark's second cousin. She had come about four o'clock on Monday afternoon. She had quarreled with the old man and said that men like him ought to be dead.

"Not that I listened," Florrie Watson said. "More than I could help, anyway. But she raised her voice. And not that I blame her, mind you."

But that was Monday. Twenty-four hours from early Wednesday afternoon do not stretch back to Monday. However—

Joan Phipps had still been in the house on Monday when Florrie left at five o'clock. Talking loudly. "About money," Mrs. Watson said. "I can't deny I heard that much. Or that she and her mother need it—need it bad. You'd think even *he*—but there, he's dead now, the poor old soul."

Heimrich had known Mary Phipps, Aaron Stark's cousin and now presumably his heir—known her slightly, incuriously, as one knows a pleasant, hurried waitress. She had sometimes served Heimrich at the Old Stone Inn. A plump, quick, smiling woman in her late forties she was.

Driving from the drafty house toward "The Flats," Heimrich recalled vaguely that she had quit the job sometime in the early fall. Something about her health. Yes, that was it.

He drove slowly on NY 11-F, which is Van Brunt Avenue through the Center, but only a number when it reaches the closely set, rundown little houses of "The Flats." He kept his spotlight on rural mail boxes. At one marked "Phipps" he pulled to the side of the road.

The little house seemed to shake in the wind as he stood on the porch and knocked. After some seconds, the door opened with a kind of violence and a tall, gangling girl looked at him. She said, "What do you want?"—with anger in her young voice. Heimrich told her who he was. The girl said, "How do I know?"—and Heimrich showed his badge.

It was not warm in the room she led him into—the room reeked of kerosene from a two-burner heater, but the room was not warm. The girl wore sweater over sweater, and a woolen skirt. She was, Heimrich guessed, about sixteen—tall and thin, with high shoulders, with cheekbones which made her face a triangle, with very wide eyes. And with red hair. The mouth was wide, too, its corners turned down—a bitter mouth. Altogether, a sulky, angry girl. Quite possibly with reason, Heimrich thought, and asked if he could see her mother.

"No, you can't," Joan Phipps said. "She's sick. You can leave her alone." She did not suggest that he sit down; she stood herself. "Leave us both alone," she said. "That's what everybody does." She was a lean young cat, snarling and spitting at the world.

"It's about your cousin," Heimrich said. "Your mother's cousin."

"All right," the girl said. "So he's dead. How do they tell the difference?"

Heimrich said, "Now, Miss Phipps."

"You want me to cry?" she said. "Go boo-hoo? Because he was always so good to us? Helped when it happened to mother? When I had to quit school? When all he had to do—" She made an angry gesture with her thin hands.

"You told him this on Monday?" Heimrich said. "When you went there. When—"

"Say it," the girl said. "When I went begging. When—" Again she stopped, but this time, Heimrich thought, there was wariness in the wide, red-brown eyes. "So what?" she said. "He didn't give me anything. He didn't die of giving me something. Not that it wouldn't have killed him."

"He died," Heimrich said, "of a fractured skull. From a blow of some sort. You went to ask help. He refused. You were angry. You shouted at him."

"Florrie Watson," Joan said. "Couldn't wait to blab, could she?"

But the voice was not the same. She was keyed up to my coming, Heimrich thought, keyed up to attack. Only she's a hurt child. Not what she wants to think she is. And—a frightened child?

"A fractured skull?" she said, and Heimrich merely nodded his head. "It couldn't be," she said. "All I did—you're trying to trick me."

"No," Heimrich said. "You hit him?"

"She can't live like this," the girl said. "Look—she can hardly move. When I have to go to work and leave her and—" She changed again. "You're like all of them," she said. "People like

175

us are made to be pushed around. Just the way he—"

There could be no doubt why she stopped this time.

"He pushed you?" Heimrich said. "And—"

"Said things," she said. "All right, you've got what you came after. Things about—about mother. And grabbed me and started to push and—I tell you, *I won't be pushed!* I won't—" But now she was near to tears.

"You hit him?" Heimrich said. "With what?"

"This," she said, and shook her closed right fist. Two knuckles of the fist were still reddened, bruised.

"He fell?"

"Fell? Of course not. He said—he called me a name and started toward me again—and I ran. And he locked the door after me. I heard it. So he was all right and—" Once more she stopped. "He *was* all right?" she said, and questioned like a child.

"It doesn't always take much," Heimrich said. "How was he dressed, Miss Phipps?"

She repeated vaguely, "Dressed?" And then she said that Stark had worn ordinary things—gray trousers and a sweater, she thought.

"Joan?" a shaking voice called from another room—from, Heimrich suspected, the only other room. "Is somebody there?"

The girl looked at Heimrich. And Heimrich shook his head, turned to the door, and went out of the little house.

He would have to come back, of course—first check with the doctor and then come back—when he had verified formally what he knew to be true: that a relatively light blow may fracture a thin skull; that the victim may not lose consciousness for hours and then go into a coma and die; that a man hurt that way might very well lock a door and even undress and go to bed and wake up later and start a search for help. And die hours after the blow. Of—what was it?—a subdural hemorrhage in the brain. That was it. So an angry girl, striking back like a child, might have killed the old man.

The radio in Heimrich's car squawked at him. He was to telephone Dr. Robert Bender, county coroner, at his first opportunity. Heimrich telephoned from the inn. He listened. He said, *"What?"* in a tone of incredulity. Then, "Come again, Doctor."

"A quite easy mistake to make," Dr. Bender said. "Even a

much more experienced man might have been misled during a preliminary examination. With further examination, Dr. Smith himself would—er—have realized that the fracture was post-mortem. I don't doubt that. I—"

"All right," Heimrich said. "I've no doubt Dr. Smith is a very able man. Ice in the skull expands and separates skull sutures and—"

"The coronal suture in this case," Dr. Bender said. "Very similar to ante-mortem fracture on first—"

"All right, Doctor," Heimrich said. "What you're telling me now is that old Stark *froze* to death. And that his brain turned to ice, expanded, and broke his skull? And that if he was hit earlier, say, that had nothing to do with his death?

"That's it," Dr. Bender said. "Got to you with it as fast as I could."

Heimrich thanked him for that much and put the telephone back in its cradle. He looked hard at it as if it were to blame.

It had been so simple—an angry child, a blow, an old man's thin skull. And now— Now he had a man freezing to death in a warm house—a house with a thermostat set at 80°. Because nobody would have gone out of a house in nightshirt and bathrobe with the bottom falling out of the thermometer and stayed outside long enough to freeze—and then— Then what? Walked back in again and lain down on the living-room rug?

A problem for a detective—a nagging problem. Nagging? Why—?

Oh, Heimrich thought, and made two telephone calls. Power had not been off Monday night in the area. The five hundred and fifty gallon oil tank in the basement of Aaron Stark's house had been filled only a week before. So.

Heimrich went back into the cold night and drove away. He drove past Stark's big drafty house and a mile and a half on down the road. Florrie Watson was still up—it was as if she had been waiting. She looked up at him with fear, without surprise.

"Mrs. Watson," Heimrich said, and went into the very warm—the almost stifling—living room of her little house. "Mrs. Watson, Mr. Stark froze to death. You knew that, didn't you?"

She pushed at straggling gray hair and looked quickly away, and then nodded her head.

"You did go to the house yesterday," Heimrich said. "And turned the furnace on again, and the thermostat up high.

When you found him dead. Thinking—thinking nobody'd ever know you'd turned the furnace *off* the day before?"

"He was always nagging," the little woman said in a voice from far away. "How was I to know it would get so cold?"

The radio had carried the forecast, the warning of a severe cold wave. It had been in all the newspapers. Which didn't matter too much.

"He always kept the place like a morgue," she said in the same distant voice. "Wouldn't let me turn the thermostat up—wasted oil, he said. Always nagging about it. I said, 'You want me to get pneumonia?' and—" Her voice died away. Heimrich waited.

"Put the mop and things back in the basement before I left Monday," she went on. "And there was the switch—the furnace switch—and I thought, I'll show him. I'll save his oil for him." Again she stopped. But then she put her hands up to her flat chest and began to back away from Heimrich.

"I didn't know!" she said, and her voice was almost a scream. "I didn't mean it to happen. *All I wanted was to teach him a lesson!"*

Drafty old houses on hilltops—such houses cool quickly when the wind rages and the temperature drops hard. Old men might wake up shivering in such houses, get out of bed to find out what had gone wrong, get up too suddenly into bitter cold. Faint from shock, perhaps? They would never know, precisely. That, also, didn't matter too much.

Mrs. Watson had taught her lesson, if that was really all she had had in mind. Others would have to decide about that.

"You'd better come along with me, Mrs. Watson," Heimrich said kindly. "Wrap up warm. It's cold outside."

CLANCY AND THE
SHOESHINE BOY

BY ROBERT L. FISH

Robert L. Pike is the pseudonym of Robert L. Fish. He was born in 1912 in Cleveland, Ohio. His first story, the first of his famous Sherlock Holmes parodies, "The Adventure of the Ascot Tie," was published in *Ellery Queen's Mystery Magazine* in 1960. Under his pseudonym he has written police procedural novels and short stories about Lieutenant Clancy of New York's 52nd Precinct. *The Fugitive* (1962) won an Edgar from the Mystery Writers of America for best first novel. In 1968 the movie *Bullitt,* based on his *Mute Witness,* also won an Edgar, as did his short story, "Moonlight Gardener," in 1971. He and his wife live in Connecticut.

11:30 A.M.

STAN WAS SITTING in Clancy's office that Monday morning, his hat thrust back on his head, chair tilted against the wall, face frowning.

"Damnedest thing you ever saw, Lieutenant," he said wonderingly. "Newspapers piled up in stacks all over the place, you couldn't hardly get through the hall. Junk? My God! Telephone directories from the year one, tin cans, barrels, magazines, rags, cigar boxes . . . One room was filled with empty orange crates—you know, them slat things they use for oranges. It's the truth. You'd have to see it to believe it."

Clancy was taking notes, nodding. "Any idea how he was killed?"

Stanton shook his head. "He was lying there with his arms around his stomach, like he had a gutache, and his legs all pulled up. If he didn't have that bloody nose, we'd probably have figured he passed out natural, but his nose was broke. Doc Freeman said he'd call you when he comes up with something."

Clancy marked it down. "Anything to show how the killer got in?"

"Broke in, I guess. At least the back door looked like it was pried open. Or it may have been like that all the time, for all we know. The windows are all boarded up with planks, nailed shut, and not a sliver of glass. They weren't touched. Some tramp probably figured the place was deserted and bust in. The old man must have been there and started a fuss, and the tramp popped him to shut him up. And killed him."

Clancy leaned back, twiddling his pencil. "Anything missing?"

Stanton shrugged, nearly unbalanced, and then settled his chair carefully back against the wall. "To tell you the truth, I don't see how you could even tell in that place. You ought to see it—it's hard to explain. A real junk heap. I talked to one of the neighbors and he told me the old man was real screwy. Picked up any piece of junk he saw. He didn't know the old man too well—I guess nobody did—but he said one day the old man was feeling friendly and started to brag about a stamp and coin collection he had. So far we haven't found a sign of either one.

Which doesn't mean too much—it could be hidden any one of a million places in that mess. Plus which, we haven't really looked yet."

"Nobody's looked?"

"Nobody yet," Stanton said. "Timmons found him. The front door was open, first time since Timmons has been on the beat. The boys from downtown are all through; I left Keller there until I get back. I figured on a bite of lunch and then going over and hitting up some more of the neighbors." He glanced at his wrist and eased his chair back to the vertical. "Anything special you want me to do, Lieutenant?"

Clancy laid down his pencil and swiveled toward the open window. The bright, warm June sunlight lit the small room that served as his office, dissipating some of its normal drabness.

"Better keep Keller there with you," Clancy said. "Go over everything in the place. The old man had to live somehow. And see if you can find any trace of that stamp or coin collection." He paused, considering, then shook his head. "Although I doubt if a philatelist or numismatist killed him."

Stanton, having no idea of what a philatelist or numismatist was, nodded his head solemnly. "Will do." He pushed his hat straight and started for the door. "I'm catching a sandwich over at the bar across the street. Can I bring anything back for you, Lieutenant?"

"All right. Roast beef sandwich and a cup of coffee. Black, lots of sugar."

Stanton nodded and disappeared, to be immediately replaced in the doorway by Kaproski, who stuck his head in a trifle apologetically. "Sorry to bother you, Lieutenant," he said, "but I got a customer here won't talk to anybody but the chief salesman."

"Bring him in."

Clancy pushed back the notes he had taken and leaned back as Kaproski came in trailed by an old man carrying a battered homemade shoeshine box. There was great dignity to the deep-lined, brown face; his clothes were old and worn, with leather knee-patches, but the attempt at neatness could be discerned in the clean shirt buttoned to the throat, and the highly polished wrinkled shoes.

The old man hesitated in the doorway as if he were suddenly sorry he had come, but the weight of his problem drew him farther into the room. He stared at Clancy gravely.

"You boss?"

"Yes," Clancy said, equally grave. "What's your trouble?"

The old man looked about the room carefully before returning his eyes to Clancy's. "I been stole," he said simply.

Clancy nodded his head. "How much?"

The old man hesitated once more, as if fearful that the sum he was about to mention might not be believed. "Seesteen dollar," he finally said. The honesty of his jet-black eyes challenged objection.

Clancy merely nodded again. "Where did you keep it?"

This time the hesitation clearly showed a fear of revealing his hiding place to strangers, but memory that this hiding place could never again serve him broke down his reserve. He lifted the shoeshine box a trifle higher. "Here. Ol' empty can polish."

Clancy asked, "When did you miss it?"

"Now. I look. I don't know why. Money gone."

"Live alone?"

"Wit' gran'son." A shadow of alarm crept across the old man's face as he foresaw the possible direction the questioning might take. "But he's no take it. He's good boy."

"How old is he?"

"I tell you he's no take it. Someone else he's take it." He tore his eyes from Clancy's, as if by breaking their common glance he might also remove all danger of the other's suspicions. "He's go to school, study hard. He's no take it."

"Yeah." Clancy sighed, twirling his pencil. "Sure. Kaproski. Take his name and address, all the facts." He turned back to the old man. "We'll look into it. We'll try and find your sixteen dollars. Don't worry about it."

The old man shrugged fatalistically. He hadn't really expected any help—it was his panic at discovering the loss that had brought him to the precinct house. He followed Kaproski out of the room dejectedly.

Stanton came in moments later, carrying a damp bag. He set it on the desk and jerked his head toward the door. "What's old Martinez doing here?" he asked.

Clancy slit the stained bag up one side and took out a sodden sandwich and a cardboard cup with a loose cover. He looked at the unappetizing combination dubiously, picking up the sandwich. "Martinez?"

"The old man with the shoeshine box. What's his trouble?"

The sandwich tasted as bad as it looked. "You know him?"

"Sure. He shines shoes in front of Haley's Cigar Store over on Amsterdam. He's okay—a good joe."

The coffee was almost cold and had a faintly oily taste. It also tasted more than a little of cardboard. Clancy shuddered. "Know his grandson?"

"Also. Unfortunately. What's the beef?"

Clancy shoved the sandwich to one side. "Claims he's missing sixteen dollars he had hidden in his shoeshine box. In an old empty can of polish." Stanton snorted. Clancy looked at him curiously. "What's the matter? Don't you believe it?"

"Sure I believe it," Stanton said. "I never knew the old man to lie. But this is a mystery? Hell! His grandson took it. Who else?"

"The old man doesn't think so."

Stanton looked at Clancy with deep pity. "The old man wouldn't think so if he had caught the kid with his paw in the box. The old man thinks the sun rises and sets on that little punk." He sighed in disgust, shaking his head. "Well, anyways, I'm on my way. Keller called in and he's waiting for me. We'll give the place a real shakedown. Anything else?"

Clancy dropped the half-eaten sandwich into the wastebasket. He didn't even look at the coffee. "Yeah. This afternoon, on your way back from the house, stop by the school and bring in young Martinez." He looked up at Stanton. "You know where he goes to school?"

"He goes to Wilson High," Stanton said in a stunned voice, "but my God! We got a hundred important things on the fire, Lieutenant."

"Now we've got a hundred and one," Clancy said evenly. "Bring him in. After school."

"But, Lieutenant! For sixteen lousy bucks . . ."

Kaproski had come back in and was listening. Clancy allowed his glance to flicker between the two men; then he swiveled his chair, staring out of the window across the dirty tenements that formed the skyline.

"Where do you draw the line?" he asked quietly, as if he were really asking himself, as if he would really have liked to know. "If the bank on the corner was robbed of sixteen thousand dollars, would it make a case?"

"Well, sure, of course, but . . ."

"If Haley's was knocked off for sixteen hundred—" there was an almost dreamy quality to Clancy's voice—"would we be right in sending a man around?"

"Sure, but look, Lieutenant . . ."

Clancy swung around suddenly, savagely. "So I ask you, where do you draw the line?"

Kaproski always felt nervous when people got too serious. "Look, Lieutenant," he said helpfully. "We could raise sixteen bucks for the old man, just around the precinct here." He added, explaining, "If the kid took it, it's probably gone into the pool tables by now, anyhow."

Clancy looked at him with irritation. "This is a police station," he said coldly. "If that kid swiped sixteen bucks, or sixteen cents, I want to see him." He turned back to Stanton. "I said *if*. Which means you pick him up quietly, with no fuss. None of his friends need to know."

"What I'm getting at," Stanton said patiently, "the old man won't prosecute anyway, so why bother?"

"Look, Stanton," Clancy said in a tone of finality. "That old recluse that got killed this morning, that Willie-what's-his-name, he won't prosecute, either." He pushed the cold cup of coffee away from him in sudden anger. "I said I want to see the kid, and I want to see him!" He paused. "Anyway, I'd like to see the kind of kid an old man like Martinez breaks his back for!"

3:40 P.M. The telephone rang stridently. Clancy pushed aside the report he was working on, reaching across the wide, battered desk to scoop up the receiver.

"Clancy?"

"Yeah."

"Doc Freeman here. About that old man we found dead this morning."

"Yeah." Clancy reached for a pencil, inching his pad closer.

"It looks like he got a sharp poke in the stomach, high up, right under the rib cage. We opened him up and he had a chest cavity full of blood from a ruptured aorta. I'd judge it didn't take too much to break it. He wasn't in very good shape."

"How about the bloody nose?"

The doctor's voice became thoughtful. "In all probability, they were caused by the same thing. It looks like he was jabbed at with something—in the face, breaking the nose, and also in the stomach."

"Any idea of what that something could have been, Doc?"

"Something like an umbrella, maybe, or more probably something a bit thicker. The bruise area on the chest was very

184

restricted and quite regular. Something about as big around as a broomstick, I'd say offhand. It's hard to be definite, Clancy."

Clancy thought a while, twiddling his pencil. "Could it have been a crowbar, Doc? The back door looked like it might have been pried open, by a tramp, maybe."

"It would depend on what kind of a crowbar, Clancy. If he was poked with the sharp end, you'd expect a more linear bruise, or possibly even a lesion. And, of course, if the same tool was used to poke him in the face, a crowbar should have done a lot more damage. Personally, I would be inclined to doubt it was a crowbar."

There was silence for several seconds. Clancy sighed. "Well, thanks, Doc. When will I get it in writing?"

"It's being typed up now. Your copy should be out there by tonight. In more technical language, of course. We have to maintain and protect the profession, you know."

Clancy smiled. "Sure." A sudden thought came to him. "Say, Doc, what about his clothes?"

"They must still be downstairs. He was baby-naked when I got him. Hold the line. I'll switch."

Clancy waited while voices intermingled on the line; finally one dominated and the others disappeared. "Hello? Yes?"

"Jimmy? This is Lieutenant Clancy at the Fifty-second. That old man Doc Freeman just finished working on—what did you find in his clothes?"

"That's a funny thing, Lieutenant. Did you see him?"

"No."

The morgue attendant laughed. "You should of had. This character has on long underwear, them old-fashioned kind, bedroom slippers, each one different, a pair of patched work pants, one of them printed vests like them Mississippi gamblers used to wear, and on top of everything one of them turtle-neck sweaters. In June, yet! What a farce!"

"Hilarious," Clancy said drily. "What did you find in his pockets?"

"Not very much. In his pants pocket he had a rag I guess maybe he used for a handkerchief, and a key, maybe to the front door. In his fancy vest he had a couple of coins. Nothing else."

Clancy leaned forward. "Coins? What kind of coins?"

"Foreign, I guess. Anyhow, not U.S. One of the boys down here says they don't have no special value, though. One of them

185

was an English penny, I remember he said. Size of a lollipop."

Clancy made a note on his pad. "Jimmy, put the coins in an envelope and make out a receipt. I'll have them picked up."

"Want his other things?"

"Yeah. Send the sweater along, too. And the vest. Thanks, Jimmy."

"Any time, Lieutenant."

Clancy eased the receiver back on the bar, and the telephone rang immediately. He picked it up again, pulling his pad closer.

"Lieutenant? This is Stanton." There was deep satisfaction in the voice. "Guess what? Whoever clipped that old man this morning should have stuck around. We've been going through those old telephone directories. The first stack was clean, but after that we really hit paydirt. They've loaded. One and two-dollar bills stashed between the pages all over the place. Some of them old horse-blanket size, even—you remember them? So far we've got over four hundred bucks, and there's lots more phone books to go through, yet."

"How about the coins and stamps?"

"Oh, yeah. We found some stamps—three cigar boxes full." His voice became dubious. "I don't know anything about stamps, Lieutenant, but my guess is these ain't worth anything. Just regular stamps, torn off envelopes. If stamps are worth anything, they keep them in special books, don't they? These were just stuffed into cigar boxes."

"All of the stamps U.S.?"

"No. All sorts of countries. I'll bring them back with me— maybe one of the brains downtown can tell if they're worth anything. On the coins, not a sign."

"Okay. Leave Keller there and come on in. Let him keep looking." Clancy glanced at his wrist watch. "And don't forget to stop by and pick up young Martinez."

Stanton's voice dropped a notch. It was apparent he had been hoping Clancy would have forgotten. "Okay, Lieutenant. I'll also bring in the stamps and the dough we found so far." He could not keep a touch of malice from his voice. "I'll sit on it so the little punk don't swipe it!"

5:15 P.M. The boy was about seventeen, short but well-built, tightly packed into faded levis, with a loose-flowing black shirt open at the throat and buttoned at the wrist with white buttons. His hair glistened in a curving ducktail; his soft black eyes with sweeping lashes were expressionless in the mahogany face. He stood facing Clancy at ease, a slight smile on his full lips.

"You wanted to see me?" he asked.

"Sit down," Clancy said.

"If you don't mind, I'll stand," said the boy, smiling broadly.

Clancy's voice hardened. "Sit down!"

The boy's smile faded and he perched on the edge of a hard chair before the desk.

"Say, what is this, anyway? What's the big idea?"

Clancy just stared at him. The boy began to work up a frown of indignation. "I haven't done anything," he said finally, tight-lipped. "You can't hold me. What's the big idea?"

"Sixteen dollars is the big idea."

"What sixteen dollars?"

"You know what sixteen dollars," Clancy said.

"I don't know anything about any sixteen dollars," the boy said.

Clancy professed astonishment. "You don't know about the sixteen dollars your grandfather's missing?"

"He must have lost it," the kid said sullenly. "Keeping it in a stupid old tin can!"

"When did you find out about it?" Clancy asked softly.

The kid was silent, biting his lip, his brain working fast. "I heard some of the kids talking about it this morning at school."

"What kids? What were their names?" Clancy became efficient, reaching for his pad and pencil, eyeing the worried face sharply.

Stanton leaned over. "Exactly what time did you hear it? Think hard. What class were you in? Who were they? How many were there? Two? Three? Four? Come on, *think!*" The boy stared at his feet; fear had begun to creep into his eyes.

Kaproski leaned over, getting into the act. "What's the matter you can't remember? It's your own grandfather's dough, he supports you with it. Don't you want to help your grandfather? I thought you people stuck together in your family beefs? It's your own grandfather!"

The boy seemed to have shrunk on the edge of the chair. He wet his lips.

"All right," Clancy said quietly. "Why did you take it?"

The boy looked up, beaten. "I was only borrowing it," he said, suddenly looking about five years younger. "I was going to pay it back."

187

"When?" Stanton asked witheringly. "1975? When you got out of reform school?"

Clancy raised his hand. "Well, now," he said in a reasonable tone of voice. "If you were only borrowing it, that's a different matter. There's no law against borrowing money." The boy watched him suspiciously. "Of course, there's a law that says you have to pay it back. Just how do you plan on doing that?"

The boy looked at Clancy bitterly. "I'll pay it back. Don't worry."

Clancy shook his head. "I'm not worried. I know you'll pay it back. Sooner than you think." He rose to his feet, motioning Stanton and Kaproski to follow him into the corridor. "Stick around. Don't go away! I'll be right back."

Outside, Clancy took out his wallet and extracted a bill. "Kaproski, go out and get the complete fixings for shining shoes—polish, rags, brushes, the works. And don't forget to bring back a receipt." Kaproski grinned and taking the money, left. Clancy turned to Stanton. "How many men do we have altogether in the precinct?"

Stanton stared at him. "Full complement eighty-six. You know that, Lieutenant."

"Now that you mention it, I do indeed." A faint smile appeared on Clancy's face. "Well, you have the desk sergeant tell them as they come in that I'm not satisfied with the appearance of this precinct. From now on this is going to be the shiniest precinct in the city."

Stanton looked at him as if he were mad; then, shrugging, he went out toward the front desk.

Clancy went back into his office and sank into his chair, facing the sulky boy. "Tell me, son, what's your name?"

"Paulo."

"Paulo Martinez?"

The dark eyes flashed for a second. "Paulo Ignacio Maria de Martinez y Bertrand."

Clancy nodded his head. "That's quite a name." The sullen face across from his remained granite-like. "Well, Paulo, tell me: have you ever shined shoes?"

"Who, me?" The young voice was hesitant. "No."

"Well," Clancy said philosophically, "it's never too late to learn."

"What do you mean?" The suspicion in the boy's voice owed everything to fear of being made fun of.

"I mean what I say," Clancy said coldly. "I mean you're going to earn back the money you swiped from your grandfather—by shining shoes. All the shoes in the precinct."

There was a few minutes of silence; then Kaproski came in with a bundle and laid it on the desk. Clancy unwrapped it and pushed the contents across the desk toward the boy.

"You're in business." He turned to Kaproski. "Our friend here is going to earn back the dough he borrowed—by shining coppers' shoes. You better be the cashier. I'm not so sure he has a good head for financial matters."

"How much does he charge?" Kaproski asked interestedly.

"Twenty cents," Clancy said.

The boy started to speak and then had to stop to clear his throat. "The old—my grandfather gets twenty-five a shine. And tips."

Clancy looked at the boy coldly. "Your grandfather knows how to shine shoes." He thought a minute. "On the other hand, if you don't do them right the first time, you'll have to do them over. I'll go along with the quarter a shine. But no tips."

The kid picked up the bundle of polish and brushes wrapped in a clean flannel cloth. Without another word he turned toward the door.

"By the way," Clancy said. "Is there anywhere we can get in touch with your grandfather to let him know you'll be getting home late?"

"He never expects me before midnight anyway." The boy paused. "He usually leaves me something on the table to eat when I get back from school. Can I go home to eat?"

"I'll send out for a sandwich for you," Clancy said. "And milk. That'll be another fifty or sixty cents." He sighed deeply, shaking his head. "You keep borrowing at this rate, and you'll never get out of debt!"

11:45 A.M. Stanton was really impressed. "The telephone directories had nine hundred and seventy-five dollars," he said the next morning. "Keller is going though the newspapers and magazines now. All of the cigar boxes were empty except for those three that held the stamps. Of course we're miles from being finished looking, but nothing on any coins so far. The brains downtown say the stamps aren't worth anything."

Clancy turned to Kaproski, who began his report, referring to papers in his hand.

189

"Records say the house was in his name, free and clear. Taxes are paid every year by some law firm downtown—Ryder and Wilson. His father set the deal up in his will way back in 1919." He looked at the other two innocently, anticipating their reaction to his next announcement. "Willie also had a slight bank account. Of a little better than three hundred thousand bucks." Stanton whistled. Kaproski nodded, pleased with the result. "Yeah. A nut—a real nut." He returned to his notes. "The law firm says Willie never made a will. They were trustees for his old man—Willie got a hundred dollars every month. I guess when his old man set that up, it looked like a lot of money. Anyway, the lawyers say Willie never asked for any more."

"The economical type," Clancy said. "What else?"

"That's it. Oh, yeah, he has—had—has, I guess, a sister, a Mrs. Henry Jorrens. I guess she'll get the works. She lives over on West End."

Clancy nodded. "I know. I've asked her to drop in this afternoon, after lunch. Anything else?"

"That's it, so far."

Clancy cleared his desk and reached into a drawer, bringing out the sweater and vest, and a small envelope which he placed to one side. "These are the things he had on, up on top, when he got it. There's blood on the sweater up around the neck from his bloody nose, but that's all. What interests me is this tear here—Doc doesn't think he could have been hit by anything sharp like a crowbar, but I figure his clothes might have softened the blow. And the sweater's torn."

Kaproski leaned forward. "That ain't torn. Not recently, anyways. You can see where he passed a crochet neddle through to catch the ends and fix it. That was yarn-sewn. He sure didn't do that after he was hit."

"Crochet needle?" Clancy looked at Kaproski in astonishment.

"Yarn-sewn," Stanton said, smiling. "Mother Kaproski!"

"Sure I know about knitting," Kaproski said defensively. "Eight months in a Naval hospital—physical therapy, they called it."

Clancy took up the vest. It was an old-patterned type, with button-down pockets, patched under one arm, but intact and clean in front. With a sigh he swept the sweater and vest into a drawer.

"Well," he said, "that wasn't much help. I'd certainly like to know what he was killed with. I've a feeling it would help." He opened the envelope, upending it. Two coins rolled out, which he neatly trapped and slid before the others. "An English penny and what's this? One cruzeiro? That's Brazil." He lifted it. "Feels like tin." He spun it with his fingers, watched it come to a teetering halt, and pushed the coins together. "So? What do we know?"

"We know he was a nut," Stanton said. "We also know he's dead. And that's just about all we do know."

"He may have been a nut," Kaproski said, as if in defense of the dead man, "but he was a rich nut."

"Yeah," Clancy said. "That may still be the answer." He glanced at his wrist watch. "Anyway, it's time for lunch."

"Want a sandwich from across the street, Lieutenant?"

"Artists and writers," Clancy said, sweeping the two foreign coins into his pocket. "Maybe they need to starve to do a good job, but I never heard it said of detectives. I'm getting a decent meal today." He pushed himself to his feet. "One o'clock back here. Ready or not."

2:00 P.M. The woman sitting opposite Clancy was dressed in dark, drab colors, and had a worried, motherly air. Clancy judged her to be well into her fifties, about five-four in height, about one-fifty in weight. The fur-piece about her neck had obviously seen better days. The whole family, Clancy thought sourly, likes to dress warm.

"Over thirty years," she was saying. "It was a terrible shock when we heard. Willie was—odd, you know. Papa felt Willie needed some sort of—well, protection, but Willie . . ." Her voice faded as she smiled at them doubtfully, twitching her fur to a new position where it once again assumed an obedient, shape-less slump.

"Yeah," Clancy said. He glanced down at his notes. "The estate was divided evenly between you and your brother?"

The woman leaned forward, opened her mouth to speak, and then paused. A slight edge crept into her motherliness. "I'm sure you are familiar with the terms of my father's will, Lieutenant," she said, a bit sharply. "Fortunately, Henry and I have never lacked for anything, so that never made any differ-ence. When Papa left everything to Willie, we were quite pleased." She examined her words and revised them slightly. "At least, we weren't displeased. And nobody can *say* we were.

191

After all, Willie was incapable of supporting himself, and that has never been Henry's problem."

Clancy's eyes avoided the bedraggled fur-piece, the worn and shiny blouse, the hair in need of a permanent. "Your brother never tried to contact you in all these years?"

"My brother . . ." She looked about and seemed to find sympathetic support in the frozen faces of Kaproski and Stanton. "Willie always felt that we didn't understand him—that is, that nobody understood him. When Henry and I were first married we offered Willie a place to live with us, but he preferred to live alone."

"Your husband always got along well with . . . ah, Willie?"

"My husband? Henry? Of course. Actually, they haven't seen each other in years and years, but when we were all young, they were quite good friends." She laughed nervously. "My husband is a bit of a recluse himself, you see, nowadays. He was wounded in the war and always felt that younger men should have . . ." Her voice faded dramatically as her smile encompassed them all, as if to say, These Men!

Clancy plowed on. "Tell me, Mrs. Jorrens, do you remember your brother being particularly interested in stamps? Or coins?"

"Oh, yes!" She sat up straighter, as if happy that she could finally be helpful. "He collected stamps and coins ever since I can remember. Papa started him off, you know. Papa used to travel quite a bit when he was younger, and he brought back these stamps and coins and always gave them to Willie. Tell me, Lieutenant, do you think Willie was killed for his collections?"

"It's happened," Clancy said noncommittally. "People have killed for less." He looked at the notes he had taken, then back to the taut face before him. "Thank you very much, Mrs. Jorrens. If there is anything else, we'll know where to get in touch with you."

The woman rose hesitantly. "Lieutenant," she said. "I'd like to offer a reward. For anyone who brings in information . . ."

"Of course," Clancy said, avoiding her eyes. "How much are you thinking of offering?"

She looked at the three silent faces in turn. "I don't know," she finally said vaguely. "I don't know about these things. Would five hundred dollars be all right?"

"As much as you want," Clancy said. "I'll tell them downtown. If you wish, they'll advise the press."

192

"That will be fine," she said, relieved, as if the hardest and most important part of her trip had been accomplished. "Thank you very much, Lieutenant."

Clancy rose as she swept out, her fur-piece sliding from her neck as if it had been caught unawares by her sudden move and was hurrying to catch up. There was a few minutes of silence after she had left. Stanton was the first to break it.

"I think maybe Papa had a funny idea of protecting Willie," he said softly.

"Maybe," Clancy said. "Maybe not. Anyway, it gives us some work to do." He sat down again, pulling his pad toward him, as Stanton and Kaproski hunched closer.

7:00 P.M. "I got some more dope on brother Willie," Kaproski said the next day, reaching for his notebook.

"Let's hold it," Clancy said. "Stanton called in a while ago—he'll be here in a few minutes. Might as well look at it all together." A short dark figure passed in the hall. "Reminds me. How's that Martinez kid doing?"

"Not bad," Kaproski said in a pleased voice. "He catches on fast. Personally, I think he's beginning to even like it. The boys have been pretty good with him. He's not so hard-mouth like he was at first."

"How much is in the kitty?" Clancy asked.

"Over fifteen bucks as of late last night," Kaproski said. "Of course, there's still the outfit to pay for—that's three-forty, plus the fifty cents from Monday and sixty-five from yesterday. He brought his own sandwiches along today."

"Good," Clancy said. The young head poked itself in the doorway just then, and encouraged by the silence, came in carrying a new shoeshine box.

"Lieutenant," he said softly. "Can I get you now?"

"What? Oh, sure." Clancy slid one foot onto the top of the box. "Where'd you get the new outfit?"

The boy grinned. "Made it in wood-working class."

"Like shining shoes, huh?"

The grin faded. "I like making money," he said suddenly, almost harshly. He got out his rags and went to work as Stanton came in, pushing his hat back on his head.

"Let's go," Clancy said. He turned to Kaproski. "All right. What else did you find out about Willie?"

"He never got close to the war," Kaproski said. "The lawyers

193

said that Henry blew his stack once about Willie being a slacker. Actually, the draft board turned Willie down for being too old, bum health, and also because he was slightly nuts."

"Henry should talk," Stanton said derisively. "He managed to get a desk job as a result of some pretty fancy wire-pulling, pals from the good-old-days. And that famous war wound of his—he got that in London. He was run down by a bread truck during a blackout. They did a bum job on his leg, and it left him crippled." He looked at Clancy steadily. "Our friend Henry uses a cane."

Clancy drummed the desk with his fingers.

"A cane could have done it," Kaproski said.

"Sure," Clancy said. He felt a prod at his foot and automatically switched feet on the shoeshine box. "Sure a cane could have done it. Also a crutch, or a pool cue. Or a drum-major's baton, or a hoe handle." He sat thinking, his fingers tapping the desk. "If it was Henry, why did he wait thirty years?"

Stanton shrugged. "Maybe he didn't need the dough until now."

"His old lady," Kaproski said, "she didn't look like they were in the chips."

Clancy frowned. "If we could only place him there," he said absently. "You sure none of the neighbors saw anybody? Nobody?"

"We can check them again," Stanton said. "Maybe that reward will wake some of them up, but we went over them pretty carefully." He grinned. "Laugh like hell if the old lady put husband Henry on the spot with that reward gimmick."

"We'll have to go over the neighbors again," Clancy said. "And Kaproski, you go back to that law firm and find out what you can about Henry's bank account. Maybe he developed a taste for blondes, or the horses, late in life." He felt a professional tap on his shoe, lifted his foot free, and admired the gleam. "Good job," he said, reaching into his pocket, and then giving the boy a coin.

The young face fell. "Aw, shucks, Lieutenant," the boy said. "Not twice! I'll never get off the hook that way!"

Clancy looked down in surprise to see what the complaint was. He saw that he had inadvertently handed the boy the Brazilian cruzeiro. With a smile he started to take back the coin, when his hand suddenly stiffened.

"Not twice?" he said slowly. "What do you mean, not twice?"

He looked down at the pouting face below him steadily. "Who slipped you the other one?"

The boy froze. Suddenly both Stanton and Kaproski saw the light.

"Who gave you the other one, kid?" Kaproski asked softly.

The boy sat there, biting his lip. Stanton exploded.

"Damn it! Who gave it to you, you little punk?" he cried.

The boy wet his lips. "I can take it," he mumbled.

Stanton took him by the shoulder, shaking him. "What kind of an answer is that?" he roared. " 'I can take it!' What kind of a stupid answer is that?"

Kaproski brushed Stanton's hand from the boy's hunched shoulder. "Let me do it, Stan," he said. He leaned over quietly. "Look, son, nobody's trying to pin anything on you. We just want to know one thing—who gave you a coin like that one? It's important, son."

The boy looked up, hesitating. "One of the cops," he finally said. His eyes dropped to the floor. "I figured he was just trying to give me the needle, so I kept my mouth shut. I can take it," he added defiantly.

"Which one of the cops?" Kaproski asked, still in the same quiet voice.

"I don't know his name," the boy said sullenly. "A big one. With red hair."

"Timmons!" Clancy said, striking one fist into the other palm. "It wasn't a cane—it was a patrolman's night stick!" He looked at Stanton. "Where is he now?"

"Should be on his beat," Stanton said.

"Kaproski, go through his locker. And then you and Stanton check his home." Clancy turned to the boy. "You stay here, son. Right in this room. You may be a valuable witness."

10:45 P.M. "He had the coins in an old suitcase on a shelf in his bedroom," Stanton said, as if Timmons were not in the room at all, sitting quiet and narrow-eyed, watching them all. "And over a thousand bucks, some of them that old-fashioned big-bill kind." He looked over at the silent uniformed figure contemptuously, as if it were a desk, or a cabinet—anything but a human body. "He must have thought he had the works before he rang in. Or maybe he was pressed for time. And I guess he didn't clean out his pockets too good if he left that coin in with the change."

195

"We found a stamp collection, too," Kaproski added. "A regular one, in them big books. I guess he took one look at them stamps in the cigar boxes and knew they weren't worth anything." His eyes also flickered over the quiet figure as if it weren't there. "I guess maybe he don't know too much about coins."

Clancy looked at the silent figure sitting beside his desk. "Well, Timmons?"

"The old man was nuts," Timmons said, speaking slowly, thinking. "He come at me like a maniac and I had to cool him. It was self-defense," he added darkly.

"Sure," Clancy said. "And, of course, once he was dead you took the dough so the rich old man wouldn't have any trouble getting into heaven. Very commendable."

"So I took the dough," Timmons said. "So what's that? So I get kicked off the force and maybe six months. So what?"

"How did he come at you?" Clancy asked interestedly. "Did he have a weapon?"

Timmons hesitated, trying to remember what the others had found. "No. But he had his hands, and you should have seen him. I put up my club and he run right into it, smashing his nose. And when he seen the blood, he really went nuts. He plowed at me like a crazy guy, so I poked him in the stomach." He shrugged. "He folded over and when I looked at him, he was dead."

Clancy glared at him. "God, I hate a crooked cop!" he muttered. "The day you burn will be a personal pleasure for me!"

"Burn?" Timmons' voice was almost scornful.

"Burn," Clancy said in a tight voice. "Yeah, I said burn!" He leaned over his desk, enumerating on his fingers. "One: there's no jury in the world is going to believe that a cop weighing over two hundred pounds needs to use a night stick to cool a sick, old man. Two: you poked him in the stomach first, knocking him out; and then, when he was on the floor, helpless, you laid your club across his face."

"Who, me?" Timmons said.

"You," Clancy said. "If you had poked him in the face first, like you said, there would have been blood on your night stick, and some of it would have come off when you jabbed him in the stomach. It would have marked his sweater—*but his sweater wasn't marked*. No, you poked him in the stomach first, and when he was down, out cold, you laid your club across his face."

196

He looked at the silent cop with disgust. "Take him away," he said, swinging his chair toward the open window and the soft screams of children running in the June night below. "Take him out of my sight!"

Stanton dragged the shocked man to his feet. "You're stupid," he said conversationally. "Real stupid. If you'd said you found him dead, it might have held us up a while—not long, but a while." He pulled the unresisting arm to the door.

The boy had sat there wide-eyed. Now he cleared his throat. "Lieutenant," he asked.

"Yeah? What?" Clancy looked over at him, as if seeing him for the first time.

"Is he—did he kill that old man?"

"Yes, he killed him," Clancy said savagely.

The kid said softly, "I'm sorry I stole that dough from my grandfather."

Clancy suddenly realized the connection. "You earned it back, kid, plus a reward. You're in for a reward, son." He straightened up in his chair, erasing the last interview from his mind. "Five hundred bucks. What do you think you'll do with it?"

The boy thought carefully, this new intelligence wiping the thought of Timmons and his crime from his mind.

"I don't know," he said slowly. "Will five hundred dollars pay for a regular shoeshine stand, Lieutenant? Big enough for me and my grandfather?"

"I honestly don't know," Clancy said wearily. "I don't know what pays for anything any more."

The kid sat silent after this inexplicable statement. Kaproski cleared his throat. "Better go along, kid," he said gently, and eased the boy from the room. He turned to Clancy. "Lieutenant," he began.

"God, but I hate a crooked cop!" Clancy said bitterly.

Kaproski nodded. "Sure. But at least you did something for that kid. If you hadn't helped him, he could have ended up like Timmons, or maybe even worse."

Clancy sighed. His eyes fell to his gleaming shoes, and he looked up at Kaproski somberly. "Yeah. Well, you can't lose them all, I suppose."

SMASH AND GRAB

BY HENRY WADE

(No photograph available of Mr. Wade)

Henry Wade is the pseudonym of Major Sir Henry Lancelot Aubrey-Fletcher, born in 1887 in Surrey, England. Of his twenty detective novels, only thirteen have been published in the United States, and his two most important volumes of short stories have never appeared here. His major fictional creation was Inspector John Poole. He was important in defining post-World War II values in England and in explicating the psychology and mores of the English people. His early novels, such as *The Verdict of You All* (1926), question the entire legal system of Great Britain. He died in 1969.

CRASH! AND THE TINKLE of falling glass.

In a few seconds a group of staring people had collected outside the broken window of a jeweler's shop in Old Bond Street. A police constable who had just previously turned into Burlington Gardens came hurrying across the road; a young man who had been passing in a coupé car pulled up at the curb, jumped out, and pushed his way through the crowd behind the policeman.

"Now then; what's this?" demanded the latter, with no great originality.

Two hatless gentlemen in morning coats, who had hurriedly emerged from the doorway of Marto's, broke into eager speech, declaring that an attempt had been made to rob their shop. The voice of a small boy penetrated through the hubbub.

" 'E done it. I see 'im."

The urchin was pointing at a little man in a shabby black coat, who instantly blushed and stammered unintelligible denials.

"Anyone know anything about this?" demanded the policeman fiercely. "Anyone see anything?"

No one, it appeared, had seen anything, except the errand-boy, who had seen the little man in black passing Marto's when the crash occurred. After one glance at the suspect the policeman commanded silence.

"No car seen?" he asked. "No one jumping out or running away?"

"I was passing in my car," said the well-dressed man who had followed the policeman through the crowd. "I didn't notice anything. I don't think any car stopped or drove away."

The lack of witnesses would have been mysterious at any other time of day, but Bond Street in the luncheon hour is deserted.

Another policeman had by now appeared and, at the request of the first, was taking names and addresses—the errand-boy, Jack Smirke, employed by Toole Brothers, fruiterers, Piccadilly; the suspect, Robert Wallop, clerk to James and James, solicitors of Lincoln's Inn; the young man in the coupé, Lord Feathergill, the "Albany."

"I want to cover this, constable," whispered the young peer.

199

"I'm a gossip-writer, you know, for the *Sunday Post*, but if I can get a scoop on this it'll do me good with my paper. If you've done with these chaps . . ."

In the meantime the first constable had entered Marto's shop and put a call through to Vine Street police station.

"Another smash-and-grab, sir, in Old Bond Street, Marto's," said the station-sergeant to Divisional Detective-Inspector Halliday. "Nothing stolen, Porter thinks, and no clear evidence as to what happened."

"Hell!" said Inspector Halliday. "I'll go round at once. You'll have to pass this on to Chief-Inspector Holby at the Yard. Quick as you can."

Grabbing his bowler hat, Inspector Halliday was gone.

Normally an incident like this would be dealt with by the divisional detective without any reference to Scotland Yard, but it happened that there had been a recent epidemic of smash-and-grab raids and the Commissioner of Metropolitan Police, irritated by pinpricks from the Press, had put the whole subject in the hands of Chief-Inspector Holby, at Headquarters, to "correlate, co-ordinate, explore all avenues," and generally take the blame.

Like Halliday, Chief-Inspector Holby also cursed when he got Vine Street's message. These raids were maddening; they were extraordinarily difficult to anticipate—you could not have a constable outside every jeweler's shop—and they usually ended in the discovery of a stolen car abandoned in a side street; there was a lot of hard work and no kudos at all.

But like Halliday, also, Chief-Inspector Holby wasted no time.

"Car!" he snapped at his clerk. "Sergeant Bevan and two detective-constables. Jump to it."

So it was that John Bragg entered upon his first case as a member of the C.I.D. Chief Constable Thurston had been as good as his word; the country policeman had said good-bye to his Downshire comrades, had passed through a vigorous process of training, education, and general smartening-up, had rediscovered his London, renewed his old friendships, refurbished his powers of observation and deduction . . . and was ready. A telephone call, a sharp order, and Detective-Constable Bragg stepped into the police car behind Chief-Inspector

Holby and in an indecently short time was stepping out in Old Bond Street.

The crowd had by now dispersed, a constable standing outside Marto's door to keep onlookers on the move and to guard the broken window. Inside, Divisional Detective Inspector Halliday was amplifying the inquiries already begun by the first police-officer on the spot. There were no customers in the shop, but Jack Smirke, Robert Wallop, Lord Feathergill and two other passers-by had been asked to await the arrival of Chief-Inspector Holby.

The young gossip-writer had made two unsuccessful applications for the use of the telephone—to tell his story to his editor; he was now looking fidgety and annoyed. Chief-Inspector Holby, who knew him by name and reputation, heard what little he had to say and let him go. A closer questioning of the lad Smirke soon broke through the tissue of imagination which had cloaked his story, and Robert Wallop's ordeal was at an end. Of the two other witnesses, one had been attracted by the passing of Lord Feathergill's car, and one by the complete absence of any "grab" in connection with the smash. Chief-Inspector Holby dismissed them all and gave his orders.

Detective-Sergeant Bevan was to question shopkeepers, commissionaires, etc., on the opposite side of Bond Street, from which a view of the incident might have been obtained. Bragg was to do the same on the near side of the street. The other detective, Patterson, would stay with Chief-Inspector Holby.

Having set his subordinates to work, Holby turned his attention to the staff of the shop. The manager reported that, so far as he could tell, nothing had been stolen; indeed it would not have been possible to "grab" anything from the outside because a fine steel grille protected the contents of that part of the window. When the smash occurred there had been a rush to the door of the shop but there had only been two customers in at the time and the manager had instantly placed himself close to the window in a position from which he could see to it that nothing was taken from the inside, while carefully watching the rest of the shop. He produced a large lump of shapeless lead which had fallen between the glass and the steel grille. He had himself extracted it, using a handkerchief so as not to mark it with his own fingerprints.

"Good man," said Chief-Inspector Holby.

"What I can't understand," said the gratified manager, "is

why anyone should smash the window at all. It seems obvious that that thing couldn't smash the grille."

"Yes," said Holby, "but it seems fairly clear that no attempt was made to grab; there's some other explanation of this game, I fancy."

In the meantime Bragg, inwardly boiling with excitement, was settling down to his first C.I.D. job. The premises next to Marto's on the north side were occupied by a firm of furriers. There was no commissionaire and the only man in the place was a packer and general handyman; he had been in his own cubby-hole at the back of the shop and, though he had heard the commotion, he had seen nothing. The manageress reported that her establishment had been empty at the time; when the crash was heard she and her assistants had, naturally, hurried to the door to see what was happening—these raids were rather getting on everyone's nerves, the manageress explained, and furs could be grabbed almost as easily as jewels—but they had seen nothing beyond the gathering of the crowd.

Next door to the furrier was a hairdresser; here a commissionaire was commonly employed but he had been "off" for his lunch at the time and had only returned after the event. There had been just enough business doing to keep the lunch-hour staff employed; nobody could tell Bragg anything.

So it continued up that side of the street for another fifty yards and then Bragg retraced his steps and started on the other side of Marto's—the Piccadilly side. Here was an art gallery; in the window was one oil painting which appeared to the detective quite remarkably dull and unattractive; velvet curtains partly screened the interior of the gallery. Here again there was no commissionaire, and Bragg, not looking like a wealthy collector of art treasures, was received by the manager with chilly dignity. The manager admitted hearing the crash of glass; there had been three visitors in the gallery at the time, besides the two assistants and himself; everyone, he thought, had gone straight to the door to see what had happened but, so far as he knew, no one had seen anything significant; certainly he had not himself. The two assistants confirmed this.

It occurred to Bragg that he ought, perhaps, to question the customers who had been present in the neighboring shops; it was not likely that they had seen any more than the staff, but "no stone must be left unturned."

"Can you tell me the names of your customers who were here at the time, sir?" asked Bragg.

The manager, who had thawed somewhat on learning the detective's identity and business, gave a wintry smile.

"I don't know that I can exactly describe them all as customers," he said. "In a gallery like this we have a number of visitors who have no intention whatever of buying anything. Some of them come because they love to see beautiful things, some because they like to be able to say they have seen them—we have many *objets d'art* which are world famous, details of which appear in the Press and are talked about at dinner-tables.

"This morning, for instance," continued the manager, "we had old Lord Bicester. He comes two or three times a week, generally during the luncheon hour when he can examine at his leisure; to the best of my belief he has never bought anything, but he has once or twice brought friends who have bought, and in any case he has 'an air'—we welcome him."

Then there had been, this morning, a young lady who had been two or three times recently; she had evidently been fascinated by the collection of *chinoiserie* which he was showing this month—the manager pointed to a series of shelves at the end of the room; on one occasion she had brought a young gentleman and it would appear that she had been tempting him to buy something for her—but the young man had not fallen; nevertheless . . .

"Who was this young lady?" asked Bragg, his patience wearing thin.

The manager shrugged. "We have had no occasion to ask either her name or her address."

"Oh, well, it probably doesn't matter. And the other one? I think you said there were three customers . . . visitors here at the time."

"Ah, the other one," said the manager, brightening visibly; "the other one was Mr. Hiram Potter, collector for Mr. Drew Pierman of San Francisco. Now Mr. Potter, when he comes, comes on business. This morning he wished to see . . ."

Bragg learned—in time—that Mr. Potter might be found at Grey's Hotel in Albemarle Street.

So the budding detective continued his walk down the west side of Bond Street, learning nothing but gathering a list of customers to be questioned—a list which became rather overpowering in its length.

Bragg returned to the Yard and reported his failure to discover anyone who could throw any light on the incident.

"Shall I go and see all these customers whose addresses I got, sir?" he asked.

"Not worth it," said his chief. "It's fairly clear that there was no real attempt to grab; quite likely that the whole thing was a practical joke."

Bragg hesitated, undertain of his own status in this new sphere; he did not want to court a snub, but he felt an urge never to leave a case alone till it was cleared up.

"Might I have a look through your report when it's ready, sir?" he asked.

Chief-Inspector Holby raised his eyebrows; a snub was imminent, but he had heard something about Bragg's record in Downshire.

"Got an idea?" he asked.

"Not at the moment, sir. I don't know enough."

"All right. Write out your own report first and then you can see mine and Sergeant Bevan's."

An hour later he was back in the chief-inspector's room.

"Well, what about that idea?" the latter asked.

"I just wondered, sir, whether this window-smashing was just a bit of camouflage to distract attention from something else."

"You mean the grab might have been done from the inside? I thought of that, but nothing's missing. Besides, I made inquiries about both the customers who were in Marto's at the time; one was young Bellowby in the Blues, choosing an engagement ring; the other was Mrs. Hilton-Carstairs bringing her tiara to be re-set. Both full of money and hardly partners in a smash-and-grab raid. One of the assistants might have been in it, of course, but they've all got cast-iron reputations and in any case, how could they get away with the stuff? If anything had been stolen they'd all have been watched and probably searched."

Bragg's large chin, symbol of obstinacy, led him on when no doubt it would have been wiser to retreat.

"There's other shops, sir; maybe there was a theft in one of them."

Chief-Inspector Holby stared at him. Gradually a smile spread over his face.

"Well, you've got the right spirit, my lad," he said. "Go and find out . . . if you can."

So Bragg returned to Old Bond Street and, choosing first the most promising objective, re-entered the art gallery on the Piccadilly side of Marto's. As it was now very near to closing-time he was not received with open arms, but his first question startled the manager, Mr. Dolphin, into acute attention.

"You've not missed anything yourself, I suppose, sir?"

"Missed anything? What do you mean?"

"It's just an idea that occurred to me, sir. There was nothing stolen from Marto's, but it's just possible that someone may be taking advantage of this smash-and-grab scare to cover a different game. Do you mind telling me, sir, what happened in here when that crash was heard? I think you said you all went to the door, customers and staff, to see what was happening."

"Yes, we did; certainly we did. It was only natural to do so, because there have been so many of these raids lately that we jumped to the conclusion that this was another—there being a jeweler's next door."

"Exactly, sir. And is it possible that in the confusion something got stolen? I've no reason for saying that that happened here any more than in any other shop, but you told me that you'd got a lot of very valuable articles—some of them not too big to slip into a pocket, perhaps."

"Good heavens, what a horrible idea," said Mr. Dolphin. "But no, certainly I should have missed anything at once if it had been taken. I know exactly what is displayed—"

"Yes, sir," interrupted Bragg, "but would you mind making sure?"

The manager looked quickly round, his assistants followed suit. One of them bent over a table in the center of the gallery, where half a dozen small green figures—bronzes—were displayed on the table.

"Mr. Dolphin, would you look here, sir, please."

The manager hurried to the table and after a whispered colloquy, thrust a pair of glasses on to his nose and picked up one of the bronzes with trembling fingers. He gave a gasp of horror.

"My God! This . . . this is not . . . this is a fake! Someone has substituted this! . . ."

Bragg suppressed a chuckle of satisfaction.

"A valuable article, sir?" he asked.

"Valuable? These are the Pallas bronzes! I bought them myself at the Ruppell sale last month. I paid . . . that is to say, in the proper quarter they are worth four figures apiece."

"And they have all been . . . exchanged, sir?"

By this time Mr. Dolphin had completed his examination of the six figures. He put down the last with a sigh of relief.

"No, thank goodness," he said. "Only two—these two."

"Just go nicely into the tail pockets of a gentleman's coat, sir . . . or perhaps into a lady's vanity bag if it was a good-sized one." Mr. Dolphin gasped. "Could it have happened some other day, sir, and you did not notice it till now?"

"Certainly not! These are good imitations but they would have been noticed directly they were handled. I put them away myself every night . . . I should have put them away in a few minutes now . . . I should have noticed at once . . ."

"I wonder," thought Bragg to himself. "You had to have a good squint at them through your glasses before you made sure, even when you were looking for trouble." Aloud he said: "How could those figures have been copied, sir? They have not been out of your hands?"

"Not for a moment."

"Could anyone have drawn them . . . or photographed them?"

"No . . . but yes! They were photographed, with other items from the Ruppell collection, at the time of the sale."

One of the assistants, who had been rummaging in a desk at the back of the Gallery, appeared with a page taken from the previous month's *Collector*. On the page were some excellent photographs of two bronze figures, taken from different angles: the two figures which had been "exchanged."

With patient thoroughness, Bragg questioned Mr. Dolphin and his staff as to the exact movements of every person in the gallery when the crash was heard. At first, it seemed, only Mr. Potter and the unknown young lady, with one of the assistants, had gone to the door; then, as the excitement outside increased, all had followed suit, even Lord Bicester so far forgetting his dignity as to jostle for a view. And for part of that time neither Mr. Dolphin nor his assistants could swear as to the exact whereabouts of the unknown young lady; she had been the first to dash to the door but after that, it appeared, had given way to the slower but no less anxious males—given way . . . and slipped back into the room? just for the few seconds required in which to exchange two slim bronze figures with two others taken from her bag? It was not impossible.

But who was she? No one in the gallery knew. Her description was vague, as derived from the observation of three men whose eye for beauty was accustomed to judge inanimate objects. "A pretty girl"; "fair hair"; "no, brown"; "about normal height"; "about twenty-five"; "no, younger"; "older"; "a dark coat and skirt"—this latter appeared the only object of common consent; pretty hopeless. Bragg asked them all to think it over at their leisure and returned to tell his tale to Chief-Inspector Holby.

With the Downshire Constabulary, Bragg had been inclined to keep things to himself until his case was practically complete, but here in the C.I.D. he was only a very small cog in a highly specialized machine. He had to make his report, and then do just what he was told. Chief-Inspector Holby was interested but doubtful; Bragg's theory postulated team-work of a very high order.

If the unknown young lady had taken the opportunity caused by the commotion to make that exchange she must have known that the commotion was about to occur. The throwing of the lump of lead had not been seen by anybody; that implied that someone had very carefully watched his time and opportunity. Who? An errand-boy strolling along with a basket?—no one would notice him if he dawdled; a young gentleman in a motor car, cruising the streets? a little black-coated clerk admiring the pretty things in the windows?—what, by the way, had Mr. Wallop of Lincoln's Inn been doing in Bond Street in the luncheon hour?

All those points required further investigation, and investigated they would be by the machinery of the Yard. But the most immediate question appeared to be the identity of the young lady interested in *chinoiserie*, and to that task Chief-Inspector Holby generously detailed his new recruit. Bragg spent two days on the job, questioning Lord Bicester and Mr. Potter, questioning the commissionaires and staffs of neighboring shops, questioning taxi-drivers and policemen and scavengers, re-questioning Mr. Dolphin and his staff . . . and learning nothing.

Then a new line of inquiry occurred to him and, rashly, he followed it on his own initiative without reference to his chief. The photographs of those figures in the *Collector* and other papers; millions of people had seen them and anyone might

207

have worked on those copies from the mere photographs in the papers. But could anyone have had better opportunity to study them, to measure, to handle? Consulting Mr. Dolphin's observant young assistant, Bragg learned that photographs of the bronze figures had appeared in the *Collector*, the *World of Art*, the *Sentinel*, the *Sunday Post*, and the *Weekly Critic*. He also learned the name of the auctioneers who had conducted the Ruppell sale.

Messrs. Bosby are world-famous auctioneers and do not welcome inquiries from the police. Still, Bragg learned that the photographs appearing in the papers had been taken by Messrs. Bosby's own photographer, who had been in their employ for thirty years and was a man of unfathomable respectability; the photographs had been supplied to a representative of the Press on request. On this point of interest Messrs. Bosby assured Bragg that only one request for photographs had come from the Press, and that was made by a representative of the Waterfield Group—yes, of course, that would include the *Collector*, the *World of Art*, the *Weekly Critic*, the *Sentinel* and the *Sunday Post*.

Disappointed but vaguely conscious of some chord of familiarity, Bragg returned to the Yard and re-read the *dossier* of the case. Twenty minutes later he was back at Bosby's. Yes, wearily, Waterfield's representative, besides asking for photographs, had asked for information about various items of the Ruppell collection on which to base an article; he had been allowed to examine what he wished and might possibly have been able to measure and even weigh in his hand such items as the Pallas bronzes—naturally, under observation.

Hot on his new scent, Bragg repaired to the huge edifice which houses the Waterfield group of papers and asked for the Editor of the *Sunday Post*; the latter in due course informed Bragg that an article on the Ruppell collection, with photographs, had been put in by Lord Feathergill, who not only was responsible for the *Post's* gossip page but from time to time contributed articles on artistic subjects.

After that things ran smoothly enough for the police—up to a point. On further inquiry little facts about Lord Feathergill emerged in support of Bragg's theory. Lord Feathergill was left-handed and so could have thrown a lump of lead through the near-side window of his coupé as he cruised down Bond Street; Lord Feathergill had been a cricketer and so could have thrown the said lump with accuracy and despatch; Lord Feathergill had been wearing gloves—a point well remembered by the first constable on the scene—and so could have avoided leaving his fingerprints upon the missile, which had in fact been free of any such evidence.

Doubts were raised as to why, if he had thrown the missile, Lord Feathergill had been so foolish as to thrust himself before the attention of the police, but here Chief-Inspector Holby's wide experience suggested that the young peer had been wise; if he had merely driven on someone might very easily have noticed it as a suspicious action and taken the number of the car; by stopping and thrusting himself under the official nose he might well have hoped to disarm suspicion. Besides, what was there to suspect? . . . until connection was made with the "exchange" in the art gallery; and it was very possible that if Bragg had not gone there with his inquisitive nose that connection might not ever have been made.

Why, asked the doubters, had the gossip-writer written that article on the Ruppel Collection and submitted photographs for publication—drawing attention to the very objects that must subsequently prove to have been stolen? Because, to obtain information for the making of the copies, he had to go to Bosby's as a representative of the Press, and, having gone, it would, if inquiries were subsequently made, have looked very suspicious if he had *not* written his article and put in his photographs. Too clever, perhaps, but clever rogues must take risks.

And the other rogue? Now that Lord Feathergill's connection with the theft was reasonably well established, it was a simple matter to follow him to Chelsea and discover that one of his most intimate friends was a sculptress—Miss Nina Beavis. This discovery seemed to Bragg nearly the last stage of the case, and it was in fact the point at which he came up against a brick wall. Although he knew Miss Beavis was the woman in the case he could not prove it. Chief-Inspector Holby refused to apply for a warrant either for Feathergill or Beavis; until, he said, the girl was identified and/or the stolen figures found, there was not enough evidence to justify arrest.

Bragg's first view of Nina Beavis certainly did not tally with the descriptions given him by the staff and customers at the Art Gallery; Miss Beavis had straight black hair parted in the middle and plastered against the side of her head; her face was dead white and her lips colorless. Still, either this or the other might be a deliberately altered appearance. He proposed to take Mr. Dolphin down to have a look at her, in the hope of recognition.

"If you do, my lad, you'll not be able to use that identification in court; no judge would admit it. Didn't they teach you the rules in Downshire?"

Bragg flushed, but in the end his chief had to consent to something of the kind being done. Bragg had learned that it was Miss Beavis' custom to lunch every day at a small restaurant in Chelsea where many others of her profession also lunched; on three consecutive days he sat in a police car or a taxi outside the restaurant with Mr. Dolphin or one of his assistants, not pointing out Miss Beavis but asking them to look carefully at all the young women who came in and out of the restaurant. The result was a blank and Bragg was not surprised; apart from her own appearance, the girl's dress was completely different from the neat coat and skirt in which she had visited the Gallery. He dared not take the manager and his staff inside the restaurant because, of course, they were well known to Miss Beavis by sight and it was essential that neither she nor Lord Feathergill should at this stage be alarmed.

Doggedly, persevering, Bragg tried to get hold of Mr. Potter, one of the other customers at the Gallery, but Mr. Potter, he found, had just sailed for America. There remained only Lord Bicester and Bragg felt very diffident about approaching him.

But the old peer fell in with the suggestion quite readily.

"We'll lunch there, too," he said. "She'll spot you if you keep on hanging about outside in a car. What time does she lunch? All right; we'll get there first and sit next to the door."

Bragg hesitated. Lord Bicester was a man of striking appearance, a tall, erect figure, gray mustache brushed up, sleek gray hair, smartly cut clothes, and eyeglass. The girl would almost inevitably recognize him.

The old man chuckled.

"I know what you're thinking," he said; "you wait."

He disappeared and ten minutes later there came into the room an untidy-looking old fellow in a tweed suit, baggy at knees and elbows; a gray mustache straggled over his mouth, gray hair rumpled on his head, a pair of steel-rimmed glasses on his nose; the erect figure was stooping and the whole appearance completely altered.

"Do a thing thoroughly if you do it at all," said Lord Bicester, "and come to that, you can't go to a Chelsea restaurant looking like a detective. Watts! Put out a pair of Mr. George's flannel trousers and a tweed coat; he's about the same build."

In due course the quaint couple squeezed themselves on to two stools in the little restaurant.

"My God, I hope no one from Boodle's sees me here," muttered Lord Bicester.

Presently Nina Beavis appeared, dressed in a green skirt and orange jumper. Lord Bicester took no notice of her, though she sat down at a table next to them—as Bragg had known she probably would.

Solemnly they ate their simple meal. At last it was over; Lord Bicester signaled for the bill, paid it, and led the way out into the street, Bragg following with a feeling something like despair? What was he to do next? How . . .?

"Well, that was her all right."

The detective could hardly believe his ears.

"You recognized her, sir?"

"Oh, yes, I recognized her, but not by her face nor by her clothes."

"Then how, sir?"

"Her hands, man. I remember, now that I've seen them again, that I noticed them when she was looking at those Chinese things; they're unmistakable—lovely long hands, the hands of an artist but . . . she's got spatulate fingers. I think you said she was a sculptress—that explains it."

"Yes, I think that identification will do," said Chief-Inspector Holby, "but I'd like just to find those figures to make sure."

"If you arrest them, sir, we might get a search warrant at the same time. Probably they're hidden in her studio."

"In a plaster cast, eh? Like your Franks corpse. Well, maybe they are, but I've got another idea. Give me that copy of *The Times*."

Holby ran his eye down the shipping columns.

"I may be able to tell you something about noon tomorrow," he said. "You're not the only man who's been busy on this case, Bragg."

And a little before one next day, the young detective was summoned to the chief-inspector's room.

"We've clicked all right," said the big man. "Your Mr. Hiram Potter was searched as he left the *Berengaria* at New York this

211

morning and the bronze figures found in his trouser pockets."

Bragg stared.

"Potter, sir? That American billionaire's buyer?"

"Yes, Mr. Drew Pierman's buyer, no less."

"But surely, sir, Mr. Pierman wouldn't . . . those figures aren't worth all that to him . . . theft, I mean."

"Not to Mr. Pierman, no, but to Mr. Potter, oh yes. Mr. Potter's a salaried servant and a hundred or two extra won't come amiss to him. No doubt he paid that young couple anything up to four hundred for those two figures; in course of time he'll sell them to Mr. Pierman, saying he's bought them legitimately, for something nearer a thousand—and produce a properly receipted bill for them, forged. A pretty game the unscrupulous Mr. Potters can play with their employers—but once too often sometimes."

Bragg made no attempt to conceal his admiration.

"I never for a moment thought of suspecting him, sir," he said.

Chief-Inspector Holby laughed. He was not proof against admiration, even from a subordinate.

"No, but you led me to him, Bragg," he said. "You've done well; you've got imagination and perseverance. But let me give you a word of advice; don't let your imagination skip you over the obvious. Here's a case in point. One of the first questions I ask myself is: how does the thief get his price? Here's a theft of some works of art, not easily negotiable through an ordinary fence. But that's just the stuff that is bought by an unscrupulous collector. Collector? Where did I hear of a collector? Why, in that very gallery—an American professional buying for his chief. Right on the spot, all handy to help distract attention from the little lady. So I just had a little talk on the telephone with New York and there's someone to meet our Mr. Hiram P. on the gangway."

Bragg looked crestfallen.

"I've been a fool, sir," he said.

Chief Inspector Holby patted him on the arm.

"I wouldn't go so far as that," he said, "but you've still got something to learn. And now we'll pull in this bright young couple."

212

THE MOTIVE

BY ELLERY QUEEN

Ellery Queen is the pseudonym of Frederic Dannay and the late Manfred B. Lee. These Brooklyn-born cousins created and made world-famous the character of Ellery Queen. Ellery Queen has appeared in 33 novels, 78 short stories and novelets, and more than 300 radio plays, as well as in movies, and on stage and television. *Ellery Queen's Mystery Magazine* was initiated in 1941. Ellery Queen's first novel was *The Roman Hat Mystery* (1928), and the authors have won an unprecedented five Edgars from the Mystery Writers of America. Frederic Dannay presently lives in Larchmont, New York, with his wife, Rose.

YOUNG SUSAN MARSH, red-haired librarian of the Flora G. Sloan library, Northfield's cultural pride, steered the old wreck of a Buick around the stanchion blinker in the center of town and headed up Hill Street toward the red-brick Town Hall, coughing as the smoke came through the floorboards. Susan did not mind. She had discovered that the 1940 sedan only smoked going up steep grades, and the road between town and her little cottage in Burry's Hollow three miles out of Northfield, her usual route, was mostly level as a barn floor.

The vintage Buick had been given to Susan a few weeks before in October, by Miss Flora Sloan, Northfield's undisputed autocrat and, to hear some tell it, a lineal descendant of Ebenezer Scrooge.

"But Miss Flora," Susan had exclaimed, her ponytail flying, "why me?"

" 'Cause all that robber Will Pease offered me on her was a measly thirty-five dollars," Miss Flora had said grimly. "I'd rather you had it for nothing."

"Well, I don't know what to say, Miss Flora. She's *beautiful*."

"Fiddle-de-sticks," the old lady had said. "She needs a ring job, her tires are patchy, one headlight's broken, the paint's scrofulous, and she's stove in on the left side. But the short time I had her she took me where I wanted to go, Susan, and she'll take you, too. It's better than pedaling a bike six miles a day to the Library and back, the way you've had to do since your father passed on." And Miss Flora had added a pinch of pepper, "It isn't as if girls wore bloomers like they used to when *I* was twenty-two."

What Miss Flora had failed to mention was that the heater didn't work, either, and with November nipping up and winter only weeks away it was going to be a Hobson's choice between keeping the windows open and freezing or shutting them and dying of asphyxiation. But right now, struggling up Hill Street in a smelly blue haze, Susan had a much more worrisome problem. Tom Cooley was missing.

Tommy was the son of a truck farmer in the Valley—a towhead with red hands, big and slow-moving like John Cooley, and sorrow-eyed as his mother Sarah, who had died of pneumonia the winter before. Tommy had a hunger for reading rare in Northfield, and Susan dreamed dreams for him.

"There's not an earthly reason why you shouldn't go on to college, Tommy," Susan had told him. "You're one of the few boys in town who really deserves the chance."

Tommy had said, "Even if Pa could afford it, I can't leave him alone with the farm."

"But sooner or later you've got to leave, anyway. In a year or so you'll be going into the Army."

"I don't know what Pa'll do." And then he quietly switched the subject to books.

There was a sadness about Tommy Cooley, a premature loss of joy, that made Susan want to mother him, high as he towered above her. She looked forward to his visits and their snatches of talk about Hemingway and Thomas Wolfe. Tommy's chores kept him close to the farm; but on the first Monday of every month, rain, snow, or good New England sunshine, he showed up at Susan's desk to return the armful of books she had recommended the last time and go off eagerly with a fresh supply.

On the first Monday in November there had been no Tommy. When he failed to appear by the end of that week, Susan was sure something was wrong, and on Friday evening she had driven out to the Cooley place. She found the weather-beaten farmhouse locked, a tractor rusting in a furrow, the pumpkins and potatoes unharvested, and no sign of Tommy. Or, for that matter, of his father.

So on Saturday afternoon Susan had closed the Library early; and here she was, bound up Hill Street for Deputy Sheriff Linc Pearce's office on an unhappy mission.

It had to be the county officer, because Northfield's police department was Rollie Fawcett. Old Rollie's policing had been limited for a generation to chalking tires along Main and Hill Streets and writing out overtime parking tickets for the one-dollar fines that paid his salary. There was simply no one in Northfield but Linc Pearce to turn to.

Susan wasn't happy about that, either.

The trouble was, to Linc Pearce she was still the female Peter Pan who used to dig the rock salt out of his bottom when old Mr. Burry caught them in his apples. Lengthening her skirts and having to wear bras hadn't changed Linc's attitude one bit. It wasn't as if he were immune to feminine charms; the way he

215

carried on with that overblown Marie Fullerton just before he went into the Army, for instance, had been proof enough of *that*. Susan had counted on the Army's taking a boy and returning a man, and in a way it had; Linc came home quieter, more settled, and he was doing a fine job as Sheriff Howland's deputy in the Northfield district. But he went right back to treating Susan as if they were still swimming raw together in Burry's Creek.

She parked the rattletrap in the space reserved for Official Cars Only and marched into Town Hall with her little jaw set for anything.

Linc went to work on her right off. "Well, if it isn't Snubby Sue," he chuckled, uncoiling all six foot three of him from behind his desk. "Leave your specs home?"

"What specs?" Susan could see the twitch of a squirrel's whisker at two hundred yards.

"Last time I passed you on the street you didn't see me at all."

"I saw you, all right," Susan said coldly, and drew back like a snake. "Linc Pearce, if you start chucking me under the chin again—!"

"Why Susie," Linc said, "I'm just setting you a chair."

"Well." Susan sniffed, off-guard. "Is it possible you're developing some manners?"

"Yes, ma'am," Linc said respectfully, and he swung her off the floor with one long arm and dropped her into the chair with a smack that jarred her all the way up to the teeth.

"Some day! . . ." Susan choked.

"Now, now," Linc said gently. "What's on your mind?"

"Tommy Cooley!"

"The silk purse you're working on?" Linc grinned; and Susan said to herself, Steady, girl. Her cultural interest in young Tom had been a source of amusement to Linc for a long time. "What's Plowboy done now, swiped a library book?"

"He's disappeared," Susan snapped; and she told Linc about Tommy's failure to show up at the Library and her visit to the deserted Cooley farm.

Of course, Linc looked indulgent. "There's no mystery about John. He's been away over a month looking to buy another farm as far from Northfield as he can find. John took Sarah's death last winter hard. But Tommy's s'posed to be looking after the place."

"Well, he's not there."

216

Linc shrugged. "Probably took off on a toot."

"Leaving a four thousand-dollar tractor to rust in a half-plowed lot?" Susan's ponytail whisked about like a red flag in a high wind. "Tommy's got too much farmer in him for that, Linc. Besides, he's not that kind."

"He's seventeen, isn't he?"

"I tell you I know Tommy Cooley, and you don't!"

Deputy Sheriff Lincoln Pearce looked at her. Then he reached to the costumer for his hat and sheep-lined jacket. "S'pose I'll never hear the end of it if I don't take a look."

Out in the parking space Linc walked all around Susan's recent acquisition. "I know," he said gravely. "It's John Wilkes Booth's getaway car. Where'd you dig her up?"

"Miss Flora Sloan *presented* her to me three weeks ago when she won that Chevrolet coupé at the Grange bazaar raffle!"

Linc whistled. Then he jackknifed himself and got in. "Is it safe? The chances I have to take on this job!"

He went on like that all the way into the Valley. Susan drove stiffly, cheeks smarting in the November wind.

But as they turned into the Cooley yard Linc said in an altogether different kind of voice, "John's home. There's his jeep."

"He must have just got back, then," Susan said. "I tried phoning this morning and there was no answer."

They found John Cooley crouched in a Morris chair in his parlor, enormous shoulders at a beaten-down slope. The family Bible lay on his massive knees, and he was staring into space over it. He was still dressed in his blue Sunday-meeting suit.

"Hi, John," Linc said from the doorway. Susan looked in from under his propping arm.

The farmer's head came about. The bleached gray eyes were dazed.

"My boy's gone, Lincoln." The voice that rumbled from his chest had trouble in it, deep trouble.

"Just heard, John."

"Ain't been home for weeks, looks like." He peered through the dimness of the parlor. "Where's Tommy at, Sue Marsh?"

"I don't know, Mr. Cooley." Susan tried to keep her voice casual. "I was hoping you did."

The farmer rose, looking around as if for a place to put the Bible.

He was almost as tall as Linc and half again as broad, a tree of a man struck by lightning.

"When did you see Tom last, John?"

"October the second, when I went off to look for a new place." John Cooley swallowed. "Found me one down in York State, too. Figured to give Tommy a new start, maybe change our luck. But now I'll have to let it go."

"You hold your horses, John," Linc said cheerfully. "Didn't the boy leave you a note?"

"No." The farmer's breathing became noisy. He set the Bible down on the Morris chair, as if its weight were suddenly too much.

"We'll find him. Sue, you saw Tom last on the first Monday in October?"

Susan nodded. "It was October the third, I think, the day after Mr. Cooley says he left. Tommy came into the Library to return some books and take out others. He had the farm truck, I remember."

"Truck still here, John?"

"Aya."

"Anything of Tom's missing?"

"His twenty-two."

Linc looked relieved. "Well, that's it. He's gone off into the hills. He'll show up any minute with a fat buck and forty-two kinds of alibis. I wouldn't worry."

"Well, I would," Susan said. She was furious with Linc. "Tommy'd never have left on an extended hunting trip without bringing my library books back first. He knows I always give him two weeks more than the rules allow as it is."

"There's female reasoning for you," Linc grinned. But he went to Cooley and touched the heavily muscled shoulder. "John, you want me to organize a search for him?"

The shoulder quivered under Linc's hand.

But all the farmer said was, "Aya."

Overnight, Linc had three search parties formed and the state police alerted. On Sunday morning one party, in charge of old Sanford Brown, Northfield's first selectman, headed west with instructions to stop at every farm and gas station. Rollie Fawcett took the second, going east with identical instructions. The third Linc took charge of himself, including in his party Frenchy Lafont and Lafont's two hound dogs. Frenchy owned the Northfield Bar & Grill across Hill Street from Town Hall. He was the ace tracker of the county.

"You take her easy, John," Lafont said to John Cooley before they set out. "Me, my dogs, we find the boy. Why you want to go along?"

But the farmer went ahead packing a rucksack as if he were deaf. Frenchy glanced at Linc and shook his head.

Linc's party disappeared into the heavily timbered country to the north, and they were gone a full week. They came back bearded, hollow-cheeked, and silent. John Cooley and Frenchy Lafont and his two hounds did not return with them. They showed up three days later, when the first snowfall made further search useless. Even the dogs looked defeated.

Meanwhile, Linc had furnished police of nearby states with handbills struck off by the Northfield Times job-press, giving a description of Tommy Cooley and reproducing his latest photograph, the one taken from his high school yearbook. Newspapers, radio and TV stations cooperated. Linc sent an official request to Washington; the enlistment files of the Army, Navy, Marine Corps, and Air Force were combed. Registrars of colleges all over the country were circularized. The F.B.I. was notified.

But no trace of Tommy Cooley—or his hunting rifle—turned up.

Linc and Susan quarreled.

"It's one of those things, I tell you." The cleft between Linc's eyes was biting deep these days. "We haven't been able to fix even the approximate time of his disappearance. It could have been any time between October third and the early part of November. Nobody saw him leave, and apparently no one's seen him since."

"But a grown boy doesn't go up in smoke!" Susan protested. "He's got to be *somewhere,* Linc."

"Sure," Linc said. "In Canada prospecting for uranium, or hunting Mau Maus in Kenya. Kids are pretty irresponsible characters."

"So are some grown men I know," Susan said through her teeth. "Tommy did *not* run away from home, he *isn't* irresponsible, and if you were half the sheriff's whitehaired boy you think you are you'd find out what happened to him."

This was unreasonable, and Susan knew it; for a thrilling moment she thought Linc was going to get mad at her. But, as usual, he let her down. All he said was, "How about you taking my badge, half pint, and me handing out library books?"

"Do you think you might just be able to locate the right one on the shelves?"

Susan stalked out. After the door banged, Linc got up and gently kicked it.

Once, in mid-December, she drove out to the Cooley farm. The rumors about John Cooley were disturbing. He was said to be letting the farm go to seed, mumbling to himself, poring over his Bible night and day.

She found the rumors exaggerated. The house was dirty and the kitchen piled with unwashed dishes, but the farm itself seemed in good order, considering the season, and the farmer talked lucidly enough. Only his appearance shocked Susan. His ruddy skin had grayed and loosened, his hair had white streaks in it, and his coveralls flapped on his frame.

"I've fetched you a blueberry pie I had in my freezer, Mr. Cooley," she said brightly. "I remember Tommy's saying blueberry's your favorite."

"Aya." Cooley looked down at the pie in his lap, but not as if he saw it. "My Tom's a good boy."

Susan tried to think of something to say. Finally she said, "We've missed you at Grange meetings, church. . . . Isn't it awfully lonesome for you, Mr. Cooley?"

"Have to wait for the boy," John Cooley explained patiently. "The Lord would never take him from me without a sign. I've had no sign, Susan. He'll come home."

"Sometimes—" Susan began. But she stopped. There was a look on the farmer's face that it would have been sheer sin to dispel. She prayed silently that the fanatical light might never have reason to go out.

But it was a vain prayer. Tommy Cooley was found in the spring.

The rains that year were Biblical. They destroyed the early plantings, overflowed ponds and creeks, and sent the North-field River over its banks to flood thousands of acres of pasture and bottomland. The main highway, between Northfield and the Valley, was under water for several miles.

When the waters sank they exposed a shallow hole not two miles from the Cooley farm, just off the highway. In the hole lay the remains of John Cooley's son. A county crew repairing the road found him.

Susan heard the tragic news as she was locking the Library for the day. Frenchy Lafont, racing past in his new Ford convertible, slowed down long enough to yell, "They find the Cooley boy's body, Miss Marsh! Ever'body's goin' out!" He was gone before she could open her mouth.

How Susan got the aged Buick started in the damp twilight, how she knew where to go, she never remembered. She supposed it was instinct, a blind following of the herd of vehicles stampeding from town onto the Valley road, most of them as undirected as her jalopy. All Susan could think of was the look on John Cooley's gray face when he had said the Lord had given him no sign. . . .

She saw the farmer's face at last, and her heart sank. Cooley was on his knees in the roadside grave, clawing in the muck, his eyes blank and terrible, while all around him people trampled the mud-slimed brush like a nest of aroused ants. Linc Pearce and some state troopers were holding the crowd back, trying to give the bereaved man a decent grieving space; but they need not have wrestled so. The farmer might have been alone in one of his cornfields. His big hands alternately caressed and mauled the grave's mud, as if he would coax and batter it into submission to his frenzy. Once he found a button rotted off his son's leather jacket sleeve, and Linc came over and tried to take it from him; but the big hand became a fist, a mallet, and Linc turned away. The big man put it into the pocket of his checkered red mackinaw along with a pebble, a chunk of glass, a clump of grass roots—these were his son, the convenant between them, Mizpah. . . . Occasionally he lifted a corner of the canvas that had been dropped on the body after it was lifted from the grave—peering, trying to make sense out of the jumbled clay. His face was a dirty gray abomination; and for the first time Susan wept.

Afterward, when the heap under the canvas had been taken away by Art Ormsby's hearse, and most of the crowd had crawled off in their cars, Susan was able to come close. They had John Cooley sitting on a stump near the grave now, while men hunted through the brush. They were merely going through the motions, Susan knew; time, the ebbing waters, the feet of the crowd would have obliterated any clue.

She waited while Linc conferred with a state trooper lieutenant and Dr. Buxton, who was the coroner's physician for Northfield. She saw Dr. Buxton glance at John Cooley, shake his gray head, and get into his car to drive back to town. Then

221

she noticed that the lieutenant was carefully holding a rusty, mud-caked rifle.

When the trooper went off with the rifle Susan walked up to Linc and said, "Well?" They had hardly conversed all winter.

Linc squinted briefly down at her and said, "Hello, Sue." Then he looked over at the motionless man on the stump, as if the two were connected in his mind, painfully.

"That rifle," Susan said. "Tommy's?"

Linc nodded. "Tossed into the hole with the body. They're going to give it the once-over at the state police lab in Gurleytown, but they won't find anything after all this time."

"How long—?"

"Hard to say." Linc's firm lips set tight. "Doc Buxton thinks offhand he's been dead five or six months. Even a post mortem, he says, probably won't permit him to fix the date closer than that."

Susan's chest rose, and stayed there. "Linc . . . was it murder?"

"The whole back of his head is smashed in. What else there is we won't know till Doc does the autopsy."

Susan swallowed the raw wind. It was impossible to associate that canvas-shrouded lump with Tommy Cooley's big, sad, eager self, to realize that it had been crumbling in the earth here since last October or early November.

"Who'd want to kill him?" Susan said fiercely. "And why, Linc? *Why?*"

"That," Linc said, "is what I have to find out."

She had never seen him so humorless, his mouth so much like a sprung trap. A wave of warmth washed over her. For the moment Susan felt very close to him.

"Linc, let me help," she said breathlessly.

"How?" Linc said.

The wave recoiled. There was no approaching him on an adult level, in the case of Tommy Cooley as in anything else. Susan almost expected Linc to pat her shoulder.

"It's a man's job," Linc was mumbling. "Thanks all the same."

"And are you the man for it, do you think?" Susan heard herself cry, as from far away.

"Maybe not. But I'll give it a try." Linc took her hand, but she snatched it away. "Now, Susie," he said. "You're all upset. Let me do the sweating on this. With the trail being five-six months old . . ."

Susan sloshed away, trembling with fury.

In the weeks that followed, Susan kept tabs on Linc's frustration almost with satisfaction. She got most of her inside information from Dr. Buxton, who was a habitué of the Library's mystery shelves, old Flora Sloan, and Frenchy Lafont. Miss Flora's all-seeing eye encompassed events practically before they took place, and Frenchy's strategic location opposite Town Hall gave him the best informed clientele in town.

"Linc Pearce's bellowing around like a heifer in her first season," Miss Flora remarked one day, in the Library. "But that boy's all fenced in, Susan. There's some things the Almighty doesn't mean for us to know. I guess the mystery of poor Tommy Cooley's one of 'em."

"I can't believe that, Miss Flora," Susan said. "If Linc is fenced in, it's only because it's a very difficult case."

The old lady cocked an eye at her. "Appears to me, Susan, you take a mighty personal interest in it."

"Well, of course! Tommy—"

"Tommy my foot. You can fool the men folks with your straight-out talk and your red-hair tempers, Susan Marsh, but you don't fool an old woman. You've been in love with Lincoln Pearce ever since *I* can remember, and I go back to bustles. Why don't you stop this fiddling and marry him?"

"Marry—!" Susan laughed. "Of all the notions, Miss Flora. Naturally, I'm interested in Linc—we grew up together—this is an important case to him—"

"Fiddle-de-sticks," Miss Flora said distinctly, and walked out.

Frenchy Lafont said to Susan in mid-May, when she stopped into his café for lunch, "That Linc, he's a fool for damsure. You know what, Miss Marsh? Ever'body but him know he's licked."

"He's *not* licked, Mr. Lafont!"

Susan saw Linc that same day. He was striding up Sanford Street toward Hill, past the Library. He looked so gaunt and squeezed out, such a leaning tower of trouble, that Susan wished a great wish that he would look up, to be comforted by an old friend's smile through the doorway, which was wide open to the opportunity. But Linc passed by without a glance.

The fact was, there was nothing for Linc Pearce or anyone else to grab hold of. The dead boy's skull had been crushed from behind by a blow of considerable force, according to Dr.

223

Buxton. His shoulders and back showed evidences of assault, too; apparently there had been a savage series of blows. But the weapon was not found.

Linc went back to the site of the shallow grave time after time to nose around in a great circle, studying the road and the brush foot by foot . . . long after Tommy Cooley was buried in the old Northfield cemetery beside his mother. But it was time wasted. Nor were the state police technicians more successful. They could detect no clue in the dead boy's clothing or rifle. All they could say was that the rifle had not been fired—"and old Aunty Laura's blind cow could see that!" Susan had snapped— so that presumably the boy had been killed without warning or a chance to defend himself. Tommy's rifle had been returned to his father, along with the meaningless contents of his pockets. John Cooley had broken down then, collapsing in tears.

Linc retraced the ground covered by his November search parties, trying to find someone who might remember seeing Tommy Cooley after October third. But no one did. So even the date of the murder was a mystery.

Motive was the darkest mystery of all. It had not been robbery: Tommy's wallet, containing most of the hundred dollars his father had left with him, had been intact in the grave. Linc went into the boy's life and through his effects, questioned and requestioned his friends, his old high school teachers, canvassed every farmer and field hand within miles of the Cooley place. But the killing remained unexplained. The boy had had no enemies, it seemed, he had crossed no one, he had been involved with no girl or woman . . .

"John," Linc had pleaded with Cooley, "can't you think of anything that might tell why Tommy was murdered? Anything?"

But the farmer had shaken his head and turned away, big fingers gripping his Bible. The Book was now never far from his hand. He plodded about his farm in the spring aimlessly, doing no planting, letting the machinery rust. Once a week or so he drove into Northfield to shop in the supermarket. But he spoke to no one, and after a while no one spoke to him.

One night toward the end of May, as Susan was sitting on her porch after supper, rocking in the mild moonlight and listening to the serenade of the peepers in the pond, the headlights of a car swung into her yard and a tall familiar figure got out.

224

It couldn't be! But it was. Linc Pearce come to Burry's Hollow. The mountain to Mohamet . . .

"Susie?"

"Well, if it isn't Lanky Linc," Susan heard herself say calmly. Her heart was thumping like an old well-pump. "Come on up."

Linc hesitated at the foot of the porch steps, fumbling with his hat. "Took a chance you'd be home. If you're busy—"

"I'll put my dollies away," Susan said, "for you."

"What?" Linc sounded puzzled.

Susan smiled. "Sit down, stranger."

Linc sat down on the bottom step awkwardly, facing the moon. There were lines in his lean face that Susan had never noticed before.

"How've you been?" Susan said.

"All right," he said impatiently, and turned around. "See here, Susie, it's asinine going on like this. I mean, you and me. Why, you're acting just like a kid."

Susan felt the flames spread from her hair right down to her toes. "*I'm* acting like a kid!" she cried. "Is that what you came here to say, Linc? If it is—"

He shook his head. "I never seem to say the right thing to you. Why can't we be like we used to be, Susie? I mean, I miss that funny little pan of yours, and that carrot top. But ever since this Cooley business started—"

"It started a long time before that," Susan retorted, "and I'd rather not discuss it, Linc, *or* my funny pan, *or* the color of my hair, if you don't mind. What about the Cooley case?"

"Susie—"

"The Cooley case," Susan said. "Or do I go to bed?"

Linc almost said something sharp. But then he shut his mouth and scowled into the blackness of the willow grove bordering Susan's pond.

"All right—" she began.

"What do you want me to say? There's nothing to tell."

"Nothing at all?"

"Hopeless. It'll never be solved."

"Because you haven't been able to solve it?"

"Me or anybody else," Linc said, shrugging. "One of those crimes that makes no sense because it never had any. Our theory now is that the Cooley boy was attacked on the road by some psychopathic tramp, who buried him in a hurry and lit out for other parts."

225

"In other words, the most convenient theory possible."

Linc said with elaborate indifference, "It happens all the time."

"And suppose it wasn't a psychopathic tramp?"

He looked at her then. "What do you mean?"

"I think it was somebody in Northfield."

"Who?"

"I don't know."

"Why?"

"I don't know that, either."

Linc laughed.

"I think you'd better go, Linc Pearce," Susan said distinctly. "I don't like you any more."

"Now, Susie—"

The phone rang in the house. It was three rings, Susan's signal, and she stamped inside.

"It's for you, Linc," she said coolly. "The bartender over at Frenchy Lafont's."

"Bib Hadley? Should have known better than to tell Bib I was stopping in here on my way home," Linc growled, unfolding himself from the step. "Some drunk acting up, I s'pose. . . . What is it, Bib?"

Discussing me in a bar! Susan thought. It was the last straw. She could see Bib Hadley's belly jiggling under the beer tap, and the knowing leers on the faces of the barflies. Susan turned away in cold rage.

But then she heard Linc say, "I'll get right on out there, Bib," and hang up; and something in the way he said it made her turn back.

Linc's sunburned face was ludicrously like a Hallowe'en pumpkin, a lumpy orange mask set in a ghastly grin.

"What's the matter?" Susan said quickly.

"Another murder."

An icy hand seized her heart.

"Who, Linc? Where?"

"Frenchy Lafont." Linc's voice sounded thick. "Some kids out in a hot rod found his body just off the Valley road. Whole back of his head caved in."

"Like Tommy Cooley," Susan whispered.

"I'll say like Tommy Cooley." Linc waved his long arms futilely. "Bib says they found Frenchy lying in the exact spot where we dug up Tommy's body!"

226

The Valley road was a wild mess of private cars and jeeps and farm trucks, some racing around slowpokes, slowpokes chugging desperately, drivers cursing, and every visible face a livid glimmer as Linc and Susan wormed past. In one car Susan saw Miss Flora Sloan. The withered despot of Northfield was driving her new Chevrolet like a demon, the daisies in her straw hat bobbing crazily.

Linc had to keep his siren going all the way.

We're scared witless, Susan thought. She almost said it aloud. But one look at Linc, and she did not.

Two state police cars had set up roadblocks near the site of the new horror. Linc plowed onto the soft shoulder and skidded around into the cleared space. The road in both directions was a double string of lights. Everywhere Susan looked, people were jumping out of cars and running along the road. The only sounds were the squeals of distant tires and the thud of running feet. In a twinkling the fifty feet of highway between the roadblocks was rimmed with eyes. . . . Susan suddenly recalled a hunting trip with her father when she was eleven years old. They had pitched camp for the night in a clearing in the dense woods, and her father had had to build the fire up when she became frightened at the glittering holes in the black wall of the unknown surrounding them. For years afterward she had had nightmares in which a ring of fiercely glowing little planets closed in on her from outer space; she still awoke occasionally in a sweat.

But this was worse. This was the menace of the known. The known turned evil. Old neighbors, good people, transformed into a hostile mob.

Susan almost trod on Linc's heels.

She peeped around his long torso at what lay just off the road on the north side. It sprang at her, brutally detailed, in the police flares. Susan jerked back, hiding her eyes.

She was to remember that photographic flash for the rest of her life. The mound of sandy earth where the grave had been refilled after the removal of Tommy Cooley's body, pebbled, flint-spangled, scabby with weeds; and across it, as on one of Art Ormsby's biers, the flung remains of what had been Frenchy Lafont.

Susan could not see his wound; she could only imagine what it looked like. They had turned him over, so that his face was tilted sharply back to the stars. It did not look the least bit like

227

Frenchy Lafont's face. Frenchy Lafont's face had been dark and vivid, lively with mischief, with beautiful lips over white teeth and a line of vain black mustache. This face looked like old suet; the mouth was a gaping black cavern; the eyes stared like dusty pieces of glass.

"Just like the Cooley kid," one of the troopers was saying in a high-pitched voice. "Just like."

His voice raised a deep echo, like a far-off growl of thunder. There was more than fear in the growl; there was anger, and under the anger, hate. The troopers and Linc looked around, startled.

"Sounds like trouble, Pearce," one of the older troopers muttered to Linc. "They're your people. Better do something."

Linc walked off toward one of the police cars. For a moment Susan almost ran after him; she felt as if she had been left standing naked in the flares.

But the eyes were not on her.

Linc vaulted to the hood of the car and flung his arms wide. The rumble choked and died. Susan could not decide which was more terrifying their noise or their silence.

"Neighbors, I knew Frenchy Lafont all my life," Linc said in a quiet way. "Most of you did, too. There isn't a man or woman in Northfield wants more to identify the one who did this and see that he gets what's coming to him. But we can't do it this way. We'll find Frenchy's killer if you'll only go home and give us a chance."

"Like you found the killer of my boy?"

It was John Cooley's hoarse bass voice. He was near the west roadblock, standing tall in his jeep, his thick arm with the flail of fist at the end like a wrathful judgment. Linc turned to face him.

"Go home, John," Linc said gently.

"Yeah, John, go home!" a shrill voice yelled from behind the other barrier. "Go home and get yourself murdered like Tommy was!"

"That's not helping, Wes Bartlett," Linc said. "Use your head, man—"

But his voice went down under a tidal wave.

"We want protection!"

"Aya!"

"Who's next on the list?"

"Long as *he's* deputy—"

228

"Resign!"

"New sheriff's what we need!"

"Aya! Resign!"

In the roar of the crowd the clatter of Linc's badge on the hood of the police car was surprisingly loud.

"All right, there's my badge!" Linc shouted. "Now who's the miracle man thinks he can do the job better? I'll recommend him to Sheriff Howland myself. Come on, don't be bashful! Speak up."

He gave them glare for glare. The glares dimmed, the answering silence became uneasy. Something embarrassed invaded the night air.

"Well?" Linc jeered.

Somewhere down the line a car engine started. . . .

Ten minutes later, except for a cluster of cars around the roadblocks, the highway was empty and dark.

Linc jumped off the police car, reached for his badge, and went over to the troopers.

"Nice going, Sheriff," Susan murmured.

But he strode past her to the edge of the burial mound, rock-hard and bitter.

"Let's get to it."

At first they thought it had been a murder in the course of a robbery. Frenchy Lafont's wallet was found untouched on the body, but an envelope with the day's café receipts, which he had been known to have on him earlier in the evening, was missing. The robbery theory collapsed overnight. The envelope of money was found in the night depository box of the First National Bank of Northfield on Main Street when old Sanford Brown, first vice-president of the bank, unlocked the box in the morning.

The weapon was not found.

It was the Tommy Cooley case all over again.

Everything about the café owner's murder was baffling. He was a bachelor who lived with his aged mother on the old Lafont place off the Valley road, a mile out of town. His elder brother, a prosperous merchant of Quebec, had not heard from him in months. The brother, in town to make the funeral arrangements and take charge of the mother, could shed no light on the mystery. Old Mrs. Lafont knew nothing; she spoke little English, was acquainted with few of her son's associates, and could not even say whether or not he had been home that evening. He always ate dinner at his café, and she had gone to bed early.

On the evening of his murder Lafont had left the café shortly before nine, alone, taking the day's receipts with him. He drove off in his new Ford. An hour or so later he was dead some six miles out of town, on the site of the Cooley tragedy. His car was found near the mound. It was towed into the police garage at the Gurleytown barracks and gone over by experts. It yielded nothing but Frenchy Lafont's fingerprints. No blood, no indication of a struggle, no clue of any kind. The fuel tank was almost full.

"He dropped the envelope into the slot at the bank," Linc told Susan, "stopped in at Howie Grebe's gas station to fill up, and drove off west on the Valley road. He must have gone straight to his death. Nothing to show that he was waylaid and held up—nothing was taken, and Frenchy didn't touch the pistol he carried in his glove compartment. Bib Hadley says he was his usual wisecracking self when he left the café, and Howie Grebe says the same thing."

"You think he had a date with somebody he knew?" Susan asked.

"Well, Hadley says he got a phone call at the café," Linc said slowly, "about eight o'clock that night."

"I hadn't heard that! Who phoned him, Linc?"

"Bib doesn't know. Frenchy answered the call himself, and he didn't say."

"Did Bib Hadley overhear anything?"

"No."

"Was Frenchy excited—concerned—alarmed? There must have been *something*, Linc!"

"Bib didn't notice anything unusual. The call might have had nothing to do with the case."

"Maybe it was some woman Frenchy was fooling with. I've heard stories about him and Logan Street." Susan colored. Logan Street was a part of Northfield no respectable girl ever mentioned to the opposite sex.

"So far all alibis have stood up." Linc passed his hand over his eyes like an old man. "It's no good thinking, theorizing. I have to *know*, Sue, and there's not a fact I can sink my teeth into."

"But there's got to be a reason for a man's getting the back of his head knocked in," Susan cried. "*Why* was Frenchy murdered? *Why* was his body dumped on the spot where the murderer had buried Tommy? You can hardly say it was another psychopathic tramp, Linc."

"Maybe it was the same one."

"Oh, rot."

Linc looked at her in a persecuted way. He was glassy-eyed with exhaustion. But he merely said, "Could be. Only there doesn't seem to be any more sense in Frenchy's death than in Tom Cooley's. Look, Susie, I've got work to do, and talk won't help me do it, even with you. If you'll excuse me . . ."

"Certainly," Susan said frigidly. "But let me tell you, Linc Pearce—when these murders are solved it'll be talk and theories and *thinking* that solve it!" And she swept out of Linc's office thoroughly miserable.

Northfield was a strange town these days. People came in to shop, exchange tight greetings, and go swiftly home. A PTA dance scarcely met expenses. The 4-H Club canceled a fair at the order of parents. At night the deserted streets were patrolled by state police cars Northfield had never seen when it was murder-free.

Burry's Hollow took on a sinister shape. Susan, who had been born there and had a pet name for every tree and boulder, found herself locking the cottage doors at night. Monsters lurked in every berry patch and clump of willows, great featureless things armed with clubs.

She kept tossing night after night, asking herself unanswerable questions. Why had Tommy Cooley been killed? Why had Frenchy Lafont followed him in death? What was the connection between the two? And—the most frightening question of all—who was going to be the next victim?

A week after Lafont's murder Susan was waiting at the café entrance when Bib Hadley came to open up.

"You must hanker after a cup of my coffee real bad, Miss Marsh," the fat bartender said, unlocking the door. "Come on in. I'll have the urn going in a jiffy."

"What I want, Bib, is information," Susan said grimly. "I'm sick and tired of moping around, waiting to get my head bashed in."

The bartender tied a clean apron around his ample middle. "Seems like every Tom, Dick, and Mary between Northfield and Boston's been in for the same reason. Even had a newspaperman in yesterday from one of the city wire services, made

231

a special trip just to pump ol' Bib. So get your list in now, Miss Marsh, while Frenchy's brother makes up his mind what to do with this place. What do you want to know?"

"The connection between Tommy Cooley and Frenchy Lafont," Susan said.

"Wasn't any," Bib Hadley said. "Next?"

"But there must have been, Bib! Did Tommy ever work for Mr. Lafont?"

"Nope."

"Did Tommy ever come in here?"

"Tell you the truth, Miss Marsh," the bartender said, lighting the gas under the urn, "I don't believe Frenchy would have known young Tom Cooley if he'd tripped over him in broad daylight. You know how Frenchy was about teenagers. He'd stand 'em all treat over at Tracy's ice cream parlor, but he wouldn't let 'em come into his own place even for coffee. Gave a good bar a bad name, Frenchy used to say."

"Well there was a connection between Tommy and Frenchy Lafont," Susan said positively, "and these murders won't ever be solved till it's found."

"And you're going to find it, I s'pose, Sue?"

Susan jumped. There he was, in the café doorway, jaws working away like Gary Cooper's in an emotional moment. She knew this was Crisis.

"I saw you ambush Bib from my office window," Linc said bitterly. "Don't you trust me to ask the right questions, either?"

I don't know why I'm feeling guilty, Susan thought furiously. This is a free country!

Linc jammed his big foot on the rim of the tub holding the dusty palm. "You want my badge, too, Sue? Don't you think I've asked Bib every question you have, and a whole lot more? This is a tough case. Do you have to make it tougher for me by getting underfoot?"

"Thanks!" Susan said. "People who won't accept help when they're stuck from people trying to unstick them are just—just perambulating *pigheads*."

"We stopped playing tag in your dad's cow barn long ago, Sue," Linc said, jaws grinding powerfully. "When are you going to grow up?"

"I've *grown* up! Oh, how I've grown up, Linc Pearce—and everybody knows it but you!" Susan screamed. "And do we have to stand here screaming in front of people?"

"I'm not people," Bib Hadley said. "I ain't even here."

"Nobody's screaming but you." Linc drew himself up so tall Susan's neck began to hurt. "I thought we knew each other pretty well, Susie. Maybe we don't know each other at all."

"I'm sure of it!" Susan tried to say it with dignity, but it came out so choky-sounding she fled past Linc to her jalopy and drove off down Hill Street with the gas pedal to the floor.

Two nights later the body of Flora Sloan, autocrat of North-field, was found by a motorcycle trooper just off the Valley highway.

The back of her head had been battered in.

As in the case of Frenchy Lafont, the old lady's body had been tossed onto Tommy Cooley's winter grave.

Flora Sloan had attended a vestry meeting in Christ Church, at which certain parish and financial problems had been argued. As usual, Miss Flora dominated the debate; as usual, she got her way. She had left the meeting in lively spirits when it broke up just before ten o'clock, climbed into her Chevrolet, waved triumphantly at Sanford Brown, who had been her chief antagonist at the meeting, and driven off. Presumably she had been bound for the big Sloan house on the western edge of town. But she never reached it; or rather, she had bypassed it, for the Valley road ran by her property.

When her body was found shortly after midnight by the motorcycle trooper, she had been dead about an hour.

Had Flora Sloan picked someone up, someone who had forced her to drive to the lonely spot six miles from town and there murdered her? But the old lady had been famous for her dislike of tramps and her suspicion of hitchhikers. She had never been known to give a stranger a lift.

Her purse, money untouched, was found beside her body. A valuable ruby brooch, a Sloan family heirloom, was still pinned to her blue lace dress. The Chevrolet was parked near the grave in almost the identical spot on which Frenchy Lafont's Ford had been abandoned. There were no fingerprints in the car except her own, no clues in the car or anywhere in the vicinity of the grave.

Three nights after Flora Sloan's murder, Sanford Brown, first selectman of Northfield, called a special town meeting. The city fathers, lean old Yankee farmers and businessmen, sat

233

down behind the scarred chestnut table in the Town Hall meeting room under an American flag like a panel of hanging judges; and among them—Susan thought they looked dismally like prisoners—sat County Sheriff Howland and his local deputy, Lincoln Pearce.

It was an oppressive night, and the overflow crowd made the room suffocating. Old ladies Susan had not seen since Election Day were there in choker-collared force. Susan saw Dr. Buxton, Art Ormsby, Howie Grebe, Will Pease, Bib Hadley, Frenchy Lafont's Canadian brother, old Mrs. Lafont in rigid mourning. She saw everyone she knew, and some faces she had forgotten.

Old Sanford Brown rapped his gavel hard on the table. A profound silence greeted him.

"Under the authority vested in me," old Brown said rapidly through his nose, "I call this town meetin' to order. As this is special, we will dispense with the usual order of business and get right to it. Sheriff Howland's come down from the county seat at the selectmen's request. Floor's yours, Sheriff."

Sheriff Howland was a large perspiring man in a smart city suit and a black string tie. He got to his feet, drying his bald head with a sodden handkerchief.

"Friends, when I was elected to office in this county I looked for the best man I could find to be my deputy in your district. I asked round and about and was told there wasn't finer deputy material in Northfield than young Lincoln Pearce. I want you and him to know I have every confidence in his ability to discharge the duties of his office. Linc, you tell your good folks what you told me today."

The buck having been deftly passed to him, Linc rose. His blue eyes were mourning-edged and he was so pale that Susan bled for him.

"I'm no expert on murder, never claimed to be one," Linc began in a matter-of-fact voice, but Susan could see his knuckles whiten on the edge of the table. "However, I've had the help of the best technical men of the state police. And they're as high up a tree as the 'coon of this piece. And that's me."

An old lady chuckled, and several men grinned. Humility, Linc? Susan thought in a sort of pain. Maybe one of these days you'll get around to me. . . .

"Three people have been beaten to death," Linc said. "One was a boy of seventeen, son of a dirt farmer, quiet boy, Congregationalist, never in trouble. One was a bar and grill owner,

234

French-Canadian descent, Roman Catholic, one of the most popular men in town. The third was the last survivor of the family that founded Northfield—rich woman, tight-fisted, some said, but we all know her many generosities. She just about ran Northfield all her life. She was a pillar of Christ Episcopal Church, on every important committee, with her finger in every community pie."

He thinks he has them, Susan thought, glancing about her at the long bony faces. Linc, Linc . . .

"The bodies of these three were found in the same spot. So their deaths have to be connected some way. But how? There doesn't seem to be any answer—at least, we haven't been able to find one so far.

"We know nothing about Tommy Cooley's death because of the months that passed before we found his body. Frenchy Lafont was probably lured to his death by a phone call from somebody he knew and wasn't afraid of. Flora Sloan probably picked her killer up as she left the church meeting, which she wouldn't have done unless it was someone she knew. Tommy Cooley's clothing was too far gone to tell us anything, and the rains this spring wiped out any clues that might have been left in his case. But we found dirt on the knees of Frenchy's trousers and Flora Sloan's skirt, so maybe Tommy was made to kneel on that spot just like Frenchy and Miss Flora afterward—and hit from behind a killing blow."

You can talk and talk, Linc, they won't let you alone any more, Susan thought. They won't do anything to you—they'll just ignore you from now on. . . .

"That's all we have," Linc said. "No connection among the three victims—not one. No motive. Not gain—nothing was taken in any of the three cases far as we know. Tommy Cooley had nothing to leave anybody, Frenchy Lafont's business and house he left to his eighty-one-year-old mother, and now we're told that Flora Sloan willed her entire estate to charity. No motive—no woman or other man in the case, no jealous husband, wife, or sweetheart. *No motive.*"

Linc stopped, looking down. Susan shut her eyes.

"When someone kills for no reason, he's insane. Three poeple died because a maniac is loose in our town. It's the only answer that makes sense. If anyone here has a better, for God's sake let's all hear it."

Now the noise came back like a rising wind, and Sanford

Brown banged it back to silence. But it was still there, waiting.

"I want to say one more thing." And Susan heard Linc's pride take stubborn voice again. Linc, Linc, don't you know you've had it? Old Sanford, the selectmen, Sheriff Howland—they all know it. Don't you? "I'm not going to hand over my badge unless Sheriff Howland asks for it. Want it, Sheriff?"

The politician squirmed. "No, Linc, course not—unless the good folks of Northfield feel—"

Poor Linc. Here it comes.

"Let Linc Pearce keep his badge!" a burly farmer shouted from the floor. "The boy's been doin' his best. But he's just a boy, that's the trouble. What we need's a Committee o' Safety. Men with guns to stand watch near that grave site . . ."

"Mr. Chairman!"

Susan slipped out of the meeting room as motions and resolutions winged toward the table from every corner. She caught up with Linc on the steps of the Town Hall.

" 'Lo, Susie," Linc said with a stiffish grin. "Come after me to watch me digest crow?"

"Committee of Safety, men guarding the grave," Susan said bitterly. "What do they expect him to do, walk into their arms? Linc, *please* let me help. You're not beaten yet. Let's you and I talk it over. There must be something you missed! Maybe if we put our heads together—"

"You know something?" Linc put his big hands about her waist and lifted her to his level like a doll. "All of a sudden I want to kiss you."

"Linc put me down. Don't treat me as if I were a child. Please, Linc?"

"My little old Susie."

"And *don't* call me Susie! I loathe it! I've loathed it all my life! Linc, put me down, I say!"

"Sorry," Linc looked genuinely surprised. He deposited her quietly on the step. "As far as the other thing is concerned, my answer's got to be the same, Sue. They can make up all the committees and posses they want—this is my job and I'll do it by myself or go bust. . . . Can I drive you home now?"

"Not *ever!*" And Susan fled to the safety of the old Buick that Flora Sloan had given her, where she could burst into tears in decent privacy.

Linc sat in his office long after the last selectman had gone and Rollie Fawcett had darkened the building. He was blackly conscious of the thunderstorm that had sprung up. The rain lashing his windows seemed fitting and proper.

There must be something you missed. . . .

Linc was irritated more by the source of the phrase going round in his head than by its persistence. That little fire-eater! She'd been singeing his tail from the start. Talk about one-track minds . . .

But suppose she's right?

The thought was like his collar, chafing him raw.

What *could* he have missed? What? What hadn't he followed up?

He'd been over the three cases a hundred times. He couldn't possibly have missed anything. Or had he? . . .

Linc Pearce finally saw it—appropriately enough, during a flash of lightning. The bare office with its whitewashed walls for an instant became bright as day, and in that flash of illumination Linc remembered what he had missed.

It had happened on that first night of the long nightmare. The night Tommy Cooley's body had been found washed out of its roadside grave by the receding waters of the spring flood. John Cooley had been kneeling in the grave, his hands scrabbling in the mud for some keepsake of his son. The pitiful little things he had found and tucked away in the pocket of his checkered red mackinaw . . . *suppose one of those things, unknown to Cooley, had been a clue?*

Linc grabbed a slicker and ran.

The Cooley farmhouse was dark. Linc turned off his lights and ignition, skin prickling at some danger he could not define.

The rain had turned into a tropical downpour. Lightning tore the sky open in quick bursts, like cannon salvos, lighting up the shade-drawn windows, the porch with the rickety rocking chairs turned to the wall, the wide-open door of the nearby garage . . .

John Cooley's jeep was not in the garage.

Linc reached for a flashlight and jumped out of his car. He splashed over to the garage and swung his light about. Yes, the farm truck was here, but the jeep was out. . . .

Linc relaxed. He had not noticed John Cooley at the town meeting, but he must have been there. If he was, with a committee of safety forming, he'd surely be one of the men to be staked out in the brush near the site of Tommy's grave.

Linc went up on the porch and tried the door. It was not locked, and he opened it and stepped into the hall.

"John?" He could be wrong. There might be a dozen explanations for the missing jeep. "John?"

No one answered. Linc went upstairs and looked into the bedrooms. They were empty.

He went back to John Cooley's old-fashioned bedroom and played his flash about. Of course, the chifforobe. He opened the doors. It was filled with winter garments.

And there was the red mackinaw.

Linc breathed a prayer and put his hand into the right pocket.

They were still there, all right.

He took them out one by one carefully, turning them over in his fingers. The button from young Tom's rotted leather jacket. A pebble. A chunk of dirt-crusted glass . . .

The piece of glass!

It was thick, ridged glass with a curve to it, a roughly triangular piece cracked off from something larger. It was . . . it was . . .

My God, Linc thought.

He went over it again and again, refusing to believe. It couldn't be that simple. The answer to the murders that had happened. The warning of the murder that was going to happen.

The murder of Susan Marsh.

Of Sue.

For a moment of sheer horror Linc saw her flying red hair, the familiar little face, the snub nose he used to tweak, the brookwater eyes, the impudent mouth that had tormented him all his life.

He saw them all soiled and still.

A world without Sue . . .

Linc never knew how he got out of the house.

Susan had gone to bed swollen-eyed. But she had been unable to sleep. The mugginess, the storm, the thunder crashes, the lightning bolts bouncing off her pond, made the night hideous. She had never felt so alone.

She crept out of bed, got into a wrap, and pattered about clicking switches. She put on every light in the house. Then she went into her tiny parlor and sat there, rigidly listening to the storm.

Oh, Linc, Linc . . .

Her first thought when the crash came and the curtains began blowing about and a cold spray hit her bare feet was that the gale had blown the front door loose.

She looked up.

John Cooley stood in her splintered doorway. He had Tommy's hunting rifle cradled in his arm. In the farmer's eyes Susan saw her death.

"They're watching at the grave," John Cooley said. His voice was all cracked and high, not like his bass at all. "So I can't take you there, Susan Marsh."

"You killed them," Susan said stiffly. "You."

"Get down on your knees, girl, and pray."

He was insane. She saw that now. He had been tottering on the brink ever since Tommy's disappearance, his only son, the child of his beloved Sarah. And he had toppled over when the body was found. Only no one had seen it, not Linc, not she, not anyone.

Linc, Linc.

"Not Tommy," Susan whispered. "You loved Tommy, Mr. Cooley. You wouldn't—couldn't have killed Tommy."

The farmer's twitching face, with its distended eyes, softened into something vaguely human. Tears welled into the eyes. The heavy shoulders began to shake.

Oh, dear God, let me find a way to keep him from killing me as he killed Frenchy Lafont and Miss Flora. . . .

"I know you didn't kill Tommy, Mr. Cooley."

With the metal-sheathed butt of Tommy's hunting rifle. That was the weapon that had crushed out Frenchy Lafont's and Miss Flora's lives . . . dear God . . . I mustn't faint, mustn't . . . those dark smears on the butt . . . get him talking . . . maybe the phone . . . no, no, that would be fatal . . . What can I do! Oh, Linc . . .

"Not Tommy. Somebody else killed Tommy, Mr. Cooley. Who was it? Why don't you tell me?"

The farmer sank into the tapestried chair near the door. The rain beat in on him, mixing with his tears.

"You killed him, Susan Marsh," he wept.

"Oh, no!" Susan cried faintly.

"You, or the Frenchy, or the old woman. I knew from the

239

hunk of glass in the boy's grave. A hunk of headlight glass. Headlight from an old auto. He was run over on the road, hit by an auto from the back . . . from the back. You killed him with an auto and you put him in a dirty hole and piled dirt on him and you ran away. You, or the Frenchy, or the old woman."

Susan wet her lips. "The Buick," she said. "My old Buick."

John Cooley looked up, suddenly cunning. "I found it! Didn't think I would, hey? I looked all over Northfield and I found the auto it come from. I looked for a smashed headlight, and the auto the old woman gave you was the one the hunk of glass fitted. Was it you run Tommy over? Or the old woman, who run the car before you? Or the Frenchy, who owned the Buick before the old woman?"

"Frenchy Lafont sold that car to Flora Sloan—in October?" Susan gasped.

"Didn't think I'd track that down, hey?" John Cooley said with a sly chuckle. "Aya! Lafont sold it to the old woman when he bought his new Ford. And she gave it to you a couple weeks later when she won a Chevrolet in the Grange bazaar. Oh, I tracked it all down. I was careful to do proper justice." The eyes began to start again; he whimpered. "But which one, which one? I didn't know which one of you killed Tommy in October, 'cause nobody knows what day in October he was run over. So I got to kill all three of you. That way the Lord's vengeance is mine. The wrath. With the boy's gun. I phoned that Lafont and I says meet me at the grave, I have to talk to you . . . I walked into the town and I waited for the old woman to come out of the church, and I stopped her and made her drive out to the grave. 'Pray, Flora Sloan,' I says. 'Get down on your murdering knees, sinner, and pray for your damned soul,' I says. And then I used the Lord's gun butt on her."

The room was shimmering.

John Cooley was on his feet, the great eyes shining.

"Pray, Susan Marsh," he thundered. "Down on your knees, girl, and pray."

Now the steel hand was at the back of her neck, forcing her to her knees.

Dear God . . . Linc, you're the one I love, the only only one I've ever . . .

The last thing Susan saw as she strained against the paralyzing clutch on her neck was that exultant face, terrible in

240

triumph, and the rusty blood-caked butt of the rifle held high above it.

She fainted just as Linc Pearce plunged into the room and hurled himself at the madman.

Susan opened her eyes. She was in her own bed. Linc's long face was close to hers.

"I thought I heard you say something, Linc, a million years ago," Susan murmured. "Or maybe it was just now. Didn't you say something, oh, so nice?"

"I said I love you, Susie—Susan," Linc muttered. "And something about will you marry me."

Susan closed her eyes again. "That's what I thought you said," she said contentedly.

They never did find out which one had accidentally run Tommy Cooley over, whether Frenchy Lafont or old Miss Flora. They argued about it for years.

CAUSE FOR SUSPICION

BY GEORGE HARMON COXE

George Harmon Coxe was born in Olean, New York, in 1901. He quit college after two years and did some newspaper work, then switched to advertising. After three years, he returned to writing. The first of his more than sixty hardcover mysteries was published in 1935. His most famous fictional detectives are Flashgun Casey and Kent Murdock, who are Boston news photographers. His books have usually been favorably reviewed, and one of his most well known is *The Groom Lay Dead* (1944). The Mystery Writers of America presented him with their Grand Master Award in 1963. He and his wife live in Old Lyme, Connecticut.

THE FIRST NIGHT THAT Dr. Standish went to Arlene Walton's apartment, he went not as the medical examiner but as Paul Standish, M.D. At that, it was a near thing. Any great delay in finding her and he might well have been called in his official capacity. But as it was, the switchboard operator at the Belmont Arms, a youth by the name of Klein, remembered that Dr. Standish lived close by.

Klein's phoned diagnosis had saved a lot of time:

"It looks like she took an overdose of sleeping tablets," he said. "Can you come right away, Doc?"

The Belmont Arms was only a block and a half away, and Standish made the foyer in three minutes. Klein was holding the elevator.

"She's still alive," he said. He said other things on the way to the third floor and down the hall to the room at the end. But Paul Standish wasn't listening, nor was he more than vaguely aware of the two men beside the studio couch.

All he saw was the woman, a small figure in a blue house coat, her chestnut hair spread across the pillow. Noting her color and the bottle of pills on the end table, he examined her eyes, checked her pulse, and prepared his hypodermic.

He called over his shoulder to order an ambulance, and heard someone talking on the telephone; then he was injecting a massive dose of amphetamine sulfate intravenously.

"Will she live, Doctor?"

Paul Standish stepped away from the couch. There was a film of moisture on his lean, well-boned face, for the night was warm and the room was heavy with a gardenia-like scent.

"Yes," he said. "She'll live."

The man let his breath out in a whistling sound and sank into a chair. Standish saw that he was a short, stocky fellow of perhaps twenty-eight, with curly reddish hair and a solid jaw.

"Who found her?" Standish glanced at the second man, who stood two or three inches taller than the doctor's own six feet and looked immaculate in his dinner jacket.

"I guess I got here about five minutes after they did."

"We found her," the stocky man said. "Billy and me." He indicated young Klein.

His name, he said, was Harry Gibney. He was a friend of Arlene Walton's and lived on the top floor, and he had knocked at her door around eight thirty. When he got no answer, he had gone upstairs. At ten forty he had telephoned her, and then asked Billy Klein if he knew where she was.

"Billy said she had come up at seven," Gibney said, "and he hadn't seen her go out. Yet she didn't answer her phone. I got scared."

"So did I." Klein was standing in the doorway. "Mr. Gibney said I should get a key and see if anything was wrong. I met him outside, and we came in and found her like that."

Paul Standish had been moving about the room as the others talked, and now he examined the half-filled bottle of tablets, noting the date the prescription had been filled.

"She didn't leave any note?"

Gibney glanced at Billy Klein. He shook his head. "No," he said. "I didn't see any."

Standish brought his gaze back to the tall man. He asked if he hadn't seen the other somewhere and the man smiled.

"Probably," he said. "I'm Victor Keenan. I have the orchestra at Castle Inn. . . . I phoned Arlene at ten thirty," he said, when Standish nodded. "She told me she'd be in tonight, and the boy here"—he indicated young Klein—"said he didn't know why she didn't answer. So I had one of my men take over the band and came right out. They were calling you when I came in and saw her."

Standish moved to the woman, finding her pulse improved. He asked, "What was her trouble?"

The silence that followed was abrupt, and he sensed an odd tension in the room where none had been before. He turned, his glance taking in Keenan and Gibney.

The two men were staring at each other, their animosity unmistakable. Gibney was leaning forward in his chair, his rocky jaw set, his mouth tight, his eyes hard with hatred. Keenan's manner seemed more defiant than aggressive.

"We used to go together," he said, turning finally to Standish. "I—I broke it off last week. I got engaged to someone else. I didn't think she would—"

He did not finish, because Gibney cut in on him, speaking through his teeth. What he said was not distinct but its cadence was profane and he might have said more if steps in the hall had not announced an intern and ambulance attendants.

Standish told the intern that he would be along presently. Victor Keenan said if there was nothing he could do he would get back to his band, and went away with Billy Klein. Harry Gibney lingered in the doorway, his brown eyes anxious.

"You're sure she'll be all right, Doctor? . . . When can I see her?"

"Tomorrow afternoon should be all right," Standish said, and waited until the other started down the hall before stepping back into the room for a final look around. He saw now that the furnishings were colorful but cheap, like the building itself. He went to the couch, examined the floor around it and behind it. When he was sure there was no suicide note he went out.

In the main foyer a man was leaning over the switchboard talking to Billy Klein, a short, round-bodied man in a black homburg. The doctor recognized the florid, heavy face, though the name escaped him until young Klein spoke.

"Mr. Cormack was just asking about Miss Walton. . . . This is Dr. Standish," he said.

"Oh, yes," Cormack said. He shook his head and looked grieved. "From what the boy tells me, I guess it's lucky you got here when you did, Doctor. I've been worried about Arlene," he said and shook his head again, "but I never dreamed she'd try suicide."

Standish placed Cormack now as a politician of sorts who had worked his way from ward heeler to building commissioner and was now exploring greener fields. He replied perfunctorily to Cormack's questions, wondering casually why the man should be calling at this hour, but otherwise uninterested. And since there was nothing unusual in the incident, he thought nothing more about Edward Cormack—until later.

Arlene Walton was sitting up in bed when Paul Standish stopped at the hospital the following afternoon, and she had company.

"You can't talk like that to me," Arlene was saying with some asperity. "I've told you before how it was, and that's the way it's got to be."

The object of the lecture was Harry Gibney. When he glanced round and saw Standish, the tightness was still in his face, and so was the flush in his cheeks. He accepted Standish's apology with ill-concealed truculence.

"It's okay, Doc," he said flatly. "I was just leaving. . . . So long," he said to the girl, "but don't get the idea that I've finished."

Arlene Walton stared at the door long after it had closed, and Standish, seeing how upset she was, examined her chart.

"You had a close one," he said. "It was a silly thing to do. Been having trouble with the boy friend?"

"I've always had trouble with Harry. But not the kind you mean. What happened wasn't on his account. And anyway," she added, "it was kind of an accident."

Standish smiled crookedly, his eyes wise. "You had a headache and took a couple of pills and later you woke up and forgot you took them and swallowed some more." He shook his head. "The trouble with that story is that the prescription was filled three days ago and half the bottle was gone."

She lowered her glance, color showing in her face. She was quite tiny, lying there in bed, not more than five feet one, but with a certain voluptuousness for all of that. About twenty-six, Standish thought, though she looked older, with good features and a face that was pretty in spite of the tiredness around the hazel eyes and the slackness of skin beneath the chin. When he found her watching him, he said:

"What do you do—for a living?"

"I'm a manicurist."

"And before that?"

She moved her shoulders. "Oh—this and that." She hesitated, continued softly, "I guess I should be grateful to you."

"To Gibney and Billy Klein for finding you when they did."

She thought it over, and Standish, sensing that she did not want to talk, stood up. "When can I go home?" she asked.

"In twenty-four hours," he said, "if you're good."

She smiled at this, and it was, apparently, a good omen, for when he stopped in, the following afternoon, she was packing her things.

"I'll drive you home," he said.

She talked easily in the car, telling him how she had left home at sixteen because of her ambition to go on the stage. "I wound up clerking in a five-and-dime," she said, "and after that there were other jobs in other stores. I checked hats in night clubs and sold cigarettes." She laughed shortly. "That was as close as I ever got to the theater."

She was still talking when Standish stopped his car in front of

246

the Belmont Arms, and what he did then surprised him almost as much as it did the girl. He suddenly heard himself asking her to dinner.

Arlene Walton eyed him curiously. Then she smiled. "All right," she said. "I'd like that."

Standish had to stop at his office, but it was a mistake to have asked his guest up. For the office was presided over by Mary Hayward, young, blonde, and, as his combination nurse, secretary and girl Friday, jealous of the doctor's time—and quite possibly of his affections. Mary's green eyes struck sparks when she saw Arlene. Presently he was driving through the outskirts of the city with Arlene.

Arlene expressed a preference for the Castle Inn. Once they were seated, Standish remembered Victor Keenan and knew why. Victor had a ten-piece band and it was pretty good. Victor looked good too, with his blond hair and dinner jacket and professionally winning smile. So did the slim young brunette who sang with him.

"Is that the girl?" Standish asked.

"That's her," said Arlene. "Helen Shirley. She's got money."

The name was familiar to Standish. While not exactly first family, John Shirley had made considerable money in the construction business.

"I was good enough for him when he had nothing but a saxophone," Arlene said, "but now it's different." Then the story came out.

Victor Keenan had come to town three years ago with an orchestra and had stayed on to work with one of the local radio stations. Until recently he had taken odd jobs and got along as best he could. But during the summer he had organized a band, made some good arrangements and the beginning of a reputation. This was his last week at the Castle Inn. He had a few radio dates left to fill, and after that he was taking the band on the road—with Helen Shirley as vocalist.

As Arlene's moodiness increased Standish offered certain platitudes by way of consolation. He said Keenan hardly seemed worth suicide. He said it was tough to take right now, but she'd get over it and probably find someone else a lot better, and anyway it worked both ways: you loved someone and it didn't do any good, and all the time some other guy you didn't want loved you.

"I guess you're right," she said finally. "I was in love with Vic, and Harry Gibney can't see anyone but me. He's a good enough guy, but he's just not for me. Only he can't see it. He says if he can't have me, nobody can."

She opened her handbag and the smell of gardenias was strong, reminding Standish of her apartment.

"What does Gibney do?"

"He's from somewhere out West. He runs a bowling alley with another fellow. It's just down the street from the beauty parlor where I work."

Standish said, "Maybe you ought to go away. You can get a job anywhere these days."

Arlene nodded and now the slackness was more apparent in her face. "Maybe I ought to," she said. "Maybe that's an idea. And I could get the money. I had an offer just the other day."

She paused, then continued, her voice thick with drink: "There's a man here in town—you'd know the name if I told you—who'd pay me to leave. He and I used to—well, we had an arrangement. He was separated from his wife then, but now they're back together again and he wants to be county judge and he's scared I'll talk. I never asked him for a dime after we split up and he came to see me the other day and—" She hesitated again. "Why not?" she said.

"Why not," agreed Standish, "if that's what he wants?"

"Also," said Arlene, "there's another citizen who might pay. If you went to prison for assaulting some girl out in Toledo and got paroled and then someone could turn you in, wouldn't *you* pay?"

Standish felt strangely shocked at what she was saying.

"That sounds like blackmail," he said.

Her eyes opened wide and there was innocence in them. "I thought blackmail was when you kept collecting over and over for something."

"There's more than one kind."

"But I wouldn't ask for much," she said. "And if I left town, what harm could it do?"

Standish said he guessed she should think it over before she did anything, and suddenly he'd had enough and wanted to get home.

But he was unable to dismiss the girl from his thoughts. In the morning, as his mind went back, he was singularly depressed by it all.

Mary Hayward gave him a stony glance and a distant good

248

morning. She took a long time straightening his desk. Normally Mary's manner during office hours was one of strict formality; but occasionally she bullied and scolded him with the proprietary intensity of a woman in love. She did not approve of his work as medical examiner.

"It isn't bad enough to waste your time on Lieutenant Ballard and medical examiner cases," she said. "Now you have to take patients to dinner and hold their hands."

"I didn't hold her hand," Standish said glumly. "I only wanted to cheer her up. She's had a tough time and—"

"Oh, I know," Mary said with studied irony. "I'm sure everything will be just perfect now."

It was in the middle of the following week that he got the call from the Belmont Arms. He was shaving at the moment—seven thirty in the morning. This time the call was official. He was to go to the alley behind the apartments, where a row of garages stretched to the corner.

A sergeant from the precinct house was in charge. "The motor was running," he said, and indicated the six-year-old coupé. "The guy in the next garage heard it as he was going to work and saw the door was shut, so he took a look. When he saw her, he shut off the motor and called in."

The doors of the coupé stood open now, and Paul Standish, moving to the driver's side, saw the small crumpled figure of Arlene Walton behind the wheel. She wore a print dress and no stockings. Her head was slumped forward so that her chestnut hair hung down, obscuring her face, and when Standish parted the hair and saw the color of the skin he knew how she had died. He reached for the handbag that lay beside her on the seat. That was when he noticed the smell of whiskey inside the car.

"Found this next to the bag," the sergeant said, and handed the doctor a small sheet of paper folded in the middle.

Standish handled it gingerly, scanning the one-paragraph suicide note. He turned it over, holding it close to his face, then he opened his bag, tore two sheets from a notebook and put the note between them.

He opened her purse and the familiar gardenia-like scent came to him, strong and distinctive. There was a hard line to his jaw as he closed the bag and stepped back.

"You'd better phone headquarters," he said to the sergeant. "You'd better get Lieutenant Ballard out here." He was moving round the car, noting the bits of tar in the tire treads, glancing at the doors, estimating the angle of turn from the alley.

"Ballard?" The sergeant's tone was questioning. "I thought Ballard was a homicide man."

"He is," Standish said. "That's why we need him. . . ."

It was late afternoon before Paul Standish was ready to make a report. When he walked into Ballard's office he found the lieutenant slumped in his chair with a look of acute displeasure on his face. Ballard greeted his visitor with a grunt.

"You still say it's murder?" he asked. "Did she die of carbon monoxide?"

"Yes," said Standish. "Also she was drunk."

"Okay. She sits in her car, drinking until she's ready to pass out, and then starts the motor."

"What did she drink out of?" Standish knew no bottle had been found.

"All right," Ballard said. "She got drunk somewhere else, tossed out the bottle, and—"

"No." Standish shook his head. "The p.m. showed she was pretty drunk, Tom. I doubt if she could drive. I'm sure she never could have made the turn into the garage without scraping a fender on the door. She got drunk somewhere outside all right. But someone else drove her home, left the motor running, planted the note, and closed the doors."

"That note looked awfully good," Ballard said. "It was in her handwriting."

Standish moved to a nearby table and examined Arlene's bag and the contents which had been spread out beside it. Selecting the billfold, he sniffed it, and the odor of gardenias was there, faint but unmistakable.

"She wrote the note before she left her house, because she didn't carry a pen. Did you find out when she left?"

"Around nine," Ballard said. "I talked to that guy Gibney you told me about. He sat up until one o'clock waiting for her."

"She wore a print dress," Standish said. "With no pockets. So where did she carry the note? If it had been in the bag it would smell of perfume, like these other things. I smelled it this morning. There was no perfume on that note, and I say she didn't have it. I think she wrote that note when she took those sleeping tablets and someone picked it up and saved it."

Interest quickened in Ballard's gaze. He wanted to know who

had found Arlene Walton the night she tried suicide. When he had all the details, he said, "Then, if you throw out the kid on the switchboard, Gibney's the only guy who could have got the note."

"Unless Cormack came earlier and found her and walked out."

"How would he get in?"

Standish told of his conversation with Arlene. He said he believed that Cormack was the politician she had referred to as being willing to pay her to leave town. He might still have a key to her apartment. Then, remembering what she had said about the possibility of collecting from some parole violator from Toledo, he passed that information along to Ballard.

The lieutenant made some notes. "It's a lead," he said. "I can probably check that and then narrow it down and get prints forwarded." He leaned back as Standish stood up. "Anything else?"

Standish thought it over. He said he had noticed tar in the tire treads.

"Maybe you'd want to find out what roads have been freshly tarred. Maybe out by the river. There are some parking places up that way. There's a chance the girl's car parked there. If so, maybe that's where the drinking was done."

"And maybe they killed the bottle and tossed it out the window," Ballard said, keeping pace with the doctor's suggestions. "If we're lucky we might find the bottle with the dame's prints on it and maybe someone else's. Is that it?"

Standish shrugged. "It was just a thought," he said.

"All right." Ballard hesitated and his voice was mildly ironic when he continued. "What's that pat line of yours about your job being only to find the cause of death and if anyone is culpable? Well, I guess you have, all right. You've made it murder, and now I guess you dump it in my lap and walk out on me, hunh?"

Standish was familiar with the approach. He had been needled by Ballard before. He heard himself say, "If I can help any, I will."

He did not know why he drove from headquarters to the Belmont Arms either, but he did, and presently he was in the garage and climbing behind the wheel of Arlene Walton's coupé. He lit a cigarette and slid far down in the seat.

He was not looking for clues, for that was Ballard's job, but his mind was busy, remembering the dead girl and the things she had said—feeling somehow a personal interest beyond the routine of the job. He wanted Ballard to find the whiskey bottle that had been thrown away; Ballard had the manpower at his disposal. But would this be enough?

He sat up slowly, his eyes on the rear-view mirrow, watching the window panel at the back move into his line of vision. The idea came to him then, and he leaned quickly forward, a new alertness growing in him as his tension mounted.

With handkerchief in hand he reached for the mirror, tipping it one way and then another. That was how he happened to see the mark there—a distinctive mark imprinted on the glass by someone's thumb or finger. That there would be other prints upon the metal back, Standish was certain. What he did not know was whether they, or this one, would be a man's or a woman's. . . .

The city maintained an office for the medical examiner at the morgue. Adjoining this office was a conference room, and it was here that Paul Standish conducted his inquiry the following evening after Lieutenant Ballard had notified him that he was ready.

Ballard was waiting with a stenographer and a fingerprint expert when Standish arrived, and grouped around the long table were the three men he had summoned: Harry Gibney, Victor Keenan, and Edward Cormack. Standish nodded to them and sat down as Ballard began his preliminary remarks by stating that Arlene Walton had been murdered and explaining the circumstances of her death. He removed some papers from a bulging brief case as he spoke, and now, spreading them out before him, he turned to Edward Cormack.

"At two forty on the afternoon of the fifth," he said, "you drew five thousand in cash from your Second National account. Did you give it to Arlene Walton or not?"

Cormack's face was impassive.

"Who says I intended to give it to her?"

"She did." Ballard glanced at Standish as he expertly stretched the truth. "She told the doctor you'd offered her cash to leave town, and she told him why. Do you want me to go into that here, or would you rather answer my question?"

"I gave her the money that afternoon," Cormack said quietly.

"She didn't have it in her purse when we found her," Ballard said, "and we couldn't locate it in her apartment. Maybe we can find out what happened to it," he said, and turned to Victor Keenan, checking his notes again as he began to review the big man's association with the dead woman.

Keenan denied nothing. He sat straight-backed in his chair, not bothering with the charm and personality he offered to customers, but deadly serious as he admitted that he had broken off his affair with Arlene Walton because he wanted to marry someone else.

Ballard seemed satisfied. He selected the suicide note from among his papers and explained Standish's theory that it had been written before.

"You arrived at her apartment five minutes after Gibney found her that first night," he said to Keenan. "Did you see this note—or any note? . . . Okay," he said when the other shook his head. "I guess that leaves you," he went on, turning to Harry Gibney.

Gibney stared morosely back at him, his rocky jaw set and a look of tension in his squat powerful body, "I didn't see any note," he said, "and I didn't kill her."

"Maybe the switchboard operator swiped the note," Ballard said sarcastically. "Maybe we don't care, now that we know it's murder. The guy that took the note killed her and framed the second suicide and here's how he did it."

He took his time telling how Arlene Walton had left her apartment sometime before nine—in her car—and had picked up a man downtown and driven out along the river. "We got a little break on that," he said and told about the tar in the tire treads. "Only one road had been tarred this week, and when we found out where it went, we knew there were just three good parking places where a guy and a girl might park to do a little drinking."

He took a pint bottle from his brief case, and the rear-view mirror Standish had seen before. "We picked up twenty-one empties," he continued, "and all but three had women's finger-prints on them. One of them—this one—had Arlene Walton's prints on it. It also had a man's prints on it, and those prints checked with a fellow who did time for assault in Toledo and violated his parole. He had another name then, but it doesn't matter. He's the same guy and his prints are also on this rear-view mirror, and so if you gentlemen will just let my fingerprint man have a look at you—"

253

Standish cut in. He hadn't known about the prints checking. Now he said:

"I don't think you need to bother with the prints now. If the ones on the mirror check with the others, you've got enough." He paused to glance about, aware that Ballard did not understand what he meant. "Arlene Walton was five feet one. The man who drove her home when she had passed out had to be careful. He didn't want an accident and the mirror was no good to him until he changed—"

The sentence ended abruptly as a chair scraped. Standish jumped up, with Ballard ahead of him. The lieutenant could move fast, but this time Harry Gibney was faster. He charged down the table and around, a step ahead of Ballard, a wild light in his eye. The lieutenant yelled, but it did no good. Gibney drove in, shoulders hunched and a snarl in his throat.

He slammed both fists savagely, and Vic Keenan went back against the wall. He tried to slide along it, but Gibney caught him, clubbing him down with rights and lefts and jumping on his chest.

Ballard caught him there, Ballard and the fingerprint man and the stenographer. They hauled him off, and it took the three of them to hold him.

"Cut it out!" Ballard stormed as Gibney fought. "If you kill him now, you'll get the chair. Take it easy! The state'll take care of it."

The words got through to Gibney and he dropped his arms. Ballard looked down at the bruised and unconscious Victor Keenan. He glanced up at Standish. "What was that about the mirror?"

"Arlene Walton was short," Standish said. "So are Cormack and Gibney." He explained how he had sat behind the wheel of the coupé and noticed the angle of view. "The mirror was adjusted for a tall man—taller than I am. I figured if there were prints on it, they should be Keenan's."

Ballard grunted. "You caught on quick," he said to Gibney. "But you missed the note that first night."

"I wasn't looking for it," Gibney said.

"Keenan picked it up," Standish said. "He could see what had happened; he was afraid his name would be in the note, and he probably stuck it in his pocket."

"He wanted her to die," Gibney said. "But you saved her, and he kept the note—"

254

"—and decided to use it," Ballard said, "when she asked him for money. He knew if she ever talked he would go back to prison instead of marrying the Shirley dame and her money. So he faked the suicide. He probably grabbed the five thousand bucks you gave her, Cormack."

As he reached for the telephone his glance fastened on Standish.

"I still don't know how you spotted it as a phony," he said. "I talked with the sergeant from the precinct house. He said you acted suspicious from the minute you stepped into that garage. Even before you had a chance to read the note you acted like something was wrong. Don't tell me it was just a hunch."

"You might call it that," Standish said. "You see, I never happened to run into a case where a woman had committed suicide that way. I wondered about it and looked up some statistics put out by New York City officials. Out of twelve hundred and ninety-five suicides in one year, there were twenty-five or twenty-six deaths from motor exhausts—*all of them men!*"

"Oh," said Ballard.

"Yes," said Standish. "I don't say there aren't exceptions, but any time you find a woman dead under such circumstances you've got a right to be suspicious."

"I'll remember that," Ballard said, and then, his hand still on the telephone, a slow smile came about his eyes. Like Standish, he had taken a certain amount of criticism and adverse comment from Mary Hayward when he made demands on the doctor's time. This must have occurred to him now, because he said, "You ought to tell your nurse about this next time she needles you about wasting your time."

The suggestion fell on fertile soil. It seemed suddenly important to Standish that he see Mary Hayward.

"I'll tell her tonight," he said.

Lieutenant Ballard understood. He was still grinning as he lifted the telephone and dialed the operator.

THE STOLLMEYER SONNETS

BY JAMES POWELL

James Powell was born in Canada and graduated from
the University of Toronto. He studied and taught in
France for three years, then worked for a New York
publisher and later for a newspaper in the Midwest. His
first short story, "The Friends of Hector Jouvet," appeared in the April 1966 issue of *Ellery Queen's Mystery
Magazine.* Later stories introduced his popular series
character, Acting Sergeant Maynard Bullock of the
Royal Canadian Mounted Police. Ellery Queen has
praised Powell for his "range of theme and subject
matter, his scope of interest and preoccupation, and his
unusual and individualistic point of view."

THERE HAD BEEN SKIRMISHING between Tasmite and Amalek tribesmen that weekend. Otherwise, world attention would certainly have been focused on the tiny republic of San Marino where the foreign ministers of the Little Three—San Marino, Monaco, and Liechtenstein—were about to sit down to an historic meeting.

But there was one man quite content to have the eyes of the world turned elsewhere. Acting Sergeant Maynard Bullock of the Royal Canadian Mounted Police was traveling incognito. At each turn of the road as his bus wound up and around the base of the crag on which the city of San Marino stood, he repeated to himself, "I am Bob Jones, a Hudson Bay blanket salesman."

Two other voices spoke inside his head. One called him Maynard: "You'll do just great, Maynard." That was his wife, good old Mavis. The other belonged to Inspector McNaughton: "For gossake, try not to boot this one, Bullock."

The bus stopped in the lower part of town. Bullock savored his disguise as he waited for his bags amid the humble, foreign-looking passengers. "If only they knew," he thought, stroking his trim mustache with a thumbnail.

"Acting Sergeant Bullock?" A sandy-haired man with glasses stood at Bullock's elbow.

The Mountie looked him up and down. "That depends," he said.

"I'm Wickett, the Canadian cultural and military attaché," said the man. "We expected you yesterday."

"This isn't the easiest place in the world to get to, you know," said Bullock gruffly.

"All I meant was, we've been looking forward to having a real Mountie here," said Wickett, who insisted on carrying Bullock's bags to the car. "I guess you do a lot of this kind of work," he added.

"As a matter of fact, for the last couple of years I've been guarding the flowerbeds in front of the Parliament Buildings in Ottawa," said Bullock. "It's exciting work in its own way. You never hear the bee that has your name on it."

"How did you happen to get picked for this assignment, then?" asked Wickett.

Bullock smiled sadly. "Last week was the Mounties' Annual Picnic," he said. "By a strange quirk of fate I came in last in the sack race. They had already started in on the lobster salad by the time I crossed the finish line and the ground was scarlet with tunics. The entire Headquarters Barrack was down with food poisoning, present company excepted."

Bullock eyed Wickett's tiny white Fiat suspiciously before squeezing himself into the front seat. "Well now," he said, "put me in the picture. What kind of a mess have you fellows gotten yourselves into this time?"

"I'm not sure how to begin," said Wickett, starting the car up the steep ascent into the city.

"Just put it in your own words," said Bullock.

"Well," said Wickett, "how are you on geopolitics?"

Bullock reflected for a minute. "I haven't really gone into it since grade school."

"All it boils down to is that any country worth its salt has a sphere of influence," said Wickett. "Traditionally, Liechtenstein has been in the Canadian sphere. You might say that Canada is like Liechtenstein's kindly big brother. San Marino and Monaco, the other members of the Little Three, are in the spheres of influence of Albania and Yugoslavia respectively. So far so good?"

"Check," said Bullock.

"The national economies of the Little Three," continued Wickett, "are based on postage stamps. But your stamp collector is a real fanatic. Left to his own devices he'd soon impoverish himself and his family to satisfy his unnatural craving. So the Little Three agreed, under the terms of the Monte Carlo Convention of 1947, to restrict the number of stamps and new issues they printed each year. You might say," said Wickett, turning to Bullock with a sly chuckle, "that they were content to milk the goose that lays the golden egg."

"Check," said Bullock grimly.

"Then about a year ago," said Wickett, "the lid blew off the Monte Carlo Convention and we found ourselves with a real knock-down-drag-'em-out stamp war on our hands with printing presses on all three sides going full blast."

"Wait," whispered Bullock, putting a finger to his lips. "We're being followed. Some guy in a leather overcoat on one of those scooters."

"A Vespa with diplomatic license plates?" said Wickett. "A big

258

fellow with one of those black handlebar-type mustaches?"

"Check," said Bullock.

"I'm afraid that's Major Glinka of the Iron Hats, as the Albanians call their Secret Police."

"Who let the cat out of the bag?" said Bullock. "Only you and the Ambassador knew I was coming."

"I know you'll understand," said Wickett hopefully. "It bothers Mrs. Wickett that the other Embassies are always having some big high muckity-muck or other visit San Marino. So when I told her you were coming she called the newspapers. You made the social notes."

"I can understand her excitement," said Bullock. "But, good Godfrey, Wickett—"

"Hear me out," said Wickett, "and I'll bet you'll want to keep an eye on Glinka. And if he's following you around, what could be easier?" Bullock grumbled but waved him on.

"Well, the stamp war was escalating," said Wickett. "New issues nearly every week, and in all denominations. The small collectors were going under. And how much longer could the big ones keep on buying? In panic, Monaco came up with the ultimate weapon: the megafranc stamp. They printed hundreds of thousands of stamps—millions—of this astronomical denomination. Unless the insane stamp war stopped, Monaco threatened to dump its megafranc stockpile on the market.

"Overnight, Liechtenstein and San Marino had megafranc stockpiles of their own. The Little Three were eyeball to eyeball to eyeball. A hasty move could bring on a philatelic Armageddon that could destroy them all and stamp collecting as we know it today.

"Meanwhile, clear heads in Ottawa came up with a really ingenious plan of inspections and controls to guarantee the Monte Carlo Convention and to supervise the trilateral destruction of megafranc stockpiles. The Ottawa Plan for Postal Peace. Liechtenstein, of course, was all for it. But the Yugoslavs got Monaco to counter with the Belgrade Plan, identical to ours except in name. And the Albanians sold San Marino some rubbish about the historical inevitability of San Marino's surviving the holocaust and picking up the pieces.

"Fortunately for us, however, Yugoslav-Albanian relations have recently soured. Border incidents. The Yugoslavs claim when their sheep wander over the border the Albanians send them back sheared. Just to spite the Albanians, it looked as

259

though they might be ready to vote for the Ottawa Plan."

Wickett turned to Bullock. "Now you're going to ask me, "All right, Wickett, where the heck do I come in?' "

Bullock considered that for a minute. "All right," he said.

"Three days ago Baron Stollmeyer of Liechtenstein had a manuscript stolen from his castle," said Wickett. "A sonnet cycle written by the Baron when he was a young man. I gather it's pretty racy stuff, all about the youthful indiscretions of some of his country's leading citizens. We believe the Albanians stole the manuscript and will use the threat of publication to force Liechtenstein to vote aginst the Ottawa Plan. Your job is to recover the manuscript."

"If it's in the Albanian Embassy that shouldn't be too difficult," said Bullock. "I once gained entry into a counterfeiters' den just by walking through the door and shouting a hearty 'Meter man!' " He saw no reason to mention they had locked the cellar door after him and escaped, printing presses and all. "Another trick I sometimes use is to put in a false fire-alarm and then follow the firemen carrying a nozzle or something."

"I thought you'd like to begin your investigation with Baron Stollmeyer," said Wickett. "So I asked him to meet us at our Embassy in an hour. That will give you a chance to freshen up at the hotel. It's back to the Embassy for me. Somebody has to answer the phone. There's only the Ambassador and myself, but with the grousing season here, I don't see much of him."

"Check," said Bullock, who had turned to see if Major Glinka was still behind them.

"By the way," said Wickett, "I've heard that Glinka is a pretty ugly customer. A master of Montenegrin savate. His heels are hard calluses. He can kill a man with his bare feet. If he starts taking his shoe off, watch out."

"If he tries anything with me," said Bullock, "I'll fix his wagon with a little taste of the old Marquess of Queensbury."

Flattening himself against the wall, Bullock peeked out the window of his hotel room. Glinka was still there, waiting across the street. "The hunter has become the hunted," thought Bullock and shook his head. Then he unpacked, hanging his uniform tenderly in the large clothes closet. He fingered one bright but stripeless sleeve. Still Acting Sergeant. How long had it been? "You'll show them, Maynard," Mrs. Bullock had said confidently.

260

During washup, as he scrubbed the back of his neck, Bullock thought, "Geopolitics, eh? Well, a man needs a specialty. 'This one involves a lot of tricky geopolitics,' Inspector McNaughton would say, scanning the ranks. 'Another case right up your alley, Bullock.' And someone would murmur, 'Lucky dog!' " Bullock smiled as he combed his mustache.

Bullock set out to follow Wickett's directions to the Embassy. Half an hour later he was lost in a maze of narrow streets, while behind him Glinka muttered in audible Albanian. Stopping a passer-by, an old gentleman with cane and gloves, Bullock sang a stanza of *O Canada* and with his hands imitated a flag fluttering over an Embassy door.

"Bravo. Bravo," said the old gentleman, visibly moved. He shook Bullock's hand, then walked on.

Glinka cleared his throat loudly. Bullock turned. The Albanian was pretending to look in a store window. His hands were clasped behind his back. One of them wagged and pointed up a street to Bullock's right. Ten minutes later, with Glinka prompting him from behind all the way, Bullock stood in front of the Embassy, which was above a radio and appliance store.

With the introductions out of the way, Bullock, Wickett, and Baron Stollmeyer, a balding little man with a monocle, sat around Wickett's desk in the outer office of the Embassy.

"Mr. Wickett and I have been having a jolly time getting out the Embassy mail," said the Baron. "I licked the envelopes and he licked the stamps. Quite appropriate, now that I think of it, because that's the way our present crisis began. About a year ago Monaco came out with flavored stickums on their stamps—mint, cinnamon, and anise. The collectors went wild. My own dear Liechtenstein countered with a Swiss chocolate flavor that was not unpleasant, while San Marino experimented unsuccessfully with a variety of flavors. What is it this month, Mr. Wickett?"

"*Costolletta Milanese*," said Wickett, making a face.

"Breaded veal cutlet," said the Baron. "Well, San Marino finally declared Monaco's flavored stickum had abrogated the Monte Carlo Convention. In retaliation they launched a stamp series commemorating Dante's *Divine Comedy,* stanza by stanza. They were halfway through 'The Inferno' before Liechtenstein countered with our 'Flora and Fauna of Canada' series and Monaco began issuing its 'Great Moments in the Lives of the Grimaldis' commemoratives.

261

"Since then, issues have been proliferating all over the place. Today, as the stamp collectors of the world beg for mercy, the megafranc threat looms large on the horizon. Your being here is our only ray of hope, Acting Sergeant."

"I'll bet it is," said Bullock.

"For me, personally, this is also an occasion," said the Baron. "As a young boy I was torn between running away to join the Foreign Legion to fight the Arabs and joining the Royal Canadian Mounties to fight the lumberjacks. Of course, that was before I wanted to be poet, the source of our present difficulty."

"So Wickett tells me," said Bullock.

"The poems in question are juvenilia," said the Baron. "But not, I like to think, without merit. As a patriot, however, I must forgo the satisfaction of seeing them in print. My sonnets, you see, are thinly disguised accounts of the early, amorous exploits of some of our leading citizens. Octagon, for example, the shepherd who spies on the goddess at her bath, is our present Minister of Justice, while the nymph Florabella, who runs through the poems in various stages of deshabille, is the wife of the Prime Minister. So you see, if the Albanians have my sonnets, we are in their power."

"Why don't you take it from here, Bullock?" said Wickett.

Bullock furrowed his brow for a moment. Then he said, "What do you say we reconstruct the crime?" When the Baron beamed approval, Bullock continued, "First off, where were the sonnets kept?"

"In my bedroom," said the Baron. "In a locked wall cabinet, the only key to which I wear on a chain around my neck."

"A chain, you say," said Bullock thoughtfully. "Tell me, Baron, how far is it from your bed to the cabinet?"

"Twenty-five feet or so," said the Baron.

"And how long is the chain?" said Bullock.

The Baron smiled with regret. "A foot and a half at most."

Bullock's brow furrowed again. "All right," he said, "let's take another tack. Suppose deft fingers—"

"I'm afraid I'm a very light sleeper," said the Baron.

"Besides," said Wickett, "that doesn't explain the oil can on the Baron's night table."

"An oil can of Albanian manufacture," said the Baron. "Such as bicycle racers use. There seems no doubt it was Rudy's. Rudy Belasco."

"Perhaps you'd better begin at the beginning," said Bullock.

"That would be about a month ago," said the Baron, "during the *Tour de Liechtenstein,* our annual eight-day bicycle race. I was out hiking in the mountains above my castle. Below me I noticed a bright speck approaching up the path. A young man on a bicycle. He bore the national colors of Albania on his racing silks, and as I was later to discover, the number thirty-eight on his back. Head down, he was pumping slowly and laboriously up the path.

"When he came abreast of me I stood to one side and as is customary I applauded. Then I walked alongside him for a few minutes and finally asked, as discreetly as I could, if he hadn't taken the wrong turn somewhere.

"Well, he looked back down the empty path and then up at the high snow of the mountain peak. Suddenly all the heart went out of him. He threw down his bicycle, jumped up and down on the spokes, and hurled the wreckage on the mountainside. Then he threw himself on the ground and sobbed his heart out.

"I sat down on a rock and smoked a small cigar. After a bit he sat up and cursed the coach of the Albanian team who, in place of giving them maps, had instructed his racers to follow the other cyclists. As Rudy Belasco remarked—for that was the young man's name—'You don't win bicycle races that way.'

"Well, he seemed so personable a young man that I invited him to stay at the castle until he had recuperated from his ordeal and repaired the bicycle. So Rudy in his shorts and bright jersey became a familiar sight at my table. In fact, he and my daughter Regina grew so close I was prepared to welcome him into the family permanently. But the morning I discovered the sonnets missing, Rudy Belasco had also disappeared, bicycle and all."

"And later that day," added Wickett, "passing the Albanian Embassy here, I saw Belasco going in with Glinka and Josef Susman, the Albanian Ambassador. Of course, I didn't know it was Belasco until I received a call from our people in Liechtenstein."

"You're certain it *was* Belasco?" said Bullock.

"I identified him from the number thirty-eight on his back," said Wickett. "I'm afraid there's no question the Albanians have the sonnets, even though, for their own twisted purposes, they haven't approached the Baron and his delegation yet."

The Baron rose to take his leave. "Recover my little brain child, Acting Sergeant," he said, "so that Liechtenstein may stand shoulder to shoulder with Canada once more."

When the Baron had left, Wickett spread a newspaper on his desk. Then he took a grouse from his *In* basket, handed another to Bullock, and began to pluck.

"The Ambassador was in a foul mood today," he said, after a bit. "Had to take his dog to the vet. Bird shot in the hind quarters. 'Cut out the cigarettes, Wickett,' he shouted. 'I may fall back on you.' The last time I retrieved for him he claimed that smoking had dulled my sense of smell." Wickett laid the plucked grouse in his *Out* basket and took another.

"By the way," he said, "I hope you realize that Ottawa sees more at stake here than a few postage stamps and a sonnet cycle. I mean, if the Ottawa Plan will work here with stamps, then why not on a global scale with disarmament and world peace? And wouldn't that be a feather in our national caps? Down the corridors of time, generations as yet unborn would bless Canada and the Ottawa Plan."

"Good Godfrey!" exclaimed Bullock, plucking excitedly.

What Bullock wanted most as he left the Embassy was a good hot soak in the tub where he could mull things over. But suddenly he had the eerie feeling he was not being followed. Major Glinka was not there. Bullock squared his shoulders and strode off resolutely into the tangle of streets.

An hour later, footsore and weary, Bullock closed the door of his hotel room and saw the shoe lying in the middle of the floor. He tapped the sole against his palm reflectively.

"A shoe," he said.

When he had started the water in the tub and tossed in a handful of bubble-bath crystals ("My only vice," as he liked to say), Bullock sat on the edge of the tub with the shoe in his hand, turning it first this way, then that, as one might a bothersome piece in a jigsaw puzzle. The ideas weren't coming. Time to slip into his scarlet tunic for a bit.

Inside the clothes closet stood Glinka, towering over him. Then the big Albanian slipped from the hook and fell, heavy and unconscious, into Bullock's arms. The back of his head was matted with blood.

"Ah, ha!" exclaimed Bullock—for one of Glinka's shoes was missing.

At that moment a small police van, its two-tone siren wailing, screeched to a stop in front of the hotel. *Carabinieri* spilled out onto the street. Quickly, Bullock dragged his burden into the bathroom and hoisted it into the half-filled tub. He turned the water on full blast and threw in another handful of bubble-bath crystals, frothing up a hill of bubbles which he peaked up carefully above Glinka's head.

The door burst open and an officer wearing sunglasses and carrying a large pistol came into the room. A dozen *carabinieri* filed in behind, dragging their rifles.

"Lieutenant Gelatti," said the officer with a tired salute. "There has been a report of foul play. Let me have your passport, please."

Gelatti sprawled on the bed and paged through the passport with the barrel of his pistol. "To Gelatti," he said, "you do not look like a Hudson Bay blanket salesman, Mr. Jones." He signaled his men, who began breaking things open with their rifle butts.

"Suppose Gelatti said he believed you to be"—the officer fumbled for a slip of paper—"Acting Sergeant Maynard Bullock of the RCMP?"

Bullock shook his head. "You flatter me," he said.

"Then," said Gelatti, "how do you explain that?"

A *carabiniere* was holding up Bullock's uniform for the admiration of his companions.

Bullock mumbled something about a mistake at the cleaners. Out of the corner of his eye he was watching two suspicious *carabinieri* in the bathroom who had fixed bayonets to put the bubbles to a closer test.

Suddenly a shot rang out. While trying on Bullock's broad-brimmed Mountie hat, a *carabiniere* had dropped his rifle which had discharged, shooting another in the leg.

Gelatti shouted in exasperated Italian. The *carabinieri* filed quickly out of the room, carrying their wounded and weeping comrade.

Gelatti stretched luxuriously on the bed. Then he smiled and snapped his fingers. "Gelatti and Mr. Jones shall play a little game," he said. "We shall pretend that you are this Bullock."

"You mean just pretend?" said Bullock. "No harm in that—in fact, it might be fun."

"You like Gelatti's little game, eh, Acting Sergeant?" laughed Gelatti.

Bullock laughed right back and assuming a deeper voice, said, "Fire away, Lieutenant."

"Well," said the officer, "Gelatti sometimes moonlights. The same day he learned of the disappearance of a certain sheaf of paper, he was engaged by Susman, the Albanian Ambassador, to follow the movements of the elusive Mr. Serge, local head of the Yugoslav Secret Police. So he asked himself, 'Gelatti, do the Albanians suspect Serge of possessing this valuable sheaf of paper?'

"But then Gelatti discovered that Serge was following Susman. 'Can it be,' thought Gelatti, that neither has the manu- —er—sheaf of paper?' So it occurred to Gelatti that by pooling their information he and this Bullock might recover the papers and sell them to the highest bidder. Or would that be naughty?"

"If I was the man I'm pretending to be," said Bullock, "I'd say"—he assumed the deeper voice again—"Lieutenant Gelatti, you are a disgrace to your uniform and I hurl your filthy proposition back in your teeth."

"Then you have signed Acting Sergeant Bullock's death warrant," said Gelatti, raising his pistol.

"First hear him out," said Bullock, "because if he were here he'd probably say something like this."

Then Bullock spoke eloquently of the honor and traditions of the RCMP, sketched the history of the Force and elaborated on the red, blue, and yellow of the uniform, symbolizing sacrifice, constancy, and virtue in general. As he spoke he had the satisfaction of seeing the pistol lowered. When he finished, Gelatti was asleep on the bed.

Bullock saw he wasn't going to get his bath. But it looked like a good time to grab a bite to eat. He threw another handful of bubble-bath crystals into the tub and left.

There was a restaurant across from the hotel. Bullock ordered a ham sandwich and a bottle of ale but had to make do with Italian beer. The sandwich was made of a foot-long loaf of bread whose crust resisted his gnawing teeth.

As Bullock sipped the unsatisfactory beer and tried to sort out his thoughts, his eyes wandered to a tropical-fish tank separating his table from the next. Tiny bright fishes cavorted about a seashell castle. Then he saw the eye watching furtively through the seaweed.

Bullock blinked. The eye vanished, reappearing immediately in the head of a short man with stainless-steel teeth standing by Bullock's table.

"I am Ambassador Susman," the man said. "Care to match wits, Acting Sergeant?"

Bullock nodded him to a chair.

"Always meet an opponent face to face," said Susman with a metallic smile. "It helps you to understand his mind, his hopes, his fears. Similarly, if you tell me what a man carries in his suitcase, I'll tell you his weaknesses."

Bullock thought of his bubble-bath crystals, but refrained from saying anything.

"Come now, what have you done with Major Glinka?" said Susman. "And how did you outwit Lieutenant Gelatti?"

Bullock grinned cryptically.

Susman smiled again. "I hope you realize I am quite desperate," he said. "You see, I have enemies at home who want me recalled to some obscure desk in the Ministry of Sheep. To thwart them I needed a masterstroke—the theft of the Stollmeyer sonnets. Interfere now and I will crush you."

"That's big talk," said Bullock. "But a little birdie tells me you don't have the sonnets."

"I wonder how much else you know," mused Susman admiringly.

Bullock gnawed on his sandwich.

"You're inscrutable, Acting Sergeant," said Susman. He rubbed his hands together. "What I wouldn't give to have you back at the Embassy where I could pick your brain."

Bullock shuddered behind his impassive exterior.

"True, the sonnets are not yet in my hands," said Susman. "But by tomorrow they will be. There is no way you can prevent that. I am the only one who can pay their price."

Glinka came into the restaurant, water squeaking in his shoes and dripping from his fierce mustache.

"Ah, Glinka, my boy," said Susman. "I was so worried I sent Gelatti up after you. Is it raining?"

Glinka glowered at Bullock. "Someone was there in the dark," he said. "Someone struck me from behind while I was taking off my shoe. Someone left me to drown in the bathtub. As for Gelatti, he was dead on the bed when I came to."

"Asleep," said Bullock. "Let's just say I put Gelatti to sleep."

"Unbelievable!" said Susman. "Glinka, can we let so dangerous an adversary run loose?" From his pocket he drew a cigarette lighter in the form of a pistol and pointed it at Bullock. "We had better take him back with us."

"I know a lighter when I see one," scoffed the Mountie.

"This is a rather ingenious invention of the novelties division of our Secret Police," said Susman. "It is a pistol disguised as a lighter disguised as a pistol. Quite as deadly as Glinka's fountain pen there." The big Albanian menaced Bullock with an ominous-looking pen.

Bullock tried for a hearty laugh. "Did you think I'd walk into a trap like this unarmed?" he said. Snatching the sandwich off his plate, he leveled it at Susman's heart. "One false move and you're a dead man," he said. For Glinka's benefit he added, "This is a repeater."

"He's bluffing," shouted Glinka.

Looking down the barrel of the sandwich, Susman began to sweat. "Perhaps," he said. "And perhaps not. A fifty-fifty chance. How humiliating to be shot by a sandwich." He lowered his pistol-lighter-pistol. "You win this round, Acting Sergeant Maynard Bullock," he said. "But we shall meet again."

Bullock backed out the door, keeping them covered with the sandwich.

A young woman with soft brown eyes and a large pigtail of blonde hair was sitting on Bullock's bed. "I'm Regina Stollmeyer, Acting Sergeant," she said. "Your door was open, so I just came in. I only arrived in San Marino a half hour ago. When father told me there was a real Mountie on the case, I dashed right over. I've something to tell you."

"Shoot," said Bullock.

Regina Stollmeyer seemed to have trouble beginning.

"I'll bet you expected me to be wearing my uniform," he said. "Maybe this will convince you." He put on his broadbrimmed hat. "Better?"

"I think it is, somehow," she said and taking a deep breath, she began. "First off, Rudy did not steal the sonnets."

"Better minds than yours have decided otherwise, Miss," said Bullock.

"Then they're wrong," she said. "I know because I stole the sonnets myself."

Bullock blinked. "Perhaps you'd better begin at the beginning," he said.

268

"It was love at first sight between Rudy and me," she said. "He was like a little boy—so serious, so determined, so bent on perfecting his craft. And he had this little lock of hair that kept falling down over his eyes. During his stay at the castle we went cycling every day. One morning we noticed two men on a scooter following us at a distance."

Bullock nodded. "A Vespa with diplomatic license plates," he said.

"Later, when we stopped to rest," continued Regina, "they stopped a few yards away. The driver, a big man in a leather overcoat, called Rudy over and spoke to him in Albanian. All three began talking in a very animated way. The big man seemed to be threatening Rudy with his foot. When Rudy returned he told me they had just wanted directions to the nearest youth hostel. But for the next few days he was morose and complained of cramps in the stomach. Finally, I told him that if he loved me he'd tell me what was wrong.

"Well, his eyes filled with tears and he threw himself on the ground. He told me those men had been Albanian officials who had learned where he was staying. Unless Rudy stole father's sonnets they threatened to send him back to Albania and see that he never raced again. And racing is his life's work!

"Rudy's room was next to father's. In desperation the poor dear had been tunneling through the wall behind the cabinet, hiding the stones under his mattress and eating the mortar so the servants wouldn't notice. He planned to break through that very night and meet the Albanians early the next morning.

" 'Now listen very carefully, Rudy,' I said. 'You are not going to eat any more mortar. And you are not going to let father's awful poems fall into the hands of perfect strangers.' Well, Rudy's lower lip trembled and he began to fuss.

" 'Now listen, Rudy,' I said. 'Tomorrow morning you are going to meet those men and tell them that you are sorry, that you know you promised to steal the sonnets, but somebody else stole them first.'

"Well, Rudy looked at me in that fierce way of his that turns my knees to water. 'You ask a Belasco to lie?' he shouted. And he started in on how his family was descended from Philip II of Macedonia, father of Alexander the Great, and even though his family had fallen on bad times since the death of Alexander, a Belasco had never been known to lie.

"So I stole the sonnets myself, so Rudy wouldn't have to lie."

269

"But how did you do it?" said Bullock.

"I crept into father's room and oiled the casters on his bed," she said. "Then while he was asleep I pushed it gently over to the wall cabinet, used the key without taking it off his neck, then pushed the bed back."

"Diabolical," said Bullock admiringly.

"I only planned on keeping the sonnets for a few days until the Albanians read about the theft in the papers. But the next morning Rudy didn't come back. They're holding him captive in the cellar of the Albanian Embassy. This morning I received a letter that he smuggled out through one of the cleaning women who is a bicycle racing fan. Rudy wrote that he's starting another tunnel! Desperate, I called Ambassador Susman long distance and agreed to exchange the sonnets for Rudy at noon tomorrow. I've been driving ever since.

"But with you here we have one last chance. Can you free poor Rudy before tomorrow noon? Otherwise I'll have to give father's terrible sonnets to Susman who threatens to break all Rudy's fingers and toes so he can never ride a bicycle again."

An hour later Bullock and Wickett were sitting in the tiny white Fiat across from the Albanian Embassy.

"The street spirals down to the frontier, all right," said Wickett. "But I still don't like this one bit."

"Just be here tomorrow morning at six sharp." said Bullock. He struggled out of the car and took his bags from the back seat. "While we're at it," he said, "is there any chance of using another car? This one makes the whole thing look comical. I am risking my life, after all."

"There's a big black Hispano-Suiza some of the other Embassies rent for espionage work. I could hire that," said Wickett.

"That sounds more like it," said Bullock, and shaking Wickett's hand he picked up his bags, squared his shoulders, and walked across the dark street to the Albanian Embassy.

Glinka opened the door and shifted an after-dinner matchstick from one side of his mouth to the other.

"Who is it, Glinka?" called Susman from within.

"It's a trick," said Glinka.

"It's Acting Sergeant Bullock," said Bullock. "I've decided you hold all the trump cards. I've come to defect."

Susman's head appeared in back of Glinka. "You realize," he said suspiciously, "that if you cross this threshold I can kill you

270

at my whim and ship your body back to Albania in diplomatic pouches?"

Bullock nodded and Susman motioned him inside, leading the way into an immense, decaying ballroom with gold columns flaking along the walls and the crystal wreckage of three chandeliers on the floor.

"I use this as my office," said Susman, indicating a card table and two folding chairs set up beneath crossed flags and portraits of Lenin, Mao Tse-tung, and a third person whom Susman referred to vaguely as "The Father of My Country."

Susman sat behind the table. "Now tell me again why you want to defect."

"Couldn't we talk about that in the morning?" said Bullock. "I don't know about you, but I'm tired and ready to turn in." Susman insisted. "Well," said Bullock, "my superiors don't appreciate me and they hint I'm a bungler. Well, I say the heck with them all." He hoped he wasn't laying it on too thick.

"What are we waiting for?" shouted Glinka with childlike impatience. "Let's kill him now."

"Quiet, you fool," said Susman. "I'm having a brainstorm." He placed a hand over his eyes. A moment later he peeked through his fingers at Bullock. "Has a Royal Canadian Mountie ever defected before?"

"Not in recorded history," said Bullock.

"Excellent," said Susman and he ordered Bullock into his uniform. "Go get your camera, Glinka," he said. "This shall be the proof of his good faith."

First Glinka photographed Bullock and Susman shaking hands. Next Susman ordered Bullock to pose saluting, in turn, the portraits of Lenin, Mao, and "What's-his-name, The Father of My Country." Finally, a smiling Bullock had his picture taken holding a small Albanian flag between thumb and forefinger.

"Excellent," said Sussman. "Tomorrow the Stollmeyer sonnets will be ours and the defeat of the Ottawa Plan assured. But here we have the means of breaking the back of Canadian prestige in this hemisphere once and for all. On Monday the newspapers of the world will carry these photographs under banner headlines: *Mountie Defects to Albania.*"

"If I can't kill him, at least let me lock him up," said Glinka, shaking a ring of keys under Bullock's nose.

"Fool," said Susman. "Where would he run to? Who would

271

take in a renegade Mountie? And think of the fine figure he'll make lecturing in full uniform to our Junior Communists League: 'I was a Fawning Lackey for the Bourgeoisie Inside the Arctic Circle.' Right, Bullock?"

"I've always liked working with children," said Bullock.

Susman did a little dance. "This is my night of triumph," he said. "A masterstroke doubled and redoubled! We are going to celebrate. Do you like parties, Bullock?"

Bullock yawned and stretched. "I'm a bit sleepy," he said. "I thought I might turn in."

"Nonsense," said Susman. "We are going to have an Albanian fiesta." He clapped his hands. "Glinka, an Albanian fiesta for three."

Glinka left the room muttering.

"We Albanians are a very festive people," said Susman. "We like to drink and sing and dance. But we are also hot-blooded and when we drink we become belligerent. And so our ancestors devised the Albanian fiesta. Ah, here we are."

Glinka had returned with three bottles of plum brandy on a tray.

Susman handed a bottle to Bullock and took one himself. "True joy is best savored in solitude," he said. "Now Glinka will show you to your room and he will go to his and I to mine. Then the three of us will drink and sing each by himself. Enjoy your fiesta, Bullock. In the morning we will talk about your future."

Bullock sat on the bed. By two in the morning the sound of breaking glass was still coming from Susman's room down the hall, while next door Glinka crooned an Albanian shepherd's song over and over. "It's past your bedtime, Maynard," he heard Mrs. Bullock say. So Bullock broke into *Allouette* to keep awake.

An hour later a distant crash told him that Susman had finally fallen to the floor, dragging furniture with him. Bullock stopped singing and lay there listening to Glinka's little melody which sounded more and more like *The Whiffenpoof Song* by the minute.

At ten minutes to six Bullock awoke with a start as Glinka's bottle smashed to the floor. For five long minutes he listened to the silence. Then Bullock picked up his bags and crept on tiptoe into the big Albanian's room.

272

Glinka was lying fully clothed on the bed. With infinite care Bullock removed the key ring from the sleeping man's pocket. "Baa, baa, baa," crooned Glinka.

At the end of a winding passageway in the cellar Bullock discovered a locked door with a bicycle leaning beside it. A minute later he was trotting back up the passageway alongside the pedaling Rudy Belasco.

"I'll miss my tunnel," said Belasco. "I find mortar is actually quite wholesome and nourishing."

"We've no time to argue about that now," said Bullock, for rounding the next corner they came face to face with Glinka.

"I was only feigning sleep," shouted the big Albanian, going down on one knee to unsheath a lethal foot. "Now I will kill you!"

Bullock took a defensive stance. "Put up your dukes and fight like a man."

"Bourgeois sentimentalist!" roared Glinka, struggling with both hands to pull off his shoe. "I have a knot in my shoelace," he added quietly, as if to explain the delay.

"Quick!" shouted Bullock and he leaped, bags and all, on the back of Belasco's bicycle which sped past the raging Albanian.

An alarm bell clanged inside the Embassy as they crowded into the back seat of the waiting Hispano-Suiza. "Head for the frontier, Wickett!" shouted Bullock.

"I'm afraid I'm the elusive Mr. Serge of the Yugoslav Secret Police," said the man behind the wheel. In one hand he held a gun. He opened the other hand to display a ball of fluff. "See that? That's three hours under your bed, Acting Sergeant. It was I who stuffed Glinka in your clothes closet. When I heard you in the hall, I hid under your bed. Gelatti's falling asleep and the arrival of Miss Stollmeyer trapped me there, so I heard all. Now the precious Mr. Belasco is mine. Now future generations will bless the Belgrade Plan and Yugoslavia for—"

The Hispano-Suiza was struck hard from behind. Serge's head bounced off the windshield. He slid to the floor.

A smiling woman in a flowered hat got out of the tiny white Fiat. "Acting Sergeant Bullock?" she said. "I'm Mrs. Wickett. My husband couldn't make it. The Ambassador went grousing and needed a retriever. And I'm afraid the car you wanted was already rented."

As Bullock and Belasco dragged the bicycle out of the Hispano-Suiza, a siren approached in the distance.

Baron Stollmeyer bowed and smiled to them from the front seat of the Fiat. "I met the Baron out walking," said Mrs. Wickett, getting back behind the wheel. "He hadn't been invited to his own daughter's elopement."

"I'm addicted to early morning walks," said the Baron, as Bullock and Belasco forced the bicycle into the back seat of the Fiat. "At one time I wanted to be a milkman."

"The laugh's on us," said Bullock. "We'll have to get in first and pull the bicycle in afterwards."

Susman came running out of the Embassy in his shirt sleeves. "Bullock," he shouted. "You can't do this! Remember the photographs."

Bullock squeezed into the back seat. "You're in for a surprise when you get them developed," he said. "In every shot I've got my fingers crossed as plain as day."

A police van entered the bottom of the street. Lieutenant Gelatti and his men lined up from curb to curb, rifles ready.

"Let's get out of here," shouted Bullock.

Mrs. Wickett drove straight down into the muzzles of the rifles. The *carabinieri* fired and jumped aside. A street lamp and two store windows shattered. Susman, running after the car, fell with a bullet in his leg. The Fiat squealed into the first turn in its spiral descent to the frontier.

"This is exciting!" shouted Mrs. Wickett.

"An elopement is always an adventure," said the Baron.

"We've got company," said Bullock. The Hispano-Suiza was behind them with Glinka at the wheel. He waved an empty shoe at them menacingly.

"I suppose that Lieutenant Gelatti will give me a ticket for this," said Mrs. Wickett.

"You are not only speeding but driving down the middle of the street," said Bullock. He dreaded the open country between the city limits and the frontier where Glinka could easily force them off the road.

"Here we go again!" shouted Belasco as they rounded a turn on two wheels.

Gelatti and his men were emerging from a side street and lining up as before. Mrs. Wickett squealed with delight.

"If they fix bayonets we're done for," shouted Bullock. But once more the *carabinieri* fired and jumped quickly aside. A web of cracks appeared in the windshield of the Hispano-Suiza which swerved out of control and up onto the terrace of a sidewalk café where a waiter with a fixed smile and a basket of breakfast rolls hurried over to it.

Lieutenant Gelatti ran out into the street and in a fine gesture saluted the departing Fiat.

When Regina Stollmeyer and Rudy Belasco had disappeared from sight on their bicycles, Mrs. Wickett, the Baron, and his sonnets headed back across the frontier to San Marino.

Bullock sat on a suitcase by the roadside. Suddenly he heard a shot and a shout: "Fetch, Wickett! Fetch!" The distant figure of a running Wickett emerged from the underbrush followed by the Ambassador with a shotgun. Bullock waved a scarlet arm but they passed on without seeing him.

Well, his work was done here. "You did it, Maynard," Mrs. Bullock would say. But this time a chorus of voices would be joined to hers—the unborn generations who would bless Canada and the great Ottawa Plan.

Bullock was embarrassed to find a lump in his throat as he flagged down the bus to Rimini with his broadbrimmed hat.

THE BOTANY PATTERN

BY VICTOR CANNING

Victor Canning was born in Plymouth, England, in 1911. While working in a government office he wrote juvenile adventure stories as a sideline. His first adult novel was *Mr. Finchley Discovers His England* (1934), which was highly successful and enabled him to devote himself entirely to writing. He has written suspense and spy fiction, which has been popular in the United States and England, under his own name and the pseudonym of Alan Gould. Many of his plots have been made into films, including *Spy Hunt* (1950) and *The Assassin* (1953), for which he himself wrote the screenplay. The *Reader's Digest* pronounced Canning one of the six finest thriller writers in the world.

NOT MANY PEOPLE, even in France, know about the Department of Patterns. It appears on no government list, never seeks publicity, and carries no sign outside its headquarters in an old house on the Quai d'Orsay—yet it is the most powerful and respected of all adjuncts to the French police service.

The Department of Patterns specializes in cases which it originates by its own research. This basic research is done by a dozen young men assigned to the Department for a two-year period from training institutions, security, and police departments. Day after day the young men sit—in what is known as the "stewpot"—sifting through masses of old criminal data, official records and photographs, newspaper reports and files, hoping that by arrangement and analysis some pattern of significance may emerge. In most people there is a strong, if subconscious, desire for order and logic in whatever they do—especially, surprising enough, in those people who step outside the law. (By the way, I must apologize if I sound rather like a lecturer in criminal psychology—but that, in fact, is what I am, at the University of Grenoble.)

At the time of this case I had been eighteen months in the Department of Patterns and had just been promoted from the "stewpot" to the position of a *chercher libre* man. In other words, I was free to roam anywhere in the Department, pursuing any trail that might interest me. My particular interest was "symbolism in murder."

All symbolism is, basically, part of an association pattern, and it is frequently met in crimes which are not committed for gain. Behind most symbolism lies a vanity which is close to mental derangement. As Papa Grand often said, more than three-quarters of unsolved cases are the work of obsessionalists who outwardly appear perfectly sane.

Anyway, after a week in the photographic gallery, I came across something which intrigued me enough to feel that I could go to Papa Grand and ask his permission for further research and for outside assistance from the police.

Papa Grand is Monsieur Alphonse Grand, the head of the Department of Patterns. He can be jovial and he can be tough. If you get no more than two black marks against you in the

Department, you go out with the rating of *Assez Bien*—and that is a high rating for most. So far I had a clean sheet.

When I went in to see him he was sitting at his desk with his back to the little attic window that looked out over the Seine. He was a big, fleshy, white-haired man of about sixty; the back of his right hand was badly scarred and one finger was missing. Nobody knew just how this had occurred. As I stood in front of him, his blue eyes lit up with a mischievous smile.

"Ha, Viaur, as I expected, you walk now with the unbowed shoulders of a man released from the burdens of the 'stewpot.' You have in your eyes the glint of a *chercher libre* man. Just to depress you, may I say that most people making the transition often find that they have jumped from the stewpot into the fire."

"I hope not, Patron."

"Hope—" he grinned, "—was declared *persona non grata* in this Department twenty years ago. Proceed."

I laid before him a sheaf of photographs.

"These—" I began, but he cut me off with a raised hand. He looked at the photographs, studying each one, and then turned them over to read the reports on the back. They were photographs from various local police concerning six murders. These murders, all of men, had occurred over the last four years in the big triangle of country enclosed by Toulouse, Bordeaux, and Cahors, a territory watered by the rivers Garonne and Lot.

The first man had been killed by a spear thrust into his ribs—an old African assegai.

The second, though no weapon had been found, had died from vicious stab wounds around the heart.

The third had been strangled with a piece of tough whipcord.

The fourth had died from a dagger wound in the heart, the weapon having been left in him.

The fifth had had his skull brutally smashed with a hammer, and the weapon had been left lying alongside him.

And the sixth had been found hanging by a rope which had been fastened high up on a tree trunk by three large nails.

Although at first nothing seemed to connect the murders or the victims, each murder had one thing in common which showed up in the photographs. I waited for Papa Grand to finish his examination, knowing that he would spot it for himself.

278

Finally he looked up at me and pushed the photographs back. "I presume, Viaur," he said, "that it is your interest in botany that attracts you here?"

"It is, Patron. So far as I can tell at the moment, these six men are not connected. They come from different places within an area of, say, one hundred square miles. They were all murdered differently—though it is possible that the sixth man hanged himself."

"Possible," said Papa Grand. "So?"

"But each murder was committed in the open, near a river or in a field not far from the road, and each man was found under a tree."

"A Judas tree in full bloom."

"Yes, Patron. A Judas tree—the symbol of betrayal. It could be—unconnected though they seem—that these six men had betrayed someone, and now a revenge pattern is being, or has been, worked out. I would like your permission to go down and make some inquiries."

"Why not? It is a pleasant part of the country. I have fished in the Lot. Maybe, if you turn up anything, I will come down with my rods for a day or two. I will phone Bardac at Cahors and tell him you are coming. But don't stay in Cahors, charming though it is. I would recommend the Chateau Mercues, a little west down the river Lot. The first murder, I see, was committed on the river bank not far from the Chateau. But, Viaur—"

He paused and eyed me quizzically. It was the kind of look which no one who had spent any time in the Department of Patterns could afford to overlook.

"Yes, Patron?"

"You did well to spot the tree. But do not let your botanical interest stop there. I feel it could be developed."

"How, Patron?"

For a moment Papa Grand frowned and I knew that I had asked the wrong question. Then the frown vanished and the blue-eyed smile came back.

"Viaur, as a good Catholic that is a question which a little thought on your part would make unnecessary. But since you ask it I am too polite not to answer. Does it not strike you as odd that a man should be hanged from a tree and instead of looping and knotting the end of the rope round a branch, a fixing is made with heavy nails? Go, Viaur—and telephone me each evening."

279

So I went down to Cahors and stayed at the Chateau Mercues, which had been turned into a country hotel, a great turreted, romantic pile that stood high on a clifftop dominating the river Lot below. Curiously enough, there was an enormous Judas tree in the courtyard of the Chateau.

On the way down I had decided to start my investigations with the first murder. The man was a Felix Seret who had lived with his aged mother in a village near Luzech, not far from the Chateau. I got a dossier on him from Bardac at Cahors—a fat plum pudding of a man who beamed with pleasure at the thought that Papa Grand might soon be making a visit. The victim Seret had been a bachelor, forty-eight years old, and had made a living as a master carpenter. His mother now lived alone in the cottage they had shared until his death.

She was a wrinkle-faced, dowdy old woman in black dress and shawl, rather like a dejected crow, who loved to sit in the sun outside her cottage and sleep. During our interview she dozed off two or three times. I asked her the usual questions and got nowhere. Her son had been a sober, industrious man, had had no enemies and no affairs with women. He had been a good son.

"And yet he was murdered?"

"Oh, yes, monsieur. But this happens to good people as well as bad. His conscience was clear. He was a good Catholic."

As she said this a bell rang in my mind. She had echoed a phrase of Papa Grand's.

I said, "Your son was murdered on his way back from working in Cahors. Do you know the exact place of the crime?"

"No—I would not like to see it." Her eyes closed briefly, then opened again. "You would like a glass of Armagnac?"

"No, thank you," I said. "Would it surprise you to know that his body was found under a Judas tree?"

She looked at me sharply, her tongue nervously wetting the edges of her lips, and I felt that something had stirred in her.

"He was a good man," she said defensively.

"Undoubtedly. But what man is there who lives his whole life without sin? It is not granted to any of us. We can gain absolution, but at some time we all sin."

"That is true, monsieur."

"Then what was your son's sin, madam?" I asked gently. "It may help to lead us to a man who has taken his life."

She was silent for a long time, looking down at her gnarled

old hands, and then slowly she began to talk—and I realized how often an investigation can go astray because the right question is not asked at the right moment, how often the truth is waiting, not to be dragged out, but merely to be invited into the open.

"He had one sin—one great sin among many smaller ones, monsieur. At first—after the war—he would not tell me about it, but I knew that it was there. He was a good son and the sin weighed heavily on him. In the end he told me about it.

"He had betrayed a man and caused his death. And it was I who told him what to do about it. He went to a priest and confessed. He was given his penances and he was absolved, and after that he was himself again—a happy, good son who never did anyone harm. Even the sin he committed was for the sake of others. Listen, monsieur, there are moments in life when a terrible choice is laid on men. . . ."

I listened to her, and as she spoke, the pattern began to clear. That night I telephoned Papa Grand and he promised to join me the following evening at the Chateau.

The next day, with Bardac, I traveled from Cahors to Toulouse and away to the west toward Bordeaux the two of us interviewed, among others, the widows and mothers of the five other dead men; and when Papa Grand arrived that evening and we all dined at the Chateau Mercues, the story was beginning to shape itself logically.

I must confess that I was quite pleased with myself. This was my first case as a *chercher libre* member of the Department and I liked the heady wine of success as much as any man. I was to learn that it is a very heady wine indeed.

It was not until after dinner, when we were sitting on the Chateau terrace overlooking the great cliff fall to the Lot, taking our coffee, that Papa Grand gave me permission to report.

"You are pleased with him, Bardac?" he asked.

"He has done well," said Bardac and then, with a sigh, added, "How lucky you are to have all the time in the world! With us, one case overlays another and the days seem never to be long enough."

"That is what we are for," said Papa Grand. "A criminal can plan at leisure. The balance must be redressed somehow. Well, Viaur, proceed."

"Patron, it is like this. During the war Seret was a member of

281

a Resistance Group that operated on the German lines of communication to the east of Bordeaux. They were a small but formidable group and Jacques Doubert who, apparently, was an outstanding character, brave, intelligent, loyal . . ."

Papa Grand sat listening to me, showing no flicker of emotion on his face, which was now grave with interest; his eyes never left me.

All six men who had been murdered were members of the Doubert Group. One day, after they had wrecked a German convoy at a small village called Pontmarde near Bordeaux, the Group had been captured. All except Doubert. The Germans, who wanted their hands on Doubert more than the others, had put a frightful proposition to the five captives. The villagers of Pontmarde had given them shelter and the Germans said that unless the Group told them where to find Doubert they intended to wipe out the village. But if they betrayed Doubert, the village would be spared, and they themselves would escape the firing squad and be given prison sentences.

It had been a fearful choice for them. Doubert was a legend, a symbol of French resistance, a great and good man—though no one knew much about him or where he had come from or even if Doubert was his real name. What were they to do? Their own lives meant nothing and they would have gladly sacrificed themselves for Doubert—but there were the villagers.

"Mon Patron, can you imagine such a choice?"

Slowly Papa Grand nodded his head. "I can, Viaur. It occurs but I thank the *bon Dieu* that I have never met it personally. So they betrayed Doubert and he was shot?"

"Yes, Patron. And the villagers were saved."

Slowly Papa Grand lit a cigar and then, tossing the match over the parapet, he said, "And this Group? I presume there were ten of them, not counting Doubert?"

I looked at him in amazement. "Yes, there were, Patron. But how—"

"Never mind for the moment, Viaur. Let us see what we have. Ten men betray, under terrible duress, their leader. Six of them have been searched out and murdered. But I cannot imagine any of the men willingly revealing such a secret, except possibly to a wife or mother. Who then has decided to avenge Doubert's martyrdom? And how could he have known about it?"

Bardac said, "We can find no trace of the Doubert family

around here. During the war—" he shrugged, "—men appeared from nowhere."

"Yet somebody knows. Somebody is avenging him. The Judas tree makes that plain. Where are the remaining four men?"

"They live, Patron," I said, "in a small village called Bauvezet twenty miles south of Cahors. We have spoken to them today and, in the strictest confidence, they have confirmed this story. They know about the other murders but until now each man has preferred to keep his secret rather than come to the police. They are men who live under a black shadow. One of them is the local doctor."

Papa Grand was silent, thinking. Below us the dusk began to gather above the river. Behind us the evening breeze sighed through the branches of the great Judas tree in the courtyard.

Finally Papa Grand spoke. "There are two things to be done. One—Bardac, I want from you as soon as possible a complete list of all the unfrocked priests within a hundred miles of this place."

"Unfrocked priests?" Bardac's face went owlish.

"Yes, Bardac. Unfrocked, or those who have voluntarily abandoned the Church. All the men in the Group had secrets. All were good Catholics. We know Seret gained absolution at the confessional. So would the others—I am sure of it. Their families would never have betrayed their secret. No practicing priest would betray the confessional. Therefore it must be an unfrocked priest. Find him for me, Bardac—and quickly.

"Secondly, Viaur, tomorrow we go to Bauvezet and see these four other men. From one of them maybe we shall find out something about Doubert which will help. Remember, it is his death which is being avenged. The person who it is—and it must be a man from the methods of the murders—must have had a great love for him. A brother? A comrade in arms? Anyway, a man of great patience who is prepared to wait for his opportunities."

A little later Bardac left us but Papa Grand and I sat on enjoying the warm night. At least, Papa Grand was enjoying it, but I was thinking hard. I'd lost no marks in the "stewpot" and I didn't want to lose any as a *chercher libre* man. But it was clear that Papa Grand knew more than I did, and equally clear—since one of the functions of the Department was to train people like myself—that I would get no help from him unless it

283

became absolutely essential for my own or someone else's safety. Help given at this stage meant a black mark.

"Come now," said Papa Grand, eventually breaking the silence, "let me have your description of the man who has done these murders."

"Well, Patron, I agree now that he must be an unfrocked priest. All these men must at some time have confessed their secret sin. Among the many priests involved, one—let us say it was Doubert's brother, and that Doubert was not the real name of the Resistance leader—learns for the first time the true nature of Doubert's death. To avenge his brother and betray the confessional he must leave the Church. But he is still a religious man, if a little unhinged."

"Why?"

"Because, Patron, of the manner of the men's deaths. This priest is obsessed by martyrdom, by crucifixion . . . The spear that killed the first is symbolic of that other spear. The stab wounds of the second—and there were five, I remember now—are the five stab wounds. The strangling whipcord of the third represents the scourging with whips. The dagger left in the heart of the next—I imagine the dagger represents the Cross. The fifth—well, the hammer is for the hammer that drove in the nails. And the three heavy nails that held the rope for the last are for the nails which . . ."

"Quite," said Papa Grand softly. "You have done well, Viaur."

"But how you could know there were ten men escapes me, Patron."

Papa Grand began to rise. "You were brought up in the town or the country, Viaur?"

"In the country, Patron."

"Then you should know the answer. The man we want is someone who knows his botany. Good night, Viaur."

The next morning we drove over to Bauvezet to see what more we could glean from the four men, particularly the doctor, named Lunel. All the way over I puzzled at the botany enigma, but I got nowhere.

Doctor Lunel was not at his house, but a maid told us that he would be found at a cafe in the village square where he was waiting with his rods to go on a fishing trip to a nearby lake. She gave us directions to the lake in case we should miss him in the village.

We found the doctor taking coffee and cognac, sitting alone at a small table under a tree. He was a white-haired, fine-looking man of great dignity.

I introduced Papa Grand to him, and almost at once he said, a little resentfully, I thought, "There is nothing more I can tell you, messieurs. I and my three friends know the danger we live in—but we accept it. What we have done we have done. We betrayed Doubert to save others. It was a terrible decision. Given the situation again we would all do the same. Over a hundred villagers were saved. Please do not question us any more about it."

"As you wish," said Papa Grand. Then, with a look at the doctor's rods, "You are going fishing?"

"Yes, monsieur. After yesterday all four of us feel we want to get away from things for a while. We have hired the village bus. I wait for it now."

Papa Grand looked at me and shrugged. Then he stood up. "We must respect the doctor's wishes, Viaur. I am going to telephone Bardac to see if he has any information for us." He moved away into the cafe to find a telephone.

Doctor Lunel finished his coffee without another word to me. A few moments later a little country bus pulled up outside the cafe. The driver, a long-faced, bright-eyed man, leaned out of the driving window and called to the doctor.

"Come on, Doctor. We shall be late picking up the others at the crossroads. It is my fault, I wanted her bright and shining for you." He laughed and smacked the door panel of the gleaming blue and white bus.

"Coming, Caussade," said the doctor, and without a look at me he got up and went to the bus. The driver jumped down and helped him load his rods and gear aboard, and I noticed that the man was wearing a flower in his buttonhole.

The blue and white bus moved away up the village street and as it passed I could read its name on the tail panel—*La Couronne. Prop.: Caussade.*

And it was that that did it for me—the name of the bus and the fact that it was painted blue and white, and the sudden recognition of the kind of flower which Caussade was wearing in his buttonhole.

I jumped to my feet and turned to get Papa Grand, but he was already coming out of the cafe. As he came up to me, he said, "What is it, Viaur?"

"Patron—" I had him by the arm and was urging him toward our car—"I think I have found him, our unfrocked priest."

"You have," he said, "if his name is Caussade. Bardac has just given me that name. He's the only unfrocked priest within fifty miles. He changed his name from Bartois to Caussade after he left the Church."

"It is he. He has just driven off with the doctor and he's picking up the other three at the crossroads." I let in the gears and accelerated up the village street. "We must hurry, Patron, if we are going to save them. Listen, Patron, he owns a bus called La Couronne, and it's painted blue and white, and in his buttonhole he wears a flower that I should have recognized before I ever let the doctor—"

"Hurry, no talk!" snapped Papa Grand, suddenly grim.

As we roared up the village street I was thinking of that flower. I realized now why Papa Grand had known there were ten men involved. The flower was a Passion Flower, the flower that according to country legend displays ten symbols of the Passion: its leaf—the spear; the five anthers, the five wounds; the tendrils, the cords or whips; the column of the ovary, the pillar of the cross; the stamens, the hammers; the three styles, the three nails; the fleshy threads within the flowers, the crown of thorns; the white color, purity; the blue color, heaven; and the calyx, the glory or nimbus.

Of the last four the bus represented three. It was called La Couronne—the crown—and it was painted blue and white. It was, however, the thought of the nimbus, the blaze of light, which made me drive furiously.

At the crossroads there was no sign of them, but I knew the road to the lake and took that. After five minutes of fast driving we saw the blue and white bus ahead of us. I put my foot down hard and overhauled it. We swept ahead of it and then stopped at the roadside.

Papa Grand, fast for so big a man, was out of the car and in the middle of the road, holding up the bus. It drew up and the driver's lean face looked down at us inquiringly.

Papa Grand jerked the door open and shouted to the four men inside, "Get out of this bus quickly. Quickly—if you wish to live!"

For a moment they looked at him blankly. Then he reached for the doctor and grabbed his arm. "Out!" Papa Grand cried.

They came out then quickly, alarmed by the urgency in his

voice. As the last one jumped to the road, Papa Grand turned to the driver, Caussade, and I saw that my Patron had an automatic in his hand. "You, too, Caussade."

For a moment Caussade looked at him and his lean face was suddenly taut, angry, and his bright eyes gleamed with a ferocious glare. Then he suddenly jerked a gear home and his foot went down. The bus leaped forward, the open door catching Papa Grand and throwing him to the ground.

The bus sped down the road as I ran and picked Papa Grand up. We stood there, the six of us, and watched it racing down the road.

"Do we follow him?" I asked Papa Grand.

He shook his head. "No, Viaur. And you know why. It would be useless."

And I knew why. We all stood there and waited—waited for the glory, the nimbus, the great blaze, the last of the ten symbols . . . for the moment which would have destroyed the four shaken men around us.

It came when the bus was about a quarter of a mile away. There was a shattering explosion, then a great sheet of flame blazing upward as Caussade set off some homemade explosive charge which he had concealed in the vehicle—the great, sheeting glory of flame which he had designed to end the lives of the four men and his own—his revenge for a loved brother completed.

When I left the Department of Patterns at the end of my time it was with the grade of Excellent—one of the only twenty ever given. Before I left Papa Grand called me in and said, "Viaur, you go now to lecture students. Remember one thing—the vanity that comes from knowledge. When a man asks a question there are some moments when it is wise to give the answer rather than to urge him to seek for the answer himself. Sometimes the answer could come too late."

It was, I knew, his way of giving himself a black mark.

287

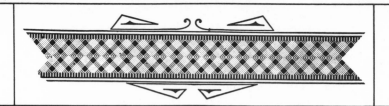

H AS IN HOMICIDE

BY LAWRENCE TREAT

Lawrence Treat was born in 1903 in New York City. He is well known for his significant contribution to the development of the contemporary police-procedural story. His first procedural novel was *V As in Victim* in 1945. He wrote six more procedurals about Mitch Taylor before moving on to other work, but in 1963 he was persuaded to revive Mitch Taylor for a series of short stories for *Ellery Queen's Mystery Magazine*. The second story in that series, "H As in Homicide," won an Edgar from the Mystery Writers of America in 1964, and all sixteen stories in the series were accorded Honor Roll rating by Anthony Boucher in *The Best Detective Stories of the Year*. He is married and lives in Martha's Vineyard, Massachusetts.

SHE CAME THROUGH THE DOOR of the Homicide Squad's outer office as if it were disgrace to be there, as if she didn't like it, as if she hadn't done anything wrong—and never could or would.

Still, here she was. About twenty-two years old and underweight. Wearing a pink, sleeveless dress. She had dark hair pulled back in a bun; her breasts were close together; and her eyes ate you up.

Mitch Taylor had just come back from lunch and was holding down the fort all alone. He nodded at her and said, "Anything I can do?"

"Yes, I—I—" Mitch put her down as a nervous stutterer and waited for her to settle down. "They told me to come here," she said. "I went to the neighborhood police station and they said they couldn't do anything, that I had to come here."

"Yeah," Mitch said. It was the old run-around and he was willing to bet this was Pulasky's doing, up in the Third Precinct. He never took a complaint unless the rule book said, "You, Pulasky—you got to handle this or you'll lose your pension."

So Mitch said, "Sure. What's the trouble?"

"I don't like to bother you and I hope you don't think I'm silly, but—well, my friend left me. And I don't know where, or why."

"Boy friend?" Mitch said.

She blushed a deep crimson. "Oh, no! A real *friend*. We were traveling together and she took the car and went, without even leaving me a note. I can't understand it."

"Let's go inside and get the details," Mitch said.

He brought her into the Squad Room and sat her down at a desk. She looked up shyly, sort of impressed with him. He didn't know why, because he was only an average-looking guy, of medium height, on the cocky side, with stiff, wiry hair and a face nobody remembered, particularly.

He sat down opposite her and took out a pad and pencil. "Your name?" he said.

"Prudence Gilford."

"Address?"

"New York City, but I gave up my apartment there."

"Where I come from, too. Quite a ways from home, aren't you?"

"I'm on my way to California—my sister lives out there. I answered an ad in the paper—just a moment, I think I still have it." She fumbled in a big, canvas bag, and the strap broke off and the whole business dropped. She picked it up awkwardly, blushing again, but she kept on talking. "Bella Tansey advertised for somebody to share the driving to California. She said she'd pay all expenses. It was a wonderful chance for me . . . Here, I have it."

She took out the clipping and handed it to Mitch. It was the usual thing: woman companion to share the driving, and a phone number.

"So you got in touch?" Mitch prodded.

"Yes. We liked each other immediately, and arranged to go the following week."

She was fiddling with the strap, trying to fix it, and she finally fitted the tab over some kind of button. Mitch, watching, wondered how long *that* was going to last.

Meanwhile she was still telling him about Bella Tansey. "We got along so well," Prudence said, "and last night we stopped at a motel—The Happy Inn, it's called—and we went to bed. When I woke up, she was gone."

"Why did you stop there?" Mitch asked sharply.

"We were tired and it had a Vacancy sign." She drew in her breath and asked anxiously, "Is there something wrong with it?"

"Not too good a reputation," Mitch said. "Did she take all her things with her? Her overnight stuff, I mean."

"Yes, I think so. Or at least, she took her bag."

Mitch got a description of the car: a dark blue Buick; 1959 or 1960, she wasn't sure; New York plates but she didn't know the number.

"Okay," Mitch said. "We'll check. We'll send out a flier and have her picked up and then we can find out why she left in such a hurry."

Prudence Gilford's eyes got big. "Yes," she said. "And please, can you help me? I have only five dollars and the motel is expensive. I can't stay there and I don't know where to go."

"Leave it to me," Mitch said. "I'll fix it up at the motel and get you a place in town for a while. You can get some money, can't you?"

"Oh, yes. I'll write my sister for it."

"Better wire," Mitch said. "And will you wait here a couple of minutes? I'll be right back."

"Of course."

Lieutenant Decker had come in and was working on something in his tiny office which was jammed up with papers and stuff. Mitch reported on the Gilford business and the Lieutenant listened.

"Pulasky should have handled it," Mitch said, finishing up. "But what the hell—The kid's left high and dry, so maybe we could give her a little help."

"What do you think's behind this?" Decker asked.

"I don't know," Mitch said. "She's a clinger—scared of everything and leans on people. Maybe the Tansey woman got sick and tired of her, or maybe this is lesbian stuff. Hard to tell."

"Well, go ahead with an S-Four for the Buick. It ought to be on a main highway and within a five-hundred-mile radius. Somebody'll spot it. We'll see what cooks."

Mitch drove Prudence out to the motel and told her to get her things. While she was busy, he went into the office and spoke to Ed Hiller, who ran the joint. Hiller, a tall, stoop-shouldered guy who'd been in and out of jams most of his life, was interested in anything from a nickel up, but chiefly up. He rented cabins by the hour, day, or week, and you could get liquor if you paid the freight; but most of his trouble came from reports of cars that had been left unlocked and rifled. The police had never been able to pin anything on him.

He said, "Hello, Taylor. Anything wrong?"

"Just want to know about a couple of dames that stayed here last night—Bella Tansey and Prudence Gilford. Tansey pulled out during the night."

"Around midnight," Ed said. "She came into the office to make a phone call, and a little later I heard her car pull out."

Time for the missing girl to pack, Mitch decided. So far, everything checked. "Who'd she call?" he asked. "What did she say?"

Hiller shrugged. "I don't listen in," he said. "I saw her open the door and then I heard her go into the phone booth. I mind my own business. You know that."

"Yeah," Mitch said flatly. "You heard the coins drop, didn't you? Local call, or long distance?"

Hiller leaned over the counter, "Local," he said softly, "I think."

"Got their registration?" Mitch asked. Hiller nodded and handed Mitch the sheet, which had a record of the New York license plates.

That was about all there was to it. Nobody picked up Bella Tansey and her Buick, Prudence Gilford was socked away in a rooming house in town, and Mitch never expected to see her again.

When he got home that night, Amy kissed him and asked him about things, and then after he'd horsed around with the kids a little, she showed him a letter from her sister. Her sister's husband was on strike and what the union paid them took care of food and rent and that was about all; but they had to keep up their payments on the car and the new dishwasher, and the TV had broken down again, and could Mitch and Amy help out for a little while—they'd get it back soon.

So after the kids were in bed, Mitch and Amy sat down on the sofa to figure things out, which took about two seconds and came to fifty bucks out of his next pay check. It was always like that with the two of them: they saw things the same way and never had any arguments. Not many guys were as lucky as Mitch.

The next morning Decker had his usual conference with the Homicide Squad and went over all the cases they had in the shop. The only thing he said about the Gilford business was, the next time Pulasky tried to sucker them, figure it out so he had to come down here, personally, and then make him sweat.

Mitch drew a couple of minor assault cases to investigate, and he'd finished up with one and was on his way to the other when the call came in on his radio. Go out to French Woods, on East Road. They had a homicide and it looked like the missing Tansey woman.

He found a couple of police cars and an oil truck and the usual bunch of snoopers who had stopped out of curiosity. There was a kind of rough trail going into the woods. A couple of hundred yards in, the Lieutenant and a few of the boys and Jub Freeman, the lab technician, were grouped around a dark blue car. It didn't take any heavy brainwork to decide it was the Tansey Buick.

When Mitch got to the car, he saw Bella Tansey slumped in the front seat with her head resting against the window. The right hand door was open and so was the glove compartment, and Decker was looking at the stuff he'd found there.

He gave Mitch the main facts. "Truck driver spotted the car, went in to look, and then got in touch with us. We've been here about fifteen minutes, and the Medical Examiner ought to show up pretty soon. She was strangled—you can see the marks on her neck—and I'll bet a green hat that it happened the night before last, not long after she left the motel."

Mitch surveyed the position of the body with a practiced eye. "She wasn't driving, either. She was pushed in there, after she was dead."

"Check," Decker said. Very carefully, so that he wouldn't spoil any possible fingerprints, he slid the junk he'd been examining onto the front seat. He turned to Jub Freeman, who was delicately holding a handbag by the two ends and scrutinizing it for prints.

"Find anything?" the Lieutenant asked.

"Nothing," Jub said. "But the initials on it are B.T.W."

"Bella Tansey What?" the Lieutenant said. He didn't laugh and neither did anybody else. He stooped to put his hands on the door sill, leaned forward, and stared at the body. Mitch, standing behind him, peered over his head.

Bella had been around thirty and she'd been made for men. She was wearing a blue dress with a thing that Amy called a bolero top, and, except where the skirt had pulled up maybe from moving the body, her clothes were not disturbed. The door of the glove compartment and parts of the dashboard were splotched with fingerprint powder.

Mitch pulled back and waited. After about a minute the Lieutenant stood up.

"Doesn't look as if there was a sex angle," Decker said. "And this stuff—" he kicked at the dry leaves that covered the earth "—doesn't take footprints. If we're lucky, we'll find somebody who saw the killer somewhere around here." He made a smacking sound with his thin, elastic lips and watched Jub.

Jub had taken off his coat and dumped the contents of the pocketbook onto it. Mitch spotted nothing unusual—just the junk women usually carried; but he didn't see any money. Jub was holding the purse and rummaging inside it.

"Empty?" the Lieutenant asked sharply.

Jub nodded. "Except for one nickel. She must have had money, so whoever went through this missed up on five cents."

"Couldn't be Ed Hiller, then," Mitch said, and the gang laughed.

"Let's say the motive was robbery," Decker said. "We got something of a head start on this, but brother, it's a bad one. Why does a woman on her way to California make a phone call and then sneak off in the middle of the night? Leaving her girl friend in the lurch, too. Doesn't sound like robbery now, does it?"

"Sounds like a guy," Mitch said. "She had a late date, and the guy robbed her, instead of—"

"We'll talk to Ed Hiller about that later," the Lieutenant said. "Taylor, you better get going on this. Call New York and get a line on her. Her friends, her background. If she was married. How much money she might have had with her. Her bank might help on that."

"Right," Mitch said.

"And then get hold of the Gilford dame and pump her," Decker said.

Mitch nodded. He glanced into the back of the car and saw the small overnight bag. "That," he said, pointing. "She packed, so she didn't expect to go back to the motel. But she didn't put her bag in the trunk compartment, so she must have expected to check in somewhere else, and pretty soon."

"She'd want to sleep somewhere, wouldn't she?" Decker asked.

"That packing and unpacking doesn't make sense," Mitch said.

Decker grunted. "Homicides never do," he said grimly.

Mitch drove back to headquarters thinking about that overnight bag, and it kept bothering him. He didn't know exactly why, but it was the sort of thing you kept in the back of your mind until something happened or you found something else, and then everything clicked and you got a pattern.

But, what with organizing the questions to ask New York, he couldn't do much doping out right now. Besides, there was a lot more information to come in.

He got New York on the phone and they said they'd move on it right away; so he hung up and went to see Prudence. He was lucky to find her in.

She was shocked at the news, but she had nothing much to contribute. "We didn't know each other very long," she said, "and I was asleep when she left. I was so tired. We'd been driving all day, and I'd done most of it."

"Did she mention knowing anybody around—anybody in town?" Mitch asked. Prudence shook her head, but he put her through the wringer anyhow—it was easy for people to hear things and then forget them. You had to jog their memories a little. And besides, how could he be sure she was telling all she knew?

He felt sorry for her, though—she looked kind of thin and played out, as if she hadn't been eating much. So he said, "That five bucks of yours isn't going to last too long, and if you need some dough—"

"Oh, thanks!" she said, sort of glowing and making him feel that Mitch Taylor, he was okay. "Oh, thanks! It's perfectly wonderful of you, but I have enough for a while, and I'm sure my sister will send me the money I wired her for."

By that afternoon most of the basic information was in. Locally, the Medical Examiner said that Bella Tansey had been strangled with a towel or a handkerchief; he placed the time as not long after she'd left the motel. The Lieutenant had questioned Ed Hiller without being able to get anything "hot." Hiller insisted he hadn't left the motel, but his statement depended only on his own word.

Jub had used a vacuum cleaner on the car and examined the findings with a microscope, and he'd shot enough pictures to fill a couple of albums.

"They stopped at a United Motel the first night," he recapitulated, "and they had dinner at a Howard Johnson place. They ate sandwiches in the car, probably for lunch, and they bought gas in Pennsylvania and Indiana, and the car ate up oil. There was a gray kitten on the rear seat some time or other. They both drove. Bella Tansey had car trouble and she bought her clothes at Saks Fifth Avenue. I can tell you a lot more about her, but I'm damned if I've uncovered anything that will help on the homicide. No trace in that car of anybody except the two women."

The New York police, however, came up with a bombshell. Bella Tansey had drawn $1800 from her bank, in cash, and she'd been married to Clyde Warhouse and they'd been divorced two years ago. She'd used her maiden name—Tansey.

"Warhouse!" the Lieutenant said.

Everybody knew that name. He ran a column in the local

paper—he called it "Culture Corner"—and he covered art galleries, visiting orchestras, and egghead lecturers. Whenever he had nothing else to write about, he complained how archaic the civic architecture was.

"That's why she had the W on her bag," Mitch said. "Bella Tansey Warhouse. And Ed Hiller didn't lie about the phone call. She made it all right—to her ex-husband."

Decker nodded. "Let's say she hotfooted it out to see him. Let's say she still had a yen for him and they scrapped, that he got mad and lost his head and strangled her. But why would he take her dough? She must've had around seventeen hundred with her. Why would he rob her?"

"Why not?" Mitch said. "It was there, wasn't it?"

"Let's think about this," Decker said. "Prudence says Bella unpacked. Did Bella start to go to bed, or what?"

"Prudence doesn't know," Mitch said. "I went into that for all it was worth, and Prudence *assumes* Bella unpacked—she can't actually remember. Says she was bushed and went right to sleep. Didn't even wash her face."

"Well," Decker said, "I guess Warhouse is wondering when we'll get around to him. I'll check on him while you go up there." The Lieutenant's jaw set firmly. "Bring him in."

Mitch rolled his shoulders, tugged on the lapels of his jacket, and went out. The first time you hit your suspect, it could make or break the case.

Clyde Warhouse lived in a red brick house with tall white columns on the front. Mitch found him at home, in his study. He was a little guy with big teeth, and he didn't really smile; he just pulled his lips back, and you could take it any way you pleased.

Warhouse came right to the point. "You're here about my former wife," he said. "I just heard about it on the radio, and I wish I could give you more information, but I can't. It's certainly not the end I wished for her."

"What kind of end were you hoping for?" Mitch asked.

"None." The Warhouse lips curled back, telling you how smart he was. "And certainly not one in this town."

"Let's not kid around," Mitch said. "You're coming back with me. You know that, don't you?"

The guy almost went down with the first punch. "You mean—you mean I'm being arrested?"

"What do *you* think?" Mitch said. "We know she phoned you and you met her. We know you saw her."

"But I didn't see her," Warhouse said. "She never showed up."

Mitch didn't even blink.

"How long did you wait?" he asked.

"Almost an hour. Maybe more."

"Where?"

"On the corner of Whitman and Cooper." Warhouse gasped, then put his head in his hands and said, "Oh, God!" And that was all Mitch could get out of him until they had him in the Squad Room, with Decker leading off on the interrogation.

The guy didn't back down from that first admission. He knew he'd been tricked, but he stuck to his guns and wouldn't give another inch. He said Bella had called him around midnight and said she must see him. He hadn't known she was in town, didn't want to see her, had no interest in her, but he couldn't turn her down. So he went, and he waited. And waited and waited. And then went home.

They kept hammering away at him. First, Mitch and Decker, then Bankhart and Balenky, then Mitch and Decker again.

In between, they consulted Jub. He'd been examining Warhouse's car for soil that might match samples from French Woods; for evidence of a struggle, of Bella's presence—of anything at all. The examination drew a blank. Warhouse grinned his toothy grin and kept saying no. And late that night they gave up on him, brought him across the courtyard to the city jail, and left him there for the night. He needed sleep—and so did the Homicide Squad.

At the conference the next morning, Decker was grim. "We have an ex-wife calling her ex-husband at midnight and making an appointment; we have his statement that he went and she never showed up; and we have a homicide and that's all."

"The dough," Bankhart said.

Decker nodded. "When we find that seventeen hundred, then we might have a case. We'll get warrants and we'll look for it, but let's assume we draw another blank. Then what?"

"Let's have another session with Ed Hiller," Mitch said.

They had it, and they had a longer one with Warhouse, and they were still nowhere. They'd gone into the Warhouse background thoroughly. He earned good money, paid his bills promptly, and got along well with his second wife. He liked women, they went for him, and he was a humdinger with them, although he was not involved in any scandal. But in Mitch's book, he'd humdinged once too often. Still, you had to prove it.

For a while they concentrated on The Happy Inn. But the motel guests either couldn't be found, because they'd registered under fake names with fake license numbers, or else they said they'd been asleep and had no idea what was going on outside.

The usual tips came in—crank stuff that had to be followed up. The killer had been seen, somebody had heard Bella scream for help, somebody else had had a vision. Warhouse had been spotted waiting on the corner, which proved nothing except he'd arrived there first. Every tip checked out either as useless or a phony. The missing $1700 didn't show up. Decker ran out of jokes, and Mitch came home tired and irritable.

The case was at full stop.

Then Decker had this wild idea, and he told it to Jub and Mitch. "My wife says I woke up last night and asked for a drink of water, and I don't even remember it."

"So you were thirsty," Mitch remarked.

"Don't you get it?" Decker exclaimed. "People wake up, then go back to sleep, and in the morning they don't even know they were awake. Well, we know Bella packed her bag, and she was in that motel room with Prudence and must have made some noise and possibly even talked. I'll bet a pair of pink panties that Prudence woke up, and then forgot all about it. She has a clue buried deep in her mind."

"Granted," Jub said, "but how are you going to dig it up?"

"I'll hypnotize her," Decker said, with fire in his eyes. "I'll ask a psychiatrist to get her to free-associate. Taylor, ask her to come in tomorrow morning, when my mind is fresh. And hers, too."

Mitch dropped in on Prudence and gave her the message, but the way he saw things, the Lieutenant was sure reaching for it—far out. Mitch told Amy about this screwy idea of Decker's, but all she said was that tomorrow was payday and not to forget to send the fifty dollars to her sister.

That was why Mitch wasn't around when Prudence showed up. He took his money over to the Post Office and there, on account he liked to jaw a little, make friends, set up contacts—you never knew when you might need them—he got to gabbing with the postal clerk.

His name was Cornell and he was tired. Mitch figured the

guy was born that way. Besides, there was something about a Post Office that dragged at you. No fun in it, nothing ever happened. All the stamps were the same (or looked the same) and all the clerks were the same (or looked the same) and if anything unusual came up, you checked it in the regulations and did what the rules said, exactly. And if the rules didn't tell you, then the thing couldn't be done, so you sent the customer away and went back to selling stamps.

Which people either wanted, or they didn't. There were no sales, no bargains. A damaged stamp was never marked down—it was worth what it said on its face, or nothing. There was nothing in between.

Still, the Post Office was a hell of a lot better than what Decker was doing over at the Homicide Squad, so Mitch handed in his fifty bucks for the money order and said, "It's not much dough, I guess. What's the most you ever handled?"

The clerk came alive. "Ten thousand dollars. Six years ago."

"The hell with six years ago. Say this week."

"Oh. That dame with seventeen hundred dollars. That was the biggest."

Click.

Mitch said cautiously, "You mean Prudence Gilford?"

"No. Patsy Grant."

"P.G.—same thing," Mitch said with certainty. "Same girl. And I'll bet she sent the dough to herself care of General Delivery, somewhere in California."

Cornell looked as if he thought Mitch were some kind of magician. "That's right," he said. "How did you know?"

"Me?" Mitch said, seeing that it all fitted like a glove. Prudence—or whatever her name was—had strangled Bella for the dough, then packed Bella's bag, dragged her out to the car, driven it to the woods, and left it there. And probably walked all the way back. That's why Prudence had been so tired.

"Me?" Mitch said again, riding on a cloud. "I know those things. That's what makes me a cop. Ideas—I got bushels of 'em." He thought of how the Lieutenant would go bug-eyed. Mitch Taylor, Homicide Expert.

He walked over to the phone booth, gave his shield number to the operator so he could make the call free and save himself a dime, and got through to the Homicide Squad.

Decker answered. "Taylor?" he said. "Come on back. The Gilford dame just confessed."

"She—*what?*"

"Yeah, yeah, confessed. While she was in here, the strap on her bag broke and she dropped it. Everything fell out—including a money order receipt for seventeen hundred dollars. We had her cold and she confessed. She knew all about Warhouse and planned it so we'd nail him."

There was a buzz on the wire and Lieutenant Decker's voice went fuzzy.

"Taylor," he said after a couple of seconds. "Can you hear me? Are you listening?"

"Sure," Mitch said. "But what for?"

And he hung up.

Yeah, Mitch Taylor, Homicide Expert.

NIGHTSHADE

BY ED MCBAIN

Ed McBain is the pseudonym of Evan Hunter, who was born in 1926 in New York City. After teaching in New York vocational schools, he wrote *The Blackboard Jungle* (1954), a grim story of violence and racial tension in a city high school. His series of novels about the 87th Precinct, which deal with social problems at the street level, are unmatched in versatility for police-procedural stories. He has written scripts for television and films, including Alfred Hitchcock's screen adaptation of Daphne Du Maurier's *The Birds*.

THE MORNING HOURS OF THE night come imperceptibly here.

It is a minute before midnight on the peeling face of the hanging wall clock, and then it is midnight, and then the minute hand moves visibly and with a lurch into the new day. The morning hours have begun, but scarcely anyone has noticed. The stale coffee in soggy cardboard containers tastes the same as it did thirty seconds ago, the spastic rhythm of the clacking typewriters continues unabated, a drunk across the room shouts that the world is full of brutality, and cigarette smoke drifts up toward the face of the clock where, unnoticed and unmourned, the old day has already been dead for two minutes.

Then the telephone rings.

The men in this room are part of a tired routine, somewhat shabby about the edges, as faded and as gloomy as the room itself, with its cigarette-scarred desks and its smudged green walls. This could be the office of a failing insurance company were it not for the evidence of the holstered pistols hanging from belts on the backs of wooden chairs painted a darker green than the walls. The furniture is ancient, the typewriters are ancient, the building itself is ancient—which is perhaps only fitting since these men are involved in what is an ancient pursuit, a pursuit once considered honorable. They are law enforcers. They are, in the mildest words of the drunk still hurling epithets from the grilled detention cage, dirty, rotten pigs.

The telephone continues to ring.

The little girl lying in the alley behind the theater was wearing a belted white trench coat wet with blood. There was blood on the floor of the alley, and blood on the metal fire door behind her, and blood on her face and matted in her blonde hair, blood on her miniskirt and on the lavender tights she wore. A neon sign across the street stained the girl's ebbing life juices green and then orange, while from the open knife wound in her chest the blood sprouted like some ghastly night flower, dark and rich, red, orange, green, pulsing in time to the neon flicker—a grotesque psychedelic light show, and then losing the rhythm, welling up with less force and power.

302

She opened her mouth, she tried to speak, and the scream of an ambulance approaching the theater seemed to come from her mouth on a fresh bubble of blood. The blood stopped, her life ended, the girl's eyes rolled back into her head.

Detective Steve Carella turned away as the ambulance attendants rushed a stretcher into the alley. He told them the girl was dead.

"We got here in seven minutes," one of the attendants said.

"Nobody's blaming you," Carella answered.

"This is Saturday night," the attendant complained. "Streets are full of traffic. Even *with* the damn siren."

Carella walked to the unmarked sedan parked at the curb. Detective Cotton Hawes, sitting behind the wheel, rolled down his frost-rimed window and said, "How is she?"

"We've got a homicide," Carella answered.

The boy was eighteen years old, and he had been picked up not ten minutes ago for breaking off car aerials. He had broken off twelve on the same street, strewing them behind him like a Johnny Appleseed planting radios; a cruising squad car had spotted him as he tried to twist off the aerial of a 1966 Cadillac. He was drunk or stoned or both, and when Sergeant Murchison at the muster desk asked him to read the Miranda-Escobedo warning signs on the wall, printed in both English and Spanish, he could read neither.

The arresting patrolman took the boy to the squadroom upstairs, where Detective Bert Kling was talking to Hawes on the telephone. Kling signaled for the patrolman to wait with his prisoner on the bench outside the slatted wooden rail divider, and then buzzed Murchison at the desk downstairs.

"Dave," he said, "we've got a homicide in the alley of the Eleventh Street Theater. You want to get it rolling?"

"Right," Murchison said, and hung up.

Homicides are a common occurrence in this city, and each one is treated identically, the grisly horror of violent death reduced to routine by a police force that would otherwise be overwhelmed by statistics. At the muster desk upstairs Kling waved the patrolman and his prisoner into the squadroom. Sergeant Murchison first reported the murder to Captain Frick, who commanded the 87th Precinct, and then to Lieutenant Byrnes, who commanded the 87th Detective Squad. He then phoned Homicide, who in turn set in motion an escalating process of notification that included the Police Laboratory, the Telegraph, Telephone and Teletype Bureau at Headquarters, the Medical Examiner, the District Attorney, the District Commander of the Detective Division, the Chief of Detectives, and finally the Police Commissioner himself. Someone had thoughtlessly robbed a young woman of her life, and now a lot of sleepy-eyed men were being shaken out of their beds on a cold October night.

Upstairs, the clock on the squadroom wall read 12:30 A.M. The boy who had broken off twelve car aerials sat in a chair alongside Bert Kling's desk. Kling took one look at him and yelled to Miscolo in the Clerical Office to bring a pot of strong coffee. Across the room the drunk in the detention cage wanted to know where he was. In a little while they would release him with a warning to try to stay sober till morning.

But the night was young.

They arrived alone or in pairs, blowing on their hands, shoulders hunched against the bitter cold, breaths pluming whitely from their lips. They marked the dead girl's position in the alleyway, they took her picture, they made drawings of the scene, they searched for the murder weapon and found none, and then they stood around speculating on sudden death. In this alleyway alongside a theater the policemen were the stars and the celebrities, and a curious crowd thronged the sidewalk where a barricade had already been set up, anxious for a glimpse of these men with their shields pinned to their overcoats—the identifying *Playbill*s of law enforcement, without which you could not tell the civilians from the plainclothes cops.

Monoghan and Monroe had arrived from Homicide, and they watched dispassionately now as the Assistant Medical Examiner fluttered around the dead girl. They were both wearing black overcoats, black mufflers, and black fedoras; both were heavier men than Carella who stood between them with the lean look of an overtrained athlete, a pained expression on his face.

"He done some job on her," Monroe said.

Monoghan made a rude sound.

"You identified her yet?" Monroe asked.

"I'm waiting for the M.E. to get through," Carella answered.

"Might help to know what she was doing here in the alley. What's that door there?" Monoghan asked.

304

"Stage entrance."

"Think she was in the show?"

"I don't know," Carella said.

"Well, what the hell," Monroe said, "they're finished with her pocketbook there, ain't they? Why don't you look through it? You finished with that pocketbook there?" he yelled to one of the lab technicians.

"Yeah, anytime you want it," the technician shouted back.

"Go on, Carella, take a look."

The technician wiped the blood off the dead girl's bag, then handed it to Carella. Monoghan and Monroe crowded in on him as he twisted open the clasp.

"Bring it over to the light," Monroe said.

The light, with a metal shade, hung over the stage door. So violently had the girl been stabbed that flecks of blood had even dotted the enameled white underside of the shade. In her bag they found a driver's license identifying her as Mercy Howell of 1113 Rutherford Avenue, Age 24, Height 5' 3", Eyes Blue. They found an Actors Equity card in her name, as well as credit cards for two of the city's largest department stores. They found an unopened package of Virginia Slims, and a book of matches advertising an art course. They found a rat-tailed comb. They found $17.43. They found a package of Kleenex, and an appointment book. They found a ballpoint pen with shreds of tobacco clinging to its tip, an eyelash curler, two subway tokens, and an advertisement for a see-through blouse, clipped from one of the local newspapers.

In the pocket of her trench coat, when the M.E. had finished with her and pronounced her dead from multiple stab wounds in the chest and throat, they found an unfired Browning .25 caliber automatic. They tagged the gun and the handbag, and they moved the girl out of the alleyway and into the waiting ambulance for removal to the morgue. There was now nothing left of Mercy Howell but a chalked outline of her body and a pool of her blood on the alley floor.

"You sober enough to understand me?" Kling asked the boy with the fixation about aerials.

"I was never drunk to begin with," the boy answered.

"Okay then, here we go," Kling said. "In keeping with the Supreme Court decision in Miranda versus Arizona we are not permitted to ask you any questions until you are warned of

305

your right to counsel and your privilege against self-incrimination."

"What does that mean?" the boy asked. "Self-incrimination?"

"I'm about to explain that to you now," Kling said.

"This coffee stinks."

"First, you have the right to remain silent if you so choose," Kling said. "Do you understand that?"

"I understand it."

"Second, you do not have to answer any police questions if you don't want to. Do you understand that?"

"What the hell are you asking me if I understand for? Do I look like a moron or something?"

"The law requires that I ask whether or not you understand these specific warnings. *Did* you understand what I just said about not having to answer?"

"Yeah, yeah, I understood."

"All right. Third, if you do decide to answer any questions, the answers may be used as evidence against you, do you—?"

"What the hell did I do, break off a couple of lousy car aerials?"

"Did you understand that?"

"I understood it."

"You also have the right to consult with an attorney before or during police questioning. If you do not have the money to hire a lawyer, a lawyer will be appointed to consult with you."

Kling gave this warning straight-faced even though he knew that under the Criminal Procedure Code of the city for which he worked, a public defender could not be appointed by the courts until the preliminary hearing. There was no legal provision for the courts *or* the police to appoint counsel during questioning, and there were certainly no police funds set aside for the appointment of attorneys. In theory, a call to the Legal Aid Society should have brought a lawyer up there to the old squadroom within minutes, ready and eager to offer counsel to any indigent person desiring it. But in practice, if this boy sitting beside Kling told him in the next three seconds that he was unable to pay for his own attorney and would like one provided, Kling would not have known just what the hell to do—other than call off the questioning.

"I understand," the boy said.

"You've signified that you understand all the warnings," Kling said, "and now I ask you whether you are willing to answer my questions without an attorney here to counsel you."

"Go fly a kite," the boy said. "I don't want to answer nothing."

So that was that.

They booked him for Criminal Mischief, a Class-A Misdemeanor defined as intentional or reckless damage to the property of another person, and they took him downstairs to a holding cell, to await transportation to the Criminal Courts Building for arraignment.

The phone was ringing again, and a woman was waiting on the bench just outside the squadroom.

The watchman's booth was just inside the metal stage door. An electric clock on the wall behind the watchman's stool read 1:10 A.M. The watchman was a man in his late seventies who did not at all mind being questioned by the police. He came on duty, he told them, at 7:30 each night. The company call was for 8:00, and he was there at the stage door waiting to greet everybody as they arrived to get made up and in costume. Curtain went down at 11:20, and usually most of the kids was out of the theater by 11:45 or, at the latest, midnight. He stayed on till 9:00 the next morning, when the theater box office opened.

"Ain't much to do during the night except hang around and make sure nobody runs off with the scenery," he said, chuckling.

"Did you happen to notice what time Mercy Howell left the theater?" Carella asked.

"She the one got killed?" the old man asked.

"Yes," Hawes said. "Mercy Howell. About this high, blond hair, blue eyes."

"They're all about that high, with blonde hair and blue eyes," the old man said, and chuckled again. "I don't know hardly none of them by name. Shows come and go, you know. Be a hell of a chore to have to remember all the kids who go in and out that door."

"Do you sit here by the door all night?" Carella asked.

"Well, no, not all night. What I do, I lock the door after everybody's out and then I check the lights, make sure just the work light's on. I won't touch the switchboard, not allowed to, but I can turn out lights in the lobby, for example, if somebody left them on, or down in the toilets—sometimes they leave lights on down in the toilets. Then I come back here to the booth, and read or listen to the radio. Along about two o'clock I check the theater again, make sure we ain't got no fires or nothing, and then I come back here and make the rounds again at four o'clock, and again about eight. That's what I do."

"You say you lock this door?"

"That's right."

"Would you remember what time you locked it tonight?"

"Oh, must've been about ten minutes to twelve. Soon as I knew everybody was out."

"How do you know when they're out?"

"I give a yell up the stairs there. You see those stairs there? They go up to the dressing rooms. Dressing rooms are all up-stairs in this house. So I go to the steps, and I yell 'Locking up! Anybody here?' And if somebody yells back, I know somebody's here, and I say, 'Let's shake it, honey,' if it's a girl, and if it's a boy, I say, 'Let's hurry it up, sonny.'" The old man chuckled again. "With this show it's sometimes hard to tell which's the girls and which's the boys. I manage, though," he said, and again chuckled.

"So you locked the door at ten minutes to twelve?"

"Right."

"And everybody had left the theater by that time?"

"'Cept me, of course."

"Did you look out into the alley before you locked the door?" Carella asked.

"Nope. Why should I do that?"

"Did you hear anything outside *while* you were locking the door?"

"Nope."

"Or at any time *before* you locked it?"

"Well, there's always noise outside when they're leaving, you know. They got friends waiting for them or else they go home together, you know—there's always a lot of chatter when they go out."

"But it was quiet when you locked the door?"

"Dead quiet," the old man said.

The woman who took the chair beside Detective Meyer Meyer's desk was perhaps thirty-two years old, with long straight black hair trailing down her back, and wide brown eyes that were terrified. It was still October, and the color of her tailored coat seemed suited to the season, a subtle tangerine with a small brown fur collar that echoed an outdoors trembling with the colors of autumn.

"I feel sort of silly about this," she said, "but my husband insisted that I come."

"I see," Meyer said.

"There are ghosts," the woman said.

Across the room Kling unlocked the door to the detention cage and said, "Okay, pal, on your way. Try to stay sober till morning, huh?"

"It ain't one thirty yet," the man said, "the night is young." He stepped out of the cage, tipped his hat to Kling, and hurriedly left the squadroom.

Meyer looked at the woman sitting beside him, studying her with new interest because, to tell the truth, she had not seemed like a nut when she first walked into the squadroom. He had been a detective for more years than he chose to count, and in his time had met far too many nuts of every stripe and persuasion. But he had never met one as pretty as Adele Gorman with her well-tailored, fur-collared coat, and her Vassar voice and her skillfully applied eye makeup, lips bare of color in her pale white face, pert and reasonably young and seemingly intelligent—but apparently a nut besides.

"In the house," she said. "Ghosts."

"Where do you live, ma'am?" he asked. He had written her name on the pad in front of him, and now he watched her with his pencil poised and recalled the lady who had come into the squadroom only last month to report a gorilla peering into her bedroom from the fire escape outside. They had sent a patrolman over to make a routine check, and had even called the zoo and the circus (which coincidentally was in town, and which lent at least some measure of credibility to her claim), but there had been no gorilla on the fire escape, nor had any gorilla recently escaped from a cage. The lady came back the next day to report that her visiting gorilla had put in another appearance the night before, this time wearing a top hat and carrying a black cane with an ivory head. Meyer had assured her that he would have a platoon of cops watching her building that night, which seemed to calm her at least somewhat. He had then led her personally out of the squadroom and down the iron-runged steps, and through the high-ceilinged muster room, and past the hanging green globes on the front stoop, and onto the sidewalk outside the station house. Sergeant Murchison, at the muster desk, shook his head after the lady was gone, and muttered, "More of them outside than in."

Meyer watched Adele Gorman now, remembered what Murchison had said, and thought: *Gorillas in September, ghosts in October.*

"We live in Smoke Rise," she said. "Actually, it's my father's house, but my husband and I are living there with him."

"The address?"

"MacArthur Lane—number three hundred seventy-four. You take the first access road into Smoke Rise, about a mile and a half east of Silvermine Oval. The name on the mailbox is Van Houten. That's my father's name. Willem Van Houten." She paused and studied him, as though expecting some reaction.

"Okay," Meyer said, and ran a hand over his bald pate. He looked up and said, "Now, you were saying, Mrs. Gorman—"

"That we have ghosts."

"Uh-huh. What kind of ghosts?"

"Ghosts. Poltergeists. Shades. I don't know," she said, and shrugged. "What kinds of ghosts are there?"

"Well, they're your ghosts, so suppose you tell me."

The telephone on Kling's desk rang. He lifted the receiver and said, "Eighty-seventh, Detective Kling."

"There are two of them," Adele said.

"Male or female?"

"One of each."

"Yeah," Kling said into the telephone, "go ahead."

"How old would you say they were?"

"Centuries, I would guess."

"No, I mean—"

"Oh, how old do they look? Well, the man—"

"You've seen them?"

"Oh, yes, many times."

"Uh-huh," Meyer said.

"I'll be right over," Kling said into the telephone. "You stay there." He slammed down the receiver, opened his desk drawer, pulled out a holstered revolver, and hurriedly clipped it to his belt. "Somebody threw a bomb into a store-front church. One-seven-three-three Culver Avenue. I'm heading over."

"Right," Meyer said. "Get back to me."

"We'll need a couple of meat wagons. The minister and two others were killed, and it sounds as if there're a lot of injured."

"Will you tell Dave?"

"On the way out," Kling said, and was gone.

310

"Mrs. Gorman," Meyer said, "as you can see, we're pretty busy here just now. I wonder if your ghosts can wait till morning."

"No, they can't," Adele said.

"Why not?"

"Because they appear precisely at two forty-five A.M. and I want someone to see them."

"Why don't you and your husband look at them?" Meyer said.

"You think I'm a nut, don't you?" Adele said.

"No, no, Mrs. Gorman, not at all."

"Oh, yes you do," Adele said. "I didn't believe in ghosts either—until I saw these two."

"Well, this is all very interesting, I assure you, Mrs. Gorman, but really we do have our hands full right now, and I don't know what we can do about these ghosts of yours, even if we did come over to take a look at them."

"They've been stealing things from us," Adele said, and Meyer thought: *Oh, we have got ourselves a prime lunatic this time.*

"What sort of things?"

"A diamond brooch that used to belong to my mother when she was alive. They stole that from my father's safe."

"What else?"

"A pair of emerald earrings. They were in the safe, too."

"When did these thefts occur?"

"Last month."

"Isn't it possible the jewelry's been mislaid?"

"You don't mislay a diamond brooch and a pair of emerald earrings that are locked inside a wall safe."

"Did you report these thefts?"

"No."

"Why not?"

"Because I knew you'd think I was crazy. Which is just what you're thinking right this minute."

"No, Mrs. Gorman, but I'm sure you can appreciate the fact that we—uh—can't go around arresting ghosts," Meyer said, and tried a smile.

Adele Gorman did not smile back. "Forget the ghosts," she said, "I was foolish to mention them. I should have known better." She took a deep breath, looked him squarely in the eye, and said, "I'm here to report the theft of a diamond brooch valued at six thousand dollars, and a pair of earrings worth thirty-five hundred dollars. Will you send a man to investigate tonight, or should I ask my father to get in touch with your superior officer?"

"Your father? What's he got to—"

"My father is a retired Surrogate's Court judge," Adele said.

"I see."

"Yes, I hope you do."

"What time did you say these ghosts arrive?" Meyer asked, and sighed heavily.

Between midnight and 2:00 the city does not change very much. The theaters have all let out, and the average Saturday night revelers, good citizens from Bethtown or Calm's Point, Riverhead or Majesta, have come into the Isola streets again in search of a snack or a giggle before heading home. The city is an ant's nest of after-theater eateries ranging from chic French cafés to pizzerias to luncheonettes to coffee shops to hot-dog stands to delicatessens, all of them packed to the ceilings because Saturday night is not only the loneliest night of the week, it is also the night to howl. And howl they do, these good burghers who have put in five long hard days of labor and who are anxious now to relax and enjoy themselves before Sunday arrives, bringing with it the attendant boredom of too much leisure time, anathema for the American male.

The crowds shove and jostle their way along The Stem, moving in and out of bowling alleys, shooting galleries, penny arcades, strip joints, night clubs, jazz emporiums, souvenir shops, lining the sidewalks outside plate-glass windows in which go-go girls gyrate, or watching with fascination as a roast beef slowly turns on a spit. Saturday night is a time for pleasure for the good people of Isola and environs, with nothing more on their minds than a little enjoyment of the short respite between Friday night at 5:00 and Monday morning at 9:00.

But along around 2:00 A.M. the city begins to change.

The good citizens have waited to get their cars out of parking garages (more garages than there are barber shops) or have staggered their way sleepily into subways to make the long trip back to the outlying sections, the furry toy dog won in the Pokerino palace clutched limply, the laughter a bit thin, the voice a bit croaked, a college song being sung on a rattling subway car, but without much force or spirit. Saturday night has ended, it is really Sunday morning already, and the morning hours are truly upon the city—and now the denizens appear.

The predators approach, with the attendant danger of the good citizens getting mugged and rolled. The junkies are out in force, looking for cars foolishly left unlocked and parked on the streets, or—lacking such fortuitous circumstance—experienced enough to force the side vent with a screwdriver, hook the lock button with a wire hanger, and open the door that way. There are pushers peddling their dream stuff, from pot to speed to hoss, a nickel bag or a twenty-dollar deck; fences hawking their stolen goodies, anything from a transistor radio to a refrigerator, the biggest bargain basement in town; burglars jimmying windows or forcing doors with a celluloid strip, this being an excellent hour to break into apartments, when the occupants are asleep and the street sounds are hushed.

But worse than any of these are the predators who roam the night in search of trouble. In cruising wedges of three or four, sometimes high but more often not, they look for victims—a taxicab driver coming out of a cafeteria, an old woman poking around garbage cans for hidden treasures, a teenage couple necking in a parked automobile—it doesn't matter. You can get killed in this city at any time of the day or night, but your chances for extinction are best after 2:00 A.M. because, paradoxically, the night people take over in the morning. There are neighborhoods that terrify even cops in this lunar landscape, and there are certain places the cops will not enter unless they have first checked to see that there are two doors, one to get in by, and the other to get out through, fast, should someone decide to block the exit from behind.

The Painted Parasol was just such an establishment.

They had found in Mercy Howell's appointment book a notation that read: *Harry, 2:00 A.M. The Painted Parasol;* and since they knew this particular joint for exactly the kind of hole it was, and since they wondered what connection the slain girl might have had with the various unappetizing types who frequented the place from dusk till dawn, they decided to hit it and find out. The front entrance opened on a long flight of stairs that led down to the main room of what was not a restaurant, and not a club, though it combined features of both. It did not possess a liquor license, and so it served only coffee and sandwiches; but occasionally a rock singer would plug in his amplifier and guitar and whack out a few numbers for the patrons. The back door of the—hangout?—opened onto a side-street alley. Hawes checked it out, reported back to Carella, and they both made a mental floor plan just in case they needed it later.

Carella went down the long flight of steps first, Hawes immediately behind him. At the bottom of the stairway they moved through a beaded curtain and found themselves in a large room overhung with an old Air Force parachute painted in a wild psychedelic pattern. A counter on which rested a coffee urn and trays of sandwiches in Saran Wrap was just opposite the hanging beaded curtain. To the left and right of the counter were perhaps two dozen tables, all of them occupied. A waitress in a black leotard and black high-heeled patent-leather pumps was swiveling between and around the tables, taking orders.

There was a buzz of conversation in the room, hovering, captured in the folds of the brightly painted parachute. Behind the counter a man in a white apron was drawing a cup of coffee from the huge silver urn. Carella and Hawes walked over to him. Carella was almost six feet tall, and he weighed 180 pounds, with wide shoulders and a narrow waist and the hands of a street brawler. Hawes was six feet two inches tall, and he weighed 195 pounds bone-dry, and his hair was a fiery red with a white streak over the left temple where he had once been knifed while investigating a burglary. Both men looked like exactly what they were—fuzz.

"What's the trouble?" the man behind the counter asked immediately.

"No trouble," Carella said. "This your place?"

"Yeah. My name is Georgie Bright, and I already been visited, thanks. Twice."

"Oh? Who visited you?"

"First time a cop named O'Brien, second time a cop named Parker. I already cleared up that whole thing that was going on downstairs."

"What whole thing going on downstairs?"

"In the Men's Room. Some kids were selling pot down there, it got to be a regular neighborhood supermarket. So I done what O'Brien suggested, I put a man down there outside the toilet door, and the rule now is only one person goes in there at a time. Parker came around to make sure I was keeping my part of the bargain. I don't want no narcotics trouble here. Go down and take a look if you like. You'll see I got a man watching the toilet."

"Who's watching the man watching the toilet?" Carella asked.

"That ain't funny," Georgie Bright said, looking offended.

"Know anybody named Harry?" Hawes asked.

"Harry who? I know a lot of Harrys."

"Any of them here tonight?"

"Maybe."

"Where?"

"There's one over there near the bandstand. The big guy with the light hair."

"Harry what?"

"Donatello."

"Make the name?" Carella asked Hawes.

"No," Hawes said.

"Neither do I."

"Let's talk to him."

"You want a cup of coffee or something?" Georgie Bright asked.

"Yeah, why don't you send some over to the table?" Hawes said, and followed Carella across the room to where Harry Donatello was sitting with another man. Donatello was wearing gray slacks, black shoes and socks, a white shirt open at the throat, and a double-breasted blue blazer. His long blondish hair was combed straight back from the forehead, revealing a sharply defined widow's peak. He was easily as big as Hawes, and he sat with his hands folded on the table in front of him, talking to the man who sat opposite him. He did not look up as the detectives approached.

"Is your name Harry Donatello?" Carella asked.

"Who wants to know?"

"Police officers," Carella said, and flashed his shield.

"I'm Harry Donatello. What's the matter?"

"Mind if we sit down?" Hawes asked, and before Donatello could answer, both men sat, their backs to the empty bandstand and the exit door.

"Do you know a girl named Mercy Howell?" Carella asked.

"What about her?"

"Do you know her?"

"I know her. What's the beef? She underage or something?"

"When did you see her last?"

The man with Donatello, who up to now had been silent,

315

suddenly piped, "You don't have to answer no questions without a lawyer, Harry. Tell them you want a lawyer."

The detectives looked him over. He was small and thin, with black hair combed sideways to conceal a receding hairline. He was badly in need of a shave. He was wearing blue trousers and a striped shirt.

"This is a field investigation," Hawes said drily, "and we can ask anything we damn please."

"Town's getting full of lawyers," Carella said. "What's *your* name, counselor?"

"Jerry Riggs. You going to drag *me* in this, whatever it is?"

"It's a few friendly questions in the middle of the night," Hawes said. "Anybody got any objections to that?"

"Getting so two guys can't even sit and talk together without getting shook down," Riggs said.

"You've got a rough life, all right," Hawes said, and the girl in the black leotard brought their coffee to the table, and then hurried off to take another order. Donatello watched her jiggling as she swiveled across the room.

"So when's the last time you saw the Howell girl?" Carella asked again.

"Wednesday night," Donatello said.

"Did you see her tonight?"

"No."

"Were you supposed to see her tonight?"

"Where'd you get that idea?"

"We're full of ideas," Hawes said.

"Yeah, I was supposed to meet her here ten minutes ago. Dumb broad is late, as usual."

"What do you do for a living, Donatello?"

"I'm an importer. You want to see my business card?"

"What do you import?"

"Souvenir ashtrays."

"How'd you get to know Mercy Howell?"

"I met her at a party in The Quarter. She got a little high, and she done her thing."

"What thing?"

"The thing she does in that show she's in."

"Which is what?"

"She done this dance where she takes off all her clothes."

"How long have you been seeing her?"

"I met her a couple of months ago. I see her on and off,

316

maybe once a week, something like that. This town is full of broads, you know—a guy don't have to get himself involved in no relationship with no specific broad."

"What was your relationship with *this* specific broad?"

"We have a few laughs together, that's all. She's a swinger, little Mercy," Donatello said, and grinned at Riggs.

"Want to tell us where you were tonight between eleven and twelve?"

"Is this still a *field* investigation?" Riggs asked sarcastically.

"Nobody's in custody yet," Hawes said, "so let's cut the legal jazz, okay? Tell us where you were, Donatello."

"Right here," Donatello said. "From ten o'clock till now."

"I suppose somebody saw you here during that time."

"A *hundred* people saw me."

A crowd of angry black men and women were standing outside the shattered window of the store-front church. Two fire engines and an ambulance were parked at the curb. Kling pulled in behind the second engine, some ten feet away from the hydrant. It was almost 2:30 A.M. on a bitterly cold October night, but the crowd looked and sounded like a mob at an afternoon street-corner rally in the middle of August. Restless, noisy, abrasive, anticipative, they ignored the penetrating cold and concentrated instead on the burning issue of the hour—the fact that a person or persons unknown had thrown a bomb through the plate-glass window of the church.

The beat patrolman, a newly appointed cop who felt vaguely uneasy in this neighborhood even during his daytime shift, greeted Kling effusively, his pale white face bracketed by earmuffs, his gloved hands clinging desperately to his nightstick. The crowd parted to let Kling through. It did not help that he was the youngest man on the squad, with the callow look of a country bumpkin on his unlined face; it did not help that he was blonde and hatless; it did not help that he walked into the church with the confident youthful stride of a champion come to set things right. The crowd knew he was fuzz, and they knew he was Whitey, and they knew, too, that if this bombing had taken place on Hall Avenue crosstown and downtown, the Police Commissioner himself would have arrived behind a herald of official trumpets.

This, however, was Culver Avenue, where a boiling mixture of Puerto Ricans and Blacks shared a disintegrating ghetto, and

317

so the car that pulled to the curb was not marked with the Commissioner's distinctive blue-and-gold seal, but was instead a green Chevy convertible that belonged to Kling himself; and the man who stepped out of it looked young and inexperienced and inept despite the confident stride he affected as he walked into the church, his shield pinned to his overcoat.

The bomb had caused little fire damage, and the firemen already had the flames under control, their hoses snaking through and around the overturned folding chairs scattered around the small room. Ambulance attendants picked their way over the hoses and around the debris, carrying out the injured—the dead could wait.

"Have you called the Bomb Squad?" Kling asked the patrolman.

"No," the patrolman answered, shaken by the sudden possibility that he had been derelict in his duty.

"Why don't you do that now?" Kling suggested.

"Yes, sir," the patrolman answered, and rushed out. The ambulance attendants went by with a moaning woman on a stretcher. She was still wearing her eyeglasses, but one lens had been shattered and blood was running in a steady rivulet down the side of her nose. The place stank of gunpowder and smoke and charred wood. The most serious damage had been done at the rear of the small store, farthest away from the entrance door. Whoever had thrown the bomb must have possessed a good pitching arm to have hurled it so accurately through the window and across the fifteen feet to the makeshift altar.

The minister lay across his own altar, dead. Two women who had been sitting on folding chairs closest to the altar lay on the floor, tangled in death, their clothes still smoldering. The sounds of the injured filled the room, and then were suffocated by the overriding siren-shriek of the second ambulance arriving. Kling went outside to the crowd.

"Anybody here witness this?" he asked.

A young man, black, wearing a beard and a natural hair style, turned away from a group of other youths and walked directly to Kling.

"Is the minister dead?" he asked.

"Yes, he is," Kling answered.

"Who else?"

"Two women."

"Who?"

318

"I don't know yet. We'll identify them as soon as the men are through in there." Kling turned again to the crowd. "Did anybody see what happened?" he asked.

"I saw it," the young man said.

"What's your name, son?"

"Andrew Jordan."

Kling took out his pad. "All right, let's have it."

"What good's this going to do?" Jordan asked. "Writing all this stuff in your book?"

"You said you saw what—"

"I saw it, all right. I was walking by, heading for the pool room up the street, and the ladies were inside singing, and this car pulled up, and a guy got out, threw the bomb, and ran back to the car."

"What kind of a car was it?"

"A red Volkswagen."

"What year?"

"Who can tell with those VWs?"

"How many people in it?"

"Two. The driver and the guy who threw the bomb."

"Notice the license-plate number?"

"No. They drove off too fast."

"Can you describe the man who threw the bomb?"

"Yeah. He was white."

"What else?" Kling asked.

"That's all," Jordan replied. "He was white."

There were perhaps three dozen estates in all of Smoke Rise, a hundred or so people living in luxurious near-seclusion on acres of valuable land through which ran four winding, interconnected, private roadways. Meyer Meyer drove between the wide stone pillars marking Smoke Rise's western access road, entering a city within a city, bounded on the north by the River Harb, shielded from the River Highway by stands of poplars and evergreens on the south—exclusive Smoke Rise, known familiarly and derisively to the rest of the city's inhabitants as "The Club."

MacArthur Lane was at the end of the road that curved past the Hamilton Bridge. Number 374 was a huge graystone house with a slate roof and scores of gables and chimneys jostling the sky, perched high in gloomy shadow above the Harb. As he stepped from the car, Meyer could hear the sounds of river traffic, the hooting of tugs, the blowing of whistles, the eruption of a squawk box on a destroyer midstream. He looked out over the water. Reflected lights glistened in shimmering liquid beauty—the hanging globes on the bridge's suspension cables, the dazzling reds and greens of signal lights on the opposite shore, single illuminated window slashes in apartment buildings throwing their mirror images onto the black surface of the river, the blinking wing lights of an airplane overhead moving in watery reflection like a submarine. The air was cold, and a fine piercing drizzle had begun several minutes ago.

Meyer shuddered, pulled the collar of his coat higher on his neck, and walked toward the old gray house, his shoes crunching on the driveway gravel, the sound echoing away into the high surrounding bushes.

The stones of the old house oozed wetness. Thick vines covered the walls, climbing to the gabled, turreted roof. He found a doorbell set over a brass escutcheon in the thick oak doorjamb, and pressed it. Chimes sounded somewhere deep inside the house. He waited.

The door opened suddenly.

The man looking out at him was perhaps seventy years old, with piercing blue eyes; he was bald except for white thatches of hair that sprang wildly from behind each ear. He wore a red smoking jacket and black trousers, a black ascot around his neck, and red velvet slippers.

"What do you want?" he asked immediately.

"I'm Detective Meyer of the Eighty-seventh—"

"Who sent for you?"

"A woman named Adele Gorman came to the—"

"My daughter's a fool," the man said. "We don't need the police here." And he slammed the door in Meyer's face.

The detective stood on the doorstep feeling somewhat like a horse's neck. A tugboat hooted on the river. A light snapped on upstairs, casting an amber rectangle into the dark driveway. He looked at the luminous dial of his watch. It was 2:35 A.M. The drizzle was cold and penetrating. He took out his handkerchief, blew his nose, and wondered what he should do next. He did not like ghosts, and he did not like lunatics, and he did not like nasty old men who did not comb their hair and who slammed doors in a person's face. He was about to head back for his car when the door opened again.

"Detective Meyer?" Adele Gorman said. "Do come in."

320

"Thank you," he said, and stepped into the entrance foyer. "You're right on time."

"Well, a little early actually," Meyer said. He still felt foolish. What the hell was he doing in Smoke Rise investigating ghosts in the middle of the night?

"This way," Adele said, and he followed her through a somberly paneled foyer into a vast dimly lighted living room. Heavy oak beams ran overhead, velvet draperies hung at the window, the room was cluttered with ponderous old furniture. He could believe there were ghosts in this house, he could believe it.

A young man wearing dark glasses rose like a specter from the sofa near the fireplace. His face, illuminated by the single standing floor lamp, looked wan and drawn. Wearing a black cardigan sweater over a white shirt and dark slacks, he approached Meyer unsmilingly with his hand extended—but he did not accept Meyer's hand when it was offered in return.

Meyer suddenly realized that the man was blind.

"I'm Ralph Gorman," he said, his hand still extended. "Adele's husband."

"How do you do, Mr. Gorman," Meyer said, and took his hand. The palm was moist and cold.

"It was good of you to come," Gorman said. "These apparitions have been driving us crazy."

"What time is it?" Adele asked suddenly, and looked at her watch. "We've got five minutes," she said. There was a tremor in her voice. She looked suddenly very frightened.

"Won't your father be here?" Meyer asked.

"No, he's gone up to bed," Adele said. "I'm afraid he's bored with the whole affair, and terribly angry that we notified the police."

Meyer made no comment. Had he known that Willem Van Houten, former Surrogate's Court judge, had not wanted the police to be notified, Meyer would not have been here either. He debated leaving now, but Adele had begun to talk again.

". . . is in her early thirties, I would guess. The other ghost, the male, is about your age—forty or forty-five, something like that."

"I'm thirty-seven," Meyer said.

"Oh."

"The bald head fools a lot of people."

"Yes."

"I was bald at a very early age."

"Anyway," Adele said, "their names are Elisabeth and Johann, and they've probably been—"

"Oh, they have names, do they?"

"Yes. They're ancestors, you know. My father is Dutch, and there actually were an Elisabeth and Johann Van Houten in the family centuries ago, when Smoke Rise was still a Dutch settlement."

"They're Dutch. Um-huh, I see," Meyer said.

"Yes. They always appear wearing Dutch costumes. And they also speak Dutch."

"Have you heard them, Mr. Gorman?"

"Yes," Gorman said. "I'm blind, you know—" he added, and hesitated, as though expecting some comment from Meyer. When none came, he said, "But I have heard them."

"Do you speak Dutch?"

"No. My father-in-law speaks it fluently, though, and he identified the language for us, and told us what they were saying."

"What *did* they say?"

"Well, for one thing, they said they were going to steal Adele's jewelry, and they did just that."

"Your *wife's* jewelry? But I thought—"

"It was willed to her by her mother. My father-in-law keeps it in his safe."

"Kept, you mean."

"No, keeps. There are several pieces in addition to the ones that were stolen. Two rings and also a necklace."

"And the value?"

"Altogether? I would say about forty thousand dollars."

"Your ghosts have expensive taste."

The floor lamp in the room suddenly began to flicker. Meyer glanced at it and felt the hackles rising at the back of his neck.

"The lights are going out, Ralph," Adele whispered.

"Is it two forty-five?"

"They're here," Gorman whispered. "The ghosts are here."

Mercy Howell's roommate had been asleep for nearly four hours when they knocked on her door. But she was a wily young lady, hip to the ways of the big city, and very much awake as she conducted her own little investigation without so much as opening the door a crack. First she asked them to spell their names slowly. Then she asked them their shield numbers. Then she asked them to hold their shields and I.D. cards close to the door's peephole, where she could see them. Still unconvinced, she said through the locked door, "You just wait there a minute."

They waited for closer to five minutes before they heard her approaching the door again. The heavy steel bar of a Fox lock was lowered noisily to the floor, a safety chain rattled on its track, the tumblers of one lock clicked open, and then another, and finally the girl opened the door.

"Come in," she said, "I'm sorry I kept you waiting. I called the station house and they said you were okay."

"You're a very careful girl," Hawes said.

"At this hour of the morning? Are you kidding?" she said.

She was perhaps twenty-five, with her red hair up in curlers, her face cold-creamed clean of makeup. She was wearing a pink quilted robe over flannel pajamas, and although she was probably a very pretty girl at 9:00 A.M., she now looked about as attractive as a buffalo nickel.

"What's your name, Miss?" Carella asked.

"Lois Kaplan. What's this all about? Has there been another burglary in the building?"

"No, Miss Kaplan. We want to ask you some questions about Mercy Howell. Did she live here with you?"

"Yes," Lois said, and suddenly looked at them shrewdly. "What do you mean *did*? She still *does*."

They were standing in the small foyer of the apartment, and the foyer went so still that all the night sounds of the building were clearly audible all at once, as though they had not been there before but had only been summoned up now to fill the void of silence. A toilet flushed somewhere, a hot-water pipe rattled, a baby whimpered, a dog barked, someone dropped a shoe. In the foyer, now filled with noise, they stared at each other wordlessly, and finally Carella drew a deep breath and said, "Your roommate is dead. She was stabbed tonight as she was leaving the theater."

"No," Lois said, simply and flatly and unequivocally. "No, she isn't."

"Miss Kaplan—"

"I don't give a damn what you say, Mercy isn't dead."

"Miss Kaplan, she's dead."

"Oh, God," Lois said, and burst into tears.

The two men stood by feeling stupid and big and awkward and helpless. Lois Kaplan covered her face with her hands and sobbed into them, her shoulders heaving, saying over and over again, "I'm sorry, oh, God, please, I'm sorry, please, oh poor Mercy, oh my God," while the detectives tried not to watch.

At last the crying stopped and she looked up at them with eyes that had been knifed, and said softly, "Come in. Please," and led them into the living room. She kept staring at the floor as she talked. It was as if she could not look them in the face, not these men who had brought her the dreadful news.

"Do you know who did it?" she asked.

"No. Not yet."

"We wouldn't have wakened you in the middle of the night if—"

"That's all right."

"But very often, if we get moving on a case fast enough, before the trail gets cold—"

"Yes, I understand."

"We can often—"

"Yes, before the trail gets cold," Lois said.

"Yes."

The apartment went silent again.

"Would you know if Miss Howell had any enemies?" Carella asked.

"She was the sweetest girl in the world," Lois said.

"Did she argue with anyone recently? Were there any—"

"No."

"—any threatening telephone calls or letters?"

Lois Kaplan looked up at them.

"Yes," she said. "A letter."

"A *threatening* letter?"

"We couldn't tell. It frightened Mercy, though. That's why she bought the gun."

"What kind of gun?"

"I don't know. A small one."

"Would it have been a twenty-five caliber Browning?"

"I don't know guns."

"Was this letter mailed to her, or delivered personally?"

"It was mailed to her. At the theater."

"When?"

"A week ago."

"Did she report it to the police?"

"No."

"Why not?"

"Haven't you seen *Rattlesnake*?" Lois said.

"What do you mean?" Carella said.

"*Rattlesnake*. The musical. The show Mercy was in."

"No, I haven't."

"But you've heard of it."

"No."

"Where do you live, for God's sake? On the moon?"

"I'm sorry, I just haven't—"

"Forgive me," Lois said immediately. "I'm not usually—I'm trying very hard to—I'm sorry. Forgive me."

"That's all right," Carella said.

"Anyway, it's a big hit now but—well there was trouble in the beginning, you see. Are you *sure* you don't know about this? It was in all the newspapers."

"Well, I guess I missed it," Carella said. "What was the trouble about?"

"Don't *you* know about this either?" she asked Hawes.

"No, I'm sorry."

"About Mercy's dance?"

"No."

"Well, in one scene Mercy danced the title song without any clothes on. Because the idea was to express—the hell with what the idea was. The point is that the dance wasn't at all obscene, it wasn't even sexy! But the police *missed* the point, and closed the show down two days after it opened. The producers had to go to court for a writ or something to get the show opened again."

"Yes, I remember it now," Carella said.

"What I'm trying to say is that nobody involved with *Rattlesnake* would report *anything* to the police. Not even a threatening letter."

"If she bought a pistol," Hawes said, "she would have *had* to go to the police. For a permit."

"She didn't have a permit."

"Then how'd she get the pistol? You can't buy a handgun without first—"

"A friend of hers sold it to her."

"What's the friend's name?"

"Harry Donatello."

"An importer," Carella said.

"Of souvenir ashtrays," Hawes said.

"I don't know what he does for a living," Lois said, "but he got the gun for her."

"When was this?"

"A few days after she received the letter."

"What did the letter say?" Carella asked.

"I'll get it for you," Lois said, and went into the bedroom. They heard a dresser drawer opening, the rustle of clothes, what might have been a tin candy box being opened. Lois came back into the room. "Here it is," she said.

There didn't seem much point in trying to preserve latent prints on a letter that had already been handled by Mercy Howell, Lois Kaplan, and the Lord knew how many others. But nonetheless Carella accepted the letter on a handkerchief spread over the palm of his hand, and then looked at the face of the envelope. "She should have brought this to us immediately," he said. "It's written on hotel stationery, we've got an address without lifting a finger."

The letter had indeed been written on stationery from The Addison Hotel, one of the city's lesser-known fleabags, some two blocks north of the Eleventh Street Theater, where Mercy Howell had worked. There was a single sheet of paper in the envelope. Carella unfolded it. Lettered on the paper in pencil were the words:

PUT ON YOUR
CLOSE, MISS!

The Avenging Angel.

The lamp went out, the room was black.

At first there was no sound but the sharp intake of Adele Gorman's breath. And then, indistinctly, as faintly as though carried on a swirling mist that blew in wetly from some desolated shore, there came the sound of garbled voices, and the room grew suddenly cold. The voices were those of a crowd in endless debate, rising and falling in cacophonous cadence, a mixture of tongues that rattled and rasped. There was the sound, too, of a rising wind, as though a door to some forbidden landscape had been sharply and suddenly blown open to reveal a host of corpses incessantly pacing, involved in formless dialogue.

The voices rose in volume now, carried on that same chill

penetrating wind, louder, closer, until they seemed to over-whelm the room, clamoring to be released from whatever un-earthly vault contained them. And then, as if two of those dis-embodied voices had succeeded in breaking away from the mass of unseen dead, bringing with them a rush of bone-chill-ing air from some world unknown, there came a whisper at first, the whisper of a man's voice, saying the single word "Ralph!"—sharp-edged and with a distinctive foreign in-flection.

"Ralph!"—and then a woman's voice joining it saying, "Adele!"—pronounced strangely and in the same cutting whis-per.

"Adele!"—and then "Ralph!" again the voices overlapping, unmistakably foreign, urgent, rising in volume until the whis-pers commingled to become an agonizing groan—and then the names were lost in the shrilling echo of the wind.

Meyer's eyes played tricks in the darkness. Apparitions that surely were not there seemed to float on the crescendo of sound that saturated the room. Barely perceived pieces of furniture assumed amorphous shapes as the male voice snarled and the female voice moaned above it.

And then the babel of other voices intruded again, as though calling these two back to whatever grim mossy crypt they had momentarily escaped. The sound of the wind became more fierce, and the voices of those numberless pacing dead receded, and echoed, and were gone.

The lamp sputtered back into dim illumination. The room seemed perceptibly warmer, but Meyer Meyer was covered with a cold clammy sweat.

"Now do you believe?" Adele Gorman asked.

Detective Bob O'Brien was coming out of the Men's Room down the hall when he saw the woman sitting on the bench just outside the squadroom. He almost went back into the toilet, but he was an instant too late; she had seen him, so there was no escape.

"Hello, Mr. O'Brien," she said, and performed an awkward little half-rising motion, as though uncertain whether she should stand to greet him or accept the deference due a lady. The clock on the squadroom wall read 3:02 A.M. but the lady was dressed as though for a brisk afternoon's hike in the park—brown slacks, low-heeled walking shoes, beige car coat, a scarf around her head. She was perhaps fifty-five, with a face that once must have been pretty, save for the overlong nose. Green-eyed, with prominent cheekbones and a generous mouth, she executed her abortive rise, and then fell into step beside O'Brien as he walked into the squadroom.

"Little late in the night to be out, isn't it, Mrs. Blair?" O'Brien asked. He was not an insensitive cop, but his manner now was brusque and dismissive. Faced with Mrs. Blair for perhaps the seventeenth time in a month, he tried not to empathize with her loss because, truthfully, he was unable to assist her, and his inability to do so was frustrating.

"Have you seen her?" Mrs. Blair asked.

"No," O'Brien said. "I'm sorry, Mrs. Blair, but I haven't."

"I have a new picture—perhaps that will help."

"Yes, perhaps it will," he said.

The telephone was ringing. He lifted the receiver and said, "Eighty-seventh, O'Brien here."

"Bob, this's Bert Kling over on Culver—the church bombing."

"Yeah, Bert."

"Seems I remember seeing a red Volkswagen on that hot-car bulletin we got yesterday. You want to dig it out and let me know where it was snatched?"

"Yeah, just a second," O'Brien said, and began scanning the sheet on his desk.

"Here's the new picture," Mrs. Blair said "I know you're very good with runaways, Mr. O'Brien—the kids all like you and give you information. If you see Penelope, all I want you to do is tell her I love her and am sorry for the misunderstanding."

"Yeah, I will," O'Brien said. Into the phone he said, "I've got two red VWs, Bert, a 'sixty-four and a 'sixty-six. You want them both?"

"Shoot," Kling said.

"The 'sixty-four was stolen from a guy named Art Hauser. It was parked outside eight-six-one West Meridian."

"And the 'sixty-six?"

"Owner is a woman named Alice Cleary. Car was stolen from a parking lot on Fourteenth."

"North or South?"

"South. Three-o-three South."

"Right. Thanks, Bob," Kling said and hung up.

"And ask her to come home to me," Mrs. Blair said.

"Yes, I will," O'Brien said. "If I see her, I certainly will."

"That's a nice picture of Penny, don't you think?" Mrs. Blair asked. "It was taken last Easter. It's the most recent picture I have. I thought it would be helpful to you."

O'Brien looked at the girl in the picture, and then looked up into Mrs. Blair's green eyes, misted now with tears, and suddenly wanted to reach across the desk and pat her hand reassuringly, the one thing he could not do with any honesty. Because whereas it was true that he was the squad's runaway expert, with perhaps fifty snapshots of teenagers crammed into his bulging notebook, and whereas his record of finds was more impressive than any other cop's in the city, uniformed or plainclothes, there wasn't a damn thing he could do for the mother of Penelope Blair, who had run away from home some time last June.

"You understand—" he started to say.

"Let's not go into that again, Mr. O'Brien," she said, and rose.

"Mrs. Blair—"

"I don't want to hear it," Mrs. Blair said, walking quickly out of the squadroom. "Tell her to come home. Tell her I love her," she said, and was gone down the iron-runged steps.

O'Brien sighed and stuffed the new picture of Penelope into his notebook. What Mrs. Blair did not choose to hear again was the fact that her runaway daughter Penny was twenty-four years old, and there was not a single agency on God's green earth, police or otherwise, that could force her to go home again if she did not choose to.

Fats Donner was a stool pigeon with a penchant for Turkish baths. A mountainous white Buddha of a man, he could usually be found at one of the city's steam emporiums at any given hour of the day, draped in a towel and reveling in the heat that saturated his flabby body. Bert Kling found him in an all-night place called Steam-Fit.

Kling sent the masseur into the steam room to tell Donner he was there, and Donner sent word out that he would be through in five minutes, unless Kling wished to join him. Kling did not wish to join him. He waited in the locker room, and in seven minutes' time, Donner came out, draped in his customary towel, a ludicrous sight at any time, but particularly at 3:30 A.M.

"Hey!" Donner said. "How you doing?"

"Fine," Kling said. "How about yourself?"

329

"Comme-çi, comme-ça," Donner said, and made a seesawing motion with one fleshy hand.

"I'm looking for some stolen heaps," Kling said, getting directly to the point.

"What kind?" Donner said.

"Volkswagens. A 'sixty-four and a 'sixty-six."

"What color?"

"Red."

"Both of them?"

"Yes."

"Where were they heisted?"

"One from in front of eight-six-one West Meridian. The other from a parking lot on South Fourteenth."

"When was this?"

"Both last week sometime. I don't have the exact dates."

"What do you want to know?"

"Who stole them."

"You think it's the same guy on both?"

"I don't know."

"What's so important about these heaps?"

"One of them may have been used in a bombing tonight."

"You mean the church over on Culver?"

"That's right."

"Count me out," Donner said.

"What do you mean?"

"There's a lot of guys in this town who're in *sympathy* with what happened over there tonight. I don't want to get involved."

"Who's going to know whether you're involved or not?" Kling asked.

"The same way *you* get information, they get information."

"I need your help, Donner."

"Yeah, well, I'm sorry on this one," Donner said, and shook his head.

"In that case I'd better hurry downtown to High Street."

"Why? You got another source down there?"

"No, that's where the D.A.'s office is."

Both men stared at each other—Donner in a white towel draped around his belly, sweat still pouring from his face and his chest even though he was no longer in the steam room, and Kling looking like a slightly tired advertising executive rather than a cop threatening a man with revelation of past deeds not

330

entirely legal. They stared at each other with total under-standing, caught in the curious symbiosis of law breaker and law enforcer, an empathy created by neither man, but essential to the existence of both. It was Donner who broke the silence.

"I don't like being coerced," he said.

"I don't like being refused," Kling answered.

"When do you need this?"

"I want to get going on it before morning."

"You expect miracles, don't you?"

"Doesn't everybody?"

"Miracles cost."

"How much?"

"Twenty-five if I turn up one heap, fifty if I turn up both."

"Turn them up first. We'll talk later."

"And if somebody breaks my head later?"

"You should have thought of that before you entered the profession," Kling said. "Come on, Donner, cut it out. This is a routine bombing by a couple of punks. You've got nothing to be afraid of."

"No?" Donner asked. And then, in a very professorial voice, he uttered perhaps the biggest understatement of the decade. "Racial tensions are running high in this city right now."

"Have you got my number at the squadroom?"

"Yeah, I've got it," Donner said glumly.

"I'm going back there now. Let me hear from you soon."

"You mind if I get dressed first?" Donner asked.

The night clerk at The Addison Hotel was alone in the lobby when Carella and Hawes walked in. Immersed in an open book on the desk in front of him, he did not look up as they approached. The lobby was furnished in faded Victorian: a threadbare Oriental rug, heavy curlicued mahogany tables, ponderous stuffed chairs with sagging bottoms and soiled antimacassars, two spittoons resting alongside each of two mahogany paneled supporting columns. A genuine Tiffany lampshade hung over the registration desk, one leaded glass panel gone, another badly cracked. In the old days The Addison had been a luxury hotel. It now wore its past splendor with all the style of a dance-hall girl in a moth-eaten mink she'd picked up in a thrift shop.

The clerk, in contrast to his antique surroundings, was a young man in his mid-twenties, wearing a neatly pressed brown

331

tweed suit, a tan shirt, a gold and brown rep tie, and eyeglasses with tortoise-shell rims. He glanced up at the detectives belatedly, squinting after the intense concentration of peering at print, and then he got to his feet.

"Yes, gentlemen," he said. "May I help you?"

"Police officers," Carella said. He took his wallet from his pocket, and opened it to where his detective's shield was pinned to a leather flap.

"Yes, sir."

"I'm Detective Carella, this is my partner, Detective Hawes."

"How do you do? I'm the night clerk—my name is Ronald Sanford."

"We're looking for someone who may have been registered here two weeks ago," Hawes said.

"Well, if he was registered here two weeks ago," Sanford said, "chances are he's still registered. Most of our guests are residents."

"Do you keep stationery in the lobby here?" Carella asked.

"Sir?"

"Stationery. Is there any place here in the lobby where someone could walk in off the street and pick up a piece of stationery?"

"No, sir. There's a writing desk there in the corner, near the staircase, but we don't stock it with stationery, no, sir."

"Is there stationery in the rooms?"

"Yes, sir."

"How about here at the desk?"

"Yes, of course, sir."

"Is there someone at this desk twenty-four hours a day?"

"Twenty-four hours a day, yes, sir. We have three shifts. Eight to four in the afternoon. Four to midnight. And midnight to eight A.M."

"You came on at midnight, did you?"

"Yes, sir."

"Any guests come in after you started your shift?"

"A few, yes, sir."

"Notice anybody with blood on his clothes?"

"Blood? Oh, no, sir."

"Would you have noticed?"

"What do you mean?"

"Are you generally pretty aware of what's going on around here?"

"I try to be, sir. At least, for most of the night. I catch a little nap when I'm not studying, but usually—"

"What do you study?"

"Accounting."

"Where?"

"At Ramsey U."

"Mind if we take a look at your register?"

"Not at all, sir."

He walked to the mail rack and took the hotel register from the counter there. Returning to the desk he opened it and said, "All of our present guests are residents, with the exception of Mr. Lambert in two hundred and four, and Mrs. Grant in seven hundred and one."

"When did they check in?"

"Mr. Lambert checked in—last night, I think it was. And Mrs. Grant has been here, I think it's four days. She's leaving on Tuesday."

"Are these the actual signatures of your guests?"

"Yes, sir. All guests are asked to sign the register, as required by state law."

"Have you got that note, Cotton?" Carella asked, and then turned again to Sanford. "Would you mind if we took this over to the couch there?"

"Well, we're not supposed—"

"We can give you a receipt for it, if you like."

"No, I guess it'll be all right."

They carried the register to a couch upholstered in faded red velvet. With the book supported on Carella's lap they unfolded the note that Mercy Howell had received, and began to compare the signatures of the guests with the only part of the note that was not written in block letters—the words, *The Avenging Angel.*

There were fifty-two guests in the hotel. Carella and Hawes went through the register once, and then started through it a second time.

"Hey," Hawes said suddenly.

"What?"

"Look at this one."

He took the note and placed it on the page so that it was directly above one of the signatures.

"What do you think?" he asked.

"Different handwriting," Carella said.

"Same initials," Hawes said.

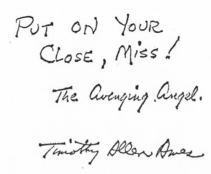

Put on your
close, Miss!

The Avenging Angel.

Timothy Allen Ames

Detective Meyer Meyer was still shaken. He did not like ghosts. He did not like this house. He wanted to go home to his wife Sarah. He wanted her to stroke his hand and tell him that such things did not exist, there was nothing to be afraid of, a grown man? How could he believe in poltergeists, shades, Dutch spirits? Ridiculous!

But he had heard them, and he had felt their chilling presence, and had almost thought he'd seen them, if only for an instant. He turned with fresh shock now toward the hall staircase and the sound of descending footsteps. Eyes wide, he waited for whatever new manifestation might present itself. He was tempted to draw his revolver, but he was afraid such an act would appear foolish to the Gormans. He had come here a skeptic, and he was now at least *willing* to believe, and he waited in dread for whatever was coming down those steps with such ponderous footfalls—some ghoul trailing winding sheets and rattling chains? Some specter with a bleached skull for a head and long bony clutching fingers dripping the blood of babies?

Willem Van Houten, wearing his red velvet slippers and his red smoking jacket, his hair still jutting wildly from behind each ear, his blue eyes fierce and snapping, came into the living room and walked directly to where his daughter and son-in-law were sitting.

"Well?" he asked. "Did they come again?"

"Yes, Daddy," Adele said.

"What did they want this time?"

"I don't know. They spoke Dutch again."

Van Houten turned to Meyer. "Did *you* see them?" he asked.

"No, sir, I did not," Meyer said.

"But they were *here*," Gorman protested, and turned his blank face to his wife. "I heard them."

"Yes, darling," Adele assured him. "We *all* heard them. But it

334

was like that other time, don't you remember? When we could hear them even though they couldn't quite break through."

"Yes, that's right," Gorman said, and nodded. "This happened once before, Detective Meyer." He was facing Meyer now, his head tilted quizzically, the sightless eyes covered with their black glasses. When he spoke his voice was like that of a child seeking reassurance. "But you *did* hear them, didn't you, Detective Meyer?"

"Yes," Meyer said. "I heard them, Mr. Gorman."

"And the wind?"

"Yes, the wind, too."

"And felt them. It—it gets so cold when they appear. You did feel their presence, didn't you?"

"I felt something," Meyer said.

Van Houten suddenly asked, "Are you satisfied?"

"About what?" Meyer said.

"That there are ghosts in this house? That's why you're here, isn't it? To ascertain—"

"He's here because I asked Adele to notify the police," Gorman said.

"Why did you do that?"

"Because of the stolen jewelry," Gorman said. "And because—" He paused. "Because I've lost my sight, yes, but I wanted to—to make sure I wasn't losing my mind as well."

"You're perfectly sane, Ralph," Van Houten said.

"About the jewelry—" Meyer said.

"*They* took it," Van Houten said.

"Who?"

"Johann and Elisabeth. Our friendly neighborhood ghosts."

"That's impossible, Mr. Van Houten."

"Why is it impossible?"

"Because ghosts—" Meyer started and hesitated.

"Yes?"

"Ghosts—well, ghosts don't go around stealing jewelry. I mean, what use would they have for it?" he said lamely, and looked at the Gormans for corroboration. Neither of the Gormans seemed to be in a substantiating mood. They sat on the sofa near the fireplace, both looking glum.

"They want us out of this house," Van Houten said. "It's as simple as that."

"How do you know?"

"Because they said so."

"When?"

"Before they stole the necklace and the earrings."

"They told this to you?"

"To me and to my children. All three of us were here."

"But I understand the ghosts speak only Dutch."

"Yes, I translated for Ralph and Adele."

"And then what happened?"

"What do you mean?"

"When did you discover the jewelry was missing?"

"The instant they were gone."

"You mean you went to the safe?"

"Yes, and opened it, and the jewelry was gone."

"We had put it in the safe not ten minutes before that," Adele said. "We'd been to a party, Ralph and I, and we got home very late, and Daddy was still awake, reading, sitting in that chair you're in this very minute. I asked him to open the safe, and he did, and he put the jewelry in and closed the safe and . . . and then *they* came and . . . and made their threats."

"What time was this?"

"The usual time. The time they always come. Two forty-five in the morning."

"And you say the jewelry was put into the safe at what time?"

"About two-thirty," Gorman said.

"And when was the safe opened again?"

"Immediately after they left. They only stay a few moments. This time they told my father-in-law they were taking the necklace and the earrings with them. He rushed to the safe as soon as the lights came on again—"

"Do the lights always go off?"

"Always," Adele said. "It's always the same. The lights go off, and the room gets very cold, and we hear these strange voices arguing." She paused. "And then Johann and Elisabeth come."

"Except that this time they didn't come," Meyer said.

"And one other time," Adele said quickly.

"They want us out of this house," Van Houten said, "that's all there is to it. Maybe we ought to leave. Before they take *every-thing* from us."

"Everything? What do you mean?"

"The rest of my daughter's jewelry. And some stock cer-tificates. Everything that's in the safe."

"Where *is* the safe?" Meyer asked.

"Here. Behind this painting." Van Houten walked to the wall

336

opposite the fireplace. An oil painting of a pastoral landscape hung there in an ornate gilt frame. The frame was hinged to the wall. Van Houten swung the painting out as though opening a door, and revealed the small, round, black safe behind it. "Here."

"How many people know the combination?" Meyer asked.

"Just me," Van Houten said.

"Do you keep the number written down anywhere?"

"Yes."

"Where?"

"Hidden."

"Where?"

"I hardly think that's any of your business, Detective Meyer."

"I'm only trying to find out whether some other person could have got hold of the combination somehow."

"Yes, I suppose that's possible," Van Houten said. "But highly unlikely."

"Well," Meyer said, and shrugged. "I don't really know what to say. I'd like to measure the room, if you don't mind, get the dimensions, placement of doors and windows, things like that. For my report." He shrugged again.

"It's rather late, isn't it?" Van Houten said.

"Well, I *got* here rather late," Meyer said, and smiled.

"Come, Daddy, I'll make us all some tea in the kitchen," Adele said. "Will you be long, Detective Meyer?"

"It may take a while."

"Shall I bring you some tea?"

"Thank you, that would be nice."

She rose from the couch and then guided her husband's hand to her arm. Walking slowly beside him, she led him past her father and out of the room. Van Houten looked at Meyer once again, nodded briefly, and followed them out. Meyer closed the door behind them and immediately walked to the standing floor lamp.

The woman was sixty years old, and she looked like anybody's grandmother, except that she had just murdered her husband and three children. They had explained her rights to her, and she had told them she had nothing to hide and would answer any questions they asked her. She sat in a straight-backed squadroom chair, wearing a black cloth coat over blood-stained nightgown and robe, her handcuffed hands in

337

her lap, her hands unmoving on her black leather pocketbook.

O'Brien and Kling looked at the police stenographer, who glanced up at the wall clock, noted the time of the interrogation's start as 3:55 A.M., and then signaled that he was ready whenever they were.

"What is your name?" O'Brien asked.

"Isabel Martin."

"How old are you, Mrs. Martin?"

"Sixty."

"Where do you live?"

"On Ainsley Avenue."

"Where on Ainsley?"

"Six hundred fifty-seven Ainsley."

"With whom do you live there?"

"With my husband Roger, and my son Peter, and my daughters Anne and Abigail."

"Would you like to tell us what happened tonight, Mrs. Martin?" Kling asked.

"I killed them all," she said. She had white hair, a fine aquiline nose, brown eyes behind rimless spectacles. She stared straight ahead of her as she spoke, looking neither to her right nor to her left, seemingly alone with the memory of what she had done not a half hour before.

"Can you give us some of the details, Mrs. Martin?"

"I killed *him* first."

"Who do you mean, Mrs. Martin?"

"My husband."

"When was this?"

"When he came home."

"What time was that, do you remember?"

"A little while ago."

"It's almost four o'clock now," Kling said. "Would you say this was at, what, three thirty or thereabouts?"

"I didn't look at the clock," she said. "I heard his key in the door, and I went in the kitchen, and there he was."

"Yes?"

"There's a meat cleaver I keep on the sink. I hit him with it."

"Why did you do that, Mrs. Martin?"

"Because I wanted to."

"Were you arguing with him, is that it?"

"No. I just went over to the sink and picked up the cleaver, and then I hit him with it."

338

"Where did you hit him, Mrs. Martin?"

"On his head and on his neck and I think on his shoulder."

"You hit him three times with the cleaver?"

"I hit him a lot of times. I don't know how many."

"Were you aware that you were hitting him?"

"Yes, I was aware."

"You knew you were striking him with a cleaver."

"Yes, I knew."

"Did you intend to kill him with the cleaver?"

"I intended to kill him with the cleaver."

"And afterwards, did you know you had killed him?"

"I knew he was dead, yes."

"What did you do then?"

"My oldest child came into the kitchen. Peter. My son. He yelled at me, he wanted to know what I'd done, he kept yelling at me and yelling at me. I hit him too—to get him to shut up. I hit him only once, across the throat."

"Did you know what you were doing at the time?"

"I knew what I was doing. He was *another* one, that Peter."

"What happened next, Mrs. Martin?"

"I went in the back bedroom where the two girls sleep, and I hit Annie with the cleaver first, and then I hit Abigail."

"Where did you hit them, Mrs. Martin?"

"On the face. Their faces."

"How many times?"

"I think I hit Annie twice, and Abigail only once."

"Why did you do that, Mrs. Martin?"

"Who would take care of them after I was gone?" Mrs. Martin asked of no one.

There was a long pause, then Kling asked, "Is there anything else you want to tell us?"

"There's nothing more to tell. I done the right thing."

The detectives walked away from the desk. They were both pale. "Man," O'Brien whispered.

"Yeah," Kling said. "We'd better call the night D.A. right away, get him to take a full confession from her."

"Killed four of them without batting an eyelash," O'Brien said, and shook his head, and went back to where the stenographer was typing up Mrs. Martin's statement.

The telephone was ringing. Kling walked to the nearest desk and lifted the receiver. "Eighty-seventh, Detective Kling," he said.

"This is Donner."

"Yeah, Fats."

"I think I got a lead on one of those heaps."

"Shoot."

"This would be the one heisted on Fourteenth Street. According to the dope I've got it happened yesterday morning. Does that check out?"

"I'll have to look at the bulletin again. Go ahead, Fats."

"It's already been ditched," Donner said. "If you're looking for it try outside the electric company on the River Road."

"Thanks, I'll make a note of that. Who stole it, Fats?"

"This is strictly *entre nous*," Donner said. "I don't want *no* tie-in with it *never*. The guy who done it is a mean little guy—rip out his mother's heart for a dime. He hates blacks, killed one in a street rumble a few years ago, and managed to beat the rap. I think maybe some officer was on the take, huh, Kling?"

"You can't square homicide in this city, and you know it, Fats."

"Yeah? I'm surprised. You can square damn near anything else for a couple of bills."

"What's his name?"

"Danny Ryder. Three-five-four-one Grover Avenue. You won't find him there now, though."

"Where *will* I find him now?"

"Ten minutes ago he was in an all-night bar on Mason, place called Felicia's. You going in after him?"

"I am."

"Take your gun," Donner said.

There were seven people in Felicia's when Kling got there at 4:45. He cased the bar through the plate-glass window fronting the place, unbuttoned the third button of his overcoat, reached in to clutch the butt of his revolver, worked it out of the holster once and then back again, and went in through the front door.

There was the immediate smell of stale cigarette smoke and beer and sweat and cheap perfume. A Puerto Rican girl was in whispered consultation with a sailor in one of the leatherette-lined booths. Another sailor was hunched over the juke box thoughtfully considering his next selection, his face tinted orange and red and green from the colored tubing. A tired, fat, fifty-year old blonde sat at the far end of the bar, watching the sailor as though the next button he pushed might destroy the entire world. The bartender was polishing glasses. He looked up when Kling walked in and immediately smelled the law.

Two men were seated at the opposite end of the bar.

One of them was wearing a blue turtleneck sweater, gray slacks, and desert boots. His brown hair was clipped close to his scalp in a military cut. The other man was wearing a bright orange team jacket, almost luminous, with the words *Orioles, S.A.C.* lettered across its back. The one with the crewcut said something softly, and the other one chuckled. Behind the bar a glass clinked as the bartender replaced it on the shelf. The juke box erupted in sound, Jimi Hendrix rendering *All Along the Watchtower.*

Kling walked over to the two men.

"Which one of you is Danny Ryder?" he asked.

The one with the short hair said, "Who wants to know?"

"Police officer," Kling said, and the one in the orange jacket whirled with a pistol in his hand. Kling's eyes opened wide in surprise, and the pistol went off.

There was no time to think, there was hardly time to breathe. The explosion of the pistol was shockingly close, the acrid stink of cordite was in Kling's notrils. The knowledge that he was still alive, the sweet rushing clean awareness that the bullet had somehow missed him was only a fleeting click of intelligence accompanying what was essentially a reflexive act.

Kling's .38 came free of its holster, his finger was inside the trigger guard and around the trigger, he squeezed off his shot almost before the gun had cleared the flap of his overcoat, fired into the orange jacket and threw his shoulder simultaneously against the chest of the man with the short hair, knocking him backward off his stool. The man in the orange jacket, his face twisted in pain, was leveling the pistol for another shot.

Kling fired again, squeezing the trigger without thought of rancor, and then whirled on the man with the short hair, who was crouched on the floor against the bar.

"Get up!" he yelled.

"Don't shoot!"

"Get *up!*"

He yanked the man to his feet, hurled him against the bar, thrust the muzzle of his pistol at the blue turtleneck sweater, ran his hands under the armpits and between the legs, while the man kept saying over and over again. "Don't shoot, please don't shoot."

He backed away from him and leaned over the one in the orange jacket.

"Is this Ryder?" he asked.

"Yes."

"Who're you?"

"Frank Pasquale. Look, I—"

"Shut up, Frank," Kling said. "Put your hands behind your back. Move!"

He had already taken his handcuffs from his belt. He snapped them onto Pasquale's wrists, and only then became aware that Jimi Hendrix was still singing, the sailors were watching with pale white faces, the Puerto Rican girl was screaming, the fat faded blonde had her mouth open, the bartender was frozen in mid-motion, the tip of his bar towel inside a glass.

"All right," Kling said. He was breathing harshly. "All right," he said again, and wiped his forehead.

Timothy Allen Ames was a potbellied man of forty, with a thick black mustache, a mane of long black hair, and brown eyes sharply alert at 5:05 in the morning. He answered the door as though he'd been already awake, asked for identification, then asked the detectives to wait a moment, closed the door, and came back shortly afterward, wearing a robe over his striped pajamas.

"Is your name Timothy Ames?" Carella asked.

"That's me," Ames said. "Late to be paying a visit, ain't it?"

"Or early, depending how you look at it," Hawes said.

"One thing I can do without at five A.M. is humorous cops," Ames said. "How'd you get up here, anyway? Is that little jerk asleep at the desk again?"

"Who do you mean?" Carella asked.

"Lonnie Sanford, or whatever his name is."

"Ronald—Ronnie Sanford."

"Yeah, him. Always giving me trouble."

"What kind of trouble?"

"About broads," Ames said. "Acts like he's running a nunnery here, can't stand to see a guy come in with a girl. I notice he ain't got no compunctions about letting *cops* upstairs, though, no matter *what* time it is."

"Never mind Sanford, let's talk about you," Carella said.

"Sure, what would you like to know?"

"Where were you between eleven twenty and twelve to-night?"

"Right here."

"Can you prove it?"

"Sure. I got back here about eleven o'clock, and I been here ever since. Ask Sanford downstairs—no, he wasn't on yet. He don't come on till midnight."

"Who *else* can we ask, Ames?"

"Listen, you going to make trouble for me?"

"Only if you're in trouble."

"I got a broad here. She's over eighteen, don't worry. But, like, she's a junkie, you know? But I know you guys, and if you want to make trouble—"

"Where is she?"

"In the john."

"Get her out here."

"Look, do me a favor, will you? Don't bust the kid. She's trying to kick the habit, she really is. I been helping her along."

"How?"

"By keeping her busy," Ames said, and winked.

"Call her."

"Bea, come out here!" Ames shouted.

There were a few moments of hesitation, then the bathroom door opened. The girl was a tall plain brunette wearing a short terrycloth robe. She sidled into the room cautiously, as though expecting to be struck in the face at any moment. Her brown eyes were wide with expectancy. She knew fuzz, she knew what it was like to be arrested on a narcotics charge, and she had listened to the conversation from behind the closed bathroom door; and now she waited for whatever was coming, expecting the worst.

"What's your name, Miss?" Hawes asked.

"Beatrice Norden."

"What time did you get here tonight, Beatrice?"

"About eleven."

"Was this man with you?"

"Yes."

"Did he leave here at any time tonight?"

"No."

"Are you sure?"

"I'm positive. He picked me up about nine o'clock—"

"Where do you live, Beatrice?"

343

"Well, that's the thing, you see," the girl said. "I been put out of my room."

"So where'd he pick you up?"

"At my girl friend's house. You can ask her, she was there when he came, Rosalie Dawes. Anyway, Timmy picked me up at nine, and we ate, and we came up here around eleven."

"I hope that's the truth, Miss Norden," Carella said.

"I swear to God, we been here all night," Beatrice answered.

"All right, Ames," Hawes said, "we'd like a sample of your handwriting."

"My *what?*"

"Your handwriting."

"What for?"

"We collect autographs," Carella said.

"Gee, these guys really break me up," Ames said to the girl. "Regular night-club comics we get in the middle of the night."

Carella handed him a pencil and then tore a sheet from his pad. "You want to write this for me?" he said. "The first part's in block lettering."

"What the hell is block lettering?" Ames asked.

"He means *print* it," Hawes said.

"Then why didn't he say so?"

"Put on your clothes, Miss," Carella said.

"What for?" Beatrice said.

"That's what I want him to write," Carella explained.

"Oh."

"Put on your clothes, Miss," Ames repeated, and lettered it onto the sheet of paper. "What else?" he asked, looking up.

"Now sign it in your own handwriting with the following words: The Avenging Angel."

"What the hell is this supposed to be?" Ames asked.

"You want to write it, please?"

Ames wrote the words, then handed the slip of paper to Carella. He and Hawes compared it with the note that had been mailed to Mercy Howell:.

"So?" Ames asked.

"So you're clean," Hawes said.

At the desk downstairs, Ronnie Sanford was still immersed in his accounting textbook. He got to his feet again as the detectives came out of the elevator, adjusted his glasses on his nose, and said, "Any luck?"

"Afraid not," Carella answered. "We're going to need this register for a while, if that's okay."

"Well—"

"Give him a receipt for it, Cotton," Carella said. It was late, and he didn't want a debate in the lobby of a rundown hotel. Hawes quickly made out a receipt in duplicate, signed both copies, and handed one to Sanford.

"What about this torn cover?" Hawes asked belatedly.

"Yeah," Carella said. There was a small rip on the leather binding of the book. He fingered it briefly now, then said, "Better note that on the receipt, Cotton." Hawes took back the receipt and, on both copies, jotted the words: Small rip on front cover. He handed the receipts back to Sanford.

"Want to just sign these, Mr. Sanford?" he said.

"What for?" Sanford asked.

"To indicate we received the register in this condition."

"Oh, sure," Sanford said. He picked up a ballpoint pen from its desk holder, and asked, "What do you want me to write?"

"Your name and your title that's all."

"My title?"

"Night Clerk, The Addison Hotel."

"Oh, sure," Sanford said, and signed both receipts. "This okay?" he asked. The detectives looked at what he had written.

"You like girls?" Carella asked suddenly.

"What?" Sanford asked.

"Girls," Hawes said.

"Sure. Sure, I like girls."

"Dressed or naked?"

"What?"

"With clothes or without?"

"I—I don't know what you mean, sir."

345

"Where were you tonight between eleven twenty and midnight?" Hawes asked.

"Getting—getting ready to come to—to work," Sanford said.

"You sure you weren't in the alley of the Eleventh Street Theater stabbing a girl named Mercy Howell?"

"What? No—no, of course not. I was—I was home—getting dressed—" Sanford took a deep breath and decided to get indignant. "Listen, what's this all about?" he said. "Would you mind telling me?"

"It's all about this," Carella said, and turned one of the receipts so that Sanford could read the signature:

Ronald Sanford
Night Clerk
The Addison Hotel

"Get your hat," Hawes said. "Study hall's over."

It was 5:25 when Adele Gorman came into the room with Meyer's cup of tea. He was crouched near the air-conditioning unit recessed into the wall to the left of the drapes; he glanced up when he heard her, then rose.

"I didn't know what you took," she said, "so I brought everything."

"Thank you," he said. "Just a little sugar is fine."

"Have you measured the room?" she asked, and put the tray down on the table in front of the sofa.

"Yes, I think I have everything I need now," Meyer said. He put a spoonful of sugar into the tea, stirred it, then lifted the cup to his mouth. "Hot," he said.

Adele Gorman was watching him silently. She said nothing. He kept sipping his tea. The ornate clock on the mantelpiece ticked in a swift whispering tempo.

"Do you always keep this room so dim?" Meyer asked.

"Well, my husband is blind, you know," Adele said. "There's really no need for brighter light."

"Mmm. But your father reads in this room, doesn't he?"

"I beg your pardon?"

"The night you came home from that party. He was sitting in the chair over there near the floor lamp. Reading. Remember?"

"Oh. Yes, he was."

346

"Bad light to read by."

"Yes, I suppose it is."

"I think maybe those bulbs are defective," Meyer said.

"Do you think so?"

"Mmm. I happened to look at the lamp, and there are three one-hundred-watt bulbs in it, all of them burning. You should be getting a lot more light with that much wattage."

"Well, I really don't know about such—"

"Unless the lamp is on a rheostat, of course."

"I'm afraid I don't even know what a rheostat is."

"It's an adjustable resistor. You can dim your lights or make them brighter with it. I thought maybe the lamp was on a rheostat, but I couldn't find a control knob anywhere in the room." Meyer paused. "You wouldn't know if there's a rheostat control in the house, would you?"

"I'm sure there isn't," Adele said.

"Must be defective bulbs then," Meyer said, and smiled. "Also, I think your air conditioner is broken."

"No, I'm sure it isn't."

"Well, I was just looking at it, and all the switches are turned to the 'On' position, but it isn't working. So I guess it's broken. That's a shame, too, because it's such a nice unit. Sixteen thousand BTUs. That's a lot of cooling power for a room this size. We've got one of those big old price-fixed apartments on Concord, my wife and I, with a large bedroom, and we get adequate cooling from a half-ton unit. It's a shame this one is broken."

"Yes. Detective Meyer, I don't wish to appear rude, but it is late—"

"Sure," Meyer said. "Unless, of course, the air conditioner's on a remote switch, too. So that all you have to do is turn a knob in another part of the house and it comes on." He paused. "*Is* there such a switch somewhere, Mrs. Gorman?"

"I have no idea."

"I'll just finish my tea and run along," Meyer said. He lifted the cup to his lips, sipped the tea, glanced at her over the rim, took the cup away from his mouth, and said, "But I'll be back."

"I hardly think there's any need for that," Adele said.

"Well, some jewelry's been stolen—"

"The ghosts—"

"Come off it, Mrs. Gorman."

The room went silent.

"Where are the loudspeakers, Mrs. Gorman?" Meyer asked.

"In the false beams up there? They're hollow—I checked them out."

"I think perhaps you'd better leave," Adele said slowly.

"Sure," Meyer said. He put the teacup down, sighed, and got to his feet.

"I'll show you out," Adele said.

They walked to the front door and out into the driveway. The night was still. The drizzle had stopped, and a thin layer of frost covered the grass rolling away toward the river below. Their footsteps crunched on the gravel as they walked slowly toward the automobile.

"My husband was blinded four years ago," Adele said abruptly. "He's a chemical engineer, there was an explosion at the plant, he could have been killed. Instead, he was only blinded." She hesitated an instant, then said again, "Only blinded," and there was such a sudden cry of despair in those two words that Meyer wanted to put his arm around her, console her the way he might his daughter, tell her that everything would be all right come morning, the night was almost done, and morning was on the horizon.

But instead he leaned on the fender of his car, and she stood beside him looking down at the driveway gravel, her eyes not meeting his. They could have been conspirators exchanging secrets in the night, but they were only two people who had been thrown together on a premise as flimsy as the ghosts that inhabited this house.

"He gets a disability pension from the company," Adele said, "they've really been quite kind to us. And, of course, I work. I teach school, Detective Meyer. Kindergarten. I love children." She paused. She would not raise her eyes to meet his. "But—it's sometimes very difficult. My father, you see—"

Meyer waited. He longed suddenly for dawn, but he waited patiently, and heard her catch her breath as though committed to go ahead now however painful the revelation might be, compelled to throw herself on the mercy of the night before the morning sun broke through.

"My father's been retired for fifteen years." She took a deep breath, and then said, "He gambles, Detective Meyer. He's a horse player. He loses large sums of money."

"Is that why he stole your jewels?" Meyer asked.

"You know, don't you?" Adele said simply, and raised her eyes to his. "Of course you know. It's quite transparent, his

348

ruse, a shoddy little show really, a performance that would fool no one but—no one but a blind man." She brushed at her cheek; he could not tell whether the cold air had caused her sudden tears. "I really don't care about the theft; the jewels were left to me by my mother, and after all it was my father who bought them for her, so it's—it's really like returning a legacy. I really don't care about that part of it. I'd have *given* the jewelry to him if only he'd asked, but he's so proud, such a proud man. A proud man who—who steals from me and pretends that ghosts are committing the crime.

"And my husband, in his dark universe, listens to the sounds my father puts on tape and visualizes things he cannot quite believe and so he asks me to notify the police because he needs an impartial observer to contradict the suspicion that someone is stealing pennies from his blind man's cup. That's why I came to you, Detective Meyer. So that you would arrive here tonight and perhaps be fooled as I was fooled at first, and perhaps say to him, 'Yes, Mr. Gorman, there *are* ghosts in your house.'"

She suddenly placed her hand on his sleeve. The tears were streaming down her face, she had difficulty catching her breath. "Because you see, Detective Meyer, there *are* ghosts in this house, there really and truly are. The ghost of a proud man who was once a brilliant judge and who is now a gambler and a thief; and the ghost of a man who once could see, and who now trips and falls in the darkness."

On the river a tugboat hooted. Adele Gorman fell silent. Meyer opened the door of his car and got in behind the wheel.

"I'll call your husband tomorrow," he said abruptly and gruffly. "Tell him I'm convinced something supernatural is happening here."

"And will you be back, Detective Meyer?"

"No," he said. "I won't be back, Mrs. Gorman."

In the squadroom they were wrapping up the night. Their day had begun at 7:45 P.M. yesterday, and they had been officially relieved at 5:45 A.M.; but they had not left the office yet because there were questions still to be asked, reports to be typed, odds and ends to be put in place before they could go home. And since the relieving detectives were busy getting *their* approaching workday organized, the squadroom at 6:00 A.M. was busier than it might have been on any given afternoon, with two teams of cops getting in each others' way.

349

In the Interrogation Room, Carella and Hawes were questioning young Ronald Sanford in the presence of the Assistant District Attorney who had come over earlier to take Mrs. Martin's confession, and who now found himself listening to another one when all he wanted to do was go home to sleep. Sanford seemed terribly shocked that they had been able to notice the identical handwriting in *The Addison Hotel* and *The Avenging Angel*—he couldn't get over it. He thought he had been very clever in misspelling the word "clothes," because then they would think some illiterate had written it, not someone who was studying to be an accountant.

He could not explain why he had killed Mercy Howell. He got all mixed up when he tried to explain that. It had something to do with the moral climate of America, and people exposing themselves in public, people like that shouldn't be allowed to pollute others, to foist their filth on others, to intrude on the privacy of others who only wanted to make a place for themselves in the world, who were trying so very hard to make something of themselves, studying accounting by day and working in a hotel by night, what right had these other people to ruin it for everybody else?

Frank Pasquale's tune, sung in the Clerical Office to Kling and O'Brien, was not quite so hysterical, but similar to Sanford's nonetheless. He had got the idea together with Danny Ryder. They had decided between them that the blacks in America were taking jobs away from decent hard-working people who only wanted to be left alone, what right did they have to force themselves on everybody else? So had decided to bomb the church, just to show them they couldn't get away with it, not in America. He didn't seem terribly concerned over the fact that his partner was lying stone-cold dead on a slab at the morgue, or that their little Culver Avenue expedition had cost three people their lives, and had severely injured a half dozen others. All he wanted to know, repeatedly, was whether his picture would be in the newspaper.

At his desk Meyer Meyer started to type up a report on the Gorman ghosts, then decided the hell with it. If the lieutenant asked him where he'd been half the night, he would say he had been out looking for trouble in the streets. The Lord knew there was enough of *that* around, any night. He pulled the report forms and their separating sheets of carbon paper from the ancient typewriter, and noticed that Detective Hal Willis

350

was pacing the room anxiously, waiting to get at the desk the moment he vacated it.

"Okay, Hal," he said, "it's all yours."

"Finalmente!" Willis, who was not Italian, said.

The telephone rang.

The sun was up when they came out of the building and walked past the hanging green "87" globes and down the low flat steps to the sidewalk. The park across the street shimmered with early-morning autumn brilliance, the sky above it was clear and blue. It was going to be a beautiful day.

They walked toward the diner on the next block, Meyer and O'Brien ahead of the others, Carella, Hawes, and Kling bringing up the rear. They were tired, and exhaustion showed in their eyes, in the set of their mouths, in the pace they kept. They talked without animation, mostly about their work, their breaths feathery and white on the cold morning air.

When they reached the diner, they took off their overcoats and ordered hot coffee and cheese Danish and toasted English muffins. Meyer said he thought he was coming down with a cold. Carella told him about some cough medicine his wife had given one of the children. O'Brien, munching on a muffin, glanced across the diner and saw a young girl in one of the booths. She was wearing blue jeans and a bright colored Mexican serape, and she was talking to a boy wearing a Navy pea jacket.

"I think I see somebody," he said, and he moved out of the booth past Kling and Hawes, who were talking about the newest regulation on search and seizure.

The girl looked up when he approached the booth.

"Miss Blair?" he said. "Penelope Blair?"

"Yes," the girl answered. "Who are you?"

"Detective O'Brien," he said, "Eighty-seventh Precinct. Your mother was in last night, Penny. She asked me to tell you—"

"Flake off, cop," Penelope Blair said. "Go stop a riot somewhere."

O'Brien looked at her silently for a moment. Then he nodded, turned away, and went back to the table.

"Anything?" Kling asked.

"You can't win 'em all," O'Brien said.